James Parsons studied art and design and then film/animation production at Northumbria University, before writing screenplays, short fiction, and then novels. He has published two science fiction books, entitled *Orbital Kin* and *Minerva Century*. This is his first horror novel. He is married and lives in Manchester, UK.

Dedication

This book is dedicated to the people of the North East of England, the coal miners and shipyard workers of the past, and the people living and working there now. The North East has a strong soul, and it will live on through all hard times into better days, as it always has done.

James Parsons

NORTHERN SOULS

AUSTIN MACAULEY PUBLISHERS™

LONDON • CAMBRIDGE • NEW YORK • SHARJAH

A CIP catalogue record for this title is available from the British Library.

ISBN 978-1-78823-006-3 (Paperback)
ISBN 978-1-78823-007-0 (E-Book)
www.austinmacauley.com

First Published (2017)
Austin Macauley Publishers™ Ltd.
25 Canada Square
Canary Wharf
London
E14 5LQ

Acknowledgments

The following books were helpful for researching local history and details:

Tyneside: A History of Newcastle and Gateshead from Earliest Times by Alastair Moffat and George Rosie

The Lindisfarne Gospels: Society, Spirituality and the Scribe by Michelle P. Brown

Lindisfarne by Magnus Magnusson

Chapter 1

Eric ran away from the funeral of his girlfriend with the police inspectors seeing him leave by the gates. He was accused, his alibi questionable, and many questions needed answering. Would they catch him and throw away the key? It greatly enraged him, as he knew he was innocent of killing his beloved Grace, but he knew how much her father, Philip, completely detested him. If Philip had sent the police inspectors after Eric right then, though, he almost wouldn't have cared. He simply wanted to end it now, his way, to end the trouble, the pain and misery and join Grace, wherever she may be. He would head to the Tyne Bridge. It would be a spectacular death.

His head was filled with questions that would not go away. Was he ill? The atmosphere at the funeral was so intense, with so many eyes on him, and the almost creeping or twisting shadows of the tall trees around the graveyard outside. Had there been strangers watching it from behind the trees? He remembered the red eyes that had watched him from deep in between the shadows of the trees and bushes at the funeral. Or was that just the relentless stress, exhaustion and anger playing with his mind?

Winds of regret and sorrow swept around the weeping souls before the burial. The loved ones gathered in mutual grief and confusion at the sudden and tragic loss. The church stood quiet and respectful, yet seemed unable to offer much hope. All family and friends felt anger within, resisting the truth, but the arching ancient trees and afternoon shadows beckoned them.

The stranger watched the cars pull up beside the church and around the grounds. His bloodshot eyes strained to observe each family member. If this truly was the mourning of the one who had interfered, he would know these people. He would find the ones who could suffer and do anything required. His cold, wrinkled hands clicked as he replaced his leather gloves.

Emma seemed to want to seek the truth of Grace's death. Well, she can try, Eric thought. Hopefully, Taylor would help her, and there would be no need for his own involvement.

Eric got into his car and drove away to the bridge, with no real care or consideration for the car or for himself.

After the funeral of his girlfriend there was nothing left for Eric but to commit suicide. He had lost the woman who had made his life worth living, and he simply wanted to die without her. There had been no obvious reason for Grace's death so far, nothing announced by the forensics or police. No reason except the argument, Eric thought. He hated himself for it, and if that was what had caused her to go, then he wanted to end the unbelievable pain and guilt as soon as possible.

They were all so sad, missing Grace. She had been a loving daughter, a true friend, and a bold young woman, taken too early from all who knew her. Her friends stood to one side of the grave, and her family on the other. Her father Philip, a respected local businessman, and her mother and sister stood close together, weeping. Her friends, including Emma, huddled around, shocked, mourning and grieving quietly, with some of the girls crying dramatically. Eric had stood at the side of them... he had watched Philip. He had then quietly walked off... with a bitter look of hate and sorrow over his pale face. He watched Philip and the other family members as the vicar finished his words. Eric then quietly walked off discreetly before anyone could stop him. Taylor and Emma then saw him, but Eric motioned to be left alone.

Eric had walked away and felt the grand, suffocating presence of the church over him, hypocritical religion and death all around him as he left to be alone. He needed to escape, to think alone about it all. It probably was not the best thing to do, but he had to do it. There was so much anger and sadness in his thoughts. He could have easily attacked anyone, smashed windows, broken just about anything to release the unending, torturous pain inside him. That was not him though, not even now. He walked away looking for signs of hope.

Were there eyes on him? Someone watching from behind? He had the feeling of someone observing him from somewhere close by, the feeling of being watched, being judged. He looked around. There was no one there, no one but a couple of passers-by who didn't seem interested in him. He decided he was just being paranoid.

If he did not do it soon, her father might help him out, he thought. Eric had caught the subtle accusations from Grace's father Philip, scathing looks aimed at him across the funeral on the grass by the grave. It was not the sort of thing Eric ever saw himself planning before. He always thought suicides were so pathetic, attention-seeking, self-pitying, that they were displays from cowards. Now, though, it sadly made sense for him, he thought. He and Grace had had so many good plans for their future together; going to university, travelling abroad, touring his band, perhaps even marriage one day. He hurt so much right then and almost saw the funeral as a farewell for both of them, their goodbye to everyone.

He would go out quietly and discreetly, though there could be no exact guarantee that there wouldn't be a bloody finish. That would be someone else's problem to clean up. He did not want life without Grace, and it seemed now to be a painful sick joke of an existence. Her father Philip could think what he wanted, Eric thought. Could he never see how deeply in love they had been, how Eric cared for her, protected her always? Eric loved Grace with an endless hunger and a painful passion.

Chapter 2

Eric drove his cheap, worn-out old car from the church graveyard before the service had completely finished, leaving discreetly onto the motorway again and out toward Newcastle. He could not help but think of many things from his life as he went; Grace, his overpowering, hypocritical father, the afterlife if it existed, some favourite songs lyrics which suited the occasion...

Was he meant to go without knowing how she had died? He just did not believe the coroner's inconclusive though not officially deemed suspicious cause of death, possibly heart trouble or a virus. There was something else, something deeper. She had only been twenty, for God's sake, he thought. The way she was before it happened was so unlike her. She was so dramatic suddenly, so paranoid, intensely angry and defensive, closed up to him emotionally but still there with him. That was not her, and something had made her like that, someone had scared her.

He reached the end of the bridge and parked his car down by the bushes. Getting out, he took a deep, sorrowful breath. He checked his pocket. Yes, the drugs were there, ready for him, so he began his walk alone to the middle of the huge bridge, to the end of his meaningless life.

The air around was cold and sharp on his face, icy but invigorating. He clung to his plan still, ignoring the beginnings of doubts that were growing. He stood casually for a minute or more, waiting for the bridge road to be vacant of cars and traffic and people. Finally, he stood where he thought was the best point over the Tyne to disappear into the deep, dark, powerful tides and be taken away forever. He climbed up quickly but carefully. He was killing himself, but did want it to be graceful and smooth, no indulgent splattering fall against the bridge as he descended, if possible.

He stood on top of the thick metal side of the bridge, and the powerful winds from the coast came heavy against him, pushing and swaying him easily. It was difficult to keep balance, but he fetched a hand into his pocket for the drugs, continuing his plan. It was to be goodbye to the world of lies, loneliness, mistakes and pain. He stood tall on the bridge side, looking out towards the sea, and thought of Grace.

The wind blew hard on him, swaying him back a little. If he fell back into the bridge, he was still around six foot high and would make a mess; an embarrassing mess, he thought. The wind pushed him forcefully again, and he tried to steady himself with his arms out, the drugs in his right hand. He accidentally dropped the pouch down into the river below. 'Fantastic, great,' he said to himself. Then the wind came back suddenly and amazingly hard on him, and he fell backwards.

As he fell, he saw someone reaching for him, somewhere in the sky before him. That's wrong, he thought, impossible. He screamed as he fell down, and landed hard onto the inner walkway of the bridge. He rolled a little, only hitting his side painfully. The breath was knocked from him, and he curled up in agony, closing his eyes. Consciousness left him.

He woke sometime later in the same place, shivering. His head was heavy like a stone as he gradually crawled up to his knees.

'I need you alive,' he heard. He turned around fast, expecting someone behind him. There was no one there, not one person around him on the bridge. Shit, he thought. I'm alive, but I've gone totally insane now, I've knocked my brain to pieces. He slowly stood, leaning against the inside of the walkway.

The cold wind was still very strong as he stood trying to focus and breathe properly once more. He looked around him, wondering what he should do. His plan had fallen apart, and he felt embarrassed and angry. But who had spoken to him?

There were always cars, he thought. He waited, watched the road on the bridge, and eventually saw a couple of cars approaching him. This will just have to do, he thought. He watched and prepared to time it right. He casually stepped nearer the edge of the path. The wind blew hard against him again and he shivered and cursed it as the cars came closer.

The first car came along then, and Eric stepped up, moved out ready. He was then hit by a force of wind so powerful that he fell back to the ground. He swore, looked up, and saw a shocking image before him. Grace smiled at him from the road as cars passed loudly through her.

Eric fell back against the inner bridge wall, scared like hell and speechless.

'How? Why?' he stammered. She vanished into the air, leaving more cars to drive on along the road in front of Eric. He stood amazed and terrified.

It was Grace he had seen, somehow. In some way, in some form she had been right there in front of him. How real that could have been, he thought. It must be a kind of post- mourning form of mild madness, he thought. He looked out into the road, confused and desperate for answers. He did not need this, any of it. His plan had been to end it, end his life, and that had been ruined. Now he was one of those miserable lonely souls who can't stop thinking about their lost loved ones, not that he wanted to really forget her at all.

Had it been her? Had she spoken to him, really? That would just mean a completely unbelievable thing. It would suggest ghosts and crap like that, he thought, but...

He had heard her speak. No one else. He was not the kind of bloke that imagined things at all; he liked real cars, real conversations, real guitars, real men, and real women. This was unreal he thought, so unreal. He looked up and down the bridge but no one was there to help him or explain it to him.

He had not managed to jump. Now he had to think of some other way, and quick, while he still had the guts to try. He was sure that Grace's father Philip would get him locked away for her death if he got the chance, or even that the local police might pin it on him for easy promotions and a reward, deciding her death was the result of some kind of sick game. He did not want to go mad in jail or give Philip that satisfaction any time soon.

Eric paced back along to his parked car at the end of the bridge and dejectedly got inside. As he located the key in his pocket, he was distracted by a faint noise, a whispering possibly, coming from somewhere around him. What the hell was all of this? He wondered if he could actually concentrate enough to drive, but then he realized that he wanted to die anyway: if he crashed, he simply crashed.

He started the engine and calmly looked in the rear view mirror. He gasped and almost screamed out. It just could not be. He saw Grace in the mirror, looking so distraught.

'Grace...are...are you there?' he said slowly, and turned around quickly to look for her in the back seats. They were empty, and he felt foolish.

'I'm with you,' he then heard.

He swallowed and looked in the mirror: no Grace there.

'Please God, you...' he bowed his head on the steering wheel '...just let me die but don't drive me crazy like this,' he said.

He gripped the steering wheel tightly in frustration.

'Help...me...Eric,' he heard. He looked up slowly out of the windscreen at the long road stretching off the bridge.

'I... hear you Grace. I saw you too. I don't want to be mad...why are you here?' he asked.

'Help me...' she said faintly. Eric looked around outside of the car as he spoke.

'How? How can I help you now?' he asked her.

There was silence and then finally she replied.

'Stop...them,' she whispered to him.

'Who? Stop who?' Eric asked.

'Tonight, at Mason Street...stop them all,' she said.

'Grace, who? Who are you talking about? Did they kill you?' he asked. 'Grace, are you still there?'

There was no more. He waited, but she was gone. It was unbelievable to him. Had he experienced real communication with the dead? He had spoken to Grace and she had answered. He had not made up the dialogue in his head, she had spoken to him. It was impossible, but it had happened. She existed somewhere, in some way, he thought.

This changed everything for him, he thought. It had to, at least for a while, until it made some kind of sense. He might still have been mad, but he was a happier madman.

He would go to Mason Street, he decided. He had to. If nothing happened, if no one was there, then he was clearly insane, for certain. But if Grace was real still, wherever she was, he would do what she asked of him, no question. Her death could not stop his love and devotion to her.

Chapter 3

The priest spoke the eulogy, talking of how special and important a person she had been, a blessing from God, a gift to all her family and friends who had known her. Her grieving father Philip felt his mind begin to wander once again that morning. He agreed with it all, believing strongly that his deceased daughter had truly been a special sweet gift to him, but he felt immeasurably angry and frustrated like he never had in his like and never would again.

Grace's death was still a tragic mystery but Eric could definitely be responsible in some way, Philip had thought. It seemed likely no matter how nice the young man had actually revealed himself be, there always seemed a reckless danger to his character, Philip thought, which he had never wanted around his daughter. Philip looked up around the church yard and grave site for a moment at all of the other many old graves and tombstones and headstones. How often were they remembered? Did tears still fall on the gravestones of these lost souls years after? Did people remember these others now they were gone?

There were many family members and friends of Grace around the grave while the priest finished his sermon, all with sad and crying faces. In between the trees and deep shadows, Philip caught strange shades and shapes passing to and fro, he was sure. His mind was exhausted, he thought, after all the preparations for the funeral, consoling his wife and younger daughter, the never ending pain and anguish warping his perception, logic, reason, and sanity.

Dark figures walked around behind the trees, between the shadows, behind the mourners.

'Mr. Pollock? You want to add your own message now?' the priest said suddenly.

'What?' Philip said, and then quietly turned to look at the priest with shock and bemused distraction in his tired eyes.

'Oh yes, of course...right,' Philip said.

He composed himself and straightened up. Looking behind everyone, at the trees and deep shadows again, he saw the dark figures had gone.

He took a deep breath, and began his speech for Grace.

As Emma left the churchyard with other friends of hers and Grace, she stepped through the gates to the street and almost walked into a tall, strikingly handsome stranger.

'Oh, I'm sorry,' a chirpy voice said.

'No problem. My fault. Sorry,' Emma told him.

'Morning is nice, isn't it?' he said.

'Excuse me?' Emma said, slightly shocked by his statement.

'The blue sky above, sunshine behind the clouds,' he said.

'Oh, right. Yes,' Emma said, understanding him then. She looked at his strange smile as she walked on with her friends.

'A friend, a young life lost?' he asked.

Emma found his questions invasive and rude.

'Yes. Goodbye,' she said, and walked away, rejoining her friends, who waited for her, all looking at the stranger.

The handsome man, possibly aged around thirty five, remained by the church gates. He watched the relatives of Grace coming out of the church side building, with their crying eyes and hurting faces. He saw Grace's mother, her sister and uncles. Then he saw Philip join them.

'There's our local hero,' the stranger said aloud, then began to walk away among the many other people shopping, walking through the streets in their ways.

Philip noticed Eric walk away, and it satisfied him easily. This young man should not be at this funeral, Philip thought. He was sure Eric had been the cause of Grace's dying in some way, but his role in the death remained unknown. The late night drunken parties, drugs of many kinds, mysterious road trips and many more things had all angered Philip. Grace seemed to gravitate toward these angry, wild, young men and this is what it had finally led to: tragically for her, Philip thought.

He was beginning to think of very nasty, horrible, sick things that could happen to Eric if he was not careful; all kinds of fatal things, things that would end him completely. No, that was no longer a legitimate line of thought, Philip knew. As a decent, upstanding and respected businessman of the North he only ever set fine moral examples for all others. Thinking that way would make him as bad as Eric, and that was not his way, certainly not. To him, Eric did seem

15

possibly guilty, even after all the police had said about there not being any real substantial or significant evidence on Eric, and how they had said that he did have a solid alibi to protect him. Still, Philip wondered, though. For an innocent man, Eric was acting guiltily beyond doubt, it seemed to him.

Philip joined his family members, along with many friends and Grace's college friends, to talk over good memories and how they loved her. He had to be strong for Grace's mother, and for Grace's sister, Elizabeth. They needed him so much now to get through it all. He accepted a double vodka from his brother-in-law Paul by the bar in the pub at the get-together after the funeral.

'We're all here,' Paul told him.

'I know. Thank you. We need you all. Thank you, indeed,' Philip said. He walked away with the glass of vodka towards a staircase in a quiet corner around the hall. He sat looking out of a small window. Outside by the church graveyard tall trees blew in the afternoon wind, leaves scattering down one by one. So many graves there, he thought, people of the North of England, passing away all the time. He thought he could probably guess at how most of the people buried there had died, but not Grace. He just did not want to believe that she had really gone from him.

A couple of men in black walked through the graveyard. They seemed focused, with a purpose, with serious faces but also with something else showing through in their eyes. More people mourning the dead, Philip thought. But they have answers for their lost ones, he thought. He saw one of them look toward him then, right at him through the window, with shocking red eyes. Holy shit, Philip thought. He shook his head, eyes closed, then rubbed them, thinking that everything must have finally got to him. He looked back out of the window at the men. They were gone.

Philip walked back through into the main room to meet his sad friends and relatives once again.

Chapter 4

For some reason, even when his first thought was to go somewhere alone for a while, Eric decided to call his close friend Taylor, who had been at the funeral earlier.

'Hello Taylor? It's me,' he said

'Christ, Eric, good to hear you, mate. Where did you get to earlier? I was worried to hell about you,' he said.

'Needed to be alone, that's all. Can you meet me soon?' Eric asked him, 'in about half an hour or so?'

'Yeah, of course I can. Where are you?' Taylor asked, like a faithful friend would.

In a short time from then they met up in a local pub near Newcastle City Centre.

'You know, I am worried about you. After her passing away...well we're like brothers,' Taylor said, sipping his cold beer.

'Yeah, okay. Well, thanks. Just stay with me if you dare to, okay?' Eric said.

He necked down his whisky and coke aggressively and looked at Taylor.

'Take it easy man. Let me know if you want a bit of weed. Take the stress down a notch, maybe listen to some good time stoner rock, Floyd, Cypress Hill, King Crimson, yeah?' Taylor offered.

'No, no, not now. Can't be a pothead now. I'd stay like that if I began. Got things to do now,' Eric said.

'What things do you mean?' Taylor asked.

'Just things. Stick with me. Can't count on many others: Mike, Ryan, Dan, they are all just being all soft on me. You take chances. You'll stick with me now, right?' he asked.

'Yes, I told you. Just don't do any mad crazy stuff, right?' Taylor said.

'I can't guarantee that I won't, Taylor. That's why you're here with me,' Eric told him.

'So, where we going and why?' Taylor asked, with a positive lilt in his voice and a supportive smile for his friend.

'I need to travel. We need to. Got some places to visit. A few days are okay, right?' Eric asked Taylor.

'A few days? Well, yes, no probs. My new boss is very flexible. I'm going up in this new branch of the company right now. No problem. Just lead the way,' Taylor said. 'Look, this isn't all about finding out what happened to Grace, is it? They're looking into it, aren't they? I mean, police can be known to take their sweet time, but right now they will be doing all they can. They have to. They don't leave things like this.'

'I would really hope to believe that, you know I should,' Eric said.

'That's it, if you're driving the next few miles now. Let's go,' Taylor said, and they walked out to the car.

Half an hour passed and both young men sat in Eric's car, parked down across from the opening of Mason Street, beside dark industrial land and empty car parks. Eric sat and focused his attention on the view before him, awaiting the arrival of anything strange.

'Life goes on, though. I mean, I don't wish to spout out all the sad clichés to you, but I'm your good pal, you know? I care about you deeply, right?' Taylor said.

'Yeah, thanks,' Eric replied, looking ahead.

'I want to help you through all of this. I know you'll want to have time alone, but I'm here anytime else, okay?' Taylor offered.

'Okay, I'll hold you to it, bud,' Eric said, not really listening much.

'I don't want you to do anything too crazy, okay? Life can still be good, really good, eventually. She'd have wanted you to keep having a good time, right?' Taylor suggested.

'Right. You're right, I know,' Eric replied.

'So why are we sat right here exactly?' Taylor asked. 'Can you tell me yet?'

'Something might happen, I think. Maybe a bad thing. Or...I don't know exactly. Just keep looking at the street,' Eric said.

Taylor was extremely concerned about his close friend, who was mourning and coming to terms with Grace's death. There were unanswered questions around the actual cause, which Taylor thought must have been a huge cause of stress for Eric.

'I'll stick with you, of course. I'm here for you,' he told Eric, with as much honesty as he could offer.

18

In what may have only been a few brief minutes a couple of police cars arrived at the area where what was left of the bodies lay in festered, rotted pieces. One police officer from each of the cars got out, and they walked together up to the building next to the remains. They seemed relaxed in attitude, casual even, as they suddenly busted the doors open, kicking them through in seconds, and entered.

These were well trained, professional police officers, prepared for all and any kinds of scenes of crime or violence imaginable. That was what they believed, at least. It was expected for them to seem unaffected or detached, but they appeared almost too at ease and relaxed with the events around them as they walked into the building.

'Sam, we've evidence of struggle, an escalated fight all around...very interesting, looks...good,' one said into a radio device as he walked around.

'Yes... over here... her hair... it was her... and him... both of them...' the other officer said in agreement as they surveyed broken chairs and upturned tables around in the dimly lit, wide room.

The first officer leaned down and noticed drying blood dripped across the side of the wall. He moved closer to it and licked at the blood. A curious, thoughtful look filled his face.

'Much to do now, much to tell...' he told the other officer.

They left the building and drove away at a startling speed down the coast road toward Newcastle.

Boredom sank in as Eric and Taylor waited in the car for over an hour and more, parked across the street from the place that Eric thought he had heard Grace tell him about, as the world drifted along under the dark night sky. No people arrived in the area, no cars, nothing at all. Eric was just about to start doubting that he had really heard or seen Grace earlier in the day. He had been to her funeral that afternoon, he thought. He had obviously just been hugely affected psychologically by it all. It had happened so fast, so suddenly. It was catching up with him while he tried to follow events.

'Maybe we should go get some fish and chips and a couple of lagers then return?' Taylor suggested.

Eric sat up quickly as he saw sudden movement down the street.

'What's up?' Taylor asked.

'Someone walked up in around the building at the end there. See them?' Eric asked.

'Not sure I did, really,' Taylor replied.

They both looked up at the dark street carefully for movement, for change of any kind.

'I'm going to have a look,' Eric said, and got out of the car.

'What? Hey, wait...Eric,' Taylor said, hesitating and unsure.

He sat and watched Eric walk off, then finally got out and ran up after him.

Eric was certain that he had seen someone enter the unused building. He had no idea who it was or what they were doing but he believed he had to find out. He approached the doorway to the tall, old building, moving forward quietly with hesitation. The door was slightly ajar, he noticed, and after briefly considering his options, he then walked through.

He stepped into a deep, incredibly dark room, which held a thick musty smell inside within the deep shadows. It seemed from what he could make out in faint slits of moonlight from high windows that the building was some neglected factory or offices. He saw pieces of rubbish, magazines, empty food cans and wrappers scattered over the floor as he walked around. Along near the deep far corner he saw a small light flicker slightly. He waited and then continued further into the wide open room. He was suddenly surprised to see a young girl crouching down among the shadows up ahead of him, lighting a lantern.

'Excuse me, hello,' he said quietly as he walked up nearer to her, as her face was cast in the dim light from the portable lantern.

She turned around fast and revealed a look of wild fear over her pale face.

'I haven't done anything wrong,' she protested.

'No, it's alright. You're not in danger, are you, are you okay?' Eric said.

'I... what do you want here? Who are you exactly snooping here?' she asked while she reached for a rucksack by her feet, which rested on a rickety wooden box.

'I heard something bad might happen here tonight. Why are you here? Are you in trouble?' he asked her.

'Is that any of your business at all? Who the hell are you?' she asked him. Her right hand went deep into her rucksack, rummaging around.

'I'm...a friend. I might be wrong about this. Completely wrong, but maybe not. You're okay then?' he asked again.

'I'm fine, thanks. Some of us just don't want the nine to five, rat-race and greed of the world. Leave and don't tell anyone I'm here.

You'll regret it if you do,' she warned him, with a strange but still malicious look.

Eric looked around the huge dark cavernous room, which seemed to be the entrance hall to the building, with a winding staircase to the right leading up to higher floors.

'Alright. Sorry to have bothered you. Goodbye, then,' he said to the young woman and walked back to the front entrance. He stopped and took a look back at her, sitting there in the dark with the small battery lantern illuminating her scowl. He met Taylor outside the building and they walked back to the car together.

'So?' Taylor asked with curiosity.

Eric was ready to reply when he saw Taylor's eyes widen like he had never seen before. He spun around and saw the back of some indescribable things between shadows lurch into the building entrance.

'What did you see?' Eric asked.

Taylor simply shrugged, unable to explain, his mouth hanging open.

'What in hell's name was that?' Eric said.

Could his eyes actually be tricking him? This looked like danger, he thought. He knew, in fact, that it really was, but he could also see that it was something he was barely prepared for.

Without rational thought, Eric returned to the doorway, and suddenly heard a piercing shrill scream from within. He hesitated, then burst in, and was shocked at the sight before him. Ahead of him, inside the long, dark room, stood some muscular, wretched, colossal thing. It towered over the girl, frightening her with its grotesque physicality. The lantern had been knocked to the floor and so Eric could only see half of the scene before him in intermittent flickers of light and shadows, which distorted and exaggerated everything before him. It was not a man, but neither was it animal. It seemed to be some form between the two, grotesque as it twisted toward the girl. She crawled slowly to one side of the floor but the thing watched her closely, intent on following after her.

Taylor came in behind Eric quietly, his mouth open in shock and disgust.

'Holy fuck,' he uttered.

'I know, no idea myself,' Eric said quietly, 'follow me.'

Eric began to step closer to the scene among the shadows. He looked over the room as he went for anything to use to attack this bizarre creature and to defend him and the girl. All he could make out were old tables, large filing cabinets, boxes of junk. Then he saw some shelving posts. He looked over to Taylor standing slightly behind to his left, and discreetly pointed, signalling to Taylor, but slipped over something which made a loud squelching noise.

The tall beast by the girl swivelled its warped head and saw both Eric and Taylor. It stormed over toward them instantly, leaving the girl. Eric looked at Taylor for help, but he was motionless, frozen in shock. As the creature came bounding closer to him, Eric jumped across the room and fell down by the pile of shelving posts. He quickly rolled over and grabbed a post as the creature came right at him. By God, Eric thought, this thing was some nightmarish beast or corpse living by mistake and pissed off beyond belief. It was repulsive to look at, all veins, scales and clawed hands, with blazing red eyes fixed on Eric.

It lifted its jagged, clawed hands and Eric took the chance. He swung out the shelving post, smacking the beast hard in the stomach. It jerked over, but still tried to grab at him while he crawled away from it. Taylor came in near them, watching.

'Help me, for Christ's sake!' Eric urged.

Taylor looked around sheepishly, and then saw the shelving posts. The beast stood once more and leapt out at both of them with rabid fury. Eric stumbled back then hit at the beast repeatedly as it came down at them, striking its side then shoulder until it grabbed the shelving, stopping him. It then reached out toward him with the other clawed hand. Taylor came up and smashed it in the face with surprising force, knocking it down successfully.

'Jesus, man!' Eric said, impressed. He then kicked it forcefully himself a couple of times.

'Finish it,' he told Taylor, who had stopped attacking to stare at the beast.

'What? God, no, I mean…can we?' he asked.

Eric looked at it, horrified but also stunned. They had no idea what this unreal abomination actually was, where it came from or how it had come to be, but it was visibly enormously powerful, evil and unpredictable.

'Fine, I'll try something,' Eric said.

He gripped the shelving post in sweating palms, held it tight high over his head and defiantly prepared to launch it down at the beast until it stopped moving. Is this what Grace wanted me to see, he thought? He swiftly plunged the post down right as the beast jumped out at him again with wide red eyes and claws coming at him. It smacked down, blood of some kind splashing around.

'Do it again!' Taylor shouted, looking aghast.

The post cut deep into the thick muscular neck of the creature as Eric repeatedly beat it, trying to finish it off. Eric leaned hard against the post, and dark crimson blood exploded up across him, gushing all over his arms and chest while the beast wailed in its dying moments.

The sight almost made Eric vomit, as the beast gagged and shook violently as it died, staring right at him in the last few seconds it lived. Eric held down with pressure until the thing finally ceased moving.

'Good God, that is just sick,' Taylor said. 'What was it? What the hell was that?'

He looked at Eric as he stood exhausted and plastered in thick red blood.

'You expected this thing?' Taylor asked.

'I... was expecting something. I didn't know it would be...this,' Eric said, pointing to the huge dead thing next to them.

'Shit, we should maybe leave in case there are more of them,' Taylor told him.

'Unless...Hang on, the girl,' Eric said, and looked around. In the dirt and tattered grass clumps at his feet he saw an A4 size card folder. It had Newcastle University logos printed on the outside. Opening it up, he saw that there were a number of clippings inside. There were some pages, documents suggesting that she was doing some history or religious degree course. Right at the very back he found a torn and very delicate-looking piece of paper inside a clear plastic slip. The paper seemed to feature some very old Celtic and Arabic wording, arranged like scripture.

'What's that you've got?' Taylor asked, peering over.

'Not exactly sure...it looks really old,' Eric replied thoughtfully.

'So how did you know all this was going to be here?' Taylor asked, but Eric walked across the room searching.

'Let's see if this girl is okay. I'll tell you how my day's been later,' Eric told him as they looked for the girl.

When they turned around, they saw that the girl was gone. The door to the far back exit of the building was open, cold air blowing in and night stars in the black sky visible.

'All that effort and she escaped and left us to deal with that bloody thing by ourselves,' Taylor said.

'There's more to all of this. A lot more. It's going to be clearer soon,' Eric said, with a nervous tone.

'Oh, I really hope not,' Taylor said.

'Come on, we'd better move on,' Eric told him.

They walked back out to the car outside with steady caution, both nervous and in a strange state of shock. Anything could happen now, Eric thought to himself. Anything at all, good or bad. If God could take his love so early in life, and leave him miserable, any number of horrors could be around the corner. All bets were off now, the logic of life gone, lost forever. They reached his car and got inside.

Chapter 5

After driving on for nearly fifteen minutes, Eric pulled the car over down off the coast road at Tynemouth. He and Taylor had both been equally quiet after defeating the unexplainable and shockingly gruesome thing back up the road. It was not of this Earth, Eric had declared, and Taylor simply nodded in agreement, equally mystified.

'You alright?' Eric asked Taylor after a deep breath. They both looked ahead out of the front windscreen.

'This is some sick nightmare, isn't it?' Taylor said.

'Yeah, and I don't see us waking up from it any time very soon,' Eric agreed.

'What next, then?' Taylor asked.

'I don't know yet. But I might soon,' Eric replied thoughtfully.

'You... knew that would be there, didn't you? How?' Taylor asked him. They looked at each other, knowing they were now involved in something deadly dangerous, a secret and macabre danger that existed deep within Newcastle and the North.

Eric got out of the car and walked over by the grass and hedge surrounding a large field to their right. He breathed in and out deeply, anxiously confused, desperately wanting clearer answers to the things they were encountering. Was he in Hell? He looked down at the drying blood on his hands. What had he done? What did it mean? They had killed some creature, something so inhuman, so unlike any animal or man, but it was something, some aggressive, hellish ghoul. Where the hell did it come from? And were there more? He just knew there were. Taylor got out of the car and joined him.

'This is mad, I mean it's insane. That thing...there's more, isn't there?' he asked.

'I think so,' Eric agreed with a sigh.

'What's this about, Eric? Was it...what was the damn thing? Because part of me is thinking some crazy things about what that fucking thing kind of looked like, but that just can't make any sense,' Taylor said.

'So what do you think it was?' Eric asked.

Taylor laughed quietly, almost afraid to speak. 'You tell me.'

'It looked like a kind of man, right. But we know it wasn't. It was no real animal. It was...it was evil, whatever it was,' Eric said uncertainly.

'What do you think about scientific experiments?' Taylor said.

'Like it escaped? No, it's a deeper thing. I know it's more,' Eric told him. He looked around then opened the car door.

'Come on, we need a place to sleep. We should rest up before we continue,' he told Taylor.

'Oh right, I'm going to have a peaceful night's sleep now. So what do you know? How do you know where they are?' Taylor asked.

'Trust me. I know…just a little. I'll know more soon. I think I have to,' Eric told him as they got back inside the car and drove away.

They drove through dark fog and rain, past tall trees and closed shops, almost expecting more beasts to run out from the dark streets, clawing and howling.

'Are there any bed and breakfasts around here?' Eric asked.

'Not sure. Maybe nearer North Shields, or Tynemouth, or Whitley Bay,' Taylor suggested.

'You know, I think we might have been seen out there earlier on,' Eric said.

'By who? You think anyone else might have seen that thing? Could anyone really have seen much in the darkness?' Taylor said.

'I'm not sure. My hands were bloody, we were...and the girl...she's gone, but...' Eric reflected.

'But no one ever does anything about anything these days anyway, so don't worry,' Taylor told him.

'I don't know. I'm just sure someone was watching, I had that feeling, you know?' Eric said. 'Could be anyone; could be police.'

'Well let's keep moving, then. We're not guilty of anything. We've got more to worry about anyway, right?' Taylor said.

'We certainly have,' Eric agreed, keeping his eyes on the buildings going by as he drove the car.

'I'm totally shocked by that damn thing back there,' Taylor said, and then turned to face Eric. 'You think we're going to see more of them,

26

don't you?' Taylor asked. 'This is what you were talking about, sticking with you to fight these fucking demon beast things?'

'Yes. You're right. Totally. Want to leave? Turn back? I'll drop you off somewhere if you just don't give a damn, okay?' Eric said, with serious rage in his voice.

Taylor turned and looked at him, considering his options. He quickly thought about what might be lying ahead for them over the next few days and nights. More wild evil beasts, unknown monsters, devils and demons, freaks of nature of unknown origin. This was some kind of unbearable waking nightmare that he was now sharing with his close friend. Even though Eric was confident, and determined to claim peace for his lost love, someone should be with him, Taylor believed. It was either he watched him, or soon enough he would be watched by police officers through a cell door window or doctors checking his symptoms instead.

'I'm sticking with you, of course,' Taylor told him.

'You really think we should stay in a cheap hotel over night?' Eric asked.

'Oh yeah, I think it'll be best. Just in case,' Taylor told him with confident reassurance.

They continued along the road in the heavy rain, finding a cheap hotel for the night a few minutes later.

Across the road from the disused building where Eric and Taylor had fought the demon, behind tall trees and under deep dark shadows, another car sat silently parked with a man behind the wheel. He had watched Eric and Taylor enter the building, heard the bizarre howls and screams, and then minutes later witnessed Eric and Taylor leave out of the rear exit. He was just about sure he could see blood glistening over the front of Eric. The dark of night cloaked their expressions slightly, though he could still see that they both seemed shaken up, with a nervous manner in their walking as they left. The looks on the faces of Eric and Taylor fascinated the man incredibly. Something seriously bad had just taken place inside there, the man thought. He finished a cigarette then took out his wallet and flipped over the front to look at the police badge on the inside.

'Detective David Raimi,' the identity card beside it read.

He looked around out of the windscreen. This really could be the reawakening of the thing which he had secretly worried about for a number of years. Only in the last few weeks had David begun to make fresh notes on a man of whom he had been suspicious for a long time, and Eric knew the man. Now that Grace had died, the mysterious death had drawn David onto the trail, and with good reason, he believed. What he had just seen, and the number of small things leading up to it – shadows, strange hair and blood samples - suggested to him that it was time to reopen the case.

He had an unwanted, uncomfortable feeling that what happened in there could be very closely linked to a thing he had seen a few years earlier which had haunted him ever since. It would make sense, though he wished to God that it would not. He himself was a police detective, a man of scientific investigation, of calm logical analysis. That was how he and people like himself knew to work, but this one peculiar case caught in his mind in the past like a poison thorn, now pushing deeper and sharper than it had in years. And it would make Philip a man to watch a whole lot more seriously. These two young men should be very careful, David thought. He had never spoken of what he had seen to anyone, because he could never really know how to explain it or describe it in any believable way. Since then, though, Philip had been an increasingly respected, powerful and significant figure in the North, a man who few would believe could ever be connected to any kind of supernatural danger to all around him.

The hotel down by the lower streets of Newcastle certainly was cheap enough, but was suitably inconspicuous for a night to keep undetected and to discuss what would happen next.

'I called you because...I need help,' Eric said flatly to Taylor.

'We both need help now after seeing that,' Taylor said.

'No, I'm not joking or saying that I'm crazy. Well...will you listen to me and not judge what I say immediately?' Eric said.

'Right, okay. Go on,' Taylor said.

Eric waited a moment, then began.

'I left the funeral, and I was going to jump off the Tyne Bridge,' he told Taylor.

'Really? Bloody hell mate,' Taylor said, visibly shocked.

'Right. It didn't happen. I stood on the bridge ready. Then the most forceful but strange wind came. It knocked me back down onto the bridge. As I fell, I saw Grace. I saw a form of her, in the sky. I didn't believe my eyes at first. I was saved by her, I fell back inside the bridge. I was not convinced or satisfied, though, so I decided to instead throw myself into the cars passing by on the bridge. When I tried, she came again. She shocked me, and I fell back, away from the cars. I heard her,

28

in my head. I saw her, really saw her. She saved me and she told me to come here,' Eric told Taylor.

'All of that happened after the funeral today?' Taylor asked, shocked but fascinated. This really was a bizarre tale, but after seeing a huge living breathing demonic beast, he could just about begin to believe anything now.

'Yes. She's alive somewhere, in some kind of way, or she exists at least. I don't know. She knows about something seriously important. Knew about that thing we just killed. We saved that girl because Grace told us about it,' Eric explained.

'Eric that's...astonishing, it's mind blowing...I believe you,' Taylor said 'After the thing that we just fought...I believe it. So, was it like her ghost, do you think?'

'Well, maybe, possibly,' Eric said. He was in a kind of overwhelmed state, in shock but honestly pleased to know that Grace still existed somewhere, somehow.

'Is there more? Grace told us to come here, kill that thing...then what?' Taylor asked.

Eric looked visibly agitated.

'I don't know. I hope...I hope she comes back to tell me,' he said.

'But if she told you about this, won't she tell you about something similar, about more things to do like this?' Taylor asked.

'I really don't know. She wanted to get out. Do her internship for a year or so, then maybe Europe or London. But...things going on around the North...not work, career things, but problems, business, old business problems...I saw her again, Taylor, do you know how I felt?' Eric said. 'She did say "Stop them, stop them all,"' he told Taylor.

You'd let her go? Down to London, or, where was it, France? Germany?' Taylor asked

'Well, my music work is building up. She believed she could hook me up with some companies and people connected to band touring, promoting around Europe. We'd travel, she'd work on the go eventually,' Eric replied

'You get what you can find. See so many trendy new shops and companies open up, but months later...gone. My college education has to get me something useful eventually but shit, I'll do what I have to do, I'll get a good life somehow,' Taylor said. 'So there are more like that thing? Shit. How does she know, do you think?'

'Damned if I know. It actually might be to do with how she died, so I hope she returns,' Eric said. He felt helpless, and all he believed he could do was simply wait to see if she reappeared to him. He prayed that wherever she may be, she was away from creatures of evil like the one he had encountered.

Chapter 6

They had stopped by an off license, bought a box of lager and a bottle of vodka before entering the cheap overnight hotel in Jesmond, just outside Newcastle City Centre. For the rest of the night they drank the lager, watched a good comedy film to distract their troubled minds from the creature and all kinds of morbid things ahead in their future. They talked about women, jobs, cars, the state of the world, almost everything other than Grace, the funeral or the thing they had killed hours earlier.

'Hell of a long day this has been, bud,' Eric slurred, around one o'clock in the morning.

'Oh yeah, strange bloody day in all. We've got our health though,' said Taylor. He looked uncomfortable.

'Going to hit the sack now, mate. See you in a few hours, okay?' Eric said to him.

'Okay. Yeah, me too. Plenty booze in me,' Taylor replied. He watched Eric with a surprising sober interest, seeming thoughtful and secretive as he nodded.

Taylor walked off to the bathroom, leaving Eric in the main room alone. Eric was happily drunk and exhausted as he began to drift to sleep on the sofa. At last it was time to end the day's traumatic thoughts and experiences, and rest his confused and nervous mind for a while. His eyelids came to close so heavily and his head span just enough to send him instantly into a deep, anguished sleep.

'Eric?' a voice called out.

Grace's voice.

He did not really notice it, his consciousness sinking below into deep, dark sleep.

'Eric? Can you hear me?' she asked. He opened his eyes, though half asleep. The room was absent of any living soul other than him, only a chair, desk and the television showing snowy static. Then she appeared before him, she came like a fog, drifting up close.

'Well done Eric,' she told him, and smiled. It warmed him to see that smile again.

'What did I kill?' he asked.

Grace looked down at him.

'Evil, Eric. It's...evil, not human. Not animal: evil. There are more,' she said.

'How many more? Why? Where are they from?' Eric asked urgently wanting to know.

She was quiet briefly then spoke again.

'Another place. Near Maylen's Bar. Tomorrow, or another night,' she told him.

'Grace, how do you know this? Why do you know?' he asked.

She stood in the room at the end of the bed, or at least seemed to stand there, but was only a trace of herself and in a different, scarcely seen mood. She was still so beautiful to him, as this spectral apparition before him. He almost cried in frustration. He was so furious, so mad at losing her and wanted to hurt someone, blame someone. He would do anything to have her back for real, in the flesh, more than this.

'Please stop them. They plan...two groups...' she said calmly.

'Two groups? Who? What groups? These things?' he asked.

She looked desperately sad but smiled at him still. She stood quiet as she looked at him.

'How can you come back? Are you alive?' Eric asked. 'Or can I be with you somehow at all? Where are you?'

'No, Eric. I don't know where I am now. I can see...see them...see dark, evil things, horrible things...there was...beautiful light before...gone,' she said. 'But I can see you, too.' She walked toward the bed and leaned over to him gradually. She kissed his cheek. He closed his eyes, and a tear rolled down his right cheek.

'Grace, tell me more. I can't do anything unless I know more, unless I understand more...how did it happen? Why did it happen?' he asked desperately. 'I'll do absolutely anything to know, anything you ask me to do, really I will,' he told her spirit before him, tears in his eyes.

'In time...now, listen,' she answered, 'and find them...'

He could hear the distance, the sorrow and sadness in her estranged voice. It killed him to feel so disconnected from her. To know she was there, but not really there. It was like a crackling distant phone line between them, a bad signal. But he could hear her on that signal, hear her message.

When he opened his eyes, she had gone, and he was alone. With his heavy, hungover head, he tried to keep in mind what she had told him. He found a pen and writing pad by the telephone on the side desk and scrawled the information down. Tomorrow he would stop more vile evil beasts, stop anything to have her back, he thought. He moved to the sofa and fell into the deepest, heaviest sleep he had had in a long time.

Emma looked at the ripening black clouds overhead as she walked out of the bakery shop with her sandwich in the morning. She passed newsagents and saw the evening paper on the stand out front.

'What the hell...?' she exclaimed.

The image on the front page held her attention. It was a slightly blurred C.C.T.V. image blown up large from a crime scene camera. There were regular images of low life crimes or gangs on the front pages, but the men in this photo looked extremely familiar to her. She would have sworn that the larger figure resembled Eric. The other could just as easily be Taylor she thought as she took a closer look.

She took the paper to the counter in the newsagents and paid for it, then quickly continued down the street while reading the article beside the large front page image. The two men were apparently suspected of causing harm, road crashes and attacks connected to missing people in the last week or more. The report suggested they might be highly dangerous, unpredictable and guilty of further serious crimes and could be somewhere in the north east area still. If anyone saw anyone who resembled either of the two young men they were to contact the local police authorities immediately, it stated. She thought that she must be just imaging the resemblances to Eric, but then she had to admit that the other man did look a lot like Taylor. Could either or both actually be involved in crime or attacks such as the paper was suggesting?

It did look so much like Eric and Taylor, she thought. If it was them, what the hell were they doing? This seriously worried her. She had hoped that Eric would be able to get through the passing of Grace with as little trouble as possible. This did now make her wonder about how well she and Grace had really known Eric. Could he really have been some kind of lowlife criminal, or a senseless violent attacker? She understood how this must have been affecting Eric, pushing him to the edges of sanity. She could not have him roaming the North with Taylor, though, taking out their anger and frustration on random strangers. It might be that they had been involved in some kind of fight or incident, and it had been distorted, overblown by the newspapers. The news does that all the time for a good story, she thought. Emma knew Eric was a level-headed, intelligent guy; he had had his troubles attending college and obeying the teachers, but he had never been a dangerous, reckless type of person, she thought. As she had hung out with Grace and him many times in the last couple of years, he always seemed a real loving, funny, sane bloke. But then death affects different people in different ways, changes people. There had never been any circumstances like these to test him in such a way, she thought.

She had still not been able to contact Eric again since after the funeral, even though she had been trying his phone about a dozen times a day. She returned to the city library, past students and a busking guitar player, while wondering if she should go to Eric's home. She had not considered it straight away, knowing that Eric usually spent very little time there, trying to avoid his father, and usually stayed at Grace's place before she had died. He could be anywhere with Taylor, she decided.

Chapter 7

Morning sunlight shone through the curtains and woke Eric from his troubled sleep. He slowly stood and walked over toward Taylor, who lay in the bed in the next room. Eric nudged him awake against his whimpered protests.

'Who...hey...you okay?' Taylor asked.

'Yeah, I'm okay. Let's get up,' Eric told him.

'Alright, no rush is there?' Taylor said, sitting up in bed.

'Listen, she came back to me, Grace. Told me of another place,' Eric explained.

'Oh, okay. There's more then?' Taylor said.

'Yes, absolutely. You still with me?' Eric asked.

'Of course. Let's get dressed and moving then. When do we go - now?'

'Yeah, I want to do a few things before we find the next thing,' Eric told him.

They got dressed and left the cheap hotel, stepping out onto the cold, grey streets near the outskirts of Newcastle, and walked on together.

They thought about what it meant and how they were involved in things. Eric was sure that they were supposed to do whatever Grace told them, and try to understand her words as well as they could. They collected some food and began to think about the things that they were up against. They wondered about just really what they were fighting, these night time monsters, whether they were scientific accidents, or real demons or devils. They had only just survived with the use of the luck of the shelving posts, but they would take some kinds of weapons if they were going to confront more creatures ahead. Of course they had seen the movies, and it was always wooden stakes, silver bullets, holy water. But that was only entertainment, which took inspiration from folk legend and the Bible. It was not real life, not real encounters with real creatures. But just what were folk legends, and what was the Bible, and other holy books, Eric wondered. He was no strong believer, and used to see things like that as simply entertainment or social tools, but just what if there really was some element of real truth in biblical stories and folk tales?

Eric and Taylor stopped in at a hardware and garden centre. Eric bought a hoe and some smaller shovels, while Taylor bought some rope, chains, and a large spade and shears. As they drove closer to the area Eric remembered something Grace had told him about. He brought up a surprising but possibly helpful notion.

'Taylor, would you mind if we quickly stop around this next street, just quickly?' Eric asked.

'No, no problem. Go for it,' Taylor answered.

They turned up the next street and they could both see the church near the middle of it. Taylor said nothing as Eric parked the car up and walked up into the church. A couple of minutes later, Eric returned quickly, carrying two small bottles. He put them in a bag in the back of the car and started the car immediately.

'You never know,' Eric said.

'Right, okay. Of course,' Taylor said, though he was not entirely sure what he was agreeing with.

That night nothing happened. They were waiting across from the place Grace spoke of but they did not encounter another evil thing like before. Taylor seemed relieved, but Eric was disappointed. It gave them time to think about it all through. Eric knew that Taylor must be wondering what the problem was, but he could not exactly phone Grace up anytime like before she died. They just had to wait; wait for her, and for the next time. They left the place, but were still ready to fight, to come up against hellish things, and save someone. They returned to the cheap hotel, drank, watched cable TV and waited for time to pass.

Eric walked through along into the bathroom alone and, closing the door, he heard Grace again.

'Now, Eric, the street in Byker. It's now,' she whispered.

He and Taylor raced out to the car. Eric drove at great speed and only just missed colliding with a sports car. Taylor watched with shocked fascination at Eric's new recklessness.

They reached the street, parked and got out of the car. The surrounding area was cloaked in the dark of night, and their breaths were visible in the cold air. Every sound and movement around the street got their attention as they viewed the area for the terror to come.

'Grace was not more specific?' Taylor asked respectfully.

'Just said this street. If she knew more, I think she'd have said,' Eric told him.

'Right, yes,' Taylor replied.

The building of Philip's company was an impressively grand, cavernous, modern home to success. The money they made was regularly in quadruple figures, giving them very adequate business security and a good reputation, making most deals and investments easy and enjoyable. They were one of the most successful Northern businesses of the previous two decades, and inevitably many other companies were envious and curious as to how they did so well again and again.

Unfortunately, though they were prepared for attempts to break in and steal secrets, valuable information, techniques, or plans, they were only ever prepared for human criminals attempting to enter and nothing more.

As employees left after six in the evening, there were a small number still lingering around but the darkness had settled outside, allowing movement. Two figures slowly crept down along beside the deep cover of tall trees. They saw a security guard patrolling the area ahead. Some might have turned and left, but not these two. This security guard was pumped up and willing for a painful fight, and he was finally in luck.

He turned, and in a fatal split second, they were on him. They dug deep, pierced, cut. Razor sharp clawed hands ripped him, and blood poured from him lavishly onto the grass. His mouth covered, he was dragged down. His bowels spilled over cold concrete beside the light of the highly placed lamp and security camera.

Quickly enough, they took his keys and pass cards. They entered through into the back corridors, and moved along, searching. Any regular men should not have been able to pass such sophisticated, expensive new security systems, but they were not any kind of ordinary men at all.

Turning corners, watching cameras overhead, and not really seeming to care, they confronted another two security officers. The officers stood no real chance. They were grabbed, struggling, then shockingly torn, butchered in sickeningly artistic ways by both dark strange figures, flesh ripped from bone, blood poured over clean white floor tiles. It happened in less than a couple of minutes. Two muscular security men murdered so fast and hideously by two mysterious figures, clawed hands dripping with blood, dissecting and splitting the bodies to pieces. Not just death, but a message to someone who might understand the meaning.

They escaped just as fast, all security cameras experiencing electrical glitches, shortening them out until minutes later. The two figures ran out under dark shadows.

'Was that enough?' one quietly asked the other as they ran.

'It will do, for now,' the other answered. 'That's what he said to do.'

They were gone, back into the hidden places of their sanctuary.

Between the still-lit night signs of newsagents and wine bars along Tynemouth, a struggle broke out between a group of men, while most others were getting into cars and heading to safety of homes and houses. The men punched and argued with force, but their captors were too strong and began cutting them, tearing their skin off their limbs as the men howled and cried with agonising pain. Bloodied hands pushed and shoved, but death claimed the two men. The bodies dropped to the ground in a mess of innards and blood at the opening of an alleyway.

The demons who so rapidly and easily slaughtered these two men initiated a system of lies and whispers. Other demons were moving around only a couple of streets from that area. The opportunity was there, ready to use. Words were shouted dramatically, signs then left in a trail of blood and marks to lead them. The bodies were soon enough found.

The other demons moved in, hearing talk as they approached.

'Jesus! The killer! The brave one, move!' was heard from someone, who appeared to have ran off then, feet steps heard in the distance. The demon stalked along and came upon the freshly mutilated corpses.

A man with numerous rings pierced through his face and a positive expression looked out at the town around and stood outside his tattoo parlour as he closed up the shutters for the evening. He then saw an attractive young woman walking his way from up the opposite street.

'Good evening Ricky, you heard of the grim tales taking place?' she enquired.

'Certainly am, actually, certainly am. The two young guys, interfering still. Problems, it seems. In all the news now, right?' he said.

'That's how it seems, yeah,' she said.

'Make you worried?' he asked.

'Only if some don't know how to react to these two. No news yet, then?' She asked.

He looked at the streets around. They knew these streets, the truths and fears. They were powerful in these streets. More than gang lords, more than politicians. The streets around were so quiet then, so bare of life.

'He managed so far. Things are just more...interesting now. Aren't they?' he said, nodding thoughtfully to himself.

'Interesting for Andrew,' she answered quietly. The tattooed and pierced man's eyes suddenly sparked and flickered red as he turned and finished locking up the shutters to his tattoo parlour.

Under street lights, Eric and Taylor walked around briefly, up the narrow dimly-lit street, where cheap restaurants and boarded up shops stood. It all seemed normal, mundane to them. There was no clear sign for them out there. It was all just normal, regular Northern streets, the places they knew, the places that had always just been boring, normal life. Eric watched a few stray people walk past along the street and felt a little useless and angry.

Across from the street, parked near a closed pet shop, David sat in his own car watching them, watching the night with them. He made notes in a small notepad and flicked his chrome lighter open and closed repeatedly as he watched the scene. He hoped to catch them with the kind of evidence that he could use not just to save the people of the North but also to save his confused mind. He wanted to know if they were personally involved in the things which haunted his mind, or if they really did simply stumble into this dark madness. Poor devils, he thought.

"Someone save their souls, and mine," he said quietly in his car as he watched.

Eric and Taylor stood around in the shadow of a shop doorway waiting for a sign of danger, with their heavy rucksacks containing their weapons on their backs. They hoped that no police stopped by and wanted to take a look at the contents.

'Eric, how precise was she last time?' Taylor asked.

'She knew, she knows about these things,' Eric told him sharply.

'But she did not know exactly, I mean precisely when or exactly where?' Taylor said.

'Right, okay, but it's important we're here anyway. Be patient,' Eric told him, 'let's look up and down the street for a few minutes'

They began walking up, casually looking down the alleys and into bars and pubs. Any kind of situation could happen, and here they were, two unlikely heroes, Taylor an unemployed rock club D.J. and Eric a sometime guitarist in a covers band studying modern art. There had only been one creature last time, but Eric wondered what would happen if there were two, three or many more the next time. Could he and Taylor actually stop them alone? If not, could they trust the police? He was not sure he should or could even begin to try to explain what these things were to them if he had to. With Grace he would stop the creatures. She knew they could, and she seemed to have faith in them, which gave him some hope at least.

'Where did it come from do you think?' Taylor asked him seriously.

'I've no idea...they're somewhere in Newcastle, hiding or waiting. They might have been around for a long time. Just imagine that...' Eric said.

They both thought about that for a moment, and it blew their minds. Had everyone been getting on with their daily lives while these strange bloodthirsty beasts, these wild killing creatures roamed hidden, existing in uncomprehending illogical ways, possibly taking lives whenever they wanted or needed?

A cold wind blew over Eric down the street. He shivered and looked in the direction that the wind had come from. He and Taylor both then felt some strange rumble underground, which seemed to travel from that direction quickly.

'Follow me,' Eric said then to Taylor and began to run up the street.

Eric knew right then that this was the cue; the time was then, their monster had arrived. The rumble rushed along, and they ran just behind it over the ground. Their feet shook as they ran onward, as if some mighty creature were burrowing along below. It then suddenly seemed to stop at the entrance to a bar right up in front of them. Eric and Taylor looked at each other then Eric put his hand to the bar door. It was closed. They must have only closed up very recently as his watch read just minutes past eleven.

'Hello? Hello? Could someone come to the door please?' he shouted, and banged on the doors for attention. Silence. He peered carefully through the frosted glass window at the dark room inside. Through drawn shutters, he could only make out slight outlines of the bar and some tables and chairs.

'There's someone near the back in there, I see movement,' he said to Taylor.

'Shout louder. I hope police don't see us,' Taylor told him.

'Hey! Come to the door! You're in danger,' Eric shouted loudly.

'Well now we're very suspicious,' Taylor sighed.

Then a noise like something big being sick or a cry in pain, or both at once, came from inside.

'Fuck, that sounds messed up,' Taylor said, alarmed.

'Hey, over here!' Eric said, banging on the door aggressively.

He saw inside the bar, between deep dark shadows, something lurching around at a fast pace. It seemed large, vast and hunched over. He also saw a woman, he thought, and a man running from the other lurching thing, pushing tables and chairs out of their way and at it in defence. The thing moved over nearer the man, who was protecting the woman behind a long table at the far end of the room. The thing then suddenly grabbed at the man, and swung him like some flimsy doll and then began to beat him against some tables, breaking him, killing him in seconds, the body broken and bloodied. The woman gasped in horror but took the chance to run straight over across the cluttered dark room, and, rattling the locks and bolts, quickly opened the door for Eric.

He came in quickly with Taylor behind him. They all looked at the hulking creature which stood growling behind two rows of long tables at the far end of the room.

'Help me, please! I don't know what it is!' the woman said to Eric and Taylor, struggling to speak in a strained, anxious rasp.

'Stay back or get outside. We'll deal with it,' Eric told her. In his head to himself, he then said some kind of frantic jumbled prayer for help or guidance. He was not actually certain of any kind of higher power, although after communicating with Grace he was much closer to believing in something. He supposed that it could not hurt to ask for help privately, especially as these evil things seemed not of this earth.

'Taylor, get ready,' he said. They both watched the beast as it saw them, and it began to move differently.

It seemed to view them with sudden interest and anger, but also Eric was sure that it seemed to be thinking. He saw in its eyes, and he was sure it was thinking like any intelligent regular man might look at another before speaking. It was not simply some powerful supernatural beast, but a thinking, conscious creature.

'Separate, use what we have, anything. Copy me,' Eric whispered to Taylor as they stepped apart then across the bar. The woman stood by the front door, then stepped outside. The beast leapt suddenly out into the middle of the room and began to launch tables and chairs wildly and

41

effortlessly at them. Both Eric and Taylor ducked away, behind shelves, pillars, other tables, and tried to creep up closer to the thing. Eric looked over at Taylor, trying to communicate to him to cover him as he approached the beast. As he quietly moved in closer, it turned around, sensing him. Just in time, Taylor caused a distraction by pushing over a couple of tables across the other side of the room with his spade.

The beast only paid attention to Eric, though, and the pair saw each other up close.

'What are you?' Eric said quietly while holding out his shears in defence. It was as if he was looking into the eyes of some secret, these red luminous eyes filled with death and murder.

It flicked out muscular, clawed hands before him, and then it let out a sound that was both bizarre and disturbing: part cackle, part howl. It went right at Eric, and he moved back while hitting out to attack it. They clashed hard, both pushing against the other. Taylor came up behind the thing, and Eric gave him a stern look, but he remained hesitant. The beast pushed harder, snarling and knocking Eric back into tables, smashing glasses and bottles behind them, and quickly slashed Eric across his chest. He crumpled down in pain and the beast growled again as it moved in close to finish him.

It grabbed at him, by his right arm. Taylor then suddenly knocked the beast with surprising force in the back with his spade. It dropped Eric, turning to face Taylor to give him a sample of Eric's pain.

'Oh fucking hell,' Taylor said. He felt trapped and so unbelievably small, the prey of some unholy predator.

Eric found the strength to rise and push the shears out and deeply penetrate the lower back of the creature. It howled shockingly loudly, turning around and wailing before Taylor. He moved in and hit it twice with the spade; once in the face, then hard in the chest. It threw its large arms around in a wild rage toward both of them, claws missing them by inches. Behind it, Eric felt around in his rucksack and pulled out a small bottle.

He opened it quickly and thrust it across the direction of the beast as it barked at him, scratching his arms. In seconds, water showered over it, and it recoiled with visible disgust and fear. Eric had found something unlikely but successful. Water he had collected from the church font, what some might call 'holy water,' had actually scared the beast. He was not sure immediately if it had actually hurt it. He could barely believe it, seeing it work like in the old horror films. It howled, smashing tables as it fell to the floor, wild eyed and caked in blood. It reached for Eric, then Taylor, who both stepped away from it carefully.

'What was that?' Taylor asked him.

'Hand of God, maybe. Or just some kind of luck,' Eric replied.

They looked at the large wounded beast as it suddenly smoked and crackled with unexpected bursts of electricity before them. In the next moment it gradually decayed, wasted away and dissolved, and then was gone, leaving only a large stain of sinewy muck, blood and bile, which reeked phenomenally.

'Jesus, that's weird,' Taylor said, perplexed and staring at the mess.

Eric looked at the mess and felt his bloody chest, which stung profusely at his touch.

'We should check the woman is okay,' he told Taylor, who nodded and began toward the front doors.

Eric looked at the clutter of astounding destruction all around the bar room, at the smashed tables, chairs, mirrors, glasses. Then he thought seriously about the creature; where it did actually come from, and where it had gone to so fast? It was not animal for sure, but not man exactly. Could it be some kind of science lab experiment gone terribly wrong? This thing had bubbled and burned out then vanished right before them. That was kind of, well, supernatural, he thought. Impossible and supernatural. These things were from outside of known reality, he thought.

This thing clearly could think in a similar level to him, though offered no English words. These bastard things could well be from some place we fear or fail to understand, he decided.

'She's alright,' Taylor shouted back in to him from the front doorway, having found the woman chain smoking outside. He prevented her from entering to look at the torn and butchered remains of her work colleague inside.

So what did this mean, Eric thought. What did this beast signify, coming to this place, this specific bar, and trying to kill these two people? He then stopped and turned to look at the woman standing next to Taylor. She was familiar in some vague sense; he recognised her face, her look, and her eyes. He had seen her somewhere before, he was almost sure. Then it came to him: the news. She had been in the news some months back, he remembered. What was it about? A protest of some kind. She had stood against something...some building or business moving in, taking over somewhere.

Was that important too now?

'Who are you?' he asked the saddened woman.

'I should ask you two the same. I'm Olivia Morrison. I own this bar with the...man, dead, in there,' she said sombrely.

'Sorry. I'm...well, we were just passing. You were in the news, right?' Eric said.

'Yes, the Abottsman contracts debate, and other things. I was against the demolition,' she said, but stopped, having to breathe deeply and focus. The sudden violence and death was almost too much to comprehend. She continued. 'The demolition of the old local churches. I'm not specifically religious, but I appreciated the aesthetic value of them, and some help the communities and children. Many religious folk did join me and we demonstrated and stood strong for a change. Stopped the demolition. We've got plans for the churches,' she explained, gradually regaining composure.

Eric began to think. He saw that she could very well have been marked out clearly. She could have been a target, as she had helped local churches to survive. Things were becoming clear, making a little sense now.

'What were the companies involved that were trying to demolish the churches?' he asked quickly.

'Oh several, these places being very desirable land. Obviously the Abbotsman company, Villo and Banks and then...Cowell Brothers Ltd. They held out and kept pressure on. Not enough, though,' she told him with a slight smile.

'Right, good to hear. Sorry about all of this. It's unbelievable, I know,' he said apologetically.

'So you were just passing by here?' she asked.

'Yes, just luck in a way. Look, I'm sorry but we have to go. You'll be okay, will you?' Eric asked.

'Yes, I'll call some friends. You go if you have to,' she said

'Okay then. Take care,' Eric said and turned to Taylor, patting him on the arm.

She nodded in agreement.

'I've no idea who or what the hell that thing was or why it came. Thank you, both of you. You take care too,' she told them. She walked them over to their car then began to phone for police and an ambulance.

'Is that it for tonight?' Taylor asked when he and Eric got in the car.

'I suppose so. Let's get back and rest. I think I've learned something useful at least,' Eric told him.

They drove back around the Northern streets. They understood that this whole thing, this hunting of shockingly horrific beasts, was going to take some time. They drove around for a short while and stopped by a different hotel, just as cheap and bland as the last. This would be a place to rest for another night or more. The two young men sat together in the quiet room thinking about the next encounter.

'These ancient gospel pieces are really important, they matter to these monstrous things. There is some link between them. They connect up,' Eric said, after a long quiet moment between them.

Taylor looked back at him with curiosity 'But what are they? Where are they from and what do they tell us?'

'That's a damn good question. The...the demons, they want the scripture relics. These things hold some secret power. If we try our best to interpret them, maybe we'll know everything we need to know. We'll maybe be able to stop all of this'

'Did Grace know where these pages were? Doesn't she know what they mean?' Taylor asked.

Eric shook his head. 'She hasn't told me that much yet. I'm thinking maybe she doesn't know everything about it all. It's old scripture, there's maybe Aramaic...'

'Yep, it's biblical stuff alright. I've seen similar stuff in Canterbury and Durham Cathedral.'

'Holy words. Holy warnings, or...instructions. Like those pieces they say they left out of the bible? They translated it right here up North, yes...' Eric agreed.

'Was it...Bede in Jesmond?' Taylor wondered.

'Somewhere else...near the coast, I think.'

Eric was glad he could count on Taylor; even for the little help he offered, he was there to stop Eric losing his sanity completely, though he was unsure either of them could remain sane much longer.

Chapter 8

David had trouble finding them at first, but eventually after making calls and being tipped off by his leads he found them and the bar they were visiting. He realized that he had turned up too late as he saw them exit the bar with the distraught-looking female bar owner. He knew her, and she added another mysterious level to the story now for him. He did not intervene still, wanting instead to continue watching, learning of what Eric and Taylor were doing. These two young men were very suspicious; there was no doubt of it, he thought. But they also seemed to be helping, not harming, but he still only saw part of the reality. He did hope that they could survive the things that might come against them. He knew they would get no help or understanding from the police or others anytime soon. They were brave men, he thought. Perhaps braver than any police or politicians. Braver, perhaps, than he had ever been or was ever likely to be.

The evenings were now quiet preparation and ominous waiting between the slaying of monsters for Eric and Taylor. They had no real clues as to how long this dangerous journey might last or what might come of it, how many they might have to fight or why, and it was almost driving both of them to the edge of sanity. They coped individually through a heavy intake of whisky, the occasional prayer, dirty jokes, and loud music through the night.

With all of these things needed to cope with trying to understand or ignore the beasts they had seen and killed, Eric did soon enough take time alone in the bathroom to think about Grace, and their times together, when life was so easy and joyful.

Eric and Taylor almost avoided all difficult questions either one of them might wish to ask the other, knowing it was Eric who would learn more whenever Grace returned to him again with more news or instructions. The alcohol and joints were numbing them to the fear of what could go wrong.

'Is this helping?' Taylor asked suddenly between vodka shots.

'Huh? How'd you mean?' Eric asked.

'With the funeral and Grace being gone?' Taylor said.

'Well, she's not gone, is she?' Eric argued, with a slur in his voice.

'No, but since it happened, you must be mega pissed and all, this shit...just us now...' Taylor said, rambling away incoherently.

'Shut your mouth now,' Eric said, a little angry with him.

'What? But I'm pointing out the weird stuff man...' Taylor said, ignorant of his offensiveness. Eric stood up.

'Get away from me!' he shouted.

'Hey, we're a team in this, we're righteous defenders,' Taylor said.

'Just fuck off with your loud mouth! Go!' Eric warned.

Taylor looked back, angry but shocked.

'Whatever, then,' Taylor replied.

Taylor did leave Eric to calm down. He left the building, walking down the stairs and out to the street. He did not mind, even in his slight drunken state. He had a place to go, to do things still connected to the events which they were trapped in.

The death of Grace had hit Taylor strongly, even though he did not personally know her too well. While Taylor was Eric's best friend, Grace had always seemed not to trust him, not choosing to offer him much attention. Before she had died, Taylor had become involved with a man who had offered him work and good times for only a few favours in return. Taylor had some kind of suspicion that knowing this man might have invited trouble to find him, Eric, Grace, and their other close friends. He had been stopping himself from thinking too much about this since he and Eric had been hunting these creatures but now he was going to meet the man called Andrew once more.

In a rarely frequented part of Byker, behind a garage and factory, Taylor walked on until he reached a doorway around a corner in near darkness. He knocked on the door as he tried to shake the lingering hangover. The door opened, and a man peered through the gap.

'Hello? Can I help?' he asked.

'Where's Andrew? I'm Taylor,' he told the man.

The door opened and Taylor was allowed into the building. It was dark and smoke-filled, and in need of repairs all around, with walls cracked and the paint peeling, and with rat and dog excrement in the corners here and there. Taylor had been introduced to many of the men and women that passed him as he was escorted down the corridor. They smiled, winked or looked at him one at a time. Shadows across the walls from the dim light suddenly stretched and bent into macabre demonic shapes, though Taylor was not afraid, as he knew where they came from.

Then he saw Andrew, the man who had given him opportunities that he could never have imagined experiencing without him.

'Taylor, glad you're back so soon,' Andrew said to him, with a smile which hid his motives.

'This is all getting very heavy, very stressful now, I'm telling you Andrew,' Taylor said.

'I understand, I do. But keep quiet. We'll sort everything out. Besides, you've lived like some kind of king, right?' Andrew said.

'Yes, I know. And thank you for it all. But Eric's really angry. It's hard to watch,' Taylor explained.

'So don't. Come out with me. Plenty for us to do; no limits, remember?' Andrew reminded him.

'I don't know. We've been...I'm getting him through Grace's death,' Taylor replied.

'Right, that's curious now. And I do hope you do that well,' Andrew said.

'Look, I have to. Okay, let's go somewhere for a short while at least, then,' Taylor said, feeling so stressed and confused.

Andrew looked at him sternly and thoughtfully.

'That's more like it. The body is safe, isn't it Taylor?' he said.

'Yes, you know it is. No problem there. It's fine,' Taylor answered.

'Okay then. Let's enjoy ourselves like only we can,' Andrew told him. He led Taylor down another corridor, passing more strange, warped shadows on the walls.

They came outside again, and walked to a car waiting for them.

'I've some gorgeous ladies waiting. And we'll get the blood flowing once more, right?' Andrew asked with a sinister grin as he got into the car.

'Certainly we will,' Taylor agreed.

And so this left Eric by himself in the cheap hotel room, sleeping and waking occasionally from uncomfortable dreams. Carl Jung and Sigmund Freud would have enjoyed dissecting his mind that night, but they would not have imagined the symbolic creatures tormenting his mind to be actually roaming the dark streets and roads around the North of England around him.

Eric knew he was doing something important, so he could forget the mess of a life he had waiting for him. His neglected college course, his dysfunctional rock band, and the unending family problems with his father could all wait while he attempted to save everyone without them even knowing at all. All those things were quite possibly meaningless, worthless. No, they were worth something, they were him and he was part of those things. But he was more than all of that, and this showed him that, and showed him bigger things, too. He thought of what more was out there, what was unknown to mankind. Scientists revealed new things all the time, but there was always something more mysterious left. All was mysterious he thought, and always would be.

He could never have predicted that he would be battling indescribably hellish beasts like these, with himself as some kind of foolish hero. Not too long before, Eric was simply hanging around between a life of selling drugs alongside his difficult studies and band with its own problems. His self-esteem had sunk too low, possibly because of his father's harsh comments and lack of interest or belief in him. Well now look at me, Eric thought.

His father was a good man, but a troubled and angry one too. His character and personality could change like the wind, unexpectedly scaring and frustrating Eric too often. He could be loyal, funny, and good to be around, but Eric could never guess when that would be. Crime had taken his father, though, not seriously but enough to make people whisper and talk behind Eric's back about the family, which always drove him to his wit's end. It was always any small chance to make a quick bit of money on the sly, a good deal for a friend or similar suspicious deeds. Eric had begun to mirror his father's ways recently, though his father would not know and would soon enough have plenty more to accuse him of.

Now Eric was feeling useful, focused and alive in a new, decent way. The job of hunting down these mysterious demon creatures for Grace was his task alone. He could see a fresh beginning in the future, if they did what Grace asked, so that he and she could be reunited once more like nothing bad had ever happened to her. His mind then travelled back to when he first knew Grace had died.

It had been Tuesday morning, nearly two weeks previously. Grace's father Philip had found her, and had soon after phoned Eric. He knew from the tone of his voice that Philip suspected him to have been involved in some way of causing her sudden, shocking death. Eric

49

immediately drove over to the house and Philip was unbelievably quiet and calm. He seemed to know how to act and what to do. Her mother and sister were meanwhile completely distraught, weeping, crying uncontrollably all day and for many more days to come. Eric himself cried with a mix of furious anger, confusion and frustrated sorrow, having to restrain himself from smashing things all around her parents' house and anywhere he went soon after in order to deal with his uncontrollable sadness and overwhelming grief.

He had screamed at Philip for answers, truth, reasons why it had happened. He wanted to know precisely what had happened to the woman he loved too much, how she had died so suddenly, and he kept wondering. He could just not believe that his perfect, beautiful girlfriend was gone, taken for no reason. Eric had seen her that morning, only hours before; had seen her sweet smile, her lovely eyes, felt her skin, felt her kiss on his lips. He thought, of course, that Philip would be feeling the same, if not even worse, but he seemed to show it in bizarrely restrained manner. Philip had no real answers to give immediately, and only expressed himself to be more sad and angry than Eric could ever be, while remaining quiet and calm. Philip tried to focus Eric, explaining that he had to comfort Grace's mother and sister through it all. Medics and police came soon enough. She was declared deceased and then shortly after they began to examine her body and condition to try to find the cause of death.

They found no real clues to explain it straight away before the funeral. She was labelled 'natural causes', though they kept the case open for any further information to reveal itself in the future. It certainly was strange how it all happened so fast; the investigation, the mourning, the funeral. That was how Eric looked at things from then on. It all passed too fast.

He had spoken with both her parents for long hours about the possible causes and continued to feel that Philip would get him arrested if there was any way at all. The unspoken hostility from Philip was constant. Eventually, Eric went to be alone, but then later met up with Taylor and Grace's close friend Emma, who both helped him to grieve through the pain of the imminent funeral. They found her death a shocking event in their lives, and each then dealt with it in their own individual ways. Like Eric, though they spent more time together, Taylor did soon disappear, which Eric saw as his need to think about it and hide his sadness. Emma, though, stayed there for him, emotional but strong, thoughtful and surprisingly ready to cope, but still with her own grief and response to the death.

With the death of Grace, Eric was not the only person suspicious of the unanswered mystery of how she had died. David overheard reports and recognized the surname called into hospital staff from the police station' He opened his thoughts afresh to his findings from a few years ago, of the unexplained mysteries, and began to consider his old notes and theories about the locally respected and admired businessman.

David would not ignore it all this time, he thought. The news that he had overheard was unbelievably significant and curious, and he could not just let it pass. No matter how outlandish, terrifying, illogical or incomprehensible, he would follow up all and every ounce of information that suggested serious social threat and connections to the events that he knew of from years before, events which had always made Philip seem dangerous but without enough connecting evidence. Until now.

In the days since the death of Grace, her father Philip had been with his wife and younger daughter, away from his hugely successful company and the demanding schedule of meetings, discussions and planning which he would usually take part in on any other day.

At the main company building, all employees were respectfully sad and sorry for his loss. All of his employees viewed him as a highly inspirational, respectable, encouraging boss and business success story who had achieved so much in only a decade or so and was such a well-known family man. While most were respectful, some employees of the company inevitably began to talk quietly. Someone always starts the gossiping, and some were soon discussing how Grace just might have passed away. Some wondered if there actually were some suspicious circumstances around the death, some unexpected thing which she was involved in. They all knew how well known and envied Philip was to other businesses and similar companies around. They wondered about how Grace might have dealt with having a hugely successful, almost perfect father, often in the newspapers, business sheets, on television news. Had she been seeking attention from him, playing the wild child, pushing the limits, doing anything to get his attention? It was so tragic, but then sometimes the best families have the darkest, most tragic tales.

Many people could imagine a number of wild, twisted stories, influenced by films and soap storylines, and many were simply afraid that what had killed Grace might be too closely connected to the business. Were any of the employees in similar danger any time soon?

The company, which dealt with international sales and the manufacture of computer software, was being steered by the ones whom Philip trusted below him: his co-managers, partners Neil Kurt and Jessica Bromwell. They continued to hold the regular meetings, oversee the work in the various building departments, and manage finances as he would expect.

During a tense day, Neil took his fellow team member Graham Benson out to an expensive Newcastle city bar for a quick lunch to break up the day.

'We're doing okay aren't we, do you think-without Philip?' Neil asked between eating a Panini.

'Right, yes. We've got it all tight and secure, no problems. Like any regular week, right?' Graham replied.

'Yes, right. Good to know Philip can be at home looking after the family right now,' Neil said soberly.

'It's is awful. Hope he holds together. It's a horrible thing. So bad,' Graham said.

Then Neil suddenly spoke very differently, a strange tone in his words.

'Graham, you...you haven't...seen him being different?' he asked.

'What? Well, you know, she's dead. His daughter has died,' Graham answered.

'No, Graham, I mean...before she died...' Neil said, not exactly sure how to explain his thoughts.

'What?' Graham asked, simply confused.

'Forget it. Just...we have to keep it all moving along. Come on, let's get back now, yeah?' Neil suggested, feeling a little embarrassed and lost.

They stood and moved to the entrance of the bar.

'Just going to the...' Graham said.

'Oh, right, okay,' Neil replied, understanding.

Neil waited outside the bar, cold wind blowing over him as the lunch hour rush of people surged past on the busy Newcastle high street. The city of Newcastle was moving on reasonably catching up with modern culture, international styles, views and opinions from the wider world outside. Between the many new thriving restaurants and businesses, Neil still felt a sadness as he knew only minutes away was the tragic street where beautiful, innocent Grace had died in such mysterious circumstances.

All the people passing by continued their own personal lives, while he stood feeling uncomfortable. He looked at the faces around, the moods in the expressions, the eyes...red eyes.

Red eyes burning deep on a strange face across the crowded street then...gone.

What the hell was that? He was quite stressed out because of holding the business steady with Jessica; it was a phenomenal amount of work to cope with. Perhaps the stress was manifesting unusual things before him, he wondered. He took a deep, anxious breath.

'You okay there?' Graham asked as he reappeared.

'Hmm? Oh shit, right, yes...I suppose so,' Neil replied.

They walked back to the offices together, Neil with a definite sense of uncertainty in himself and his surroundings.

The car park was almost empty, and Jessica walked back into the company's office building. People were walking between rooms, focused on tasks, discussing work, exchanging papers in a professional manner, like always. A woman approached her from the front reception area when she passed.

'Jessica, there's a man here wants to talk about Philip,' she told her.

'Who is he?' Jessica asked.

'He did not say. He's very...different. He said it was about some previous business,' the receptionist told her.

'Does he know Philip is not here?' Jessica asked.

'I said you might help him,' the receptionist admitted.

Jessica gave her a stern but knowing look.

'Alright, okay, where?' she asked.

The secretary then led Jessica around to the inside waiting area where they saw the tall, thin man, smiling in his dignified, slightly gothic suede suit and boots. His tied, long hair was almost greasy, but he did impress with a sculpted and bony but handsome face which smiled at them in its paleness.

'Hello there. The boss isn't here, is he?' he said.

'No, I 'm sorry, he is taking time away. Personal family matters. Is it very important, I can't really say when he will be in at the moment,' Jessica told him with a professional suspicion.

'This all his? Philip, right?' the thin man enquired, still smiling as he looked around, gesturing.

'He established this company, yes. How do you know him, may I ask?' Jessica said.

He stepped around, looked down the corridors, and looked up at the impressive interior of the long wide entrance foyer through to the other connected sections of the grand building, the modern art sculptures, the fine, expensive stained glass windows.

'I'm proud. Good for him. Old friends. Give him my regards,' he said, then instantly turned and walked straight out of the building. Both women watched him leave, stunned and baffled by his words and attitude. They were both equally confused and suspicious.

Chapter 9

Eric left the motel after an hour, needing fresh air and space to think. He walked out into the dark night, under the miserable black rainclouds. All kinds of things were happening around the world this night, he thought. Good things, bad things and all in between, and man could not explain all of it. He was not entirely sure if Taylor would return to join him, but he decided that that just might be best. If not, well that was how it would be. Perhaps Emma might be more use than he had imagined. As he walked down the quiet streets of the edge of town, he saw a crooked, old church ahead. It looked about ready to come crumbling down to the ground in pieces any second. It held a strange fascination for him, and he found himself walking closer up to it, walking up through the church yard grounds, and then he opened the front door and stepped inside.

On stepping inside he looked around the small, crumbling church. It was in much need of some loving repair and attention, with the stone wall crumbling away and paint peeling on all sides. He noticed a tall pulpit up front and etchings along the pews. There was not much light illuminating the cavernous main church room, only perhaps a dozen lit candles right up at the front and a couple down back near the door. There were no other people inside at all, and as he stepped up the aisle his shoes made sounds that echoed loudly off the stone walls in the otherwise deathly quiet around him. It was chillingly cold inside, but he realised that he liked it like that as it kept him focused and awake. As he walked towards the front, he casually observed the surprisingly fascinating and detailed stained glass windows high at either side of the building walls, showing cryptic and mysterious scenes of tales from centuries ago that he just may have known. He stopped to inspect one particular window, the scene seeming to be of some kind of sacrifice of denouncement that intrigued him. He heard breathing near him. He turned his head suddenly and found a man looking at him quietly, smiling back.

'I'm very sorry. Should I leave?' Eric said.

'No, not if you want to be here. I'm Father Gaskill. Please feel free to look around,' the man told him.

'Thank you. I'm Eric. I'm not in the way or anything?' Eric asked, checking to be sure.

'No, please. Everyone is welcome here. This is a sanctuary and a place to worship. A place of forgiveness,' Gaskill told him pleasantly. He then slowly walked away from Eric to tend to some books and bibles at a table near the side wall.

'I do pray, you know,' Eric suddenly said aloud. He instantly felt shocked and embarrassed at his words. Gaskill turned back to face Eric again.

'Well that's great news. I hope it helps. Does it?' Gaskill asked softly.

'Maybe, in some way. But right now...more than in a long time. Can I ask you a question?' Eric said, just slightly nervous.

'Go ahead, no problem,' Gaskill replied.

'Do you think most people, people who, you know, don't step foot inside a place like this...do you think they still pray, though...to God?' Eric asked.

'Yes, I think many do, if not nearly all. Perhaps not every day, but probably in times of great need, in bad times. I think people want to believe, but they're scared, cynical, afraid, confused...I think they would get much more from it if they came here to do so, but I'm obviously biased,' Gaskill said to him. He watched Eric, knowing that here was a young man with great heavy thoughts in his head, spiritual struggle, scientific scepticism and pride holding him back from a freer life. 'Do you want an Irish coffee? I was making one. It's pretty cold tonight,' Gaskill said, and Eric smiled back finally.

A few minutes later, Gaskill brought out the coffees to the front row of pews near to the altar, where Eric was waiting quietly. It felt very strange and unexpected, Eric thought, as he ate a muffin from Gaskill with the Irish coffee in the dimly lit, gothic surroundings. Perhaps not all churches were boring, irrelevant places, he thought.

'I'm tired; it's been a long week for me. The next might be even longer and harder, though,' Eric stated openly, sipping the coffee.

'Are you in trouble, Eric? If you don't mind me enquiring,' Gaskill asked.

'I just might be, actually, but not because I'm any kind of criminal. It's…difficult to explain. I've stopped some bad things from happening but I think I might get blamed for things even so. I didn't really want to do these things, get involved, you know, but I have, and I feel guilty in a way,' Eric confided. He looked at Gaskill, who seemed very interested and concerned, thoughtfully nodding as he listened to Eric.

'There are bad things in our lives, Eric. Sometimes there can simply seem to be just too many: you stop one thing and along come another. But for every bad thing, a good thing can cancel it out. The grace of God can come along with us to do this. We might not even know it until everything is fine again. We just won't know everything. Faith is useful in times like this,' Gaskill replied.

'Right. I try to listen, for Him. Recently, though, so many unbelievable things have happened, I mean really shocking, appalling things…I am getting confused, I think, not everything seems absolutely black or white like it used to be…or as real...' Eric said, and stopped hearing his words coming out.

'There are many helpful parts of scripture I can suggest. The book of Job is often useful. Trust in God, he doesn't let us down. Believe me; I've had my own hard, shitty times too. He's still there, all the while,' Gaskill said surprisingly.

'Okay, I might look those up. You have a copy I can use?' Eric asked. Gaskill reached behind the near pew and offered up a Bible, which Eric accepted.

'Father, what do you think of the things we fear? I mean things we sometimes don't acknowledge or admit to fearing more than the little things that don't matter?' Eric asked.

Gaskill sat silent for a brief moment, then answered.

'They can tempt us, and lie to us, distract us from good. Sometimes we ourselves can be a more deadly monster than anything that we might fear out there. I think you are a good person, Eric, but be aware of yourself,' Gaskill told him.

'I'm trying to do that. I should be going now,' Eric said and stood up. 'Thank you anyway, for the drink and food. And the advice.'

'I know of the woman in the news a few months back, trying to keep another local church from being demolished,' Gaskill then added. 'Interesting occurrence; she was an admitted atheist, but felt compelled, for some hard to explain reason. That church, I know, had significant relevance to the history of the saints when they travelled from Holy

Island. So very interesting...and not the only thing. There is a pressure. But I don't seek to bore you now...' he told Eric

'No, it is interesting,' Eric agreed

'Always pushing, you see, to close churches, holy buildings, they say for land, but...I see many reasons for these things. Well, you look tired still,' he said, finishing.

'Well, yes, I suppose I should make a move,' Eric replied.

They shook hands, and Gaskill walked Eric to the front doors of the church and then watched him leave.

Chapter 10

Eric wandered with many thoughts of guilt, anxiety and confusion reeling deep through his mind. He felt like a fragile sack of nerves, somehow gifted with power which could do good if he only knew how to act in the next couple of hours. He kept thinking back, thinking of when she was still alive and when she left him...

There was Eric, and there was Grace, both just out of college. They loved each other with unashamed passion and sincere lust. There was a dangerous drama in their love, though.

A fiery outburst from Eric sent Grace away angry at him and anxious to prove him wrong. Her family was good, her father an honest, hardworking business man who was well-respected and cared for his family. Eric did not seem to believe this. She would prove him wrong. Entering into her father's study one afternoon, after busting the lock, she dug deep into journals, files, computer documents, folders, and papers. She learned much of her father's early career, his travels, his life before he married her mother. He had moved through several jobs early on, then began to climb higher with more responsibilities, bigger roles in companies. She wanted to be able to explain how Philip had his very well paying job and his company, his reputation. It was hard to begin with as he had always been so very private and closed off to his children about his life.

There was not enough there, so she kept looking around, rummaging in drawers and desks. She knew he would be extremely angry if he caught her, but she did not care anymore. He owed it to her and her sister to explain his life, tell them and not hold any secrets. Why could she never know anything at all about her father, she thought, getting angry as she failed to find enough information to explain things.

Then she found the strangest reports. Some files were very confusing, and yet strangely intriguing. There was a kind of disturbing story appearing between figures, times, names, numbers, data. Some places and dates contradicted others; people mentioned who could not be around, some who were in photographs with dates and addresses which must be impossible. Names appeared, facts, mysterious reports backing up other dates, times and evidence, filling in gaps, periods in time, changes with companies. Some of the addresses she recognised. Amongst all of these pieces of information, there was deep underneath a carefully wrapped, thin bag. Unfolding it delicately, she found inside a piece of very old and mysterious paper. It looked like the examples of ancient bible or religious scriptures so old that she would not have expected to see them outside of academic text books or museums. She would look at the curious and carefully written words and paragraphs for days and nights to come.

In the following days, Grace went about locating and visiting some of the places in her father's files. Things became even more strangely disturbing. She wanted to know everything, the real truth. They were so mysterious, the names and implications. She began to realise that she really did not know all of what her father did to look after his family, and that she was not entirely sure he was a good person. She did not know how much she really could trust him at all.

After a couple of days subtly observing some of the locations, she believed her father was involved with some seriously dangerous business arrangements. These things were beyond gangland crime. She saw strange markings on the hands of a number of businessmen and women entering and leaving some buildings, and found that many of the names and titles seemed to refer to some kinds of dark magic or the occult. Eventually she decided to enter one of the buildings when one of them left. She ran inside, quiet and careful. She made sure to dress similar to one of the women she had observed leaving the building, with black jacket and trousers.

She moved around, observing rooms and meetings being held in them behind closed doors. She overheard conversations and talk between people, things that she already possibly knew, and more strange, bad things were mentioned. What was this, she thought to herself. Surely it could not be entirely secret, this business organisation. But it was not just one thing, she thought. There seemed a few small offshoot groups, all connected by some unfathomable, mysterious thing. She had heard of satanic cults, Area 51, black magic, and other things that were not officially supposed to exist but were known about, she thought.

She decided that she would not probe too far, only just enough. Over a short time, she got closer and moved in and around the other people. She spoke to a few eventually, just greetings to begin with then eventually questions. Everyone still seemed very secretive, paranoid, careful and guarded. Then a handsome man from within the building paid her obvious interest and attention. Here was her opportunity.

'I haven't seen you before,' he said to her in a quiet, friendly manner.

Her heart nearly stopped.

'I've...been away, I'm back, right in the hard work again,' she told him. 'What do you do?'

'I work along with Sirius most of the time. Watching the hold on streets of lower Newcastle, and Tynemouth some days,' he said casually.

'Oh really? Sirius, of course,' Grace said, nodding.

'You...do you know of Mr. Spruance?' she asked him.

He looked at her for a moment. She waited, wondering what he was going to do or say.

'I have heard of him. A man, he has helped us, hasn't he, at times long ago? Bruce worked with him, didn't he?' he asked her.

'That's right. I just heard someone new mention the name,' she said.

'So much talk going on. The others need to be put in place. That man did his part,' he told her.

'Yes, right. I have to go. See you around, then,' she told him.

'I hope so,' he told her, watching her walk off around the corner. Her mind raced with fear and uncomfortable questions, wondering if she was in way too deep. She did, though, now know names and real information. Her father was tangled up deep, drawn right into this group that seemed very dangerous.

The next time she returned, the horror shocked and revolted her, almost revealing her charade to the others. As she moved in around the rooms of the building, watching gambling, arguments, even possibly torture in one room, she met the handsome man, Craig, in the corridor. She wondered what kind of business it was, what the hell was happening, and if this was simply how businesses succeeded these days.

'Hello there. Good to meet you again. I'm in with Sirius, watching a performance. You want to come if you're free now?' he asked.

'Well, if you think that's okay...' she said nervously.

He led her down the corridor toward a doorway. He stopped and knocked on the door. They waited for a moment. Grace was regretting joining him. He casually smiled at her and somehow she found the courage to smile back, despite her growing fear of the happenings all around. She tried not to believe that she was not actually attracted to this young, athletic, charming man, in his tight, expensive suit, with his fresh, strange aftershave. She was using him, that was it, she reminded herself. Not the other way around, not at all.

Craig led her inside the room. There was a group of people in a semi-circle around a man sat and bound onto a chair. The man seemed frightened, shaking, talking about some confusing things. What the hell is this, she thought to herself. Her pulse raced insanely, her heart beating manically, with panic twisting her stomach.

'...Give him a couple of minutes more,' one woman said, with desensitised calm in her voice. This is surely completely illegal, Grace thought. It was just like Guantanamo Bay or some other insane hostage camp, where nothing was off limits. They must be some kind of highly organised gangland organisation, she thought. How can they get away with anything like this, she wondered in outrage as she watched.

A man stepped forward to the bound victim and took out a set of knives. Grace was alarmed, but held her silence in fear. She remembered not to scream or panic, knowing the knives would be then directed toward her instead. The man began to cut. He stepped up to the bound man, who moved around in the chair desperately.

'No more time if no more answers,' he told the bound man. Wild fear danced in the bound man's eyes, as the man with the knives suddenly stuck him very precisely, opening up bloody slices of flesh across his hands, arms and face. The victim screamed through the cloth over his mouth. The half-dozen or so men and women watching looked excited, enthralled, as if ready to join in, if allowed. As blood dripped down the victim's face and the chair, they all began to slowly approach him.

Grace looked around at the others, and decided to move forward with them. She felt her stomach trying to turn and erupt within her, triggered by the vile scenes she was seeing.

'Does Bruce not care?' one woman asked the others.

'He let Philip sort it, but look what has happened. Damn human has let us down, like we knew he always would,' the sinister blonde man told her.

'Down to the quickest way to learn anything from this mortal animal,' the man with the bloodied knives said, and spread out his arms, prompting the rest of them to copy his actions.

Grace saw them all step up and put out their hands before the bound moaning man. A spark crackled in the air, like a flash of lightning. She looked up at the lights in the ceiling but it did not seem to originate from there. Grace looked across the room, puzzled. An unusual small noise buzzed somewhere, seeming to move from one side of the room across to the other. Suddenly, blue light crackled and moved between the people around and the bloodied man. He moaned, still under his gag, afraid of the bizarre flashes of dark blue light. The blue and white flashing light snapped and danced around the heads of the people, around their hands, through his body and theirs. Grace was incredibly nervous.

She stepped back a little as she saw the man begin to judder around in the chair. The blue sparking light crackled and buzzed faster and with much more intensity, seeming to put him in hellish pain. Faces surged out of the man, faint but visible images gushed out from inside of him like smoke or steam. Each time, it seemed like he was drained more. The faces and thick energy flew quickly and deeply into all of the individual people with their hands before the man. Grace, desperately trying to disguise her shock, stepped back up near the door quietly, though she watched still while the man thrashed and convulsed.

As the energy surged out of him he finally stopped moving, resting in a crumpled heap in the bloody chair. He was dead, Grace knew. They had killed him, together. She then quickly opened the door and ran. She ran so fast and so hard back out of the building. She didn't need to know any more about any of what was happening. Her father was involved with these sick, murdering torturers with their dark, evil forces. Now she knew it all to be true, though she wished that she did not know any of it.

She quickly moved on down the streets around, running with only thoughts of getting safely away and finding her father. She wondered if she could get him out of it, take him away from the evil horrors of those buildings. He knew, he must have known, but he was a good father and so he must still be a decent man really, she thought. She could not entirely convince herself of this, she realised. She dodged cars, bikes and bemused people going along with their own business on the streets and roads of Newcastle. Eventually, after minutes of breathless running, she allowed herself to finally slow down and then stop briefly. She took a look around her, at the streets and surroundings to recognise where she had run to in delirious haste.

She was in the top end of Newcastle City Centre, behind many business buildings, close to an art gallery she knew of. There was a long road that split off and divided to her far right. She began once more, but heard a growing noise behind her. She looked around. At the top of the alley she saw a couple of men in suits running into the alley. She ran off in fear once again, but they seemed to see her.

As Grace ran, she passed many people who looked confused and intrigued at the serious panic and fear in her eyes. In minutes, she came toward the taxi rank behind the bus station and ran straight up to a waiting taxi. She climbed quickly inside and told the driver her address. As the taxi moved off down the main road, she took out her mobile phone.

'Hello, Emma? Hi, it's me, Grace. We need to meet. I seriously need some help. Call me as soon as you can, please,' she said, leaving the message to her good friend.

'Hold on, love, I'm pulling into this gas station to fill 'er up, okay?' the taxi driver told her suddenly.

'What? Shouldn't you have...fine,' Grace said, sighing. He pulled in and she sat agitatedly waiting for him.

She sat thinking about what she was going to do next. What was her father, she thought. Was he innocent, ignorant of everything or highly involved, guilty, and deeply entwined in the plans of these murderers from some obscure but incredibly dangerous occult group? Thinking back, it seemed he was definitely involved. He was at the top of that company, those people were his staff, his employees and the project names and people there all connected up with the names and notes she had found. These people were doing unbelievably horrific, sick, disgusting things. She began to think of what could be done in reality to stop these people. Would any police believe her at all if she began to describe the horrific madness and torture she had witnessed? Of course not. So what could she do, who could actually help her?

Someone tapped on the car window next to her.

'Excuse me, hello?'

It was the handsome man who had seemed fond of her from the building. She slowly wound down the window.

'Yes?' she said nervously.

'Why did you leave?' he asked her.

'I have plans. Have to be somewhere now,' she told him. She caught something strange out of the corner of her eye. There was another man moving around the other side of the taxi. Grace took the chance and leapt quickly right out of the car as the driver returned, and pushed the man away. She ran off again, not looking back at all.

The men were surely following her somehow, she thought as she ran, men who took blood, sweat and souls from others. They would not have a chance to take her blood, her own soul. No way. She ran to where she thought some small hope might wait for her. Her legs ached so badly, her body was weak and exhausted, and her head was getting dizzy. She was confused, anxious and afraid. She simply prayed to any good force out there as she ran that she would reach her sanctuary safely.

Her mobile phone rang suddenly in her coat pocket, and her nervous heart almost exploded.

'Jesus, Eric. I almost died,' she told him, seeing that it was his number.

'Where are you?' he asked.

'I'm near...the coast road. Along the golf course, I think,' she told him. 'And you?'

'Give me a couple of minutes, hon. I'll meet you there, okay? Keep safe,' he said.

She walked along the grassy narrow trail behind a long row of houses near the main road. She was exhausted, but was too afraid to stop. The images of the bizarre torture and strange, supernatural things haunted her mind, posing so many questions and making her so afraid for her life. Rain began to drip down from a dark sky above as she stumbled on. She looked around, unsure if she had heard suspicious noises behind her. No, she realised; it was her fear tricking her, eating away at her sanity. There was no one around when she looked. It always seemed like that was how it was, never another poor soul when someone needed them, she thought. She began to cry just a little, then swore to herself for being so weak and soft. She felt so vulnerable and stupid. She wasn't a weak stereotype of a girl, though; she was modern, self-assured, confident and strong, she remembered. That was her, damn right. All this time her father had been involved in such evil things, supporting his family by working with these people. It made her sick, almost physically so. She almost did not want to see him, but thought that there must be more to it than the simple horror of it all.

'Grace,' a voice said.

Chapter 11

There was a chilling wind near the small side street newsstand. Magazines pages ruffled in the racks, and leaves from the ground and street blew up, hitting some front covers. Between the magazine pages, some form of steam began to appear. It grew, drifting out wide and spreading. Was there a fire behind the newsstand? A small child stood a few paces from his mother, and held up a comic from the stand. The cover began to crackle and flicker, with sudden flames licking the pages. The mother on her smartphone had, of course, not noticed. The newsstand keeper was watching, and he smiled a peculiar and mischievous smile. He laughed quietly seeing the flames on the comic book and around the child's hands. The smoke was rising and the newsstand keeper's eyes shone crimson red with wicked delight.

As the moon looked down through black clouds, Eric walked quickly down the street in the icy cold and in the shadows of tall trees around him. His mobile phone buzzed inside his trouser pocket, and he answered it with a distracted voice.

'Hello, who is it?' he said.

'Eric, thank God. It's me, Emma. Can we talk?' she asked. 'I'm worried about you, mate. How are you doing?'

He really wanted to walk alone back to the hotel, even though he knew he could and should talk to Emma. She was a good, close friend and had been a best friend of Grace's. Emma had not seen him since he left the funeral and she must be extremely concerned, he understood.

'I'm busy right now. I'm alright, though. Thanks for being concerned for me,' he told her. 'I'll be in touch.'

Emma quickly spoke.

'Listen, I said to her I would watch out for you if anything happened. That's what I'm doing, like it or not. She wouldn't want you to go off all angry at things, would she?' Emma asked him.

He felt so annoyed at Emma. He knew she was right, of course, but she was simply the first person to be honest with him. Grace had been close to both of them, and Emma had actually known Grace before he had. He knew how Emma could be, though, so stubborn but faithful and reliable at the same time.

'I know you mean, well, I'm very grateful…' he began, but she took over.

'So tell me where you are? Just to put my mind at ease. Do you want me to think I might lose you too now after Grace?' she said, making him feel incredibly guilty 'Look, you know I think you're lazy, a dreamer who gets by on good looks, but I will just keep hounding you. Where are you?' she asked again.

'For *her* sake? Look what happened, for the love of God!' Eric said with anger. 'I don't matter at all. She did, she does still. Not me, Have you…' He nearly continued, but then decided against it and sighed to himself. He looked around the dark street, frustrated at nothing in particular.

'Have I what? Just tell me, Eric. It's me. We know each other well enough not to bullshit around, don't we?' Emma said. 'It hurts me too, so damn much. But we'll get through it,' she told him sternly with conviction.

Eric listened then and knew that they were in the same place, in the same circumstances, and feeling the same pain.

'I'm out past Durham, off the motorway somewhere. Me and Taylor came out here…we just came to…well doing bloke stuff, you know?' he told her as some kind of answer. He did want to tell her everything, but he felt it was still too soon.

'Look Emma, Taylor and I…we're dealing with some things out here…' he began to explain, but he knew that she had a strong sense of truth sometimes; she could often guess how people were feeling, and if they were lying. It was a skill of her character.

'So we can meet then? Near Durham somewhere?' she asked.

'Okay. For her, but it can't be for too long,' Eric warned.

'Tonight?' she asked

'No, tomorrow, please. In the town centre, okay?' he said.

'Fine, yes. Just look after yourself in the meantime. No stupid stunts. And tell Taylor that I want him to be a good friend, no stoned adventures alright?' she explained, with a joking edge to her voice finally.

'Yes, mother. See you soon,' Eric replied, and switched off his cell phone. He decided that maybe nothing was going to be achieved unless he knew the area better. He and Taylor were waiting on something vague that Grace had spoken of, but it was frustrating just waiting around aimlessly. In the morning he could read the local paper, maybe talk to some locals of the area in nearby pubs.

He turned to begin walking back toward the direction of the hotel, to rest and apologise to Taylor. As he did so, a screeching, sudden noise rose howling up in the streets around him. If this was the thing that he was to face, he felt unprepared. The noise changed slightly, cleared and he came to realise it was sirens, possibly from police cars, wailing like wild cats dying.

As he pushed the room door open, Eric stepped in and could not see Taylor anywhere. The room was deadly quiet.

'Hello? Tay, you in here?' Eric called out.

Eric assumed he would see Taylor asleep on the sofa or sitting stoned listening to some stoner rock or Pink Floyd. The room was bare of him, his bag also missing. Eric realised that he was annoyed as he honestly had intended to apologise, which he did not usually do while sober. He came to the conclusion that, like himself, Taylor had probably wandered off in a negative and angry state and would return soon enough. Deciding this, Eric sloped along to the worn bed, which seemed to be calling him to let his exhausted body fall deep into the curve of it for a few useful hours of needed sleep. He submitted.

'I don't know how far I can really go,' Taylor said between sips of his cold beer.

'You're doing great, okay? Loosen up. You've no worries, okay?' Andrew told him.

'I've got a fucking corpse in my old flat, for God's sake,' Taylor whispered dramatically.

'And I thank you for keeping it there,' Andrew replied, smiling as he drank his ale.

'How much longer?' Taylor asked.

'Look, forget about it. Not much longer. Leave it to me. Relax, will you?' Andrew told him.

'It's a dead body, though. Why? She's dead,' Taylor argued. This was not the first time he had asked.

'It's just a complicated thing. Hard to explain, like I said,' Andrew told him.

Taylor looked around. They had been with a number of very loose, dirty women all night, doing all number of wild, lustful things until they ached. Drugs had been shared around, and the women shared, tied down, chased around, but finally Taylor's thoughts became nervous and anxious once more. He leaned in.

'Explain it to me now,' he said to Andrew, the drink and drugs letting the words escape through his loose lips.

'Chase a girl, the brunette there is lonely I think,' Andrew said, pouring himself a whisky as half-naked men and women sauntered around them.

'No, I want answers. Give me your story. Who are you really?' Taylor asked.

'You don't need to know,' Andrew said, standing and swiftly necking back his whisky. Taylor stood also and grabbed at him by the collar of his shirt.

'Fucking tell me something more! Tell me why I've got Grace's body in a freezer for fuck's sake!' he yelled.

Andrew took him by the wrists, sneering down at him. Andrew changed. It was shocking and it worked in horrifying Taylor enough to silence him. He fell back down to the leather sofa behind, afraid and angry but speechless. This was Andrew, in some contorted, distorted way. He had hunched up, twisted out of his human shape into a more alarming form. His skin was bizarrely grey and pallid, but most outstanding were his burning crimson eyes, striking Taylor down.

'Get down and shut the fuck up,' Andrew growled.

'You can't…okay, okay,' Taylor said quietly, with stunned fear.

He looked around at the other men and women who worked with Andrew and who were simply continuing to enjoy the decadence. They also then flashed back similarly glimmering red eyes at Taylor one by one as they noted the scene.

'Have another whisky now,' Andrew suggested, proffering a full shot glass toward him.

They both sat and drank a couple more shots of whisky in silence watching each other for a long moment until Andrew spoke.

'We are things you have forgotten about. Things you all told yourselves didn't exist, were illogical, mythical. But things that most have a guilty dream of being. You don't mind that, do you?' he said as he shuddered back into his original human form.

69

'I...I...can live with it,' Taylor managed to say, though he did not make eye contact.

'Myself and the others here all succumbed to join with a way of being different from your human life. We have not fully left humankind nor stayed with it. We are between forms, and it is damn good this way. Happy?' Andrew asked.

'Maybe. Shouldn't I know more?' Taylor asked.

'How much can you handle?' Andrew said, with a smile that only killers could have.

Taylor was sick all down the wall to his right then a little down his own right leg as well until the pain ebbed away. There was no way he could suppress it; this was a horror which shocked him completely, and would stay with him forever against his will. He looked up at Andrew in fear with a sense of lost confusion. He did not know Andrew really, he realised, and perhaps did not want to know him at all now.

Andrew had shown him a much better life, allowed him to experience so many good things, and had given him access to so many great delights, and good times in the last two weeks. Taylor knew this, but he was beginning to think he might easily trade it all - the stunning slutty women, the plethora of fine drugs - to forget the bloody scene before him.

'Why?' he managed to stutter finally.

Andrew looked back, with a focused seriousness, eyes unblinking.

'Follow me, quickly. This...it's what I do,' Andrew told him.

They ran out down the dark back alley to where a car waited for them. They got in quickly, but inside Taylor sat away from Andrew. His skin was bizarrely grey and pallid, his burning crimson eyes staring Taylor out.

'This is what you do?' Taylor repeated again in a quiet voice.

'Yes. Now you know,' Andrew said casually. He flipped a cigarette lighter between his bloodstained fingertips repeatedly as he looked at Taylor, then looked out of the car window.

'But you...what did you do?' Taylor said, trying to understand what he had seen.

'Only what was needed. Well, I think, anyway. I'm a little angry right now, you see; not with you, don't worry about that,' Andrew said.

'But you...did you-eat that bloke?' Taylor uttered.

Andrew looked at him, with disappointment.

'You could think so. No, we don't 'eat' people. That's sick, Taylor,' Andrew said.

'No shit. But you...you kind of...what then? The blood, he fell to pieces and then he...what?' Taylor said.

'Listen, all these things we've done, the beautiful women, the fast cars, hard drugs...my friend...there's a price,' Andrew explained.

'I expected something, but what I saw you do...you kill people?' Taylor said, his mouth dry and voice rasping.

'It's not killing, Taylor. Don't say that. No, it's something necessary...something else...' Andrew said, annoyed by the simple definition Taylor was using.

'But didn't you kill that guy? Was it cannibalism?' Taylor asked, regaining some colour in his face.

Andrew leaned close to him in the back seat of the plush car.

'I am one of a group of beings in the North. We live a different but much better life than others; you know this. Are you staying?' he asked.

Could Taylor continue to remain in the company of this mysterious and dangerous killer? This was not even simply another human killer, but as he had seen, but tried to ignore, Andrew and the others there were very much like the demon beasts which he and Eric had been fighting. Was there enough reason to do remain with him? This was a man whose company Taylor had sincerely enjoyed in the previous fortnight. He had accepted the pleasures offered up which he knew he could never normally obtain by himself; women like those he could only usually dream of being, with let alone sleeping with, and the drugs were of such good quality he barely wanted to come down at all..

He could not forget the murder that he had seen Andrew commit minutes ago so openly in front of him, so casual and aggressive.

'That was not right,' Taylor said slowly.

'No, probably not. Doesn't matter. Only happens occasionally. Mind you, now the blood is spilling faster than usual. The others like myself, we keep a reasonably dignified, civilized routine,' Andrew told him, almost with great pride.

'That's civilized? Ripping a guy to bloody shit then he disappears in your hands?' Taylor said.

'Hey, others kill for gain. It's not new. Been happening for centuries now. It's just the way. There are others who do it much worse, and much more often with greater pleasure,' Andrew said.

This made Taylor quiet as he thought seriously about his position some more. He had left Eric for this? Oh God, he thought. How stupid am I? God help me now, he thought. What the hell am I involved in, he wondered. They drove along through the darkening streets as the night enveloped them in blackness, Andrew happily thumbing through a small pocket book of dates and notes.

'Andrew?' Taylor said nervously.

'Yes?'

'Why? I mean, doing that gets you all the good things? How? The sex and money and everything?' Taylor asked.

'It does, keeps it coming, yes. In many different ways. It has to be done. Look, people like a good steak or burger. People eat horse, chicken, and many other animals; tastes great, but someone kills it for them. There's always a bloody reality behind the way we live,' Andrew told him.

'So you're a butcher for other people?' Taylor said.

'Close enough. You like the taste it brings, right? Forget the bleeding and death, think of the end result, okay? Or...forget the end result all together. Forget the experiences,' Andrew said. It was an ultimatum.

Taylor did absolutely love the experiences so far. Could he walk away now? Would he ever get those things again? He did begin to think about the kinds of people who Andrew and his pals were murdering. Was it just any random person? No; Andrew did seem to imply that these killings were organized, specific and carefully decided upon when they happened.

'Who was that bloke, then? Was he actually chosen beforehand?' Taylor dared to ask.

'By day Taylor, I'm a very successful businessman. Hunt or be hunted. By night, I enjoy the things only I and my kind can,' he told Taylor.

Taylor was beginning to feel trapped, cornered in the car. It felt like air was being drained from inside, dizziness taking him, his heart beating erratically. He wondered if he was meant to really be with people like this, but then he did not believe that he belonged with many people elsewhere either. He also wondered how long he could trust Andrew before he himself became that torn and ripped up bloody mess he had seen.

'You're asking me to stay? To continue what we've been doing?' Taylor said. 'You want me to help you murder?'

'Do you feel the need? Taylor, if you want our life, you do this with us. All of it. It's not much to ask, is it? People die every day,' Andrew said.

'I... I don't know. Maybe...I mean...' Taylor said, unsure of himself.

'You're useful to us. Don't worry too much about your role just now,' Andrew said to him.

Taylor did not disagree with this man, who was also some form of demonic beast, and simply remained beside him, humble yet fearful, and thinking of a way out.

Chapter 12

Eric's sleep was filled with dreams that were fantastical and disturbingly sadistic in equal measure, eventually causing him to jump to consciousness. It was nearing mid-afternoon as he boiled the mini coffee maker and poured a strong drink for himself. He took a walk around and found that Taylor had still not appeared yet. This was now quite a worry for him, but it was not his main focus. He got dressed, left the hotel, and stepped out into Jesmond.

After another long, painful night with barely any good sleep, Eric returned to the local police station once more in the vain hope that some kind of new clues about how and why Grace had died had been found. Hours had elapsed, surely enough for something to show up, for some police officer or detective to come across the truth somehow. He entered the police station, and received friendly but uncomfortable responses from the reception staff, who had meet him regularly over the previous few days.

'Good afternoon, Eric. How are you feeling?' the woman at the desk asked him, with a sympathetic smile.

'Not a lot of change yet. Same pain deep in me. Same questions need answering. Hope you're well. Nice day, right. For some people. So any good news yet?' he said, trying to sound positive.

'No, Eric, I'm very sorry. We all are. We'll let you know,' she told him, feeling awkward.

'I know, I know. Thanks. Where are they? Where's Detective Lumley and Moorcock?' he enquired, and glanced down the corridor to his right.

'They're out working now. We really will let you know anything new that comes in. Please, perhaps go and be with friends and family. It should help in some way,' she suggested in a friendly manner.

He looked at her. He felt inside him a huge anger, and almost wanted to shout back at her, to look on her computer, over her desk. She might be lying, he thought. She might be keeping things from him, hiding something, like he might not be able to handle the truth. Of course he could handle it, he thought. She had died in his damn arms. The worst of it was over, perhaps, or maybe not, not at all. He looked at her and wanted to shake her until she told him the truth. But he knew really that she did not know. They did not know yet.

He turned and walked back out of the station, his thoughts heavy on his mind. Be with friends, he thought. Where the hell was Taylor then, he wondered.

Emma had walked away from the funeral of Grace with thoughts in her mind that no one else was thinking. Not terrible, offensive thoughts, rather thoughts about why, who, and where. She was thinking seriously and thoughtfully about what she was going to do next. Grace had left her with things that were so bizarre and unsettling, but Emma had to understand the meaning of these things, of all the notes, documents, papers, discs.

The note was cryptic, yet incredibly serious, like Grace had rarely ever been. Grace had usually been great fun to be with, a playful cheery girl, though thoughtful and compassionate. This was obviously a serious message from Grace, right before she had died, and Emma knew that it would begin to explain exactly how or why it had happened. She also had the deepest worrying feeling that there was a very real danger attached to the note, connected to some very shockingly unusual and bizarre things, and so had been keeping the existence of the note secret until she knew who she might be able to tell or ask for help.

Emma looked at the note again.

My dear friend Emma, I have found things recently about my father which I have always been seeking to know. The things, though, are extremely shocking, and are possibly seriously dangerous to me now I am aware of them. He is a very different, more dangerous kind of businessman than I had thought in the past. He deals in business that no one knows about, or should have to. Really horrific, sickening business, believe me. There are things happening, things which exist in and around Newcastle and the North that should not happen, should not really exist. But they do.

Supernatural things, Emma. Seriously: no bullshit. Pray to God above that you keep safe from harm now you have read this. I have been where these things are happening, witnessed some of the appalling things which they do, the people who are not people, not real like us, but something beastly, barbaric and deadly. So truly horrifying.

Here are the places:

Building 6, Clayton Street

Hayzels-Sandhill Quayside road

Orion House- Orchard Street

Get the police to these places somehow, but keep out of it. Be extremely careful. I am going to finish what I need to do. My father needs to redeem himself or to be punished.

Love,

Grace.

While the other friends and family of Grace wept and mourned her sudden passing, Emma went out alone to gather information and make sense of what Grace had told her in the letter. She initially did not visit the places Grace had listed, as she was secretly spooked and nervous of what was waiting there. It took a short while to find the courage. Instead, she made enquiries at the city library, council offices, and on the internet, about the buildings and residents of the places listed on the letter.

Information was scarce to begin with. There was little explaining who resided in the buildings or what they were really being used for without her getting inside somehow. After her lack of results, Emma boldly decided to probe further, deeper. She knew that he had to, that it was the only way. She received cautious glances and sceptical words when she questioned people relentlessly for any clues about the buildings and about anyone seen going inside or coming out.

Finally, a woman at the city library was surprisingly helpful to her.

'I have heard a few people talk of previous residents at the Orion House and Hayzel Studio. I think that people often make up tales, rumours, embellish things out of real proportion,' the woman warned Emma.

'Well yes, but there must be some actual truth about the people in these buildings, mustn't there?' Emma said.

The woman looked uncomfortable as she looked at Emma quizzically, then leaned nearer to her.

'Okay, I heard that the Orion House place might have housed some businesses suspected of financial crimes a few years ago. But now I don't know,' the woman explained.

'Not now?' Emma asked.

'I wouldn't know, and wouldn't wish to know either. Do you really need to know about these places? Why, can I ask?'

'It is important for my research into local history, business history and local changes in culture. University dissertation,' Emma told her.

'You shouldn't look around these places. Look for something safer, really. You don't need the danger. It's not for you. Leave it to others,' the woman cautioned.

'So there are people in these places that you think are doing suspicious things now still? Where did you hear of it?' Emma asked.

'I... know someone who found some things. Might know some things. Just maybe. Maybe not. I suggest you keep your research wider, in other parts of the city,' the woman advised.

'Could you put me in touch with your friend?' Emma asked.

'It... it's me. I have to go do some work elsewhere. Take care, darling, okay?' the woman said, and walked away sombrely.

'No, wait, hey!' Emma called out, but the woman walked off quickly across the library corridor away from her.

Emma did not dare tell any other friends or Grace's family of the letter left to her. She did not want to offend them, or look crazy, or even make it seem that she did not care about how people remembered Grace, or what they thought of her. Emma could not even think of how to speak to Eric about it all, though she strongly felt that she had to soon. She knew him well, and knew how close he and Grace had been until her death. She found it hard to believe that he did not know about these things, but perhaps Grace simply wanted to keep him safe.

She waited and held back, but after another day, she met up with Eric.

'You look good, you moody old dog,' she told him, breaking the ice after they had hugged in silence for a long moment.

'This dog is going to stay moody for a while,' he replied. 'Good to see you, though.'

'How are you doing?' she asked him tentatively.

'Things are...difficult, you know? She's gone. I... see her, though. I don't even want to in some ways, but she's there. It's hard. How are you?' he said.

He knew that Emma and Grace were very close friends and that she probably was hurting nearly as much as he was.

'I'm here for you, we all are. Through the pain, together. We can speak to each other, though, okay? We knew her well, better than almost everyone else. We can help each other, be there for each other, okay?' she told him. He looked at her, then out of the pub window.

'I know. Thank you, Emma,' he told her with tears in his eyes. 'I think I might move away soon. Work somewhere else, or go to university down South maybe.'

'Really? That's cool. I was thinking of doing similar things with my grades. Just don't run off, though, I mean do anything...I'm here for you,' Emma told him. They both sat there feeling sad and wanting Grace back. Emma finally spoke.

'You... haven't heard anything new about how she died, have you?' she asked Eric. He looked at her then looked away as he spoke.

'Still nothing more. They're so useless. I wish I knew more. Something, anything more. It's not right, it's bullshit. She disappeared in my arms, faded. And those blokes just watched. We argued, but not in a big dramatic way. Something happened to her. Some bad thing, or bad people...I don't know, I wish I did. You don't know more, do you?' he asked.

'Is that what you think? She got into trouble somehow?' Emma asked him.

'I really don't know. Do you? Do you know anything more? Emma?' he asked.

'I don't know,' Emma said and looked away.

'We'll get by. We knew her. We were blessed to know her, right?' He said.

'Yes, blessed to know Grace,' Emma agreed.

They promised to keep in touch over the next few days, to help each other make it through the time ahead. Emma continued investigating the streets and buildings listed by Grace, though did not decide to tell Eric just yet, or even at all, if it never came to anything of any use.

Whatever she was looking into and discovering, she thought it better she do it than Eric, in order to leave him with good memories of Grace, to cope without any sudden drama or danger. Knowing something definitely was strange with the buildings and streets listed, Emma set to learn more about the final building in Clayton Street. She found nothing out of the ordinary in many dozens of journals and internet sites and practically gave up. She walked away from the city library frustrated and angry, down a number of streets in the late afternoon sun, as heavy grey clouds drifted above her. She looked up to her left and saw a street sign on the wall: Clayton Street.

On a Thursday morning, Emma walked along to the house where Grace had lived with her family. She wore gloves and a coat with big collar to cover her face as she approached. Grace's father Philip, her mother and younger sister remained. Grace had accused her father finally of being involved with the things she had found out about, and so Emma knew to ultimately investigate him. He was not the pleasant, innocent father she had known him as for a few years before. He had secrets, which were powerful enough to kill Grace and leave no obvious marks or clues somehow. Emma would find the reasons why, she had to, for Grace and Eric.

Emma knew the house and the neighbourhood well enough to predict a perfect time to walk up to the house unseen, if timed right, and used a key that Grace had given her in great trust, knowing how strong their friendship was. She knew from speaking on the phone that Grace's parents had decided to go away for a few days to grieve, and that Grace's sister would be at college.

Emma knew to be fast but thorough in her search for what she needed to find. She would blackmail Philip if she had to sort it all out, she considered. She would do anything...wouldn't she? No, she thought. Grace would not want her in serious danger, but then the letter...There was some kind of unexplainable evil out there. Those things, whatever, whoever; they got her. Philip knew them, worked with them, she thought. She was almost sick thinking about how long she had known him, as Grace's father, as a good respected man, and neither had known what sick, vile and evil things he had been connected with. Perhaps she could ruin his life, for taking her good friend away. But Grace had been his daughter, Emma thought. He must not have expected it, surely, she thought, and must have been in just as much pain. Emma was getting confused, and was bitterly angry as she moved up and into the main study room.

She knew it was Philip's room and was sure she could find useful things there. There were many files and papers over in the cabinet and desk drawers; lots of records from his business ventures, with dates, budgets, and numbers all over them. She was not sure what she needed, but thought that she would probably know when she saw it. She would make it look like a damn robbery if she needed to just to get what she needed. Then she thought about Grace, what she might have done with the information.

Emma ran through to Grace's room, past the chairs and around the desk and bookshelf. She moved some books away, and lifted up a floorboard. She found the usual small bag of cannabis, and then also behind it some folded papers and photographs. She saw Philip in the photographs with men and women in suits; men and woman with red eyes while Philip's eyes remained blue. No time was wasted there, grabbing the documents and photos and leaving by the back and walked off down the back alley behind the houses. She instantly felt paranoid, thinking she was being watched or had been seen leaving the house. There was no one around the streets nearby right. It was a quiet, breezy morning as usual. Suddenly, though, she felt someone, somewhere, watching her. She looked around nervously, and then saw him.

A tall, thin man, maybe thirty-five years of age or more, stood and looked back at her from across the street behind her. Had he been following her? No, of course not, she thought. Really, that didn't happen in real life, did it? But the look he gave her had knowingness about it, an intimidating look. As if he knew what she was doing, who she was, or where she had been.

This has got me scared, Emma thought. I can't freak out, and must stay cool, she told herself. She continued on, ignoring the man, but began to walk a little faster and started to quickly think of how to lose him. She would go to her flat and look at the documents and photographs. After walking down two more streets, she found the courage to take a quick look behind her again, but did not see the thin man. She knew she was being paranoid, she thought. He was probably just a regular bloke who happened to look at her. People look at people, she thought.

She made it to the bus stop moments later and sat down on the bench to wait for the next bus going her way. There was a cold chill around her, while the sun flickered behind thin, grey clouds. Then she saw the man again. He stood out at the far end of the bus stop. Was he waiting for a bus next to her? It was getting unbelievable, her mind playing nervous tricks on her. She knew sometimes people could easily convince themselves of things that just are not true and this could be one of those times. Or it might not.

She subtly kept a careful eye on him, and hoped her bus would show up soon. He was not looking at her at all, it seemed, but out around the street, and then just in the direction of where the bus should come from.

Suddenly he did look in her direction, and Emma froze. The sun was bright and stung her eyes briefly when she looked away around her. She looked back and almost gasped out loud. She could swear that his eyes seemed to appear a kind of red. Was it the sunlight confusing her? No, it could not be that simple. She could see them.

She tried to casually look back, but he was gone. Emma glanced around the bus stop discreetly, wondering where he was. It truly did freak her out, and her nerves were completely on edge, making her uncertain of things and people all around her. She could not see the man around the bus stop or the street around it anywhere; he was gone.

The bus then appeared and came to the stop. Emma boarded it in seconds behind the others. Time could not pass quickly enough as she sat on the bus, watching houses and buildings going past her as she left. She felt vulnerable and wondered just how dangerous it was to have the things she had taken from Grace's house. Grace had died somehow because of the information, and she did not wish for the same fate, but knew she would do anything to expose it all.

Ten minutes later, Emma reached her street and ran up to her flat. Once inside behind closed doors, she lay out the papers and photographs on her coffee table and studied it all carefully. She still retained the feeling that she was being watched or had been followed, no matter how unlikely it seemed.

She looked out of the windows quickly, but saw no one on the street, so returned to the coffee table. As she read each sheet of information slowly and carefully, she began to piece together fragments of some disturbing story concerning Philip. It did not explain everything cohesively or in linear fashion, but she began to find clues of some sickening back story.

It was more than Emma could easily believe at first. What she was reading was so outlandish and far-fetched, but actually made a twisted kind of sense. There were things she had only heard of in old trashy horror films on cable late at night, tattered cheap novels and tales that people told small children to scare them.

Philip and a number of other people were connected to a group that seemed to practice some form of dark worship of some kind. It was like Dennis Wheatley stories or Hammer horror, she thought, but realistic, too realistic. Bizarre Latin or Greek names were written, and things were recorded that could possibly get then jailed for life. Sacrifices, murders, torture...a vile list of events, which seemed coordinated and calculated toward controlling and manipulating rich people, businesses people and the North over a number of years when Grace was growing up.

It just could not be true. It had to be wrong; this kind of thing was the thing of stories and films, she thought. Real life danger was from gangs, crime, corrupt governments, people trafficking. None of this kind of crap is ever real, she thought. After all, there isn't even a real God in this mysterious life we have. She used to like some Nietzsche, but remembered her mother quoting some fascinating C.S. Lewis saying that always made her wonder about faith.

If anything this bad, evil, dangerous or unbelievable could exist in this real world then she definitely wanted a God to trust in, to hope for and pray to in these times. That did not mean she was simple or weak, but it was what she thought. Her beliefs were now very much wider and stranger than science could answer, but there was nothing wrong with that, she thought. If these crazy things were supposed to be real, Philip's real secrets, then perhaps she should go to the places Grace had written of, she thought. These things couldn't be real, and yet...there was a disturbing truth to it, suggesting a kind of mythical, supernatural force. Grace had believed in these things just before she died. Maybe Emma would find nothing there and could then move on to look for the real things behind it.

Emma shuffled through the pieces of paper and photographs of Philip with unknown people on her coffee table while she dialled the woman at the city library once more.

'Hello, city library, how may I help?' a different woman from before said.

'Hello I'm Emma Branaghan. I would like to speak to Mrs. Appleton please,' Emma said.

'I'm sorry, that is not possible. Can I take a message at all or help?' the woman asked.

'She said I could call back today if I needed to. She was very helpful the other day. I wanted to thank her very much for what she was able to give me. Is there any way I can reach her? Is she in later?' Emma said.

'Who is this?' the woman asked. She sounded a little angry and troubled.

'I'm Emma, a student at the city university studying local history and business. She helped me a great deal with information, I wanted to thank her personally,' Emma said.

'She is...in hospital right now, I'm afraid. She might not be back at work soon. I'm sorry, goodbye,' the woman explained, and ended the call abruptly.

'Bitch,' Emma said as she put the phone down. She put it near the photographs on the coffee table and then nearly fell back as she saw something different that startled her.

One of the photographs with Philip had him standing beside a group of people, and one of them looked just like the man who had been watching her at the bus stop, the man with the red eyes. She found it hard to breathe, her chest suddenly tight and caught in fear. Emma fell back into the sofa chair behind her while still looking at the photograph. She was almost certain that she had not seen the man in the photograph seconds earlier. This was unreal, disturbing and the final thing to convince her that very bad things were very close.

Her cell phone rang and she jumped a little in shock. She took it out and answered.

'Hello?' she said nervously.

'It's me, Eric. Can we meet up?' he asked.

'Oh God, Jesus mate, you scared me then. Yes, of course we can. You want to meet right now?' she asked.

'If that's possible, yes,' Eric said.

'Course it is. Where?' Emma said.

Despite more rational thoughts troubling her mind, Emma departed the bus and approached Durham Cathedral in the late afternoon alone. The heavy sun was setting along the horizon behind her, withdrawing again, in place of encroaching dark evening. Perhaps she really was reading much too far into all possible angles from the information she was obtaining and from her interpretation of Grace's letters to her, but she felt she really should not ignore any of the suggestive connections which seemed to be rising up and becoming something significant.

The time at the city library had been a long, hard search, with so many journals and papers to go through. Then there was the library reception lady disappearing like that. So strange, Emma thought. But as Eric was still being distant and secretive, she would use the time to go further and explore the things which she was finding.

Durham Cathedral stood looming grand and ancient, cast strong and tall by long-gone hands, a magnificent icon of Northern spiritual history and worship. The information connected to the people attacked and their activities led her there. If she believed it all, she would find something to tell her much more. This cathedral held the shrine of Saint Cuthbert, a truly legendary figure, a dedicated monk and holy man from centuries before, who had come to be seen as a figure who had saved Christianity and the North of England from the Viking attacks and had also created some of the most longstanding holy written word to live by for the centuries to come.

Many tourists visited the cathedral on a daily basis to view the hugely inspiring and captivating architecture, as well as the fascinating religious history within. Emma walked on inside, observing the security as she passed the tourist shop and entrance. A number of quiet people were walking around her, admiring the many huge and elaborate stained glass windows, as well as the paintings and information plaques explaining the history of it all. What was special about this place, she thought. Now, after years, centuries, what was of importance? People were so materialistic, godless and secular now, too distracted from religion or cynical and romanced by modern scientific advances to give much time to ancient superstitions of faith and history. Bu the bigger questions were what secrets were waiting, and did she have any real idea of where to look?

Museums and historical tours usually bored her very quickly, but this held her focus, as she needed to find the truth. There was a connection here; with Grace, with other churches, with some strange things. Maybe the history of the place held clues, something to do with the land, holy men, the bible. She knew how, back in the past, there were many tales of the brutal things kings and organised religions did to control land and the population. She read a few plaques, and learned that the cathedral was much older than she imagined, so incredibly old. It dated back to the beginnings of Christian faith in this country, the very time when holy men had to put their lives at risk to defend their faith and the peace of the land. It really was strangely interesting, she found.

Had Grace come here? It didn't seem like she had made it this far. Emma wondered if it would have made a difference. It was a place of old nostalgic religious symbolism. She was sceptical and jaded with the whole religious belief thing, the known opium of the masses, guilt and blind worship passed on through generations unquestioningly as routine and repetition. There could be a God and a place where Grace now existed, but so much of organised religion seemed worthless to Emma's eyes and mind.

She remembered her notes from the library, and noticed the descriptions around. Some things began to stand out. Saint Cuthbert was the main legend here, a brave and respected monk who defended early scriptures at the most brutal times against Vikings and wicked kings. She read the many plaques; he travelled from the 'Holy Island', or Lindisfarne, just along the coast from the north, bringing the early Bible and scripture to the mainland. He and his fellow monks then translated and defended the early gospels, making it a hugely important place in British religious history. Kings and Vikings pillaged this land, but the monks, led by Cuthbert, held strong. After he died, this very cathedral continued with bishops and monks down the years following his teachings and brave guidance. And inside this huge historical building, Cuthbert remained, a shrine to his existence for all to witness.

Emma walked on with a fresh inspiration up the transepts, along the north aisle and finally toward the last room ahead. Stepping inside, she found it, the actually finely impressive and carefully crafted shrine of Saint Cuthbert.

Within the corridors of the magnificent Durham Cathedral there were clues to suggest a missing or hidden part of history, if a person observed with the right questioning eyes, hungry for more than doctrine, statues and religious nostalgia and comfort in the obvious religious eloquence around. If the items Eric and Taylor had collected up were of actual historical and religious significance, they might offer a guide to a long forgotten puzzle. There were many stained glass windows and statues featuring well-known Northern saints. The information on the small panels below stated that he had at times challenged his fellow local men of cloth and faith, and had questioned the manuscripts around old English and Latin-Anglo translation process. He had been even known to become wild, angry and erratic. In his later years he had a fight in this area near the Cathedral, where a number of religious peers were hurt and written work on gospel translation was harmed. After this came the Vikings and raiders, changing the land. It was said he had distinct visions of his faith, and he mentioned fallen angels and demons. He described nine false altars, nine faces of sin, and later these would become only two and two tribes. It was believed he foresaw the invasions and changes of the old England, but others did not heed his words.

'Are you okay, madam?' a voice asked.

She turned and saw a tall man to her right also admiring the shrine.

'Yes, it's very interesting, so historical, so much to take in. Beautiful,' she replied.

The man was evidently one of the cathedral guides from looking at his outfit, she observed. He watched her as she leaned back. Another guide man stepped in. The two guides looked at each other, then at Emma.

'Everything okay?' she asked, feeling slightly nervous.

'It is...isn't it? Really, he...he was right...' One of the men said aloud as they both watched her. They stood still, waiting as she looked back, not sure of what was happening.

'Should I... I think...' Emma began and then stepped back, away from them. She then lost her balance and fell painfully down against something behind her. She stopped herself with her left hand.

'Shit...what?'

She turned and held up her hand, which stung, and the blood flowed steadily down. It dripped easily from a clear cut along the side of her hand. She felt embarrassed and saw that the blood was spilling over the lower corner of the shrine.

'Oh shit, I'm so sorry, I didn't mean to...'

The two men simply watched her, observing her actions quietly. It was so strange and intimidating. She just had to leave, she thought. Clasping her bleeding hand, she turned and ran out of the room, out down the long corridor toward the entrance. She passed two more cathedral guide men, who noticed her and whispered as she left. She suddenly stopped when she noticed something captivating and curious. The plaque below read 'The Chapel of the Nine Altars'. There were other figures etched there, more monks and saints alongside Saint Cuthbert. She was sure then that she did recognise the faces somehow, like she had seen them in person somewhere very recently. But that would just be absurd, she thought. But...she had dreamed of such faces, she knew she had. That was right. The same old faces that she had just seen. She needed some air.

The cathedral shop clerk put a plaster and bandage over her bleeding hand, and offered more help, but Emma politely declined, before quickly leaving the grand old holy building; nine altars, nine faces, and Saint Cuthbert. The two cathedral guide men from upstairs came around to her and she stood.

'Look, I'm so sorry about that. I don't know what happened...I just kind of...' Emma said, but did not know what to tell them.

'It's okay. Listen, do you know Gaskill?' one of them asked.

'Who?' Emma said.

He looked at the other man with him, and then they looked back at her.

'Bless you. Please be careful. God bless you,' he told her. They simply looked at her as if she were some angelic vision. She had no idea what to make of them, and was so uncomfortable. She watched them and then walked away smiling, but was worried by their behaviour.

Her bloody hand still stung as she walked back towards Newcastle. The handful of cathedral guides and the vicars of the building watched her leave, with stunned, awestruck faces.

Chapter 13

Emma walked down past the tall, old theatre building and around Pilgrim Street. The Orion building was on the other side of the road. She stood and watched others pass it for a moment. No one seemed to acknowledge it or go inside, she thought. But she had to, for the truth, for answers.

'Excuse me, love,' a voice said. She looked to her left and noticed a thin man with an ill appearance glaring at her.

'Sorry, what's up?' she said reluctantly.

'Spare a bit of change please? I'm on the street tonight, honey,' he said in a sad tone.

'Really? Can't you sell Big Issue or something?' Emma asked.

'No, not everyone can. Please love, maybe buy us a coffee or a pie at the cafe, eh?' he suggested, pointing across at the small, cosy cafe as his foul and pungent breath drifted over to her.

'I'm sorry mate, I'm in a hurry now,' Emma explained, feeling guilty but distracted by the Orion building ahead.

'Oh, I see, it's like that. Another heartless, self-important person. Thought you might have been different, but no...' he said to himself.

'I am, look...' Emma said with a sigh. She looked up at the Orion building, then sighed and found change in her jacket pocket.

'Come on, then,' she said to the man. She walked with him over the road to the cafe for food and a coffee. He was smiling like he had won something and looked at her as they walked.

'Thank you love, so generous indeed,' he told her.

'Right, yeah. No trouble at all,' Emma replied. She really was a charitable person usually, but it was the most unsuitable time for it, she thought to herself.

'Maybe a chicken wrap, or a couple of muffins, or doughnuts and a pot of lovely warm tea...' the thin, horrid-smelling man said, thinking of choices to have.

A cold wind whistled through the air between them, giving Emma a sudden chill to her bones. She shivered and looked around.

'Sorry, I have to go somewhere now,' she suddenly told the thin man.

'What? No, no you don't, girl. Get me some food. You owe it to me. You and all your wealthy, bright-eyed, lucky bastard friends!' he shouted.

Emma ignored him as she quickly walked away.

'Look, have this,' she said, and passed him a couple of pound coins.

He took them from her as she quickly walked away out of the cafe, but he watched her from behind the window. She crossed the road towards the Orion building. As he saw her approach the front entrance to the building, his eyes sparked a sudden flash of red light as he picked up a muffin from the counter and bit into it, drooling as he growled.

Having left Jesmond and walked on into Newcastle City Centre, after fifteen minutes it seemed luck was with Eric as he walked into the recently renovated and rebuilt city library. It was a huge, multi-floored place of many kinds of gathered information of all sorts, he knew, but what he was after was the murky history, hidden secrets, guilty rumours and truths from years back that could possibly have been erased or misplaced when the library was renovated. He asked a pretty girl at the desk for any books or information about crime and deaths in the region, feeling it might be more reliable than the distorted guesses from the internet. She was helpful straight away, but did seem to watch him carefully. Did he look that bad, he wondered. He had slept, but he was mourning his dead girlfriend and she could not know that, but should not judge him by his appearance either. Perhaps she was keen on him, he thought. That was probably it, he thought, must be. That would help him, too, he thought as he saw her looking back. Yes, she liked him.

He put his head down and began the process of going through the pile of books and journals she had found for him. He had vaguely seen some of the stories and information before, probably on the news and spoken of by relatives as he had grown up, as his grandparents had lived in Durham before moving nearer Newcastle while he was still in primary school. He was trying to link up some of the places and buildings that they had been around so far to find more meaning somehow. Nothing came out at him. He saw plenty of street names, companies and people but nothing was really standing out significantly. The library was reasonably quiet, with a few people milling around casually behind him doing their own thing. He had never really spent too much time in any library so far, and even at college he managed to borrow enough notes from friends who spent the time there instead of him. His mobile phone buzzed in his pocket suddenly, almost frightening him. He quickly walked out to the side doors to answer it.

'Hello?'

'Hey, it's me,' Emma said. 'Where are you?'

'Durham town library right now,' he explained.

'Okay, well can you stay there until I come? Be careful, I think police have been asking about you,' she told him.

'How do you know that?' he asked.

'I went and spoke to Philip. He said they aren't pleased with you, and neither is he. What a dick,' Emma said.

On top of all the unbelievable supernatural events, he did not need even more danger from police chasing him for no good reason.

'They've been to your house. I told your father I don't know where you are,' she said. 'I'll be there soon anyway, okay?'

In just under half an hour Emma met Eric at a metro train stop near the library, and they grabbed some sandwiches before returning to the library together. He showed her the books and explained some of the events, but all the while tried to remain very vague, suggesting only a strange interest in old Newcastle history.

'You're involved in some seriously dangerous things, then?' Emma said to Eric with concern.

'You could say that. But, you know, some people have to do these things. Some people drift through life with no problems, no danger. Others face the danger head on; saints and activists, people like Gandhi, Martin Luther King Jr, Lennon...fearless men and women,' he told her.

'Eric, they fought for civil rights, end to war, peace, human rights. This is different, isn't it? They knew exactly what they were fighting. Are you fighting for something as big as that?' Emma asked.

'I think so. Really. We've got some things to help us stop some...things in their tracks. It's been working,' he explained.

'Eric, I'm impressed, but Grace might not have wanted you to put yourself in such bad situations,' Emma said, trying to gently give some cautionary advice.

Eric turned away from her and cursed her under his breath.

'Do you get it? No one else knows about these things. Not police, not anyone. And they don't want to know either. No one will know. I only know because...I just know. So I have to do this, okay?' he said, just a tad angry with her.

'Well, fine. I can't stop you. But you can see that I'm just worried about you. And I'm not saying to stop, just...be careful. That's what I'm saying,' Emma told him.

'Really?' he asked.

'Yes, but I do think we should look deeper into the importance of these buildings and who works in them. It's very important. It might explain everything, don't you think?' she asked.

He nodded in silence.

'Depends how much time we have,' Eric said eventually. 'Look, I'm going back now, before night comes. We can speak later or tomorrow,' he said to her.

'Okay. You think there's something coming soon? That we're running out of time? Before what?' Emma asked him.

'There's something. I can't say what, but I have a feeling, a bad feeling. Let's go,' he said. 'Taylor and I are looking for something important.'

'Can you tell me what exactly?' she asked. She was not stupid; he knew that, but wanted to hold back, initially for her sake. He wanted to tell her eventually. Having already lost his love, he did not wish to lose a good friend so soon after. He was tangled up in this unbelievable, shocking trail of blood and fear, and could soon be accused of many things. He could not let that happen to her, Grace's good friend.

'There's really not much to tell of interest, I think; just a, well, kind of sentimental thing that Taylor and I are trying to sort out quickly right now, then I can return to normal shitty predictable dreary Newcastle life,' he told her.

'Really?' she asked 'Eric, police are after the two of you. Why? I'm asking because I care. And don't worry about me; it's you that is in danger. Where is Taylor? What's he doing right now?'

If only I could actually answer that question, he thought.

'He's around town. So can you help us?' Eric asked. 'We can't do all of this research ourselves. Like you said, we're, well, wanted now. Call me with information or I'll call you. Is it a deal?' he asked, giving her puppy dog eyes.

'You need to know about the dark history of Newcastle?' she asked, not altogether sure about his intentions.

'It's not me, really. I'm not sick or one of those weird obsessive people that memorises facts about Charles Manson or Alistair Crowley. It's for an important thing. There's kind of a problem that only me and Taylor can actually solve. It was a kind of danger, a serious threat to all

91

around here; Durham, Newcastle, Tynemouth, all over. We are deep in, and have to finish it off. End it. Police can't do anything, nor can Government, or anyone else. Trust me, please. Help me,' he said quietly.

'It sounds a big and dangerous thing,' Emma told him with quiet concern.

'We're kind of following a trail, but the trail is weak and vague. That's where you come in. Clearing the trail, with facts, names, places, connections. We had it, but it's changed. Something's new suddenly, it has got us guessing,' Eric told her.

Emma did not know exactly what to think. She was almost saddened with sympathy for Eric. Was this all just a morbid delusion brought on to cope with the passing of Grace? Part of her thought yes, but a deeper instinct suggested that there was a disturbing truth to it all. She did not want the police to do anything to Eric or Taylor, and she knew that they just weren't weird psychopaths or anything like that, but it was so mysterious. She knew Grace would not have been happy about any of this, and would not have wanted Eric to be in danger. Eric did seem extremely nervous, tired and secretive, but he was going through mourning so she expected him to be a little out of character.

Emma had no real idea of just how dangerous the situation was other than that the police were looking around for Eric and Taylor. She decided that this was actually enough reason to help out, for now at least. These were close friends in danger, she thought, and friends are precious as life itself.

'Why history books? What's in them for you?' she enquired.

'I'm not too sure. Maybe not much, not everything is recorded, or at least not for the public to know about. Worth checking, though, anyway. I mean, some things, some events in history simply remain of memory, spoken word passed down in conversation, don't they?' he said rhetorically. 'So what are these buildings? Do you know about them?' Eric asked.

'I don't know too much - yet. Grace simply mentioned them very briefly, that's all. But they're important, I know they are. We should know as much as we can, and find out more, shouldn't we?' Emma said.

'These places were just mentioned in the letter Grace left you? Why? What did she say about them?' Eric wanted to know.

'Yes. It was strange and, well, disturbing. I mean, it scares me thinking she might have pissed off some really powerful people. The kinds of people who can do what they want if someone gets in their way,' Emma said.

'It's okay. I've been thinking non-stop about why and how she went. We'll find out, I promise that. Anyway, we can,' he told her.

'Can I see the letter?' he suddenly added.

'Well...yes, of course. If you promise to be careful and let me help you with what you're doing now,' Emma said.

'Look, it's complicated. I'm thinking of your safety,' he told her.

'And I'm thinking of yours, you bloody stubborn bloke,' she told him. 'Yes, you can see it.'

'Thank you,' he replied.

'So what are your thoughts on these businesses, in these buildings?' Eric asked.

'Could be almost anything. From the letter, Grace was vague, but I... I think maybe just very bad people but clever, wealthy people. I mean, people who get a shit load of money in the most calculated, clever ways and still look like respectable charming professionals,' Emma said. 'What do you think?'

'You might be right. Hate to think of really bad situations, but yes, could be some very powerful and clever people. But more than we could easily guess, too. It's the unexpected we should expect,' Eric said.

'You're right,' Emma agreed.

He was glad they had found a common agreement in amongst their opposing opinions which occupied their thoughts.

His cell phone rang.

'It's me, Taylor. You okay?' Taylor asked. He sounded pleased for some unknown reason.

'Where are you?' Eric asked him.

'Other side of town. Can you come over here, near the Haymarket?' Taylor asked.

'Give me half an hour or less. See you soon, you jackass,' Eric answered.

'I've found something interesting. Hurry up,' Taylor added, then ended the call.

After hanging up on Eric, Taylor looked around. He stood in a crumbling, old building by the motorway, the sound of cars humming in the air regularly. Around Taylor, two tall, dark figures moved between deep shadows. The moonlight illuminated only select parts of these strange figures near him as they watched him silently. The tallest figure stepped close to Taylor.

'We need him, or we kill him, and many others. Possibly even you,' it said to him, with a bizarre, inhuman rasp.

'He's on his way. He'll come soon. He's desperate,' Taylor explained.

'We hope that you really are something special. For your sake, if nothing else,' the thing said to him. 'Do not waste my precious time.'

'I'm wasting nothing at all,' Taylor told them. He almost felt sick, his stomach knotting up inside.

As they walked along down the quiet streets together, Eric and Emma discussed their plans.

'We have to be extremely careful now. I'll help you, but we have to watch all around us,' Emma explained to him seriously.

'I know, I agree. Even so, let's do this well,' he said. His thoughts conflicted.

'It should be your main priority. You can't do much at all if you're banged up, can you?' Emma suggested.

'Yeah, okay, I get the point. Thank you for taking the risk, Emma,' he told her suddenly.

'Whatever, don't mention it,' she said, a little embarrassed. 'So, where to?'

'I have no clear idea. I think, though, the way things are going, that it's just a matter of time before I know. Could be anytime, any time now...or I could simply end up at the right place at the right time,' he explained with a pained smile.

He knew that she did not understand much of what he was suggesting, or what he knew or had seen, but at least she was someone sympathetic and loyal that he could share his thoughts with when ready.

They continued on until reaching the metro train station entrance at the Haymarket front area.

'Look, Emma, I really appreciate your being here but soon there's probably going to be some very intense things suddenly happening. I don't want you to get hurt, okay?' he said seriously.

'I can handle myself just fine. I'm not being chased, you are. I'm sticking to you like sin,' she explained wryly.

They heard a wailing, then some fragmented moan, tortured and agonised, somewhere not far from them.

'That might be it,' Eric said. Emma looked at him, confused and scared. He seemed to wake up, eyes darting around, fully aware and alert.

'What do you mean 'it'?' Emma asked unnerved.

He didn't reply, but began to walk quickly along a narrow path through bushes and brambles across an overgrown field in the direction of the bizarre screams.

'What do you think it was?' Emma asked, following him.

'Could be anything nasty, right? Or an accident. Or it could be the thing Taylor and I are following,' he explained as he briskly walked on. 'The things we told ourselves not to fear, not to believe,' he added, only looking forward as they went.

He ran on and Emma stumbled behind in the long grass. Another strange scream rumbled out from somewhere around in the early evening as the sun was quickly setting around them. It spooked Emma as she tried to keep up with Eric. What was he heading toward? Were they prepared to confront whatever had caused the screaming? She looked up from the grass around her and found Eric gone.

'Eric? Eric...where are you?' she said, and grew nervous. No reply came, and she could not see him anywhere around. 'Shit,' she said to herself and quickly turned around on the spot, paranoid and suddenly alone. Even while Eric had yet to fully explain to her just what he and Taylor were really involved with, she had the feeling that it really was something to be afraid of. She could tell by the expressions on his face when he spoke to her. If he had been taken by the people or thing he was chasing, she was not sure that she was prepared to meet it herself so soon.

Chapter 14

He wanted this fight, needed it, Eric believed. Every one of these surreal fights was giving him an unbelievable rush of energy, a euphoric high lifting him out of the depression of grieving for Grace. He was angry, confused and bitter, and beating and killing some supernatural, unearthly thing helped. He was taking it all out on this next one, he thought. Why did Emma have to insist on getting so involved in it, though? She might ruin it all if he had to keep watch on her as well. Okay, she was a very close friend of Grace's, but all of this unreal danger was deadly. It was too much, and he wanted as few to be involved as possible. It was his trouble, his job to find out what the hell had killed Grace, and to save her soul.

There were feelings and emotions which may have led Eric through the quiet, lonely parts of Newcastle to the secretive parkland area. Some places would always be quiet and left alone after a certain time of night. There were places where even police would avoid, where even junkies, prostitutes and dealers would think twice before entering, even in the most desperate of times. Some used to speak of special leylines around parts of the country, connected to spirits or witchcraft, but those myths may be slightly off track. There are other parts which could hold powers and dangers if investigated in the wrong manner. The answers would be of a nature wholly unearthly, uncontrollable by most natural means and this park far down the winding back streets of higher Newcastle City Centre was such a place.

Shadows throbbed, winds whispered and beckoned, and nature around was darkening, enthralled and commanded by hidden hordes and fallen, brutal forces. The people of the North-East were very aware of this elaborate and extremely overgrown parkland, but would always choose to stay well away. It would often be many months between persons accidentally or foolishly walking through the entrance, or reports of it being the last place someone was seen before being declared missing, or worse.

There were tales of the park holding entire dead families, perhaps containing various homeless, crazed or insane people who were once wealthy or famous locally. How much of any of it could actually be true at all? Why should Eric be the one to learn fact from fiction? If he never returned from within the park, would he also in years to come become the next myth, an alleged cannibal, homeless cult member or sacrificed body?

The gates seemed to open up before he even stepped forward to touch them. Would that be possible? A chilling drift of air brushed his neck, some vague echo of words, or just hollow wind through the thick rows of defiant, tall trees all around. On his lonely walk ahead, the narrow path between overgrown bushes, nettles, brambles and trees, other paths opened and closed briefly. He saw patches of muddy ground, and he could look ahead and only just make out his path due to the florescent light of distant streetlamps guiding him and indicating that he had not yet fallen into some endless, black vortex. He knew that he had walked into the park because of desperate personal necessity; what would choose to live in here, spend time in this place of shadows, bugs and disturbing mysteries? In the engulfing blackness the distant, shivering light forms could almost be moving, twisting around ahead somewhere. Did they have eyes, teeth? Was he hearing some rasping breath up close to him? It could be the rustling of the many autumn leaves underfoot, or it could be something waiting for him, hungry for him. He swallowed, took a quick breath, and continued.

The night had come as he approached the park gates. He saw that they were unexpectedly wide open and unlocked, with no need to climb them. This was unusual for late evening, but he walked on through as cold night air and thin fog filled the deep darkness of the park, and the many long rows of tall trees and bushes all around obstructed his view further. He could only walk on deep into the park, looking and carefully listening for any clue as to the right direction to travel in order to find his fight. He walked into the fog, feeling vulnerable but clutching tightly onto his crowbar and bag on his shoulder, praying for guidance, for direction. Whether or not he would receive an answer was another thing altogether, he thought to himself.

Noises from deep within the darkness of the park came from around him; chirping, howling, rustling sounds. He was on edge, prepared to attack and defend himself but still uncontrollably paranoid and hesitant.

The fog began to thin out gradually, showing him an opening before further paths and long grassy areas. He had been in the park many times over the years, but rarely when it was so incredibly dark.

Shadows and branches warped and bent across the narrow opening, confusing his eyes. He was beginning to feel trapped, or out of his depth. The sounds of the night in the park were growing, distracting him. As he thought this and began to turn around, he glimpsed something different ahead, a moving shape. He turned back and looked up the pathway. It was the shadow of someone, a person nearby, he realised. Someone was approaching or coming near.

'Hello?' he called out.

The tall shadow seemed to possibly resemble the silhouette of a long-haired woman in a dress walking by. He stepped up further, curious as the shadow moved by. It came from behind or had moved around him somehow. He looked around past the trees ahead.

'Hello there? Anyone?' he said.

The woman seemed to have moved away further beyond past the closest row of tall trees, which closed off the next few pathways of the park. As Eric was there for a specific reason, he chose to keep walking ahead to look for the woman. There was a claustrophobic darkness surrounding him all around as he walked deeper into the park, hiding any potential attackers, dwellers or things there waiting, with only dim moonlight shining down from behind thick night clouds above.

Eric came out at an opening between the larger expanses of the two main areas of open park land. The woman, if that was what Eric had seen, could not been seen ahead anywhere. He shivered in the cold air, almost giving up. A noise then suddenly erupted loudly, possibly from just around the next row of trees. It sounded like some kind of distorted moan or wild scream, he thought. There was something happening then, close by, and he was not alone. He turned and caught the back of someone or something moving away behind. He jumped back, startled, then moved up towards the dark shape, which turned to face him. It was a normal, even slightly beautiful, woman, he made out through the shadows around her. Her eyes shone shockingly bright crimson red back at him as she smiled. He stumbled back a couple of paces while she disappeared quickly into the deep shadows ahead. Though she was smiling, she seemed to rush away sharply, as if running from something. But if she was one of those in some way, what was she running from?

He moved on along the far side of the trees, moving with quiet caution and expecting danger ahead. There was something, he knew it.

If that woman was different, her strange red eyes told him there were more close by. He gripped his cricket bat as he continued. Some great noise rumbled up ahead of him. He heard a woman's laughter faintly, then speaking, maybe a conversation. He had no idea what the hell was going on around him, but he would find out. The ground shook suddenly as he stood clutching the cricket bat, waiting. He staggered, unbalanced and confused. He almost regretted not bringing Taylor as he stepped closer to the next row of tall trees.

He heard uneven footsteps nearby, then voices spoke in some obscure or dead language, if it was a language at all. There were more than two, perhaps more than three or four voices, Eric thought. He gripped the cricket bat still, stepping out with grave hesitation. The noises seemed to warp from being voices one second then indiscernible growls and moans of cryptic language the next. Possibly Latin or Eastern words, he considered. Other sounds, though, were more like the wild expressions of rabid dogs or other feral beasts. Between these unusual sounds he then began to make out English words.

'…The girl…father…knows…changed…two of them…' one voice said, between other sounds.

Eric wondered which girl they were talking about. Could they be talking about Grace?

'Bastards,' Eric said aloud, then stumbled over onto the tall bushes to his right. The voices and growling became louder and he heard loud footsteps approaching. Could he take on two or three of these hellish things? He was trapped, and would have to fight no matter what, he realised. Eric glanced over his shoulder and saw that he was surrounded by the huge trees and their deep, black shadows.

'Good God, shit,' he said to himself, and took a deep breath before storming out of the only opening between the trees. The growling and talking nearby continued loudly. He stumbled forward in the dark, and was then confronted by three huge, hulking abominations looking down on him, with burning red eyes and powerful, clawed hands held out high towards him.

The three huge, misshapen monsters towered in front of him, trapping him. He was frozen with dread, fascinated and repulsed equally as he witnessed their shining, sharp fangs, their odorous, reptilian skin shining in the moonlight. The largest beast then spoke to him.

'The mighty…man. Come to fight…us…now?' it asked in surprisingly clear English.

Eric stood before the three large demons, calculating his choices. Three demons against only him this time; was this finally the end?

'Impressive...so far...man,' the closest beast said.

Was it talking to him? Giving him some kind of compliment?

'I'll do what I can. I have so far,' Eric told them, clutching the cricket bat with all his strength as they watched him.

'You...will,' the closest one agreed. The three demons watched him intensely, observing him, trapping him there.

'I have to, you took her and others,' Eric told them, not giving much of a sweet damn if they decided to suddenly rip him into pieces right there and then. Their three sets of shining red eyes glowed and intimidated him as the beasts stood silently. The large lead demon lurched down to him, and it pointed its scab-encrusted, muscular hand right at his face.

'You can...kill our kind,' it said, 'two kinds now. Men like us...you can kill them...you will,' it told him.

'Two kinds of things like you?' Eric asked, not sure of what it was telling him.

'They took your woman...part of us in them, our darkness,' it told him.

Eric and the lead demon looked at each other silently for a brief moment. There was slight admiration between them, or even respect. They lurching demon laughed in a deep, low tone, revealing its sharp teeth to Eric.

'You know my Grace? Where is she now, between afterlife or she's waiting, trapped?' Eric asked. The demon nodded back silently. Eric gripped his cricket bat, twisting it before the three demons who watched him.

'These men-demons took her, and not you?' he asked.

'Yes...' the first demon replied.

'You can get her back? Can you save her?' Eric asked.

'It is...possible...' it told him.

Eric wondered just why these huge, unearthly beasts could not stop these other demon men by themselves. Why should they need him? He was just another small, everyday human praying to God for his Grace to be saved, he thought. He had killed two of them, though, he and Taylor, and they seemed to know this, and it did seem to disturb them, even impress them.

'So where are these men demons you need killing?' Eric asked them. Sudden pained howls echoed around the park, and strong harsh winds blew past him, and possibly crows, rushed passed him in the shadows.

'Hello? Anybody?' he said, and walked on with caution as he crept around the corner of the crumbled, tall building.

'Will I do?' a voice suddenly asked. Eric spun around, alarmed. He saw a terrible vision of some blasphemous form, stretched out and unnatural, staring at him.

'What's your game tonight?' Eric asked, keeping composure. It did raise hairs on his neck and chill his blood to look at this creature, but he had overcome three of them now with some kind of help from Taylor. Where was Taylor now, he thought.

'I came to meet you. You are getting an impressive reputation,' it said to him in its low tone.

'I hope I am. Care to turn back now?' Eric asked it.

'Not this night,' it told him. They looked at each other, a brave foolish human, and a horrific abomination, each with fatal plans.

'Someone has to stop your kind,' Eric said.

'Not true. No, someone could join with us,' it said among the heavy shadows of the building. Eric could barely believe what he was hearing. Was it making him an offer?

'You butcher, kill, stop us…you enjoy it all. Yes?' it asked him.

'It has to be done. What the hell are you anyway?' Eric said.

'What the hell are you?' it repeated.

Eric looked at the beast, and wondered. It came from some cruel, otherworldly place where love did not exist. It must have been some kind of diseased, mutant man, or animal, or something, Eric thought. Some rich man and a bunch of scientists going way too far, and here was their rabid Frankenstein's monster.

'You are no man at all, but you can be a new thing…no rules, no misery, no pain…' the beast told him.

'Stop talking and return to the hell you came from, or I'll beat you to shit like the others,' Eric said.

'We are in control,' it said. It seemed so sure of its words, with a satisfied glare in its eyes.

'Not completely,' Eric said, and watched it as it walked around. Even when Taylor stood frozen or making mistakes, it was still reassuring to have him there.

'You don't know me,' Eric said.

'Quite the opposite,' the creature explained, and suddenly slipped deep in among the shadows of the building, gone from view.

Eric was relieved that it was over, though not entirely sure what any of it had meant. Who had been threatening who, he thought. But it had given him an offer then, hadn't it? He could hardly understand the proposal; was it an offer to work with them, or even be one of those soulless abominations in some way? Could that be possible? Just about anything could be possible, he thought. Why would he even consider joining with these creatures? Now that reality had changed, widening to reveal greater dangers close by, more than simply man against man, drugs or violence, these creatures, possibly actual demons or devils, seemed to now be the greatest threat to mankind he had ever seen. But if they were actual physical evil, then surely there should be some strong, supernatural form of pure good to counteract them, he thought. He couldn't say that he had seen much evidence so far, although he believed that Grace could get to a better place, from the mysterious limbo place that she was in.

He had been on their trail for days now, stopping slaughter and death at their hands. That had been until the last time, and he and Taylor only just managed to save the last one by some kind of luck. But then there was this.

Was it ending? These creatures, were they actually offering him some sort of peaceful agreement, some truce? No, he could not believe that at all, would not allow himself to consider any of it. He could not understand any of it, and only continued because of the messages from Grace, or from Grace's spirit.

He desperately wished to see her, and to know where she really was. By day, he had been growing more and more spiritual, open-minded and God-fearing in his own cynical way because of all of these unreal events. Taylor was missing, and so was Grace. He did have Emma, though, he thought. Could she get him through these encounters, he wondered. If he was to fail, could she then continue to fight them herself?

Ahead of Emma were yards and yards of tall tangled, knotted trees, their branches entwined. The night moon climbed high overhead, watching in silence and enjoying her anxious frustration. Emma was a person who usually preferred to be amongst a crowd of friends and this sudden isolation was absolutely terrifying her. She was a rational, logical person and no soft, pretty girl. Right then, though, she could not suspend a myriad of thoughts of danger and terror that filled her idle mind. For all the support that she was offering Eric, she considered that

102

he really did not seem very grateful and was maybe taking her for granted.

She took out her mobile phone and tried to dial through to his. No connection could be made. She scowled and gave up, and so simply decided to try to find her way back to the motorway and onto the city streets once more. In less than ten minutes she did just that, after gaining numerous cuts and scrapes from the tangled bushes and trees around the field and paths. She arrived at a zebra crossing on the main road, opposite some tall buildings near the old cinema across the road. There were no other people around as she crossed the road, and she turned the corner of the next street hesitantly. She knew this area, and would have finally felt reasonably secure until she looked up and saw it. Her heart jumped in shock, and she gasped aloud.

The scene she saw across the street opposite was absolutely distressing and terrifying beyond doubt. She questioned her sanity as she looked on with distressed and horrified fascination, but some part of her told her to step away quietly. Walk away, run, even; just turn and go; her mind said. But she looked on in shock and in disbelief. She saw what seemed to be two people attacking another two people so violently, with such insane aggression and savage energy. Blood poured all over the street, screams and cries echoing around in the air, as the victims wrestled against the mad attackers helplessly. Emma could see sprays of blood jetting out across the pavements as the two attackers stabbed, clawed and grabbed their prey like rabid predators in the wild. She could not make out everything clearly but the attackers seemed to appear strangely large, distorted in size and shape, with curious movement as they lurched on, hurting and killing. Emma wanted to stop them in some way, but her logic told her that she might just as easily end up right alongside the two bloodied victims there on the street within minutes. What could she do? Her words and intelligence had always been her protection, and she doubted they could help much. As she watched motionless, the two torturers looked around, as if they sensed her watching. Would they leave the people they were slaying in order to pursue her?

She ran, telling her legs to go like lightning. She could not believe what she had seen and almost in some crazy way wanted to go back to check that it had been real. She decided against it, but knew that she was feeling so much pressure after losing Grace. Who were those people and why were they killing others so openly out on the city streets? People don't do that, she thought. There was crime and violence out there, but what she had just witnessed...it was more than murder. It was like torture and sadistically brutal pleasure. She wanted to find Eric straight away, or simply get to a safe place. Where was safe, her flat? She should phone the police, she thought. Would they believe her? They should, but it was honestly very doubtful if she told them all of what she had seen, she thought. She had witnessed a truly sick atrocity, but it had been so unbelievable. She did know the area well, and knew that her place was less than twenty minutes away. The taxi ranks were close by, too.

Every sound made her shake a little as she ran steadily down the next few streets. After another couple of minutes, the town police station was right before her. Walking inside made her feel guilty that she had not tried to intervene, but she knew they would have done the same to her. She would not have done that, anyway; she was not that reckless. She had always been a good, law-abiding girl, with no criminal charges, no warnings and no trouble with police whatsoever. Even so, she could not help but feel insecure and paranoid, wondering what they might ask her or think of her as she approached the reception desk. Thinking back about how shocking, unreal and savage the attack seemed, she finally began to think about what Eric and Taylor were doing. Something very dangerous that no one would believe or understand, Eric had been telling her. Just like what I've seen, she thought nervously to herself.

She saw someone standing behind the front desk, looking at pages of a book then at a phone switch board.

'Excuse me?' Emma said curtly.

'Hello, how may I help, madam?' the policeman asked.

'Right. Well, I'm not messing you about at all, okay? I've seen the most...I lost my friend down near the big city park, right? But then I accidentally came around by the back area, Marshall Street, yeah? I saw...I saw...' She could not begin to tell him.

'Go on. Would you like to sit down, or speak in a more closed area?' he asked.

'It was just insane, brutal in fact, so sick and wrong...' she blurted out.

'Okay, slow down, madam. What are you saying you have seen and where?' he asked calmly.

'An attack, yes. Fucking insane, evil stuff. So much blood. Two people were...killed, but slowly, like some sick kind of torture just out on the street. You have to catch them now, these murderers,' Emma exclaimed dramatically.

The policeman at the desk called out another officer to take his place while he led Emma to a room.

'This was only a short time ago?' he asked her.

'Yes, must be only fifteen minutes ago,' she agreed.

'Okay, would you like to stay here, or we can take you home now if you like? I'll get some of my colleagues out around there right now. Don't you worry about this at all, you are totally safe, okay?' he explained. He spoke into the small radio piece clipped to his jacket, sending a message through.

'But my friend is out there, missing,' Emma said aloud.

'Sorry?' the policeman said, looking at her again then.

'It's...fine. Yes, I'll get a lift home. Thank you very much,' she said.

'You're okay, are you?' he asked.

'I'll be alright I think, it was just so shocking,' she told him.

'These things happen. Society has problems,' he told her. He seemed annoyed and even slightly amused. She could swear he nearly smiled. She was not sure if he was attempting to reassure her or if he was simply being arrogant and did not believe her.

'Look, I have to call this through. This is a very serious thing that you've reported. I heard that another person has seen a similar thing. As for your friend, I think he'll turn up soon,' he told her.

'Is that it?' Emma asked, surprised.

'I'm sorry, I've got to send out cross reports and record this all. You may go now. Officer Brenson is waiting out front to take you home,' he said. He hurried off away from her down the winding corridor. Emma was astonished. His behaviour was so unusual for a police officer, she thought. She almost screamed after him as he went, but then she remembered Eric.

She remembered his excuses, his manner, and began to think about the danger out on the streets. She wondered if Eric knew things about these unbelievable happenings. It could just make a twisted kind of sense. If Eric did know the hows and whys of these sick events, did he only know so much? Or did he know how to stop it? Was that what she was helping him to do? He was gone now, and she then thought about the possibility of these attackers knowing about him. Could they have caught him, done similar brutal things to him? She did not really wish to consider it.

Emma felt an urge to run home and lock herself securely inside her flat until it was all over, until others had resolved it without her, but she knew that was not going to happen. She knew, too, that her foolish friends needed her to be foolish but brave like them, too. She ran back onto the quiet, dark streets once again.

Chapter 15

There was a specific kind of future waiting ahead for Eric, Emma and Taylor in their familiar yet recently deadly home of Newcastle. They did not necessarily believe myths, religious tales, superstitions or what older generations might believe, but they knew to be fearful of a different time around them.

The Northern towns where they lived, from Newcastle to Gateshead, Tynemouth to Byker, were being ignored by the rest of the country, or it seemed that way to the people there. There were stereotypes, clichés and negative views that many lived by and which held them down in the dirt. For how long would the people of the North view it as the scrap yard, waste bin of the country, where modernity, civilized democracy and decency rarely came by? For how long would it be seen as a place of closed down coal mine industries, of shipping and building industries long dried up and forgotten, of simple lives, desperate thoughts and little money? Admittedly, unemployment was high, after regeneration. All of these things suggested returning to the overwhelmingly depressing levels of the eighties, and drug dealing and human trafficking were becoming a known presence in the North. All of these things suggested that the North was a disgrace, an embarrassment; somewhere to avoid, ignore and forget.

For Eric though, and Emma, they would not think like that. They could not.

Most harboured constant anger, frustration, and bitter jealousy towards the apparently more successful, confident image of the South of England, London in particular. And with all this anger and insecurity, the dark forces took their hold, and had done for some time.

The rules were changing, Eric saw that much. He knew what Grace had told him so far, but things were getting more unpredictable, less definite. Nothing was ever simple in life, and this would be no different, he thought. The attacks, the mystery, the places. A new challenge for him, for Taylor, also, and for Emma. So now he knew more. He had been told some of what he had wanted to know, he had found some of it, and guessed more. With it, though, had arrived a fresh set of problems - or were they?

He had spoken to them. These things had appeared at first as some wild, unknown manlike creatures, though now revealed themselves to definitely be demons, and had spoken to him, showing themselves to be intelligent yet deadly. As they had tortured and hurt others physically, their words now tormented and abused Eric. Had he been lucky or chosen, he wondered. Had a God intervened, or did some strange new possibility stand before him to consider amidst the bloodletting and violence?

He had survived so far, somehow, and knew their ways. These beasts were now communicating with him. Could they have easily killed him there and then? Just possibly, he thought. He actually felt lonely and unable to decide upon the next action without Taylor around. While Eric did regularly criticise Taylor, he relied on him in many ways which he often did not consider. He saw this then, and regretted it, but maybe it was how things worked best with both of them. At least, that was what he tried to convince himself.

Eric walked along past houses as quiet as mausoleums, windows with curtains fully drawn shut, families sleeping peacefully. He could only think about the things the beast creatures had told him or offered him and wonder. Wonder about himself, his life, his past. Wonder about saving these people sleeping or resting at home all around him, oblivious to the evil. And then he thought about how much the demons knew. How much control did they have? Grace had helped him, but it had been him and Taylor. It was simply him alone right now. Could he possibly defeat many more of these things alone?

What were they really trying to get? What were they really after? They did obviously enjoy tearing innocent people to bloody shreds but there was a purpose beyond that. He knew there were two separate groups or tribes of demons. One group were asking for him to help them kill or defeat the other. Were they telling the truth, he wondered. These were things from below, possibly not possessing guilt or fear like mankind. What if both these demon tribes were as evil and dangerous as each other? Was there any point in joining them at all? He might be used in a vile game before they decided to finish him. He was no simple fool, if he chose to play then he could play them just as well, he decided. Anything for Grace.

They obviously enjoyed it sadistically, but there was purpose to their attacks, he knew. And he was very curious to know if they had killed Grace, or if something else had happened which he did not yet know. There was a deeper story here, he thought. Grace knew. If only she could tell him more, and quickly.

He came along toward the high, old stone bridge and his mind began to slow down. The thoughts pulled his logical judgement in all moral directions as he stepped close up to the bridge. He usually had believed people who took these kinds of actions to be weak, selfish, or it could just be all that was left to choose to do at that moment. He looked from left to right. As there were no people in either direction, he climbed up onto the bridge ledge and stood, carefully balancing. Wind came teasingly, tickling his face and blowing his hair a little. In the wind, he somehow heard a whimper.

'No... time...for that now...human,' a voice said.

He recognised the voice well.

'Maybe I've done all I should. I've got my reasons,' Eric said aloud.

'I tell you the truth; you've got reason not to. You know that. Things will change. Keep walking,' the voice told him.

He stood tall and straight, with determination and bullish pride, but he knew that he had to continue. No easy exit, no sympathy or escape just for his own sanity. He swallowed, sighed and looked around. Across the bridge he could see the horizon beyond the town in the bright, beautiful moonlight. He climbed down and took a quick, shameful look to see if anyone had seen him being so selfish. He was thankful to see that they hadn't, and turned. To his right he saw the back of a tall man, who was walking away a few yards from him. Eric wondered if he knew the man. Thinking no, he went off on his way again.

Chapter 16

The music was at a level that shook his inner core, woke his soul and rattled his teeth, rumbling the bass up through his body to the pulsing electro-rock beats. Taylor sat in the nightclub, sipping a double vodka and coke thoughtfully, nervously. He watched a group of loud, leery men shouting drunkenly over the music, trying too hard to impress the many dozens of gorgeous Goth-styled rock women around the club. After watching them for a while it looked like the small group of alpha male men were deciding to leave the club, so Taylor got up casually to follow behind. He himself had enjoyed enough impressive and debauched erotic games and lustful play earlier on with a couple of enthusiastic and gorgeous rock women. His connections with a certain mysterious businessman from around the area granted him a more enjoyable level of respect and adoration, and to ease his increasing stress and fear he took good advantage of it, though after more drugs and loose sex he felt much the same.

As the confident men stepped out to the street, many more late night revellers stumbled along, fuelled by strong booze of many kinds and hungry appetites for love, lust, sex and adventures. Taylor waited to make his move, coming along stealthily behind the men, close inside the shadows of the buildings along the street. The boisterous, tall young man at the front of the group waved his arms around dramatically, making misogynistic jokes and smacking the arse of a girl wobbling close by them. Taylor walked along by the men silently yet purposefully then fell into the loud, toned man.

'Watch it, you freak!' the man shouted, excessive testosterone rattling around his heated head.

'Did I knock you there, little fella?' Taylor said with a concerned, deadpan expression on his face. The tall man immediately took a swing at Taylor, but as he had downed at least eight pints Taylor easily dodged his attack. He watched the man stumble a few steps across the road.

'Not too precise, are you, big guy? Want to give it another try?' Taylor asked sympathetically. The man and his friends moved in on him, his face red and eyes squinting. The man lunged, trying to grab Taylor. Spotting this quickly, Taylor ducked and smiled. He seemed to move shockingly fast, the other men watching speechless.

'Damn, you guys are really out of shape, aren't you?' Taylor said, laughing. 'Keep it coming, you just might scratch me if you try harder, ladies,' he added, and quickly moved away at speed, dodging them and moving towards the middle of the street. The group of four angry, drunken men came roaring after him, shouting raging abuse and threats, their fists in the air. Taylor disappeared into a side alley between buildings as they followed.

'Little pussy shit thinks he's going to get away alive tonight? No chance of that,' the lead brute announced to his friends as he looked around the street in confusion. They looked down at the back alley entrance, curious and suspecting it to be Taylor's sanctuary. They walked along past large rubbish bins deep into the shadows of the alley to claim and maim Taylor.

'Come out and face us, you mouthy piece of shit!' the tall man shouted aggressively into the shadows. Then the violence began.

All four men were suddenly dragged without mercy by their legs deeper into the alley, taken by the unrelenting wild savage claws, red eyes in the shadows, blinking back while blood poured. Clawed hands grabbed at their faces, arms, legs as they all wrestled hopelessly against the forces which caught them, pulling them into darkness, down to the ground. The men fell and crawled, shocked at the things they briefly saw small horrific glimpses of near them. They screamed like helpless children as they were cut, sliced, torn and bitten. Each of them was slowly though enthusiastically tortured until the life ebbed away from them, after a fitful, bloody resistance. The large lead man tried to struggle free from the strong arms and shocking red eyes that watched him suffer in the dark of the alley.

'Get...off me!' he called out pathetically, his voice thinner and more feminine than before. 'Who the hell...' he said, but that was all he would say, as he was pulled with pain in opposite directions. He fell over his quickly dying friends in the darkness as his face was then suddenly torn brutally from his skull. Over his crawling friends, three more creatures with red eyes floating in the dark held them down. No help came into

111

the alley while the men screamed. There was only one witness, but that person would not speak of what he saw to others, or call for help. Taylor watched silently, looking away once or twice when it was just too much to handle. He watched with sick interest, and proud triumph. The men wailed and thrashed for a painful moment, as the inner life was taken from them, and then there was silence. Taylor walked away from the alley turning his thoughts to Eric, hoping that he was having luck in finding the ones they were after.

The walk from the car to the dirty, old flats was brisk, and made Taylor more nervous than he already had been. He was wondering just what Andrew might want to do with the motionless corpse of Grace. Who was she to him? Andrew had not known Grace as far as Taylor could be sure. What use was the dead body of Grace now?

Taylor was already thinking about the significance that she must hold for Andrew and his brutal and mysterious kind. This was Grace, though, he thought; the kind, sweet, beautiful girlfriend of his best friend. He just could not imagine how she could be involved with or connected to Andrew. Taylor knew that Andrew was a kind of businessman, owning or managing at least one bar in Tynemouth where they had been horrendously drunk, and a club elsewhere, and maybe with involvement in other businesses, it now seemed. He was a businessman who killed people in some unreal way by night for some kind of business deals. How could Grace have come to be of any interest to him, Taylor wondered. Had she come to be involved in one of Andrew's morbid and dangerous business deals? He almost did not want to know. They reached the doors and Andrew stepped close.

'Here we are,' Taylor told him, and fumbled in his pocket, taking out the key and aiming it at the lock, missing at first, and then unlocking it. They walked in and descended the staircase with shadows around them, with Andrew smiling hopefully. Taylor stopped at the flat door.

'She's inside. Just like you asked for, all ready for you. Will she be okay?' Taylor asked.

'She's dead, Taylor, isn't she?' Andrew replied.

'Yes, but I mean, you won't rip her up and spit her out like that guy, will you?' Taylor asked. Andrew simply gave him a look which suggested that Taylor had hurt his feelings.

They stepped inside, and Taylor nervously watched Andrew.

'Where is she, then?' he asked.

'Over here, come with me,' Taylor said.

112

He led Andrew across the main room through to the smaller kitchen where a large long freezer stood. Taylor grabbed the lid, unlocked the top, and pulled it open with a strong groan. They looked down into the freezer cabin. There, surrounded by thick ice and a floating icy vapour, lay the motionless body of Grace. Taylor had arranged for her to look peaceful again after having been pulled from her grave in the night.

'Beautiful young lady,' Andrew commented.

'Yes, she was. Still is, really,' Taylor said in agreement. They admired her for a brief moment, although Taylor was waiting for whatever was to come with increasing guilt and fear.

'I promise I will leave her as she is now, but you should leave the room, I think,' Andrew told Taylor.

'Really? But I mean, what should I not see that can't fuck my head up more than it is already?' Taylor asked.

Andrew threw him a stern look as he leaned a hand into the freezer toward Grace.

'Alright, fine. I'll have a couple of whiskeys in the other room. Give me a shout if you need me,' Taylor said, and walked out as Andrew took hold of the delicate, porcelain-white hand of dead Grace.

Once left alone in the small neglected kitchen, Andrew was ready to begin his work on Grace to find out just how many of his secrets had escaped. He placed a hand on her neck, which began to suddenly bubble, then jerk and twist. He himself soon began to quietly moan and twitch his head, closing his eyes as his skin turned paler and his shoulders expanded. His bright red eyes then looked down on the body of Grace as he touched her neck with both of his crooked and clawed hands. Something was happening, an occurrence unholy and powerful.

He held her with a tender grip, looking into her dead eyes. Here was a dead young woman who had found them, knew about them and received death quickly afterwards for her troubles. But she had taken secrets away with her, to help her on her journey, secrets to ruin Andrew and his demon brothers and sisters.

It was time for him to connect much deeper into the further realms, to find her soul, her roaming being in the foggy plains of supernatural existence. He would channel the evil disease within and the origin for guidance and strength in his search. With it he could act in even greater supernatural ways, with dark energies and power from beyond simple Earth life, in order to control her threatening spirit.

He held Grace and began to whisper out a complex mantra of satanic prayers or callings. It was secretly against his usual way, to be so truly and honestly demonic; letting his human side slip so far away from him, but this was the most effective thing to do at that time, he believed. The ice inside the freezer cabinet melted quickly, his clawed hands warming around Grace as he held her tightly while chanting. A visible energy pushed through her, from beneath her cold skin. He let go and watched with patience.

'Bring her out to me,' he said quietly.

There was suddenly a violent shaking of the freezer, which seemed to shock Andrew himself. He watched her with keen anticipation. She was still and motionless inside the freezer.

'Bring her out,' he repeated, and bared his fangs as veins throbbed on his neck and forehead. No result came, no life moved before him. Taylor came in then, with the whisky bottle almost empty.

'How's things?' he asked cheerily, offering the bottle toward Andrew. Andrew turned to him slowly, returning to his human form in that moment.

'It is troublesome tonight. A strong evasive soul, she has,' Andrew told him.

'Is this some kind of séance or something?' Taylor asked.

'That's just foolish entertainment. This is communication, but...there's something blocking my way to her,' Andrew explained.

'You were going to actually talk to her? What, like...her ghost?' Taylor asked in disbelief.

'Give me the fucking bottle, now!' Andrew shouted at him, snatching it from Taylor and guzzling down the last of the whisky in seconds.

'You've done this before, have you?' Taylor asked, losing some of his fear towards Andrew as the situation seemed so bizarre.

'I have, though not for some time. There's been no need for a long time. It's not my style, but it has to be done,' Andrew replied, pacing the room in frustration.

'Is she really so important to you?' Taylor asked.

'Yes, I wish not, but yes. It's a big fucking accident, all her fault. It needs sorting out. She's fucked around with the way of established business, and here she is,' Andrew explained.

'You going to try again?' Taylor asked.

Andrew looked down at the still body of Grace, with melted ice water around her.

'Not now. I'll return soon,' Andrew told him with a defeated sigh. 'Let's go now. There are other things to do.'

114

He passed the bottle back and Taylor finished the whisky before locking up, and they walked out of the flat and returned to the car outside.

Chapter 17

Houses and other old buildings sat with decayed exhaustion as Emma walked along. Everywhere she looked things seemed tired, ruined, and used up. It was continually hard for her to be positive when all surroundings seemed to have given up competing with the rest of the world. The city had been getting better, showing signs of positive hope, but now all this. She decided to try to contact Eric again on her mobile phone. It rang, and she waited nervously for an answer.

'Hello? Emma?' Eric said.

'Thank God. It's me. Where did you go? Are you okay?' she asked him quickly. They exchanged recent news and less than ten minutes later they found each other at the city library entrance once more.

'I've seen death, and I know we're in danger. Look, Eric I need to talk to you about some serious things now,' Emma told him. Eric looked at her with frustration.

'Well alright, when we can. I can't stop now, I have to keep going,' he told her. 'What did you want to talk about?' he said as he walked along from the library and she followed behind.

'Eric, all of this...the things that you and Taylor are doing...I think I can understand. I will listen if you want to try to explain it to me. I'm with you on this,' she told him.

'I am sorry that I haven't explained it too clearly yet, but I thought that you said you trusted me?' he asked.

'I want to, Eric,' she told him honestly.

'Look, I really need you to do that. I can't really trust anyone else right now, and you and I both knew Grace like no one else did,' he said.

'I trust you. I do, and... I saw something in town earlier; it was horrible, Eric. Sick. Just unbelievable,' she said, and he saw that she was distressed simply telling him this. They looked at each other silently for a moment. They each had reason to be nervous and cautious with each other. Each needed the other, but neither Eric nor Emma wanted to risk losing their friendship.

'Really? What exactly?' he asked.

'Eric, I trust you now, totally,' she said to him. He watched her and realised that he really could tell her the reality of things.

'So, what have you seen?' he asked.

'I saw an attack. Two people attacked, possibly killed by...they weren't men or women, these things that tore up the two victims. It was just so horrific. I ran. It's happened before, hasn't it?' she asked.

'It has. You're right. I'm sorry you learned about them like that, I really am,' Eric said, looking out around the street.

'So you know about them? Jesus, Eric, this is what you kept from me? What are you doing?' Emma asked, shocked and angry.

'Okay, look, calm down. It is what Taylor and I have been tracking recently. We've had some very close encounters, believe me,' he told her.

'How did you know about them?' Emma asked.

'Because of Grace. She told me,' Eric said, knowing that his answer sounded strange.

'Before she died?' Emma asked, curious. 'It goes back to Holy Island, all of these things. Something from right back then, centuries ago...'

'Well, that's astounding and terrifying,' Eric said

'Yes, yes it is. Things get hidden. Some things are cared for, other things lost...these attacks, they're hunting for the pieces, the hidden gospel of Holy Island,' Emma explained.

'No, we need to go now. Things are moving on. We're completely involved now,' he said.

'So what are they, then?' Emma asked. She felt very naive and clueless.

'Do you want to know? Really?' Eric asked, not wanting to try to tell her.

'Yes, tell me,' she said. 'I know much more now, from looking further into details at the cathedral and museum. Relics, spread out for safety, but they know. Grace got involved, slowed them down, and made them angry...' Emma added 'These gospel relic pieces, the journey of the original pieces around the north coast to Holy Island, Viking attacks and invasions suggested they were possibly possessed by demons back then, which shaped events at that point. Saints Oswald, Aidan and Cuthbert each intervened over time, separating the pieces,

117

while the dark energies sunk deep in and around the North-East until this day and age. Because of the work of Cuthbert, Aidan and Oswald, the demons are limited to specific parts and areas around the Tyne and North-East. They must generally stay around the city, with only small clutches and numbers out near Tynemouth, South Shields and Durham. We could break this up even more possibly with the help of vicars and priests, but we may not have time for doing things that way. It calls for a more intense defence and attack of our own.'

'Demons, Emma; they're actually real demons. Like the biblical folk legend kind, like only preachers tell us to be scared of,' Eric said, 'from some kind of...hell. Not exactly sure if it is the Hell that people have known of for centuries, all fire and shit, but they are inhuman, evil things. They exist outside of our laws of reality or understanding,' he informed her seriously.

'So did Grace...she told you...' Emma began, but could hardly let herself ask such unreal questions. She had so many questions, and she felt they were finally going to be answered. Not that she wanted to know more of the confusing evil around, but she did want to know how to help Eric as best she could.

'Look, I don't want to draw you deep into all this,' he told her.

'Too late now. I'm there. I'm in. For some reason. I didn't even actually ask: it was right there before me. All of these things that you and Taylor know of came to me. Grace knew about them, so she's in trouble?' she asked.

'It's very difficult for me to work out, and I don't want you to be totally at risk,' he warned.

'Just accept that I'm in with it. Probably for a reason. Hey, it scared me shitless, but if I'm meant to help you two...I'm meant to, okay?' Emma told him.

'Right. Okay. So follow me,' Eric said. They both left the area, and walked together with purpose.

'Some wrote that Saint Bede of Jarrow may have looked into some of the events, but it was generally denied, it seems, to retain his local religious 'hero' status. Also, Eadfirth, Bishop of Lindisfarne, may have known something. Most have never discussed it at all in centuries, seriously,' she told him. 'Then came the Vikings and chaos and confusion. This was right up until William the Conqueror. We had the suitably-named King Eric Bloodaxe, then came Eadred and the battle of Stainmore. It all sounds gruesome and bloody. After all of this came our industrial age. It led on to the shipbuilding, coal mining, soap making, salt making, glassmaking, Charles Algernon Parsons and his steam turbine. We were a proud North then, but it crashed down. They've been manipulating our lives, our livelihoods all the while. The decline began in the twentieth century, probably when they split. The seventies and eighties…they ruined us, made us suffer,' Emma told him.

'There is just so much to all of this. Almost feels like too much to really cope with,' Eric replied quietly.

'If you and Taylor have stopped, then why? And what now?' Emma asked after a few minutes.

Eric walked in a circle briefly as he tried to focus his thoughts.

'We know that there are, it seems at least, two large groups of these demons. God, that sounds stupid, right? They are extremely dangerous, as you seem to know, murderous things. But they are very focused and do actually know what they are doing, and have some complex plans. They have, I think, been controlling most of the North-East for what may have been decades, if not longer. It might be due to our lack of faith, our greed, or any other number of things. The point is they're all over, killing whoever they want to. I think they killed Grace. So that is why I'm doing this,' Eric said.

'I met a couple of them in the park,' he said after a brief uncomfortable moment as Emma digested the information.

'What happened?' she asked.

'What happened is that I've got something to do now whether I like it or not. They talk like us, and they're damn intelligent in their own way. They have me,' Eric said and sighed.

'Sorry, what do you mean? I don't get you,' Emma said.

'Forget it. Look, tonight we have to stop it all. I'm going to try to save Grace any way that I can. Whatever the hell I have to do to put her at peace and free her, I'll do,' he explained. He sounded angry and bitter, she thought. There was pain and regret in his voice.

'How? Got priests? Vicars? Guns, or a trap to catch them?' Emma asked, with humour but honestly wondering just what could actually stop these horrific things.

'This isn't a Hollywood movie. This is real, horrific shit. No dramatic soundtrack here,' he said. 'They have plans for Newcastle tonight. I can help them and then they might just help me. One of the two groups, you see?' He explained.

'Is it safe? Aren't they just lying to you?' Emma asked, thinking of his safety.

'Well, I'm not really sure, but I don't have too many options. Time is short.'

'Can't we bargain with them?' she suggested.

'Not now. No way. You can come so far with me. Then...I don't know, pray for me, or something like that,' he told her with a solemn face.

Out around the North-East most people ran scared and fearful as news of the killings spread around, hiding and finding sanctuary from the dangers they were hearing of around them. Within the offices of the city's local evening newspaper, a number of brave or possibly foolish news reporters argued over the truth of events and how to continue.

'Report what you see, not what you think, tonight more than any other night, okay?' the editor told the staff.

'That's bullshit! You never tell us to act like that!' one of them argued.

'Well I'm telling you now. That's your orders. Two murdering young men are on the loose,' he told them.

'There's much more to it than that, sir,' one female reporter said.

'No, there won't be. It's decided. Go report,' he said.

'Chief, this is serious news. Really serious shit out there. There's two different kind of tales out there, and one of them is total shit. We have to be honest, especially now,' the first reporter said. 'It's really unusual stuff, more than just two guys. There are more of them, more going on...let us tell that.'

'Look, when the time is right, we'll probably let out more information about various theories connected, but until then, just keep it simple,' the boss told them.

'That's never been this paper's way, has it?' one woman said.

'Value your job, Melissa? Really? Then report two working-class losers on a killing spree. For now. Understood? You all know why it is handled this way. Don't like it, then feel free to go home,' the boss told them all, losing his patience.

All of the reporters looked at each other with a collective sense of futile powerlessness and silently began their work in the only way they were then allowed.

Chapter 18

There were three men with Taylor as he walked down through the city streets. He himself did not know them too well, but certainly lacked the courage to tell them to leave him be. He looked confident but slightly ill, like he might be coming down with a virus. The men with him quietly smiled and laughed amongst themselves as they walked along beside him. These were powerful, mysterious men whom Taylor had only recently come to know. He had spent much time away from Eric in their company, even since the death of Grace. These men knew of things that very few people witnessed, experienced, or acquired, and Taylor had been privileged to join them in this. All the bloodshed and screams had become part of the experience, which he endured to get to the pleasure elsewhere. He would gladly do many things to keep his chance at experiencing these secret things, possibly even join in with the killing and torture himself. He was now in a personal place of dark pleasures, sin, unending guilt and sickness. His yearning for personal gratification in all the most lustful, debased ways had thrown him trapped into the intimidating company of these demonic friends of Andrew. He smiled to himself as he continued under flickering street lamps with his intimidating friends.

'You've been greatly undervalued around these parts, Taylor, you know that?' the blonde thin man in a smart, black suede jacket told him. 'Tonight we'll show you how you are appreciated,' the man told him with a wry smile.

'Thanks. I look forward to that,' Taylor replied, lying against his will.

'It won't be completely easy going though, okay? This can be very hard work. It all pays off, though, if you stick with it. You've seen that. If you want the good times enough, you don't want to be under anyone else. They'll be your good times, then,' the man explained. He patted Taylor on the shoulder as they continued.

'We need to go to the Madina Street area. I heard they're doing some things we should know about there. Might give them a surprise,' one of the other men told Taylor, smirking.

'Sounds very good. We'll get there and sort this all out. And your old pal. What's his name, Eric?' the lead man asked Taylor. Until then, he had managed to keep any discussion of Eric very brief and had given them various excuses and apologies for the trouble that Eric had caused them.

'Whatever needs to be done,' Taylor agreed half-heartedly. 'How long have you guys actually been doing this whole thing around these parts?' he asked.

'Us? It's all different. We're different, to the first ones, the old ones. It was different when we all...arrived. Now...things have to be done to keep a hold onto what we have,' the lead told Taylor.

'We're still in control! We own the North! We do!' the red-haired, loud man exclaimed excitedly.

'Not all of us, you know that. Keep quiet, you damn fool,' the blonde man warned him, pointing a finger.

'You collect them, don't you? You all collect...what? Souls? I've seen it,' Taylor said, with a pounding heart.

'More than that,' the redhead said.

'Yes, we do. We use them. But you, you'll help us to stop your brave persistent friend before he ruins all of what we have,' the blonde man warned, and sent him a glance that suggested he would very easily kill Taylor if he needed to. Taylor sighed and continued walking.

With dark skies overhead, and the sound of crows somewhere in the trees nearby, Eric and Emma reached the city's outer main roads that led to Gateshead and Byker, and they paused to cross.

'Eric, the way you did things with Taylor...I'll be able to help like that, will I?' Emma asked.

'Well, you can try. I don't think you could be any worse than him. He really just managed to step in at the last minute. Like he wasn't really there anyway,' Eric told her encouragingly. He watched the road lanes clear of cars for a moment and then they both ran across.

'This is supernatural, then?' Emma said when they reached the other side.

'Something like that. Good against evil, that kind of thing, in some way. Sounds simple in a way, but dangerously so,' Eric said, thinking about it.

'How did you two stop them so far, then?' Emma asked.

'Well not with anything from a Hammer horror film, though Peter Cushing was the man. We've got a load of stuff together; knives, spades, blades, rope. Basically, we were trying any damn thing...and actually I used something that might sound stupid,' Eric told her.

'What was it?' Emma asked.

'I collected some water from a church...last time I gave it a chance, and...it burned those bastards in no time! My God, that was handy' he said, almost laughing

'What? Actually burned them for real?' Emma asked in disbelief.

'Really, I couldn't believe it. That kind of shit is real. Holy fucking water. Hallelujah, Amen,' Eric replied. 'I've...been kind of...praying, too. Using all these things, we have to just pound the hell out of these abominations when we find them,' he told her.

Emma did not really know what to think of it all. It was just such a strange situation. This whole experience could threaten their lives, everything they knew of their daily existence; their families, friends, teachers, everyone they knew, as well as people they did not know. All other smaller thoughts had to leave her mind, the lesser things in her life like college, boys, and music. She had to confront the importance of this and stay strong, she knew.

'The first time I did craft a sort of crucifix with some wooden pieces. Hit the damn evil thing in the stomach, with blood pouring all over it and me. Worked a treat. Don't know if the crucifix did some special spiritual thing or if it was just a psychological crutch for me, but it helped me stay in one piece,' he said, remembering it clearly.

'I think the crosses might do something. Actually, churches seem to have an effect; the creatures seemed to keep away from the churches that we passed. Maybe we really can rely on help there,' he added.

'Do they have weak points? These creatures, any weaknesses, other than the holy water? Are they actually like holy people describe them to be? I mean like back in the day when some scary preacher or vicar warned of burning and evil things? You know, like Satan and all that crazy stuff?' Emma said, a little embarrassed to speak of it seriously.

'Well, I didn't say that, but...it's God who knows right now. Apart from the couple of strange holy things, I say we just be careful, cautious and beat the living shit out of the damn things,' he admitted.

'So anything goes, then?' Emma asked.

'I think the crosses might be helpful, can't hurt right? I know it's an old horror film cliché but...keep praying, too. They can change shape as well, I've seen this. Unbelievable until you see it. Big, small, tall, thin. Men and women, and they can become sort of like animals too if they want to. Not completely, but almost convincingly so. Their real form is the disgusting, horrible sight you might have seen. I think this is when they are vulnerable,' he explained.

As he said that, police sirens could be heard somewhere not too far from them.

'And don't talk to police, either,' Eric added.

'Sorry, but...' Emma began apologetically.

'Oh you haven't?' Eric said with a sudden look of dismay. 'Why? I mean, when? What was said exactly?' he asked. He tried to remain calm and understanding. Of course she had witnessed a horrific attack, and usually anyone would go and seek help from the law.

'What?' Emma said, feeling accused. 'What do you expect? I saw people get butchered in the street before me!' she said in her defence.

'I know, I know. It's...alright. Forget it. We'll deal with it, with them, probably, soon enough. We've much worse things to fear than police,' he told her.

Chapter 19

They walked along through a very plush, middle-class-looking area. It would be hard to believe much real trouble or danger could come near these refined, respectable streets, Eric thought, as they approached the houses quietly. The owners and inhabitants of these expensive homes would be usually seen as wealthy, civilised, and morally upstanding members of society, and so Emma was surprised that Eric had brought her here. There was quiet all around the gardens and streets, ahead as if the residents were locked in their houses, fearing the outside world already, ahead of time. Eric walked up the garden path of the second house to his right, noticing how expensive and grand the front of the house appeared.

'Hey, what's here?' Emma asked him quietly from his side, a little nervous as they stood near someone's property.

'Hopefully some clue about the way things are now,' he told her.

He then knocked on the door knocker, though after only waiting a few seconds decided that was enough to suggest that they improvise. He walked around to the back garden gate and kicked it in forcefully.

'Jesus, Eric!' Emma exclaimed in shock.

They reached the back door and he took out a small set of screwdrivers and a crowbar. After fiddling near the door lock he stepped back, looked around them for onlookers then took out a crowbar from under his coat and wedged it tight in-between door and frame and forced his weight onto it. The door snapped open after a couple of attempts, and, to their relief, no alarm sounded. Emma was amazed and a little suspicious.

'My God, we can't do this!' Emma gasped out.

'Look, I think I know who lives here. And, I'm about sure they're not in. Come on,' he told her as he stepped quickly inside the silent house.

The house smelled wonderfully aromatic, a mix of potpourri spices and perfume with some rich tobacco scents. Looking around, it was the place of stable, wealthy, cultured folk. There were pictures of a small family of three - mother, father and child - on the mantelpiece, and a desk near the front windows.

'You think someone here is involved in the things we've seen? This is just a regular, boring family house,' Emma argued. Eric ignored her while he opened drawers and looked in and around desks and cupboards freely.

'I'm going upstairs, could you watch out for anyone down here?' he asked, then went off.

'Hey! Eric!' Emma said, and followed. It was a lovely home, and Emma imagined caring parents with their little girl putting her to bed at night. They must be much better than her own parents, she thought. She would have loved a close, caring home such as this a few years ago.

Eric disappeared off into a room by himself before she noticed. Quickly, she turned and ran after him. The sound of powerful wind or rain could be heard against the windows behind the drawn curtains as she passed. They were in so much trouble now, she thought. What was Eric doing? She knew that he would definitely go down for time if they were caught, all on top of the danger of the demons potentially anywhere nearby.

She entered what might have been a study and found Eric looking carefully through a pile of books, journals and papers on a desk top.

'What are you looking for? Can I help?' she asked.

'No, not yet. I'll come across something soon,' He murmured quietly.

'Eric, I think these are decent people, you must be wrong. This is all wrong, I think,' Emma said, not wishing to anger him. She was so worried about being caught. She had not considered that offering to help him might include breaking and entering or stealing. Eric stopped and looked at her.

'No, this is not a good family. It is rotten at its core. Anyone can keep up a lovely false appearance to the world; wear a deceitful smiling mask to protect them as they do corrupt things. The father of this family is deeply involved with the groups. These demon groups, helping them control the North. I know this to be true. I'm sorry for his family, I really am, but he must pay for his actions now,' Eric explained.

He continued to search for what he needed; addresses, names, information about how things worked with the groups.

'This family man? How could he be involved? What could he have done?' Emma asked.

'Too much. Here, this might help us,' he said, and held out some papers with dates on them. 'Look, it talks about the groups of Northern Tempest Holdings. The years of business changes and contracts with other companies; 1920, 1949, 1987...and so on,' Eric read out to Emma.

'So what has this guy done? Helped them use businesses around here?' she asked, not seeing how bad it could be.

'He was a middle man, he knew who he was helping, I believe. This helped them to stay around us, deeper in with us. To not just kill us whenever, but use us, torment us, hidden for such a long time, taking many of us and covering it up perfectly for decades at least,' Eric said with regret.

'So what now?' Emma asked.

'Look, these places: the Bridge Hotel, the Faulks Lodge, the Gallery House Building and the names with them. This is where we go next. These are the places we attack,' he explained.

'Okay. Well, whatever. Is that all we need? Can we go now?' she asked nervously, anxious to leave.

They crept back down the stairs through the shadows toward the back door again, careful and on guard. Eric turned the lock and opened the door. From the darkness of the night a man pushed himself into Eric suddenly. Eric stumbled, fighting the man and trying to hold him at bay. Eric fell against Emma and they all moved back into the house, the man raging against Eric.

'We're not burglars,' Emma said urgently, shocked at this strange, wild man who wrestled with Eric. Was it the man who lived here? No, it did not seem to look much like him from the photos in the next rooms.

'Who are you?' he asked loudly, staring at Eric as he held him by the throat and then at Emma. 'Why are you here?'

'Let him go you, you're hurting him. Please,' Emma cried. She quickly tried to think of some answer for the man, anything that might calm him, or at least stop him choking Eric. She grabbed the man by the wrists and tried to pull him back with difficulty.

'We're with the police. A new division of surveillance and protection unit,' she told him with a serious face.

The man held Eric still, then began to steadily release his grip. Eric gasped and giving the man a pissed off look.

'I don't believe you. Try again. I'm phoning the police,' the man told them.

'Believe what you like. We're going anyway,' Eric said defiantly.

'Really? You think so?' the man said, watching Eric closely and ready for any movement. The man moved to block the back doorway.

'You're not much threat compared to the big lads, are you?' Eric scoffed with sarcasm.

'What do you mean?' the man asked, moving close to him again. Emma watched, ready to help this time. The man then made a grab for Emma, but Eric reached out and punched him, hitting him hard against the face.

'Blessed are the dead, but not you. Not yet. This trouble you've caused,' Eric said as he held the man by the shoulders.

The screaming began. The man shook suddenly and twisted while his face distorted, stretching in on itself, then folding outward again, revealing something that resembled a bat's face, but doglike as well.

'Oh Jesus, help us,' Emma said uncontrollably, reeling back aghast. She stared at the warped face in fear while Eric still held on to the man, unimpressed.

'Keep back,' he warned Emma. The demon man in his hands then writhed violently around, gnashing its teeth at him. It screamed at him and began to claw away at the walls at either side of them.

'Is it the father?' Emma asked.

'This is your nice, decent family man. Yes,' Eric replied. He held on as the demon swung aggressively to one side, and it nearly took Eric down with him to the floor.

'Give it up. I know you. I know your damn filthy secrets,' Eric said. The demon in the family man swung from one side to the other, wheezing, then bucked at the knees and fell down heavily to the kitchen lino floor. Eric let go as the beast fell and he and Emma looked down at it with caution.

'How was he one of them?' Emma said quietly, not sure if he might rise up again. She was numb. Reality was disappearing faster all the time, and Eric was the main catalyst.

'That was a demon-possessed rich geezer. Some might argue they're all like that,' Eric told her.

'But he has a family. What about them?' she said.

'That's his problem, or theirs. He accepted this. He knew what he was doing. He should have expected this. They all should,' Eric told her. 'We're going,' he said, and pushed the corpse out of their way, squeezing out through the door.

'Come on,' he said, as he looked back at Emma. 'This is a secret war. We're helping them really, saving them,' he said, looking vexed. Emma understood, but wondered if there might be another way of doing things. They watched briefly as the corpse writhed and dissolved in repetitive spasms, blood and fluids bubbling down through the floor. Emma almost threw up, so they quickly left out of the back door again, looking around in case they were being seen leaving. They walked down through the narrow back pathway behind the gardens, leaving the expensive houses behind.

'You'd think people like that would be nice,' Emma said as they walked away quickly.

'You'd think so, but dirt gets in the cleanest places,' Eric told her.

Chapter 20

The walk with the group of strange men made Taylor extremely nervous and yet strangely confident, though he knew that it was important if he was to make progress beyond always being in the shadow of Eric's heroic acts of bravery. Andrew came along from within the deep shadows of a row of trees suddenly to join them.

'Hello, all. Hope we're making progress,' he said to them.

'So will this change it all? Can we alter the things that he has allowed?' Taylor asked meekly. He barely looked at Andrew.

'We have you, don't we? We can get to his plans sooner than we expected, I believe,' Andrew said with confidence. 'You do enjoy it all Taylor, don't you, all our crazy shit?'

'Sorry? What's that?' Taylor said, distracted.

'What we do, Taylor. You need it, don't you? We can't let just any person come along with us right now, understand?' the other lead demon man told him.

'I know that, of course. This is just what I want, really it is,' Taylor told him.

'Good. You will have to prove it. Very soon. Will you do that for us?' the man asked.

'You know I will,' Taylor answered, with sheepish respect and fear.

They continued along the quiet, empty street. Turning the corner, they approached a large roundabout in the road ahead. At the side of it sat two police cars. Andrew strolled up to the first car and leaned into the window.

'Hello Gordon. All ready and watching?' he asked the police officer at the wheel.

'Hi Andrew, yeah, no problem. Just like you all want,' the police officer replied. 'We'll get this guy before the night's out, no problem. This is our town, our business,' the officer said.

As they looked at each other, their eyes seemed to briefly glow a deep red. Andrew took a swift look at Taylor.

'Okay, we're staying around this area for a while. You get back to him. Maybe try the girl again. I'll call you soon enough,' Andrew told him.

'Alright. I'll get what we need done,' Taylor agreed.

They separated, and Taylor let out a quiet sigh of relief to himself as he walked off alone. He walked away, relieved that he could relax for a short time at least by himself. He knew, though, that he had much to do if he was to prove himself worthy and remain part of the group. He had needed a good reason for his relationship with Eric to end for a while now, and this was perfect. He could end it in style and show that he was just as brave and fearless as Eric could be. He would join these men and women with their mysterious and dangerous powers deep within the city.

With them he could be a legend, a powerful force that all would know and respect, fear and love. It was just too much, though. Beyond the sex, money, illegal highs, he could barely take it; his sanity was peeling apart, piece by piece. He reached his other place of residence in less than thirty minutes, and made sure he was not being watched as he entered. This place was unknown to Eric, and for good reason. Taylor entered the hallway, ascended the stairs and opened the door ahead. Inside, he quickly walked through into a room. He opened up the freezer chest where the body of Grace lay, still beautiful and cold.

'So here we are again,' he said aloud before turning on some ambient electro music on the nearby music player. He pulled up a chair next to the freezer chest and sat down beside it.

'We are grateful for what you've given us already. Time to add to it and really be useful. I need places, times, reasons,' he said to the motionless body of Grace, her lifeless eyes closed to him.

She simply lay there. Taylor suddenly shook his head and took out a photo from his coat pocket. Eric was in the photograph alongside Grace. It was then that she appeared.

'For God's sake, if you don't come to me Andrew will cut your dead body to bloody fucking pieces soon enough,' he said. He shook his head looking at her. He turned away, rummaging inside his coat pocket, frustrated.

The blue and grey cloud of smoke took shape up above the lumped bag on the floor.

'Hello once more,' he said and smiled wickedly.

'This...is...wrong. You...should not...' she said slowly and almost painfully.

'That's not for you to worry about. You know your dilemma. Your Eric, he's out there being a hero, we can't have this. I need more. Where is he? What is he doing now?' Taylor asked.

The ghostly smoke moved around gently in the dim light of the room, her face translucent and in pain.

'What good...don't you...know?' she said.

'Look, don't mess with me, alright? I can leave you here to rot. You know that. And he'll be the same too. Tell me what you see!' Taylor demanded, standing up.

'Poor Taylor...so...envious,' she whispered.

'Watch your damn mouth, bitch! You just tell me now!' he shouted.

He leaned over the edge of the freezer and admired her petite round breasts. He had always thought she was extremely pretty. He would not touch her. Probably. No, that would be...sick.

'Don't you...know?' she asked, surprised. He looked at her, the floating image in the air above him. He had known Grace weeks ago, before her death, and hardly liked her then. She always spent way too much time with Eric, as far as Taylor could see.

He leaned in and took her by the arm, shaking her corpse as her spirit looked down at him.

'I'll waste you, I swear I will!' he told her. She looked down at him, seeming unimpressed by his threats.

'You're new...to this,' she told him calmly.

'I know how it all works, okay? I know enough,' he answered.

'Really?' she said. 'He is going through Byker now...for them,' she told him finally.

'Right now? You're sure?' This was strange to Taylor, but could be right, he supposed. It was just unexpected, but then that was Eric sometimes.

Grace nodded at him with a look of pain on her face. She then gradually vanished away again, leaving Taylor alone once more. He let go of the body bag, took out his mobile phone and dialled.

'Hello? Got his direction,' he said.

Chapter 21

'How much of this do we have to do?' Emma asked Eric while they crept along through brambles and thick overgrown bushes.

'I don't want to do this, but we have to, Emma, everything is not clear, not just black or white answers. The truths will always be hidden away. That's how they use us,' he said, with a strange, paranoid logic.

'Really? Don't you think we're being used somehow? Us, used by one group of fucking demons against the other, and maybe this is their game. I mean when does it end? How much do we do before it stops or we're finished?' Emma asked, wanting answers.

'It'll end...when it ends. Where's that trust?' Eric said.

'Yes, but...' Emma began.

'Then just help me. We're doing well. It won't be long. Really. We're saving the North tonight, remember? People who are blissfully unaware of how every day they are used like parts of a machine, then spat out and killed randomly. We'll be unknown heroes. But we'll know that we've saved them all,' he told her.

'Do you hear that?' she said, suddenly alarmed 'Eric, stop. Do you hear that?'

'What?' he said, and looked around.

'Listen...' Emma told him.

They heard police sirens coming very near again, possibly a few streets away from them.

'That was fast,' Emma said.

'Come on, we better get out of here,' Eric warned, and took her hand. He led them off along a narrow trail between streets. He looked out between two backyards and a pathway.

'This way, I think...' he said tentatively, looking back at Emma and then moving on. She followed before they stopped to listen for the police cars.

133

'I think they've moved on, over across to our far left, a few streets away now,' Emma said, satisfied.

'No, can't be. I don't think so,' Eric said, annoyed. He looked over at her. The sound of the sirens increased second by second.

'Give me a little trust now, can you?' Emma asked.

Eric nodded. 'Come on, there's no time,' he said.

The sirens wailed, the sound floating nearer in the dark.

'Let's go over here,' Emma suggested. She began to walk while watching Eric. He stood and looked in both directions briefly. The sirens were so loud then, possibly a couple of streets away. Then, suddenly, there was silence.

Eric walked off in the opposite direction to Emma. She watched, speechless. How the hell was she supposed to help him if he just would not listen to her, she thought. The cars came around then and drove right up in her path, stopping her, trapping her in the headlights. She stood as the police officers stepped out from their cars toward her.

'Stay where you are, Miss. Where is the young man who was with you?' one of them called out to her.

'I've...no idea. He was scared and ran,' Emma said with caution. She remembered to think very carefully about what she said.

'He's getting himself in more trouble. Do you know him?' they asked her. They did not seem to know too much, thankfully, Emma thought to herself.

'Just a little. Not really. Can you help me?' she said.

'If you help us, we'll try to help you,' they told her ambiguously.

The fatal air of deadly horror continued to haunt Eric as he ran along alone. He instantly regretted leaving Emma behind. He might have made faster progress without her, but he might have possibly lost a hugely valuable partner in his crusade. This thought was not permanent in his mind, as he had been thinking that he should consider the significance of the recent events. He had been in serious danger, but he had battled against these creatures and overcome them nearly half a dozen times so far. Him, mostly, just him. The might be how it was supposed to continue, he thought. Then he remembered Taylor had called him earlier. He decided to call back to see where he was.

'Hello? Hey, it's me, Eric. Sorry I didn't meet you yet. Where did you go?' he asked.

'I... thought you needed space. Plus, I thought I'd get some weed maybe. You're okay then?' Taylor said, sounding pensive and distant.

'I'm okay. Kind of expected you around, though. So you haven't done much else?' Eric enquired.

'Like what? No, look, I'll meet you soon. I'm going to see my folks but call me later. Hang in there, mate, okay,' Taylor told him.

'Right. See you later, then,' Eric said, and hung up.

He wished that he had not ran from Emma, as it seemed Taylor was being secretive. There were lies in the air, he felt, and friends who should not be trusted so easily, he thought.

More than simply fighting and killing them, he had now communicated with them. They had shown themselves to be shockingly intelligent and surprisingly human in confrontation. He had discussed their plans, their actions, power, the killing, and more. These were not simple creatures, not merely mythical, one-dimensional beasts to be chased. Eric saw that they had cunning, stealth, discipline, judgement and their own ideologies. These darkly disturbing beasts did hold a macabre fascination to him, he acknowledged to himself. There was already a whole lot more to the way they existed than he could have guessed in the beginning. Could he manipulate them like they had been manipulating others for such a long time? Worse than that, the thought came to him that he might be able to learn something about these creatures. These were they mythical things that people had prayed to God to keep them safe from for centuries. Here they were, unleashed on the North, and gradually he was learning their weaknesses.

There was already a whole lot more to the way these things existed than he could have guessed at to begin with. There were two groups of them, he had now come to find. Two separate groups of demons, and something separated them, but he was not entirely sure of what so far. In some way, for some reason, they were warring with each other, and from what he had done one of the groups had significantly expressed a kind of respect for his bold fighting and capabilities in staying alive. Could he use this to find out much more about their ways and the whole situation? It made his mind ache to start to imagine how these things had existed hidden beneath or between society all this time. Why were they there? How did they arrive?

Since the first time he and Taylor had saved someone over two nights ago, Eric had been thinking increasingly about the notion of God, the devil, evil and good in his world. How much was myth, legend, story, and how much was true, real and relevant, he wondered. He did not previously want to be any kind of spiritual person, no Buddhist, no Jesus freak or anything like that, but he also did not consider himself an atheist. Now, though, it seemed that he had to believe something. Grace had come to him, after her death, and these demon things...it all told him that there was much more than he could easily expect in life; other existences, other places, and other beings somewhere. Was there a God somewhere in all of this?

Where was any God when these things roamed loose and free on the streets to kill and murder, he thought. Did God know that they are around here, doing all of this? God sees everything, though, he thought. At least that was what he remembered being told as a naughty child. Did these beasts rule freely? How could that have happened? Had God been tricked, or forgotten about them? That was what happened in all of the old tales, he thought. There's a wager, a bet, then someone loses and spends eternity doomed. That kind of thing is in all of the old stories, he thought. Like that old Bergman film with the knight beating Death at chess, he remembered. He almost laughed to himself.

Eric had wandered away from the orthodox faith forced upon him as a child, but the lingering ideas of Eden, God, sin, temptation, evil, redemption all remained close in his thoughts through the years up to the present time. If these unnatural beasts or demons were real evil incarnate then surely there was real, pure good somewhere also?

He could have been trapped in a rut as they tried to control him by keeping the spirit or soul of Grace, but then he would be with her eventually, wouldn't he? If he could resolve everything, destroy the grip of these evil things over the North-East, would God return Grace to him and thank him? He had to think differently, he thought, in spiritual and supernatural terms. No longer could police or human social laws get in his way. He must work with the laws of the Heavens, the deep infinite cosmos beyond everyday life and channel this understanding and work with it. This sounded obviously crazy from anyone else's point of view, but right then it made perfect sense to him.

When he had met the demons in the park, they had told him of the house in the wealthy area of town, and they had then mentioned the old cigarette factory down to the West. Eric had been told to leave a certain person there for them, as proof of his commitment: a token gesture. Only he could get to this person, though to do so could put him in even greater danger with the police. The demons he spoke to needed this man, who they said had crossed them and was due his punishment. Eric was not sure of how much truth was in that, but he had to get the man anyway. Worse, this could be them actually getting ready to finish him in some grand and sadistically satisfying way, but he felt he simply had to do it, for the meantime at least, while he gathered his thoughts and options. He believed that he did have some kind of luck in this twisted game of deadly chance.

He found the businessman soon enough in a bustling and loud bar in the city. Eric stood close by for a few minutes, listening to the conversations that the man was engaged in and deciding when and how would be best to make his move. When the man left the bar to have a cigarette outside, Eric discreetly followed behind. A brief conversation confused the man, and then Eric pulled him into the alley at the side of the street near the bar. With a quick bludgeoning thump to the head, Eric knocked the man unconscious and packed him into his car, which sat waiting at the top of the alley.

Less than ten minutes later, Eric arrived at the desolate cigarette factory in his car. He parked up close to the front doors and knocked on the doors without hesitation.

'Hello? I'm here,' he said loud enough as he surveyed the front of the building and the streets around. It was deserted of people or any living thing. Eric turned and went to the car, then unloaded the businessman from the car boot with clumsy difficulty, dropping him down to the ground haphazardly. Although he was doing this, Eric did not want to help in doing anything fatal to the man himself. He pulled the man across into the front open area of the factory.

'Hey, here's the guy you wanted. Anyone want this guy?' he called into the warehouse, and kicked the doors, watching as they slowly swung inwards. There were dozens and dozens of dusty, rusty machines and conveyor belts up and down the warehouse sitting unused and neglected. Still no reply. The businessman wriggled and rolled down by Eric's feet.

'Hey, look, just be quiet, okay?' Eric said to him, annoyed. He turned around and looked outside, concerned. He could have sworn that he heard police car sirens again. Don't say my own mind is giving me a guilt trip, he thought. The factory was all broken walls, fallen poles and timber inside. Shadows cloaked it all in potent ominous dread. He heard what could have been laughter.

'You want him?' he said. 'What do I get? I haven't time to mess around, okay?'

Maybe this is the wrong place, he thought. He was pretty sure the address was correct, though. Was it time? Yes, it seemed to be by his watch, give or take a minute or so. He began to feel that perhaps this was a trick, and he looked at the businessman in frustration.

'Maybe I'll take this little piggy back to his pigsty if there's no butcher here,' he said aloud. His words were then greeted by a sinister bluish smoke which slowly emanated forth from within the dark shadows of the warehouse. It swirled up in an almost hallucinogenic manner, seeming to be alive, growing and stretching out. The smoke carried a pungent odour with it as it drifted around toward him. Eventually, it grew into a drifting silhouette almost six foot tall. Then, all at once, a spark and the smoke filled out, thickening, filling to become a full man in a crisp navy blue suit. He instantly walked toward Eric.

'You've done well. Impressive. You might wish to leave now,' the man advised.

'You need me and you owe me my girlfriend's soul back. Pay up,' Eric told him, unshaken.

'There are a few more to collect. This is helpful, but the others are gaining strength around us. You can collect the others, if you would be so useful. It's better for you that my kind hold control here, not them. We look after you as you would prefer,' the man explained. 'You had no real trouble?' the man then asked.

'Actually no, not at all,' Eric told him.

'You will soon enough,' the man replied.

'Really?' Eric said. 'Save it. Is this it? Personally, I just don't believe much of that. Convince me. I've heard they do know how to get better hold of these towns. Problem, that, isn't it?' Eric said, with a sly smile.

'We appreciate your unique, foolish persistence. You're human, aren't you content like that?' the man asked.

'Most days, yes. Nowadays...not so much,' Eric admitted. They both looked at the body tied and bound up at the floor.

'You want more?' the man asked Eric.

'What more could I have?' said Eric, knowing this would allow the mysterious man to offer him the most tempting things.

They both watched the bound and gagged businessman rolling around down before them, rolling dramatically in a useless frenzy.

'Would you kill?' the man asked Eric suddenly.

'Who?' Eric asked quietly.

The businessman fell onto his face, still wriggling in a muddy puddle.

Eric looked at him and then around him, as if preparing to announce a carefully decided answer. The mysterious man swirled around him, unravelling partially as blue smoke once more. His eyes burned red as he watched Eric for a reply.

Chapter 22

It was an unsteady, overly stressful walk to a nearby bar for Taylor alone as he stepped in and ordered a double whisky. He necked it swiftly, then drank another. Some large, toned men looked across at him, and he nearly laughed openly at them as the drink loosened him up. Their narcissistically pumped up bodies and designer hair styles, desperate for any and all female attention, were outstandingly embarrassing to Taylor. Ironically, Taylor himself was first to claim attention of two nearby pretty young ladies looking his way.

'You like a stiff drink, do you?' he asked the blonde with icy blue eyes, who smiled and giggled at him along with her brunette friend.

'You have to grab life with both hands, ladies,' he told them, as he waved to the bartender for more drinks of the same for all three of them. The larger men to their right muttered loudly and watched Taylor with aggressive envy.

'He won't please you ladies any time soon; he's just a strange little drunk!' the first man told them. Taylor heard him and wanted to laugh, but managed to restrain himself for a while.

'You girls going anywhere else tonight or feel like an early night?' Taylor asked them with charming curiosity.

'Hey, he's not going to please you ladies like we can. He looks impotent to me!' another of the large men shouted, and laughed heartily with his friends.

'He's more of an interesting man than you pretty boys,' Stacy, the blonde, called back, while her friend Bella stuck her tongue out at the men. Taylor simply let out a joyful fit of laughter. This pushed the men into rage finally, and the three alpha males swaggered over.

'Let's see him prove how much of a big guy he really is; got any balls, little man?' the lead man asked with a gruff voice as he towered over Taylor.

140

'Yes and they probably work much better than yours, mate,' Taylor said. The man's eyes bulged furiously.

'Come here,' he barked at Taylor, and suddenly reached to grab him, but Taylor moved away in a flash. The girls watched confused, looking at each other then back at Taylor in disbelief.

'Let's take it into the gents', little man. Not wanting to shock the girls or others, right?' Taylor offered. The three men looked at him fiercely and followed him off into the gents'.

'Don't do this! You don't have to!' Bella pleaded as she and Stacy watched the men enter the toilets.

Taylor walked in and turned around to watch the men enter behind him and close the door. As it shut, Taylor smiled at them. The smoke vapours seeped into the room quickly, the men looking around surprised and angry. One of them reached out fast at Taylor, but the smoke began to solidify. An arm shot out of the smoke, grabbing the closest man with razor-sharp claws that slashed across his throat instantly. More demon men appeared from within the fog, and began to quickly hack and slice the two other men, blood splashing in all directions. Taylor watched, slightly disturbed and nauseous. He stood and was splashed over and over with crimson blood from the helpless men. He felt an uncomfortable mix of power, satisfaction, sickness, and guilt rumble inside of him, only calming slightly when the men stopped moving.

Taylor made eye contact with the demon men around him as the smoke mingled between them all and the dead men at their feet.

'Will this help?' one of them asked.

'Who knows,' Taylor answered blankly.

'We have more to do, be quick,' the nearest demon man said to him. He nodded and swallowed down the sick in his throat, stepped over the bodies and left the gents'.

The two young women watched speechlessly as Taylor came out alone to greet them cheerily.

'Shall we leave?' he asked. They left the bar and hailed a taxi from the roadside, directing the driver to one of the women's flats. Within minutes of entering the flat, all three of them were undressing each other, kissing any flesh on view between them. Taylor was thinking how unbelievably lucky he finally was after such a low number of sexual encounters of late. The two young ladies licked him, bit him, and teased him lustfully in turn. They touched and played with him as he satisfied them equally. He returned the gestures with enthusiasm until the images flashed into his head. Between the two beautiful girls came quick, shocking visions that appalled him. Flesh being ripped, anguished faces in agony, hybrid beast monsters eating each other and roaming barren lands attacking innocent people. He shook his head, trying to rid himself of the images, then felt the strong urge of erupting sickness.

He swayed to one side, though managed to steady himself against a close wall. Bella, the brunette, stroked his left arm and bit his earlobe playfully.

'Everything okay, babe?' she asked softly.

Taylor saw two winged men tearing into each other with sadistic rage, blood pouring down their bodies as they did so. They screamed and cursed each other, nails clawing flesh unceasingly. Taylor was sweating uncontrollably, horrified and shaking next to the two girls.

'What's up, honey?' Stacy asked.

'He's not so good now,' Bella said, concerned.

Taylor shook a hand in front of her, trying to gesture 'no'.

'What's up with him?' asked Bella.

'Rob, you like this, don't you? Like us here, now, right?' Stacy asked, standing in her underwear. Taylor shook his head and stumbled onto his feet. He looked around at the girls.

'Sorry...I'm...I have to work,' he suddenly told them, and walked out of the room. The girls watched, astonished and confused.

He pulled his clothes on and made it out onto the street again in a few minutes, and ran along cursing himself and the things he had seen. He looked around the street as he went, paranoid and hesitant. The area was unfamiliar to him, he realised. He stood by a tall building which could have been some bank or solicitors' offices. He regretted getting involved in the whole thing; the demons, stealing Grace's body, joining Andrew. He had watched Eric be the hero, and now some superhero of the North, God's vigilante. So Grace had died or been murdered, perhaps, and Taylor had sympathy for Eric, but it just seemed to elevate Eric into some crime-fighting martyr on a mission. And it downgraded Taylor even more, beyond the underachieving sidekick.

The visions must just be caused by all the stress, he thought. They would be gone soon enough after it was all over, Taylor thought to himself.

'Having a productive night, buddy?' a voice asked.

'Jesus!' Taylor exclaimed in shock. His eyes caught sight of a thin man, standing dressed in a dark green suede suit. It was Andrew, smiling back.

'Tonight's a big night, isn't it? Well, it was going fine. Just took a brief pit-stop. Enough of that. There'll be time to rest after this is done, right?' Taylor asked, unsure of what Andrew was thinking. He had trusted Andrew wholeheartedly. Andrew made it seem very easy, enjoyable and magnificent to be entwined with these hellish demon men and women. Taylor simply continued to listen, despite his regret and wishes to hide from them, to find Eric and save him.

'Your good friend is going to spoil all of our fun. All of the places I own, the places I use, where you and I have had good times, that might just go. You think he's your friend? A good friend? He will be stopped, agree?' Andrew asked.

'He's not going to get very far. I've got it controlled,' Taylor explained.

'Well, you are still just human. Mistakes happen...once. You like him, it's hard. He does not have to be the hero, Taylor,' Andrew told him.

'I know, you're very right,' Taylor nodded.

Of all the other demon men that Taylor had befriended in the last few days, Andrew was most accommodating, interesting and also the leader of the hybrid group. He was constantly enigmatic, mysterious, intimidating and fascinating every time Taylor was around him, which did not help him in trying to resist his offers.

'You must find him and keep close with him. Forget any stupid arguments, you must be around him. Lure him into our hands. Time is short. He's somewhere near Jesmond or Tynemouth, I hear,' Andrew explained.

'Do I have to? I mean, he's not that clever. You guys must be able to trick him anyway you want to, can't you?' Taylor asked timidly.

'No. No! We only do...some things, some times. Where we can, how we can. You and he are human, you can reach him better. Be subtle but quick. I'm telling you this. Be grateful it comes from me,' Andrew said clearly. Andrew himself found Taylor interesting and good company, a needed distraction. He even saw some of his early self in Taylor, which interested him. It was like watching a replay of his own tragic temptation all those years back. He put a hand on Taylor's shoulder. They began to walk off toward a car park nearby, with joint focus on the night's work.

Chapter 23

The night was deceptively timid as Peter the young church youth pastor looked out from the doorstep of his church's side entrance. He turned back and locked up the doors securely, as he always did. Most days were predictably similar for him recently; the same faces, the same quiet questions. He spent time with the teenagers, then time with the vicar, and then there would be some night study over thick theology and ministry books. There was still a lack of something else, and this made him feel guilty and ashamed often. Very recently he had been feeling lazy, or as if he was wasting opportunities. He was between pleasing some people and pleasing himself, and he was stuck for the right answers. As ever, he prayed for guidance, but he felt God was slow to answer sometimes. He did not want to be a person who craved much personal enjoyment and pleasure, knowing that pleasure came from helping others. It was possibly more like the knowledge that he should end up involved in something more radical, unpredictable or unorthodox which haunted him.

He had considered moving to another parish or church, maybe in a place with less social harmony, with more to do in the community; a place of more problems, crime, social unrest, but he had decided to continue where he was for the time being until a sure plan came to him. He provided a service, but was it the right thing? He wondered if he was afraid to really engage with modern society's real problems, and maybe didn't know how. He sighed and walked down to his parked car, and began to open the door when a man walking past the church gates stopped him.

'Hello, Peter. Heard about the strange trouble in the city tonight?' the man asked with a familiar, friendly tone.

'No, what things do you mean?' Peter asked, concerned.

'Some really terrible things from what I hear. A couple have been attacked, really brutally. Might be dead. Then across town some others butchered near a club. It's a bad night, alright, I tell you,' the man warned grimly.

'Oh good God. That's horrible. None of it's related, is it?' Peter asked.

'I've no idea. Might want to do very serious praying tonight. I pray God will stop this kind of thing and help those affected,' the man said.

'Absolutely, yes,' Peter agreed in shock.

The man patted Peter on the arm and then walked off slowly.

'Take care now, Fred,' Peter said as the man left him.

Peter began to think about a number of terrible scenarios, about how bad the world could be sometimes. Usually Newcastle and the North-East were fairly calm, with occasional gang trouble but no really nasty events such as these. As a man connected to the church, he did often feel secretly disconnected from the real world. He knew that he and many religious people could be ignorant and self-righteous all too often, neglecting many serious modern problems in the real world. He recently wondered if his praying did have any significant effect on other people and places in need. Earlier that night, he had listened to that strange young man with his frank and honest opinions of faith and God from behind the rest room door. Would he be better off for his prayers that night?

For nearly two hours since Eric had been to the small church, Peter had been thinking about him. He heard Eric talk of the numerous horrific events in and around town, and it made Peter think more carefully about him, but also about what was really dangerous around Newcastle and where his prayers should go. He turned and ran out down the street as it began to rain and caught the man with the dog.

'Hey, wait...excuse me, where did the last thing happen, do you know?' he asked, catching his breath.

'Well, the radio said near the Tyne. Off by Byker, too. My pal was coming back that way a while ago, he heard police around there. You okay?' the man said, seeing the curious look on Peter's face.

'Yes, I have to go somewhere now. Thank you, though. Please take care, goodbye,' Peter said.

Peter decided to head for Byker, just outside of Newcastle. He reached his car out on the street and drove along to the motorway as rain came heavy through the dark skies above. Now he was taking a chance, he thought. No more lying to himself, no looking away. He was facing the problems and dark side of the North, where a man of faith should be. This was serious, he knew, but he really did not know how serious just yet.

Chapter 24

The city of Newcastle now seemed much more foreboding with potential horror, danger and uncertainties for Emma as she tried to retrace her steps around the outskirts of the large, quiet park. She was fearful of doing so, but thought that it was possibly the only thing that could reveal anything. She reached the outskirts of Byker and saw happily boozed up groups and couples staggering through the night, merrily unaware of the supernatural carnage that had taken place only hours previously. She walked past a few of them, receiving curious looks and drunken whispers. Emma tried to be better than them and ignore the remarks, knowing these people were not thinking soberly, until she heard more serious, dramatic tones when she turned the next corner.

'Can you help us? They won't help, everything's wrong!' a young man exclaimed with two girls by him. They looked incredibly distraught as he spoke to Emma.

'There was a fight. Something wrong happened, I mean really fucking bad! Really violent. We left, but we got roped into it, and we saw it get really nasty. Really horribly nasty shit!' the young man said, shaking. His eyes were wild, pupils massively expanded in shock.

'It's the police, we needed them but they've taken some of them then joined in beating up the others. Honestly,' the first girl said.

'This is all real?' Emma asked.

'Hell yes. It's like some secret society thing or something. They're totally corrupt, these police. Just insane. Who the hell do we trust now?' the man said.

'Do you have a car, any of you?' Emma asked.

They did, and so Emma joined them in it as they began a journey down along Jesmond and around the back of Newcastle City Centre.

The night was dark, but occasionally illuminated by orange street lamps and passing car headlights.

'So you know about all about this crazy shit happening around town tonight, Emma?' one of the young girls asked her.

'Yes, I've only seen some of it nearby earlier on. My friend he was kind of involved with it. Well, he's kind of been stopping some of it somehow,' she said. They looked back, not really understanding what she meant by that.

'Really? How? Is he with the police or something?' the shorter girl asked.

'No, not at all. Just happened to get lucky,' Emma improvised.

'So he knows what's going on, does he?' another asked.

'Not completely, he just got caught up in the wrong place at the wrong time, you know?' Emma explained with difficulty.

The questions did make Emma think about how these horrific things were possibly affecting other people. Real people were being tormented, scared and chased out there, and these people would possibly see Eric, Taylor and herself being involved and wonder what they were doing, who they were, and if they were just as evil. She wondered what Eric really was doing and if he was sure of what they could do to stop it all. He had certainly confused her before they were separated, and she just could not figure out what he was planning. She could tell he was hiding some dangerous truths, keeping things back to himself. There was no time for that, she thought. To police and some people, he would already be recognised as a highly dangerous and unbalanced attacker, and that could stop them doing anything. She was not stupid, and could tell he was trying to keep her safe. But maybe he wanted to deal with all this alone; it was about him and Grace from his point of view, she knew. Did Eric actually resent Emma for interfering with him and Grace before she died? Emma tried not to think about things like that, knowing they could just get in the way of saving lives.

'Look at that, we can't turn off down that road ahead. It's blocked off. I'll have to take that ring road around and down. Bloody pain, I was sure it was open this afternoon, wasn't it?' the driver said to himself.

'Yeah, it was,' one of the girls agreed.

Emma felt nervous, knowing it to be a grim sign of something bad. She knew that she never used to feel like that, but everything was unpredictable and unexpected that night. Not one thing around seemed dependable. She was one of less than a handful of people who had any clue as to what was really occurring on the streets, and perhaps that suggested that she had a kind of responsibility and duty, she realised.

They drove along, across past the road diversion in near darkness past shady wiry trees and empty streets. From a few streets behind them a siren sounded noisily.

'Hey, there are police nearby somewhere. Do you think they're maybe two or three streets along? They might help us,' the blonde girl suggested hopefully.

'Look, it's not all police. They weren't real police, I keep saying,' the quiet young guy in the back told the others.

'He really might be right, you know,' the blonde girl said.

'Keep driving, please,' Emma asked. They just could not consider them, she thought nervously.

'Really, though, maybe they could help. Get us to a safe place. They might know about what's happening now,' the other girl said.

'No, it's not worth it. Just don't stop. They won't help us. You were right the first time. Don't trust them,' Emma pleaded seriously.

'Why won't they? What's up with you?' the driver asked, bemused.

'It's...I just have a strong feeling that the police are not going to stop. They'll not stop for us. They won't help, believe me,' she warned. She was fast running out of white lies to tell them to save them.

'Karl?' one of the girls said.

'Yes?' the driver said.

'We're near the place Emma wanted, aren't we?' the girl said.

'Well, now you mention it, I think it's not too far now,' Karl agreed.

'What?' Emma said, confused. 'No, it's still a while from around here. Look, we've all seen some very troubling things and we must keep calm and focused,' she suggested.

She was ignored, and Karl pulled the car over quickly to the side road. The door was opened for Emma by one of the girls.

'Thanks for the advice, and good luck!' the girl said to her. Emma looked at them, stunned, but as they all stared at her with accusation and suspicion, and she got out of the car. The car raced off straight away, leaving Emma standing cold and alone.

She was alone, and it was unfortunately becoming a regular thing, she realised. More of the unpredictable, savage things that kill could be waiting around any corner, behind any doorway for her, she thought, and she realised that she should be prepared for any sudden attack. She had to arm herself, perhaps like Eric with holy water and a baseball bat, or any other hard solid object she could find. She shivered. Fortunately, she saw that she did know the area of streets quite well. She realised that Eric was probably quite far away from her then, but hopefully the church which he had spoken of visiting was only minutes from her. She felt foolishly vulnerable, and actually considered collecting a loose piece of wood or a pole from fence or wall as she walked along quickly and quietly.

Seconds later, she thankfully saw the church steeple piercing the night sky above a row of houses before her. She secretly allowed herself a humble prayer of thanks to God and ran towards her sanctuary, ignoring sounds of crows or strange rumblings from the streets around her.

Chapter 25

There were all kinds of sadistic possibilities waiting ahead for Taylor and Andrew, but this was the night that finally Taylor would prove himself worthy of joining the group of lawless men and women which Andrew commanded. It all seemed very clear and simple to Taylor, but Andrew was still privately making fateful and fatalistic decisions.

'Do you really believe in what you asked me to do tonight?' he said to Andrew, who walked alongside him confidently.

'Oh I do, but will you do it in the best possible way?' Andrew asked. 'You know, I only wish to help you along. I know you have a twisted soul, my friend. I want to see it join with us permanently. Listen to me; I've been using this town and the North for many years now. I have my wicked ways. It owes it to me. There were no jobs except bad ones before. And down the country, they thought we were only capable of breeding and digging holes. They'll get the shock of the new eventually,' Andrew announced.

'This means a lot to you, doesn't it?' Taylor asked.

'I've used lives, used families, businesses, rumours, fear, paranoia, lust, desire...all to keep our freedom and opportunities that humans just don't have. You need my advice,' Andrew told him.

'I don't have too much time now. Eric is doing anything he can to make progress. He'll find a way to continue tonight. He just wants to be the great hero of Tyneside, and he can't be. It's my turn,' Taylor said, almost like a small child.

'I understand. I've seen similar rivalries of mankind dozens of times. But you have his dead woman, don't you?' Andrew reminded him.

'Damn right. She's a tough cow, but has still been useful to us,' Taylor said thoughtfully.

'You're using it, right? To stop him? It's our key to it all,' Andrew said.

'Yes, but he's been acting strange. I mean, maybe he is suspicious of me. I can't guess him or his plans. He's gone off alone. I still have to meet him soon, though. To trick him. Like you want,' Taylor said.

'It's a bluff. He knows we need him or want him stopped. He's not stupid, is he?' Andrew said. 'Well, we can play that much better than him. Use her tonight,' Andrew told him.

'I will, if you think I have to,' Taylor agreed.

'What about his family?' Andrew asked, curious.

'He actually doesn't give much of a damn about his father, and he has no mother anymore,' Taylor explained.

'You're sure? Okay. Right, his dead girl it is, then. Let me give you some more ideas,' Andrew said.

'Alright, but we can't take too long. Just try for a short while to see...' Taylor said, unsure.

'We'll see some good results, I promise,' Andrew guaranteed, with a perverse grin.

'Certainly more dramatic than I expected, all of this. Sometimes you have to just ruin things, don't you? Things have to change, or end. Can't be all good times.... Thatcher, the unions, we saw the despair, the depression...but it all comes through the shit of it,' Andrew said

'Sorry? Thatcher was years ago now,' Taylor said

'Years ago...years ago things fell apart, but now...the greatest tapestry can be picked apart,' Andrew said vaguely. 'The ones I take, I care for. They may lose their lives, but they are still useful. I put them to work; I guide them in their next new path. Hundreds, perhaps thousands I have converted, sculpted beyond simple human existence. Their fallen shifted path is a gift for them. It is more than Bruce would ever do.'

It was near eleven o'clock, Eric saw, looking at his wristwatch. He wanted to keep Taylor guessing for a while longer on his whereabouts and so still had his mobile phone switched off. Just until...well, until things were certain. Eric walked along the main street near the University of Northumbria. There were still a handful of happily unaware people wandering along to kebab shops and late night pubs a few streets away from him.

He himself had been one of the happy ones along those same streets only a couple of weeks before. He had been out with Grace for one of her friends' birthday celebrations; the drinking, the laughs, the jokes, singing, dancing, pranks and crazy times. This town of Newcastle and places around it were so familiar to him; he had known it all so well. Now, it was a place of lies and death, streets of blood and sadness. Perhaps he had known it so well before that he had wanted more. Yes, he had wanted more than his bitter, frustrating life. Now he had more than he could ever have expected; so did everyone. This was a new start, a new him that the people of the North were seeing. It was the chance to be a different Eric, the one he deserved to be; after everyone else getting the chances, now it was his turn to be successful. The hidden underside of the city's past had been revealed and it was exciting, revitalising and...

And it gave him purpose. To join the new comers, streets and their legion of lawless inhuman hosts, he wondered just how much they were asking of him. He saw that these hellish demon creatures possibly respected him for the ones he had fought and killed. They were impressed and saw in him a challenge and someone useful, a man worth knowing and working with. Could he really say goodbye to the world he lived in, a life his own but pathetically flawed? Few friends really meant much to him, and Taylor had left him. Eric would not willingly be made a fool of, especially by soulless creatures like them, and so he cautiously thought about his next steps. He would love to reunite with Grace more than anything, he knew. Hadn't he heard that suicide was not favoured by God? He just wanted to kiss her lips again, hold his love close to him tightly and not let go ever again. He had let go.

Eric was not exactly very clear of where he was to go next. Even while he considered how much trust to give the demons, he knew that he had to keep up some level of false agreement and pretence while learning more. As he began to wonder, a sharp, sudden pain sparked inside his head, convulsing, throbbing. He put a hand to his temple, scowling. As he closed his eyes to focus past the sudden headache, thoughts and words floated up in his mind. He clearly began to think of specific street names, places, images. He knew his direction. He was not exactly sure how he knew, but it was there, clearly, with fresh confidence suddenly. It was the deep, strange voice of the lead demon in his head. As he walked around toward the Monument Mall and Haymarket Street, all people had gone, leaving only lingering rubbish and a stray mongrel dog roaming along a few feet from him. He paced over the road toward the smaller back streets. This was an area of town which he had only visited a handful of times, though he knew of the businesses and shops there. Some people spoke of extremely violent gangs near that area, drug dealers, even possibly sex traffickers and black market goods. That was mostly rumour and gossip, he knew, but it did worry him. Now, though, he was willing to believe many of those rumours and whispered words. It could benefit him to keep an open mind, he realised. The dangers of demons and local terror could wait near these parts.

While he and Taylor had begun to coordinate their initial tracking of the demon attacks, they had found at least half a dozen areas around Newcastle and the North-East which suggested strong dwellings and activity of these beasts for a long time before. This saddened them, and made them wonder about the place they had grown up around and how safe they had actually been all those years.

He entered a tall building which resembled a disused old bank or theatre in a grand, art deco style. Stepping inside, he looked down the hall and saw a thin, greasy-looking guy leaning against a stairwell expectantly.

'Evening, guv'nor. Come for a chin wag again, have you?' the ugly, thin man enquired.

'Where are your sick friends right now?' Eric asked straight away.

The greasy man cracked his knuckles together as he approached Eric, smiling and sniggering.

From all around the dusty, cobwebbed hallway, smoke suddenly swished up in circles, increasing in size in the air from cracks in the floorboards. Eric watched silently as the smoke swirled quickly and thickened before him. Faces emerged in the smoke, mean looks, red eyes shining out, whistling along past him before finally solidifying into four separate solid columns of smoke which then filled out and into flesh and bone bodies. The four men walked up close to Eric and the greasy man and looked Eric in the eyes. One of them stepped forward.

'Back again, human?' the smoke man in a suit and battered leather jacket said coldly.

'Keeping my options open. You've heard what's been happening, I hope?' Eric asked.

'We know, yes. Are you proud? Did you enjoy it all?' the smoke man asked.

'Did I have to? Isn't it enough that I actually did it, these atrocities for you?' Eric asked.

'Without passion for it, you could be a cold machine. We want a new man, not a machine,' the smoke man told him.

'There are evil humans, you know the ones you have feared. But then there are us. We enjoy, we create, we manipulate...to survive,' the second smoke man explained.

'How many humans do you know who can connect you all and change things, do things that could threaten the stability of your group? Manipulate, humiliate or confuse them... Old Jacket?' Eric said giving a name to the man.

'We see your value. What do you offer us, then?' the man in the leather jacket asked him. 'What do you know about the Gateshead group?'

Eric walked along by the wall, looked around at the dusty surroundings, peeling paintwork. He could smell the deep copper of blood and something rotten not too far from him.

'I have spoken with them, I've met them. So has my partner. They were close lipped mostly but they did offer some interesting opportunities,' Eric alluded.

'You know we are powerful. They are only a shadow of us. They only ever have been jealous and desperate, not as you may believe. They know how your woman died,' the man explained.

With those words Eric was completely focused on him then.

'Excuse me? Just what do they know?' he enquired with cynical suspicion.

'They know guilt, the time, the place, reason. So you help us now?' Old jacket asked.

'For two warring groups, you have very similar boasts and warnings,' Eric informed him.

'If you want to know our power, just say the wrong thing, that is all it takes, human,' the man warned.

'I could say the same thing to you,' Eric replied.

'What we do, we do nonstop. All day, all night. It's our nature, it is us. What we exist for. Since the early times, we sank below, then began to rise to ruin and kill. If you are simply angry for now, get over it, or let us kill you,' Old Jacket offered.

'I have so much hate I could kill hundreds, if not more. Believe me,' Eric warned him.

'Come to us, tonight. Kill them with us. Do this and promise, give us blood, give us loyalty to get what you want,' Old Jacket said.

'You are going ahead with the full attack on the Quayside after midnight still?' Eric asked.

155

'Yes, it is only hours away. Make your choice clear to us or risk death soon,' Old Jacket said, growing impatient.

'Could you really kill me so easily? Would you?' Eric asked dangerously. 'You know how many of you I've slain,' Eric reminded.

The smoke men, watching him in the ominous silence as Old Jacket held back a moment with his final words.

'Luck. Everything will change over the North. Choose wisely, or lose what you have,' Old Jacket said

'I will see you there, at the Quayside. You will see me. I will make my choice before I arrive,' Eric explained.

'Very well. As ever, a man with free will,' Old Jacket said.

Eric walked away from the men with tentative, cautious steps. When he reached the doors once more he looked behind, and saw the men finally bursting apart into thick clouds of smoke and dust again, dispersing over the dirt-encrusted floorboards around. Old Jacket was the last to disperse, after watching Eric leave the building.

As time moved on, the night gradually gave Newcastle and Gateshead terrifying bloody horror like never seen in centuries. Television stations and radio stations began to report the mysterious killings and deaths, with speechless politicians and local police trying to either provide answers or evade the reporters.

Every person in the areas of Wallsend, Walker, Byker, Tynemouth, Jesmond and Gateshead was beginning to question their safety and the safety of their families and friends. Through this living nightmare, families, lovers, politicians, children and old people alike witnessed and experienced things they hoped to never truly know, see, or have to try to escape in their lifetimes.

All people of many religions were seriously praying and questioning the events, reading their religious texts for guidance, looking for how to continue and face the terrors around them as their particular faiths might show them. Each faith was interpreting the events in different ways, some seeing events as prophetic apocalyptic signs, some with less distinct understanding than others.

Besides the reluctant and tempted Eric, there were the local police, many of them, out on the streets and driving around, ready to hunt down the murderers and attackers. That was how it seemed. Unfortunately, as was only known to Taylor so far, many of those police were actually hybrid demon men or women. The hybrids either already had lives and kept them once becoming part demon, or moved into jobs and places of potential power in society that would allow constant control and manipulation of the North.

Both Eric and Taylor were individually out on the city streets, pursuing separate but similarly dangerous goals. If either would actually defeat any of the demon forces which held the North captive, it could not be a strong bet, as they fell down deep into personal confusion, temptation and evil tricks set out for them. Taylor had gone into the deadly company of Andrew and his hybrid demon friends, tasted the pleasures and sin, and was now finally seeing how extremely hollow and soulless that life was. He wanted out, but he felt strong pressure and guilt in every direction.

Taylor struggled with wondering how Eric would react if he admitted to all of his double crossing lies and to stealing the body of Grace. He assumed that Eric would instantly want to tear him to pieces on the spot. No forgiveness, understanding or seeing his point of view, he guessed. They had always been the closest friends, but Taylor had probably done things that deserved the greatest and most painful punishment. The decision to even meet up with Eric like he had asked was a hugely difficult one.

Conversely, Eric wanted in. He thought he had fallen into a pact with the original demons who had taken the North many decades earlier, who had foolishly spawned the hybrids as a kind of game or trick with the humans, which had backfired and now was a constant trouble for them, as well as an imminent threat to all people of the North-East. Eric was only beginning to see the freedom, the power and respect that Taylor had experienced unbeknownst to him, and the original demons could give him twice as much, at even more cost eventually. The pressure of his loneliness and anger could end him without hope, with only a bloody, dark present and a black, hollow future.

Both groups of demons in the North of England were exploiting e these brave, reckless young men as best they could, knowing that these two had been the only humans to actually kill and stop any of them in decades. Although there were numerous dark and sullen buildings, offices, parlours hidden below, within and between the places of everyday industry and work of humans, there were still many places among these where the demons dwelt. There were dimensions and depths which they moved between while observing and manipulating the men and women of the North-East. The places where they resided did change regularly. There was no permanent lair; it was closer to a roaming infestation and parasitic dwelling of sorts.

Both groups of demons were initially fascinated and then soon eager to know how they might use these men, after suffering demons of both tribes dying at the hands of Eric and Taylor. Both tribes saw the dark potential in them, these two ambitious young men, and both would use either one until they got what they needed, or die a lonely death surrounded by bodies along the way. This unravelling narrative was no Hollywood movie or perfect blockbuster fiction, and so an unpredictable and monumental finale could soon fall upon the towns without apology or expected reason.

Down between the tall trees and deep shadows in Tynemouth, a grotesque scene shook out violently. Two young women argued with a man who seemed drunk or simply aggressive toward them. He was trying to force himself onto the redhead girl as the brunette shouted and clawed at him, trying to prise him away.

'Hey, there's no need for that, you dirty shit, get away! Clear off!' the brunette shouted loudly, as he grinned back, swaying slightly.

'Don't give me orders, cutie, or you'll get some too,' he told her, pointing a finger her way before looking back at his trapped and scared lady.

'Hey, just get the hell away from us, will you? The police are coming anyway, so fuck off,' she warned him.

He looked at the redhead, who was giddily drunk between his arms, and the wall behind her.

'You lot need to see that what you do don't change shit, in the end. Need the latest phone or dress or car? There'll always be more below you to find you, all of you,' he said, with a maniacal grin.

'Hey, tosser!' the brunette shouted suddenly, and grabbed his right arm, twisting it. He looked over his shoulder with burning crimson eyes of fury, smoke rising from them. She grasped but held tight, causing him great pain.

'What are you?' she asked in anger and fear.

'I'm the news dear, I'm your nightmare, the disease to kill you,' he told her, laughing.

'Get away from my girl, you weird shit!' she told him, not really caring what the hell he was, just wanting to save her friend from him quickly. She kicked him in the shins, knocking him down. He looked up, angry, and flicked a hand out at her, and suddenly clawed fingers reached for her, trying to scratch out in her direction. He fumed and turned away from the redhead.

'Let me have you, then, as you are much feistier,' he said, more quietly.

'I'm a Catholic, you shit. I pray you're struck down, you bastard!' she told him, and punched him suddenly, knocking him across the jaw. He fell back with blood down his chin and a crooked smile held up at them. It slowed him, but he reached to grab her girlfriend, who moved behind her. The brunette then grabbed his arms and they fought, stumbling around as she held out against his surprising strength.

The police car sirens echoed out around them, to the relief of the women. In the next few seconds, a police car drove up around the street and pulled up near them, and they both looked at the car. The policeman stepped out and walked over with assured conviction and calm authority.

'What's going on here?' he said to the woman.

'Got a feisty young bitch spoiling our plans here, Jim,' the red-eyed attacker announced.

'No, he's attacked my friend and me as well. Lock this dirty shit up, please. Get him away from us. He's a damn rapist!' the woman told the policeman, who listened calmly.

The policeman shook his head and sighed to himself.

'Come on, Christopher, are you wasting time?' the police man asked

'Get it over with,' he said. The words shocked the life out of the young women, all hope of safety and help vanishing.

'What did you say? Aren't you going to take him away with you?' the brunette asked.

'Do you want a hand here? They're on the lists, aren't they?' the policeman asked the pervert casually. Things were very wrong all of a sudden.

'Yes, both. Well, if you want to, come on then. This one's getting out of hand, and she's irritating as hell,' the pervert explained.

'What? What the hell is this?' the brunette said loudly, confused and angry. She began to step away, pulling at her friend.

'Shit, God help us,' she said to herself.

They both looked at her and laughed between each other as they followed her. Their eyes smoked, as if they were red hot coals placed inside their eye sockets.

'This isn't fucking happening. Sweet Jesus, you sick bastards,' the brunette said, with determined aggression.

They came toward her and she looked over at her unconscious friend in her arms. She almost wished that she was similarly unaware, taken to

159

sleep, to another state of being, away from this horror before her. Before she became one more of the night's unnecessary bloody deaths, a car came swerving fast around the top corner of the street. Peter was at the steering wheel. He pulled up alongside her and opened the door.

'Do you want help?' he asked. 'Get in,' he told her.

She hesitated briefly, not sure about him.

'They're much worse than me. Promise,' he said. She looked into his eyes. He seemed an honest soul, she decided.

'Yes, alright. My friend, too,' she told him quickly. The policeman and pervert jumped at her, not pleased by the arrival of help.

'Get back, I know your intentions but I know righteousness too,' Peter declared with strong conviction. The men grimaced and looked at him quietly.

'Bullshit,' the policeman said to provoke the car driver.

'Afraid not. I got faith,' Peter said wryly. 'Get your friend,' he told the brunette. She nodded, speechless, and quickly moved with her friend as Peter stepped out to the two men.

'Brave man tonight, are you?' asked the policeman with startlingly red eyes. His teeth had seemed to narrow to fangs at the front as he smiled slyly.

'That's right. Righteous disciple. I know the score, all this nasty shit tonight. Leave these ladies, and go try something else if you dare,' Peter told them.

One ran at him suddenly, as the demon policeman looked toward the women getting into the car. Peter fell as the demon launched into him, both rolling down onto the ground struggling against each other. Peter reached into his pocket and retrieved a small bottle, like a pocket bottle of whisky or vodka. He held back the demon's hands, then quickly flicked the contents across the demon. He then punched the demon with full force hard in the gut, then again in the face.

A piercing howl erupted from the demon man as he fell to one side, clutching tightly to his burning face. Peter stood and walked to the girls. The brunette was holding back the other wild demon man, who had grown a small pair of horns on his forehead. He slashed out with dirty, long nails, and Peter knocked him to the ground. Peter turned the frenzied demon over and wasted no time, splashing the small bottle's contents over the demon. Once more, howls of pain and cursing came at them. Peter ignored them and stepped over to the women.

'What did you throw over them?' the brunette asked.

'A special secret mix. Blessed good stuff,' he explained. 'I never expected all this,' Peter said.

'It's...is it...holy water?' she said, shocked.

'Maybe, looks like it, doesn't it?' Peter agreed.

'You're a priest, then?' she asked.

'Get in the car, come on,' he told her. He started the engine while the writhing manic demons rolled around out on the bloodied ground beside the car. They drove away in safety, quickly leaving them behind.

'No, I'm not a priest - yet. I work in youth ministry. Similar, but more street cred,' Peter told her in the car.

'Thank you so much for that. I'm Lisa. Good timing,' the brunette said. 'How did you know to do that? I mean, what's going on with people acting like that?' she asked.

'It shocked me, but I've been expecting it. Some prophetic words and visions in church have hinted at things such as these tonight,' Peter told her. 'It was only earlier today that I really began to believe these things could be arriving now after meeting someone else who knew about it,' he said

'What did they know?' Lisa asked, interested by what he was telling her.

'He knows about things that seem very unreal, but things that I know are coming. Only he knows, and he knows a lot,' Peter said. 'I'll find him tonight. I have to.'

'It's like actual evil, then? Real, dangerous, spiritual stuff and mad shit like that?' she asked. 'I didn't believe in crazy shit like that, but their eyes...red eyes. They're like...devils, or demons?'

'Yes. I believe so,' Peter told her.

'I'm not sure I believe in stuff like that. I mean there's terrorists, rapists, gangs, corrupt politicians, but actual demons?' she said incredulously.

'Some times in life we think we really know how everything is, how everything can be, and don't like to accept any other alternatives or that we aren't right. Sometimes we need to stop overanalysing things and accept things and just deal with them. We got to be thankful for our mortal lives and live bravely,' Peter stated.

'Well, easy for you...' Lisa said.

'Not really. It's hard, very hard sometimes. That's faith, hope, love. Sometimes I do nearly give up. Thankfully, not before tonight. Where can I take you, then?' he asked.

She thought about it, thought about what was happening, though she simply could not understand any of it. She knew that she was scared, frightened, confused, but had this curious holy man at the wheel.

'Could we stick with you for a little while?' she asked. Peter looked at her with hesitation.

'Are you sure? I don't honestly know where I'll end up, where I'm going to right now. I don't know what I'll be faced with, more importantly,' he warned her honestly.

'The world around me just got very nasty and unpredictable to me. We feel safe with you now. We won't get in your way,' she told him softly.

'Okay. You can leave if you want to anytime, though, if you need to,' Peter agreed.

'Thank you very much,' Lisa told him, but thought that she would probably not willingly leave him anytime soon.

'Do you know where to look for this other bloke?' she asked him.

'I have a vague idea. Hopefully I'm right, or near enough. God's my satnav tonight,' he said with a straight face.

'Right,' she agreed nervously.

The roads were long and open ahead for Peter as he drove on. He had seen the evils that he suspected, and the supernatural horrors often ignored and forgotten were waiting to be stopped. He prayed he would know what to do and that he would find Eric saving lives somewhere soon enough.

Distressed families rushed past Detective Raimi as he stood at the bottom of the Byker police station steps. What he was seeing was shocking, unthinkable; there were such great numbers of people scared, hysterical and desperate for help, for any real protection. So there were killers around the North-East; they knew this, now. For days, Raimi really had been right on the mark, but should he give up his information to the main area units and just let the county chief of police take over his lead? Would he actually understand that what he thought he would tell him was true? Would he believe in the strange connections, the almost unbelievable links between attacks, suspects and something else, something...disturbing?

Chapter 26

Within minutes, Emma ran up to the front of the old, crumbling church where Eric had been only an hour or so previously. It appeared to be closed, with no lights on inside. There may not have been anyone there right then, but Emma remembered that churches used to be a place of safety; or was that just if you believed in God, she thought? She quickly said a quiet and impromptu prayer. There could not be much harm in that, she thought. If I'm a fool, no one will know it. She crept around the side of the church toward the main entrance and ornate sculpture of Christ upon the cross over the doors. The stained glass windows depicted many mysterious images of fighting, saints and bloody battles. She wondered if there might ever be windows to illustrate the battles that might be won later that night as she walked around.

It occurred to her that maybe these people did not realise how significant those battles were back then, to be immortalised in those stained glass windows for many years to come.

The church grounds were alive with insects chirping bravely in the long grass and bushes around her. Emma did in some sense experience a feeling of positive hope as she walked around in the dark mist surrounding the church. She stepped up to the huge wooden doors, which were bolted shut. Memories of being forced to attend Sunday school, of teenage doubt, came flooding back to her. None of her present friends attended any kind of church, though one was going to a temple or Mosque regularly and others simply enjoyed life without questioning any of it. She did not really go there or anywhere, instead holding out for authentic personal epiphanies that she could decide to accept or reject as she drifted into her twenties.

'Looking for something?' a voice asked. She spun around, shocked. A couple of feet away, half-draped in deep shadows of the trees and the church, stood a tall, thin figure.

'Who are you?' she asked, looking around discreetly for potential methods of escape.

'I'm Father Wilberforce. George Wilberforce. The vicar here. Can I help you?' he asked in a friendly manner. She let out her breath and relaxed slightly.

'Maybe you can. Has a young man or two men been here? They might be in trouble, but they're good really,' she asked.

'There was a young man here an hour or more back. He had troubles, but he did seem a good young guy.'

'Do you know where he went?' she asked him.

'Toward Newcastle I think. He had a lot on his mind. My youth pastor has gone to find him, I think,' he told her. He had a look of aged wisdom and patience on his dried, wrinkled face.

'Yes, that's him. You don't know where he's gone now, do you?' Emma asked.

'He left earlier on. I did too, but I came back for some books and things. Can I help in any way?' Wilberforce asked.

'Well I wanted to talk to him, the youth pastor. It's very important that I find my friend now. Do you have the youth pastor's phone number?' she asked.

'Let me see...' the vicar said, and put a hand deep into his pocket. He considered her, who she might be, and if she was telling the truth to him. He thought that she was, if bending it just a little, but ultimately he believed her. He retrieved a very modern-looking mobile phone, which surprised Emma. He scrolled through menus on the tiny screen.

'Here we are; Peter, 07923471. Do you have a phone to add it to?' he asked.

'Yes, yes,' Emma replied, and quickly got out her own mobile phone and entered the number.

'Thanks very much for that, father. Are you aware of...anything unusual or bad happening tonight around the region?' she asked, and tried to sound relaxed.

He looked at her as if troubled by some uneasy, tormenting thought.

'Not exactly, but I'll tell you that Peter did leave acting very unlike himself. It was curious, and I prayed for him then after he left. He did say that he unexpectedly had to take a long drive around town. Are bad things happening around the area?' he asked her.

Emma almost laughed at the thought. What could she tell him? Where could she begin without horrifying him with tales of shocking macabre visions of brutal bloody deaths so recent and nearby?

'There is danger out on the town right now, yes. It is completely shocking, terrifying. I've witnessed some people being killed before my eyes. I wish that I hadn't seen any of it,' Emma explained with sadness.

'Really? Dear Lord. Have you contacted the police about any of it yet?' he asked. Now he was much more concerned and disturbed.

'Father, please. Isn't our faith strong? Look, I just know that I can't trust the police tonight, maybe never again. I'm trusting myself, my friends and even possibly any God that might like to help out any time soon,' Emma told him. She began to walk off.

'He will. I know he will help us if we ask at a time like this,' Father Wilberforce said as he followed Emma out of the church gates onto the street outside.

'That would be good, especially tonight. I'd welcome it, even with my confused faith,' she said.

They looked up the street at some cars screeching along past them towards the roundabout. Emma turned to the vicar as she stood on the path near the shadows of tall trees. Instantly, a large hand came around from behind his face, clutching him tightly. His head was suddenly pulled back as he yelled, his scream stopped by the clawed hand. Emma watched, disturbed, and she stepped back in shock. A broad, muscular man with smoking, red eyes and clawed hands grabbed at the vicar, who fell.

'Get off him, you evil shit,' Emma said. She bravely threw a fist at the demon man, only punching his side as he held the vicar tightly.

'Too late, bitch, no mercy here,' he told her, and held the vicar's head. He then twisted suddenly, the flesh of the vicar's neck stretching tight like elastic. The vicar howled and grimaced in agony. Emma was in total shock and scared for her life. This was a towering man beast nearly twice her size, she saw. She felt almost entirely useless, looking around for any object to hit the thing with. As she watched, the demon wasted no time and ripped, releasing a fountain of gore and blood. The demon rubbed its hands in the blood joyfully as it watched Emma. She quickly bent down and tore off the crucifix from around the neck of the dead vicar.

'Get back to where you once belonged,' she said bravely, holding the crucifix tightly. She held it out toward the demon man.

'Confused aren't you? I don't blame you. Confusing times we live in today,' he told her, licking the vicar's blood from his clawed hands.

'I know truth. I know hope. Get back,' Emma said sternly, holding the cross out. He came at her quickly all of a sudden. Emma fell over

165

the books which the vicar had been carrying. She quickly picked up a couple and flung them hard at the demon. One missed him, but the other struck him loudly on the face. It knocked him back, and he swore in pain. She took the moment to get up fast and rammed the crucifix down hard into his screaming face, bursting his nose and cracking his jaw, his blood pouring. She held him down and stabbed with aggression again and again, the demon blood flowing over her hands. As he fell, holding his bleeding, ripped face, Emma leaned took the chance, and ran with speed and fear propelling her away, running like she had never needed to run before.

Chapter 27

Over a dozen reporters and journalists waited by the Newcastle city police station, watching the cars coming in and out of the street. As a couple of important chief inspectors stepped from a police car, they were met instantly by the many reporters.

'Where are the killers?' one asked.

'What have they done now?' another enquired.

'Who are they really?' another wanted to know.

'Are they mad or sick?' someone else asked.

These were just a few of the many questions shouted at the police chiefs as they entered the building.

'One at a time; slowly now, please,' Inspector Wakeman told them as he stood on the doorway, turning to face them.

'Why are they doing these sick things? Do you know yet? Are they terrorists?' one woman reporter asked.

'We have a number of clues which we are following up now. No, we do not believe them to be terrorists. We will stop them soon enough, we promise,' he replied calmly.

'Inspector, we have heard of a number of conflicting reports, and statements almost contradicting each other of news about strange attacks at opposite ends of the North-East in the last couple of days and last few hours. Very strange unexplainable things and sightings, similar but far apart, often around the same times. Is it really two men alone doing this?' one confident reporter enquired.

'Listen, there are many confusing reports coming in and people are certainly very scared and confused for valid reasons. We cannot explain or tell you all that we know at present. We'll speak later. Goodbye for now,' the police chief told them, and they entered the station, as the reporters continued to shout out questions at them.

Deep down among the backrooms of a dark, exclusive nightclub in lower Newcastle City Centre, a group of twelve men and women stood around a long table. They were all part of an unknown secret, a group with phenomenal political, social and supernatural power over the North. They all stood with human faces, with convincingly crafted skin, hair, and postures, though each and every one in reality originated from a realm far away from Newcastle. They worked together every day and every night, but were engaged in serious disagreement. One broad, dark-skinned man waved his hands and shook his head, then spoke loudly for attention.

'Listen, anything might happen tonight. We have to realise that. All I'm suggesting is that we think of other options,' he declared.

'Give it time!' one blonde woman said angrily.

'This could be us gone! We've had a few good decades. We might have to accept it finally,' another man added, with a grave bitter tone to his voice. The doors to the room opened up behind them and in walked two men, smiling to themselves.

'Are you lot still arguing?' one of them asked incredulously 'Where's your faith in the darkness we know? We are the true originals, right? We own this town,' one told them.

The two men stepped apart and then Eric walked out from behind into the room between them.

'Good evening, everyone. I'm here to work with you all,' he told them as he looked on the group of demons who he was to help that night. They looked at first glance like any ordinary people he might walk past on the street. Without trying to stare, he watched them as they looked at him, inspecting him. Even with their impressively human skin and clothes, he noticed a number of minute giveaway signs; they all held a just observable red shine to their eyes, and occasionally snarled and gnashed their teeth. If they were to butcher him, they really could most likely do it right them, he realised. Each one of them could draw his blood, tear into him and finish his defiant interferences. It did not happen, not then.

This night was due to be louder than many in recent times. The screams and cries of the people of Newcastle and wider North would be monumental, legendary in their volume, moans of fear and sorrow would eclipse all known joy. It was going to be more unpredictable and unbearable than any night any Northerners had known in their lifetimes; since the last war, at least. There would be no army to combat the danger this time, only a handful of defiant young people with reckless courage.

As the night progressed, various parts of the North began to buzz with whispered rumours, news of terrible atrocities told in panic and hysteria. With the sudden increasing body count all over, police followed up by racing through all town centres, main roads and close to where any incidents, deaths or violence had been reported. These police were doing what they were expected to do, though also what they themselves wanted to do. Some of the police officers driving around were decent, trustworthy men and women. They would stand before danger, crime, and violence of many kinds to protect all others in our modern society. Some of them, though, were very different. They were police too, or looked like them and sounded like them, but they were simply using the uniform to be where they wanted, and get what they wanted. Those few were demon men or women in disguise, playing a sinister game to take souls and ruin human lives.

Like real men could be sadistic, careless, selfish, these diabolically evil creatures had wanted to be like mankind, even if only to entertain themselves with the simple relationships, problems, and challenges of humankind. Once wrapped in human skin, though, they soon took advantage in order to manipulate, torment and kill in many intricate and macabre ways.

In the past few days, Eric and Taylor had initially only come head to head with the original demons. They had begun to perceive these wretched things as being only this particular way. The actions, timing, and repulsive look of these unreal entities had fixed, and the two young men set their attack, confidently supposing that they knew all they could know.

As they had successfully matched the demons repeatedly with help from the spirit of Grace, change came. A number of things instigated the unforeseen turnaround for Eric and Taylor. While Eric contemplated just what might be at the root of the terror, and Taylor seemingly followed behind sheepishly, the unknown elements took advantage while they could. Grace had ceased to visit Eric, which had forced him and Emma to investigate more clues themselves, before police and others closed in and the news of attacks spread too widely.

The North of England was at that time still trying, mostly surprisingly successfully, to equal the South in contemporary multicultural progression, and experienced economic and cultural growth like it had never before seen, whether individual Northerners appreciated it or not. It seemed the powerful figures of the North were trying desperately to impress the government and businesses of the South. All the time, they had been unknowingly manipulated by hybrid demons who tried out their own plans and operations. As people in the North-East towns began to aspire beyond simple labour jobs with the increased higher education options more frequently possible to many, the youth of the North-East began to explore with fresh confidence new cultures, new attitudes, new options and opinions about the modern world. In reality, the evil darkly pulsing heart of the North could still find ways to keep its people from escaping and finding different lives elsewhere.

A policeman named Oliver and another named Windsor stood amongst a mixed group of police officers, all around the Jesmond area investigating the phone calls and rumours of attacks and sightings. Locals and quick-witted witnesses had spread word to the police, who then arrived in less than fifteen minutes to investigate what was only one of many strange reports called in over the last couple of hours from around the area. Many of the people and police just did not know what to make of it all; could it be that Newcastle and the North of England actually contained a serial killer, or even a highly organised group of killers, or terrorists who moved like ghosts between each massacre?

The majority of the local police force was unfortunately jaded, overly masculine, and occasionally immoral. Most of the officers disguised their insecurities, confusion, and fear with overly macho parading around, joking, even politically incorrect banter, both sexist and juvenile, to keep their minds from thinking about the uncertain horror out there which people expected them to deal with. They were genuinely scared and feeling so pressured, unprepared and unsure of what they actually had to confront. Things as gruesome as this hardly ever happened outside of London. No one ever expected a Jack the Ripper up North. But a small number of them did know what was happening. They were just what the rest of them feared.

Oliver and Windsor had both been in the local police force for nearly ten years. They were both good at their job, very capable of being qualified and professional police officers; both knew all about the local area, the local crime levels, the known criminals, and the history of events in Newcastle. They knew about the local rumoured underworld, the gangs that were possibly out there in various dangerous areas across the town and further afield. They knew, because they were deep in there with it all. They were corrupt, and they were demon hybrid men. Each had individually chosen to open themselves to life-changing experiences years ago, losing much of their humanity to gain just as much hellish power. They were not alone, either. Many other men and a few women had crossed over, had been tempted, seduced, or tricked into joining them and leaving the problems of their mortal lives. They viewed human life and living in a more relaxed manner, and also could see a certain amount of the landscapes of the hellish homeland of demon kind.

'You think we'll win this feud tonight? It's tonight, isn't it? Andrew has arranged that we all meet Bruce and his lot, right?' Oliver said quietly to Windsor.

'Yeah, it's tonight. Have to, don't we? We will. We're better than the originals, no doubt. It's the real evolution. That's what was said,' Windsor told him with confidence.

'Getting wild, this night is,' Oliver said, looking out over the coast road and the many hundreds of street lamps and road lights trying to shine light upon the heinous slaughter and bloody violence below. 'It's not the way, but should be entertaining.'

'Certainly will be, pal. Let's make the most of it all, eh?' Windsor said, smiling fondly. He rubbed Oliver on the back with significant affection.

'They say he's gone with them. Been tempted, finally,' Oliver told him.

'Makes no real difference to us, does it? They're going down for good. He'll just be with them when it happens. Going to happen anyway, right?' Windsor said.

'That's right. Yes, you're right,' Oliver agreed.

Another policeman came over to them from his own parked car

'Hey, you two, they're all appearing close by the Tyne, it looks like. Around the city area. We're all going to move on out there now, Phil and his lot are coming down by here soon enough,' the policeman told them.

'That so, is it? Okay then,' Windsor said. He and Oliver nodded thoughtfully in agreement and walked to their car as the other policeman returned to his own.

'Hey, still doing what we want to on the way, are we?' Oliver asked Windsor as they climbed into their car.

'If you're quick and don't make a mess…yes,' Windsor told him. They all then drove off up the dark roads along the coast to look for what was dangerous and what was useful.

Chapter 28

At a police station at Jesmond, questions were demanding answers, by many and all around. The death, the horror was all so sudden and unexplained. Families wanted answers, explanations, results, action. Parents could not calm their children, and almost everyone felt vulnerable, unsafe, angry and terrified in some way as the night continued.

'Tell me what you do know!' a tall, lean man shouted in growing frustration at a couple of police officers at the reception desk. This man was Mr Derek Prealgate. He had been informed just over an hour previously of the extremely graphic and needlessly brutal death of his son and son's girlfriend. Prealgate was not alone in feeling the pain and helpless anger. Mrs Brenda Hearly's world had been broken into ruined pieces on hearing that her husband had been beaten and strangled down dark streets not too far from their own home less than fifty minutes previously. There were many others, growing in numbers, all furious and demanding truth, protection and justice through bitter tears and shouts of rage and anger.

'How did this happen?' Mrs. Hearly screamed at the police officers. 'Catch the bastards doing these sick, sick things! Why? Why should they do any of these things? You're all fucking useless wastes of my tax!' she shouted, with many around nodding in agreement. Her sister finally managed to pull her back from near the reception desk.

'What is going on? All of this death and killing tonight? How is it happening? Who is doing it all?' Derek asked, a little calmer than Mrs. Hearly.

'We really are doing our best to find out, everyone. Please believe us. These events are horrendous, are really terrible things indeed, and we are so sorry for you all. We will put a stop to these things and get justice for all of you; you can believe me when we say that, I swear,' the older police officer at the desk said loudly to the hysterical folk stood around. Inwardly, though, he did not know if he could believe his own words. He knew very well what some people thought of modern police these days, but he had to give them all some kind of positive words to keep them strong, himself and his team included.

There had never been an occasion similar to this. People had hardly any confidence in the police. As the situation was so extreme, a number of people personally began to consider their own means of defence or safety; some seeking spiritual guidance in churches and temples, others deciding to arm themselves with all manner of collected dangerous weapons, from knives and golf clubs to barbed wire and wooden stakes.

On better nights, many parts of the North knew how to let loose and have the most unapologetically decadent time, most notably in the world famous part of Newcastle City Centre known as the Bigg Market. Many people of all types from far and wide would turn up on the worn but familiar cobbled streets of this area to stagger between the many dozens of hospitable pubs crammed tightly into those tight labyrinthine streets, talking to strangers, joking in the merriest of drunkenly joyous ways. Toward one fetid and musty area of these streets, Andrew led Taylor into a place still securely private, yet containing much greater levels of debauched revelry than the streets around it.

'Here we are, my curious human friend,' Andrew said, and softly pushed him through the doors into a place which looked like a cross between a low rent casino and an opium den.

'Back to the place of dirty fun, drunken times and any old excess once again, my friend. No limits in here. Forget your troubles; that's an order, okay?' Andrew said with seriousness, but then suddenly let out a lively, echoing laugh.

'Of course. I'm very glad you let me in here, really. I love it all,' Taylor replied.

They walked on through the dimly lit rooms and passages, past suspicious pimps, dope fiends, and misshapen demon men and women. Andrew pointed Taylor in the direction of a room lit in shady yellow and orange light, with draped pastel scarves all around. Behind these were a number of ornate beds and baroque sofas with numerous attractive, semi-naked women lounging around. They smiled and winked seeing him enter, one or two of them already occupied by other men but open to even more company. He joined a couple of beauties, a redheaded girl and a brunette, on the ornate sofa to the left. The redhead was topless, the other in some leather garment.

'Evening, ladies,' he said, smiling but visibly distracted.

173

'Hello Taylor, good to see you. We've missed your curious hands, and charming words,' the redhead told him.

'Great, well, I'm back for a while,' he said.

'Please relax, Taylor honey. We know how to enjoy ourselves, don't we?' the brunette said, stroking his face.

'Right, yes,' he agreed. He looked around the long room and saw that Andrew must have disappeared off into another room to get his own entertainment, and so leaned in towards the two women.

'Can I tell you two ladies something very unusual?' he asked.

'Say whatever you like,' the redhead told him.

'You'll listen and not think I'm mad at all?' he asked.

'Does it matter? No, we think you're a very clever, handsome man, Taylor,' the other told him.

'Okay…girls, I've come here and enjoyed myself with you two and some of the other ladies in the last week or more…but there are some bad things happening,' he began.

'Really? What do you mean?' the redhead asked, not really seeming shocked.

'Well, look, I'm really not going mental or anything, but I mean death, murder. It's being done by…' he said, but found it difficult to finish.

'By who?' the redhead asked.

He looked around in hesitation, knowing Andrew and his friends were only in the other rooms next to them.

'There are demons,' he whispered quietly, almost inaudibly. The two ladies did hear him, and looked back with fascinated interest, though not with shock, it seemed. He waited for their reaction for what seemed like hours.

'There are many evil things around,' the redhead told him and kissed his lips.

'Many dark places where evil acts,' the brunette added, as she kissed his neck and unbuttoned his trousers. They continued undressing him as he lay back on the sofa, closing his eyes in hopeless confusion while they began to pleasure his vulnerable flesh, even quietly laughing between each other as their clawed fingers touched his chest and face.

Even as murder and death were building all around the North at unexplainable speed, there were always a number of people likely to seek out truth and thrills. The news reporters waited along the motorway at a service station area, necking black coffees and chewing on stale, overpriced sandwiches. Paul Gilby, reporter from the local evening paper, received a call on his mobile phone suddenly.

'Hey Paul, you ready to go?' a man asked. It was his close friend, Police Inspector Gattis.

'Of course. Tell me, what's happening?' Paul asked.

'Okay, you'll see us coming in from Gateshead direction, and others too. These two guys have been noticed moving along by Jesmond again. Could be the two who are killing people for some sick black magic thing, or occult bullshit, or even one of those internet pacts. Funny, but that's really what they're saying. They're both highly dangerous, both serial murderers, okay?' the police officer told him, 'get what you need but keep well back, alright?'

'You got it. Thanks again, Gattis. I owe you,' the reporter said.

'You always owe me. You're welcome. You know my whisky of preference, okay? That's your new ripper. Enjoy the fame and attention,' the officer said.

'But nothing else?' The reporter asked.

'That's enough. Tell it as it is; two serial killers, occult weird shit, or working-class anti-British anarchist bullshit, okay?' the officer said

'No problem at all. Thanks again. See you soon,' the reporter replied happily.

Chapter 29

Eric was surrounded by the things he had been chasing and killing for a fortnight. Was he trapped, helpless or were they about to be finished at his hands? They watched him with dubious suspicion, all of them uncertain as to why he actually was in the room with them and still breathing. Most of them began to move towards him, creeping up and feeling the urge to snuff this cocksure young human who had shaken their control over the North and dominance over the hybrid demons. He felt their resentful, psychotic eyes on him, dozens of inhuman red eyes.

'He has a level of agreement we can understand. I have made an agreement with him, as you know, and so we will work together for now. And so we offer respect and not pain,' Bruce told all of them as he stood at the side of Eric.

Bruce was the oldest demon to take residence over ground in the North nearly two hundred years ago. He was the leader of all others; he gave the commands, the punishments, and knew what the great dark wanted of them while they were on Earth. Until recently, he was sure that he would catch Eric and Taylor, these two restless and persistent humans who had somehow known where to find and attack demons, ruining all operations. No men had been so successful at doing that for many decades, and it had not been expected by either tribe of the warring demons due to the ways men and women of the country were living and what they believed, and did not believe any longer.

Bruce believed that he was going to give Eric the best lasting view of Hell conceivable, but then Eric had opened his mouth and managed to come to a very understandable agreement with his tempting use of examples and quick words.

Although Bruce and his fellow dark beings regularly slaughtered, abused and tortured many humans, mankind did undeniably hold a persistent fascination for Bruce. The men, women, children and old ones of Earth were always fascinating in many ways, beyond their simple self-destructive habits. The contradictions, decisions, and paths taken by them kept Bruce watching them closely. He still enjoyed manipulating men after decades at it. He would use them, play them off against each other, and watch the results. This unexpected time was so different, even kind of challenging to a scared, experienced demon such as him.

When the group of demons initially surfaced after being summoned at the end of the 1970s, they primarily took a variety of mutating forms until defining their earth-dwelling appearances. They could take almost any form of species from Earth in a crude but almost convincing manner, though with faint demonic traces showing through if studied well enough. As they did mostly remain hidden within the dark reaches of night mostly, two remained significantly demonic while the grand, feared demon which chose the earth name Bruce decided to arrange his brutal and sickening features to eventually seem almost completely human to further his secretive dealings with the ones who had called them forth.

He chose the human name of Bruce almost at random, having observed it on a film poster as he passed the famous art deco cinema building in the city streets of Newcastle. The fallen demon kind, of which the three were respected warrior demons, had their own language, but they could understand and easily speak English and other Earth languages. They were glad to have been called out to the human realm. A challenge ever few decades was fondly appreciated, especially with the chance to slaughter and massacre in innumerable ways. They could always observe humankind, but to interact, or kill, even, required the most rare specific summoning and events. But once out, it always took a hell of a lot to get them back to where they came from. Once out, they could take extreme sadistic pleasure in repetitive murder, death and anguish, before any destined supernatural ordeal might challenge them.

This omnipotent demon in the human world had now spent nearly thirty years abusing and butchering the towns and entire region around Newcastle. He had, with Philip, explored how far they could terrify, manipulate and sicken others unknowingly and have it be seen as the effects of post-war economic climate or Northern depression in the face of the successful South.

As such dark, fabled monstrosities were horrifying yet fascinating to mankind, so were humans a continual unexpected interest for Bruce and the demons out with him. He had always known of them; all demons knew of mankind, all knew of the great fall and separation, but to closely witness their sweet suffering, sadness, paranoia, fear greatly entertained him for the years to come. Until he and Philip could not so easily agree on plans; until Andrew.

Philip removed himself from their secret business dealings soon afterwards, and the two demon tribes took their places over the North, claiming streets and towns, and the secret wars started unknown to almost all of mankind.

'This man, having killed some of our kind, commands our respect. You know this. Rare it is that man defeats our kind. He offers much. We are going to take up his offer tonight,' Bruce explained to the many dozens of surrounding demons.

'Are you finally insane? This is a simple man of bone, shit and piss, all guilt, fear, panic, worries and desire. Useless and weak,' One demon shouted out to him defiantly.

'Suspend your disbelief. He knows how we work, what we do, and he understands and respects us mutually in return. With the problems unravelling tonight, this man can help us regain control once more,' Bruce offered.

'If he can't, or won't...he's dead. Tonight,' the demon with the vulture face said. The dozen or so other demons near him nodded in agreement while watching Eric.

'I know more than enough right now. More than intelligent men, more than priests and paranormal specialists might guess. And I...I should be involved. You should be involved with me. I'm bringing down demons, and you don't want to be the ones I aim for,' Eric explained.

'You know them also?' the vulture demon asked.

'He does, and he will help us if we accept. They fear him equally, as we did. With him, we rule them again. We are wasting time now,' Bruce told them.

'I'll stick around with you all. Mankind is a sham to me, a useless, cruel trick to me now,' Eric told them.

'He will help any way that he can,' Bruce added.

They all slowly nodded in silence, Bruce watching them, and then looked at Eric, who smiled back. They all collectively decided to agree and trust Bruce, as they often did, accepting Eric. They explained some rules and misunderstood myths, rumours and fallacies concerning Hell, and the spawn from deep within it.

Things were somehow both simple yet complex for Eric then, but he believed he was at least closer to the next step and in control of the situation, with a good chance of stopping them all and helping the spirit of Grace. What could he lose? She was gone, and Taylor...well, he had chosen his own path, apparently.

Bruce took Eric around the cavernous corridors of the underground nightclub which the demons had built for themselves over the years. He led him into a private, dimly lit study for a close conversation alone, closing the door behind them.

'I will admit that I hadn't expected to be doing this fight against the hybrid ones along with a human but this is how it will be. You are okay with that?' Bruce suddenly asked very seriously.

'Yes, you know I am. I will be doing anything to save my love. This I have stated, and right now that means joining with you and your kind,' Eric replied.

'Alright then. Things will go the way that they will go,' Bruce told him with a kind of secretive agreement. 'Tonight is going to be a significant night. A night of change like there has not been in the North for decades. We are to fight the other ones, the hybrids. It will happen, as agreed, down on the Quayside,' Bruce explained.

'Both demon groups? Like a fight to the death? If you can be dead?' Eric said.

'You've killed some of us, you know. We...pass into another way. We've done so much to this town Newcastle and Gateshead and further around. Do you know what we've achieved over many years?' Bruce said to Eric as they sat at two large leather chairs next to a grand table.

'I have heard of some of these things. Read of some things in reports. Men have recorded some of it, actually. Tell me more, though. I'm sure that I've only just scratched the surface, haven't I?' Eric replied.

'Stability and control. Death and birth. Your kind keeps reproducing constantly, every day, every hour of the day. You call this kind of thing genocide when you do it to yourselves. We are keeping your population down. You should be grateful. But you are, I know. Equilibrium,' Bruce explained. 'I will tell you much more after this night. You know the others though, right? Encountered them, haven't you? Do you know where they come from?' Bruce asked.

'I have wondered. It's a deep rivalry, isn't it?' Eric asked.

'Men and women might not be aware of any of it above the surface, but it could make things much worse for all of them. We control things; your lives, your opportunities, and your mortality. We are much more

179

focused, dedicated and serious. From a serious place with an age old duty, of course,' Bruce explained.

'Yes, is that right?' Eric asked, provoking Bruce.

'Those ones, they were human; still are, mostly. They are very confused, foolish, childish bastards. Waste time, waste opportunities. They spill your blood without thinking, torture and mutilate at any whim at any time. If you want revenge, fulfilment, it comes with us, in defeating them,' Bruce said with finality. 'Tonight you can begin it all. We move out soon. So much has been lost already. You can join me in claiming revenge tonight. Any way that we can, we will get it.'

'Yes I will,' Eric told him in agreement. They drank a stiff drink together before discussing the final plan of action.

'And don't worry yourself about the others, how they looked at you. Usually they would kill any of you quickly, and after what you did...but not if I tell them otherwise. I rule here. Onward then, on the road,' Bruce told him. They finished their whisky and then walked back out to meet again with the others.

Bruce led the group quietly out of the back entrance of the building and around to where a number of sleek, expensive cars waited for them. The group split between the cars, with Bruce and Eric up in the first one together.

'Are we going straight to the Quayside now?' Eric asked when they got inside, with three demon men quietly sat in the back seats with them.

'Not straight away. We're going to follow their patterns. We have our own areas which we own, control, fought for or retained. We have boundaries much like your own gangs, tribes, cultures. We did have some respect for them when they were born from us, but ultimately they retain too many human flaws. Neither men nor demons, not worth a thing to us,' Bruce explained to Eric.

Eric looked out of the car window as they drove along. They sped along through the quiet roads of Tynemouth, Cullercoats, and Whitley Bay. Some of the demons in the back of the car laughed, mumbling about recent killings and fights with the hybrids. Eric realised then with a sobering thought that he was actually sat in a car full of real murderous demons. Only a day before, he had been hunting these beasts, killing them in any way he could with Taylor. He held back the mind-blowing thoughts in his mind to try to think then of the other evil in the North he knew of; the street gangs, drug dealers, gun dealers, paedophiles, abusive parents, rapists, thieves and criminals. Knowing that these creatures were separate from humankind, he did though wonder if they were more morally considerate, useful, justified than any of these other many guilty sinful people.

'Bring it over, Riggs,' Bruce called to the demon driving the car. The demon had a very curiously fascinating face, Eric thought. It was mostly human, but the colour of his skin was a sickly grey, with some lurid veins rising to the surface around the jaw and neck. He then saw the red pupils in the eyes again when the demon looked back at Bruce and nodded before looking back at the road ahead. The demon pulled over near a school building and the start of a small shopping centre.

'What now?' Eric asked Bruce tentatively.

Bruce looked at him with restrained emotion before giving a reply.

'You and I walk,' Bruce told him. They stepped out of the car and down the front of the shopping centre together.

'Is this their turf or ours?' Eric asked, looking around at the streets near them. There were no people on the streets anymore, simply discarded carrier bags and fast food boxes blowing along the pavement.

'It's very near their area here, we know. Follow me. We need information, it won't be easy to find,' Bruce told him with a pensive face. Every step was still a step in danger to Eric.

Eric had no idea what might happen next, but kept ready for anything. He knew that he might be very vulnerable, walking beside a powerful, ancient demon in human form. Well, what would happen would happen, he thought. His old life was quite possibly lost forever to him by now anyway, with police chasing him and rumours about him all over the newspapers, but he also did not wish to be made to look foolish. He was definitely not in the mood to be used or ridiculed, and hoped that Bruce knew this. He did not want to die a quick, shameful death either, without putting up a hell of a determined fight against any damn demon to get in his way.

'Don't be threatened by human things now. Not police, not people, laws...no one will come near you, you're with us. Let's try here,' Bruce said, and pointed to the bar to their right. Bruce walked over with Eric at his side.

On entering the bar, it seemed like nearly any other modern alternative bar; neon lights, plasma televisions on the walls, mirrors, chrome panels. Mainstream chart and hip hop tunes rumbled and pounded out of the speakers around the place. People were crowded in all directions around Eric and Bruce, drinking, laughing, and shouting to each other, as they would on any other night of the week. Many men and women mixed around, dancing, flirting, and joking around. Eric felt sorry for them, but also happy in a sense, as they were some of the only people unaware of the tragedies outside. If only just some people might know of the senseless bloody killing and supernatural horrors so close and deadly, he thought, as he drank a quick shot of vodka from the bar.

He did feel slightly guilty at having Bruce by his side, Bruce being the embodiment of pain, suffering, fear, horror. Eric wanted to say some kind of prayer for these merry people, he was surprised to realise himself thinking. He looked at Bruce, who was approaching the bar. Eric suddenly wondered if anyone he knew might actually be in the bar then. He did still care for his friends and family, and he did not want to imagine them getting caught in the middle of some dangerous conflict between these demons. He still cared, he realised. Grace was dead, but there were still plenty of people who he cared for that were in real danger, he admitted to himself.

No matter how many times he told himself that he was away from everyone now, he still cared, and there were plenty of them that he hoped would not get hurt. Even if he no longer wanted to be with humans any longer, these were human feelings and thoughts. They made him, he knew, and he wanted to feel like that. He needed to care for the people who knew him, who liked and loved him back. He was still a man.

'Get this down you, quick sharp,' Bruce told him, and pointed to a small but potent drink, possibly absinthe. Eric viewed the dark amber and green liquid in the glass with suspicion as he picked it up. He saw Bruce then quickly throw back a similar drink and so decided to copy him.

'Good right?' Bruce asked, smiling. 'Down the far right, see?' he said, more quietly.

'No, who?' Eric asked, with a sudden loose, free feeling in his body and head.

'The group sat down. The guy in the old jacket, the ginger guy, the slutty girls,' Bruce told him, 'they're known around here. I've been told about them. Your turn now.'

'My turn? To do what, exactly?' Eric said, the drink tickling his grey matter.

'Get what we need. I trust you can do it,' Bruce told him. 'This lot will lead us in the right direction; we have to move along quickly tonight. I'm not sure of everything. The hybrids, they're doing different things now after you and your friend stepped in. Forget that, just work with me here. Do your stuff,' Bruce said.

Eric nodded in agreement, while the mystery alcohol trickled into delicate parts of his head. It was his chance to keep Bruce happy and trusting him, he saw. He tried to think about what Bruce had been saying, but he could not focus his thoughts like usual. Eric coughed, straightened himself, then confidently walked down the back of the bar room, up to the group Bruce had pointed to. They were talking and joking quietly until Eric came near them, then all talk stopped as they looked at him.

The old jacket guy and ginger guy stopped talking and looked up at him.

'Who's this?' Old Jacket said casually, giving an irritated look toward Eric.

'You probably do know of me, but that's not too important. Thing is, I know who you lot are and I need you to tell me a few things right now. I've no time to piss about, so just give me what I need and I'll leave you to continue,' Eric said.

'Who do you think you are, skinny man-boy shit?' Old Jacket asked, taken aback.

'I'm the bloke who's been and found your kind, kicked you up the arses, killed at least three of you and generally pissed you off. I know what I'm doing. The breaking newsflash now, though, is that I'm with the other side. The originals. You dig?' he said, and enjoyed it.

'Oh really? Is that the truth?' Old Jacket said.

'Damn right. My company is nearby, so don't mess about now. Tell me where you all are and what is happening if you value your freedom,' Eric said.

The people at the table around Old Jacket all looked up at Eric and had heard his speech. They were shocked, but all of them played it cool, as if he had asked for the time. It was him, they were thinking. The one they all talked of, the demon killer, the brave human, the one who knew, the interfering young saint himself. Old Jacket stood suddenly.

'You just don't care, do you?' he asked Eric.

'I care, but not for you. At all. I care about my business, like anyone or anything alive. You should care about yours. So tell me what I want to know,' Eric said. This was getting just a bit intense, Eric thought. He had demons behind him, demons in front of him. What a game he was playing, he thought. He looked just out of the side of his vision, not too sure he could still see Bruce supporting him back up at the bar. This is where things might fall apart, Eric thought. There were people all around them, innocent people. It was the first time he had met any kind of demon among so many unaware innocent people, and it suddenly added much more stress and responsibility to his situation.

As Old Jacket looked Eric up and down, one of the accompanying slutty-looking young women by him thrust out an arm and suddenly scratched wildly at Eric, drawing blood from his neck. He recoiled back in shock, and all of the demons laughed. Eric grabbed Old Jacket by the throat, and Old Jacket quickly took Eric by the arms, but Eric had control, only just.

'Speak now, you crusty old shit. Tell me about tonight or you'll see no more of it. I swear to Hell and back,' Eric said, with all seriousness. It must have been the drink, Eric thought. His hands seemed so much stronger, and he seemed to enjoy grasping tighter on the man, and looking right into his red demon eyes with the other ones watching.

Old Jacket and his group watched Eric. In unison, all of their eyes flared instantly to red, burning and smoking like bright coals.

'It hurts, you bastard saint,' Old Jacket exclaimed. He was in pain, Eric saw. Then he saw a dark kind of blood ebbing forth between his fingers as he held Old Jacket at the arms, the old man wrestling out of Eric's grasp while the others waited, ready to lend their claws. The ginger haired demon man stood and tried to grab Eric. Surprisingly, Eric stopped fighting and fell to one side. Bruce stepped up behind him.

'Well then?' Eric said to the quiet demons.

'Past Newcastle, right? Something like that. Don't you know? Don't know much, do you? Too human. All soppy emotions and animal ways,' Old Jacket said.

'Where and how?' Bruce said in a low menacing tone, with unflinching eyes.

'You...you don't know? That's a shame,' the ginger demon said sarcastically.

Eric squeezed Old Jacket around the neck. The other demons were ready to jump in and attack him, but they were afraid of Bruce. They always were. Old Jacket croaked and gasped, losing what colour there had been in his face.

'Our place this...these streets...ours. Our fear, our souls to...take,' Old Jacket murmured.

'Eric, do what you feel like, they won't touch you,' Bruce told him casually. Eric looked at him in a moment of uncertainty. Bruce took over.

184

'Where?' he asked Old Jacket, and then held up one of his gnarled, clawed hands to Old Jacket's face. A clawed finger roamed over the left pupil dangerously.

'Newcastle. Dunno, it's history anyway. All history. Your fault, isn't it?' Old Jacket said, and laughed nervously. Bruce flicked a clawed finger. He plucked out the red eye ball, a splash of thick blood dripping along the table, and other demons stood watching, shocked and silent. Old Jacket didn't scream or howl in pain: he simply stood and swaggered a little, as if he had been punched.

'Eric, do what you do best,' Bruce ordered.

The ginger demon moved up close to Bruce, but Bruce instantly lashed out, scratching his face, and jerked his neck around with a fierce twist between his clawed hands. As the body fell to the floor, he looked at the two girls, his eyes glowing a neon green hue, and they ran out through the back doors, through which many had already departed.

Eric looked at the man he held between his hands; a demon in human form, only just. He probably deserved death or prolonged sadistic torture due to opposing Bruce and his original demons. He found it extremely hard to think straight, as unnatural urges of violence fought for attention in his mind. Eric knew Bruce was waiting for him. It was just another one, Eric told himself. Just one more, one of the many already stopped by himself and Taylor. He looked at Old Jacket, who gave him a look with his one remaining red eye, which almost taunted him to act on those sinister urges.

A peculiar, nauseous feeling moved inside Eric then, and he closed his eyes as the pain stabbed suddenly. On opening his eyes, he saw the face of Old Jacket between his hands was scorched black. Between screams, dripping flesh, and dying flames, the face was smoking and had burned horrifyingly somehow in the seconds since he had last looked at him. Eric looked at Bruce, who stood smiling back at him.

'Very good. Let's go, then,' Bruce said to Eric. Eric dropped Old Jacket to the floor, the corpse falling in a charred, bloody heap. It sizzled and then suddenly flamed and crackled again, bursting into dust on the floor. He and Bruce quietly left the bar, with the other demons whispering while they left. Eric and Bruce came out on the street outside once again.

'I'm different, now...aren't I?' Eric said, and looked at Bruce for an answer as they drove along the motorway once more.

'Yes; not much, but enough. For now. You can help us more like this as we do what must be done,' Bruce explained.

'Okay. Thank you,' Eric said, and began to think about the implications. He had just burned someone – something, actually - to death with his own hands. Alright, it had been a demon, but he had done it. Just how was that possible? He knew Bruce had given him some kind of supernatural power, but he wondered how he could use it, and for how long. How much did it make him like them now that he could do this? Bruce had given him this strength, but had it taken away some element of his humanness in return, he wondered. How human was he still? How much demon was in him? Would this transference of evil power damage or taint his human soul? It troubled him gravely as they drove on together.

Eric did not actually really expect to become like them, at least not so very soon. Was that it? If Bruce had done this, passed this power or strength into him somehow, he wondered if he could keep hold of all of his human self. If he had been altered, had his spiritual self been altered as well? Did he believe that people had souls? What was Grace now? Was it the soul of Grace that he had spoken with in the last few days, or her ghost? Things were so damn confusing, he thought. These rival demons that he had killed, like Old Jacket minutes ago, they were hybrids, he remembered. What did that mean? They were human before, weren't they, he thought to himself. He wondered how human they still were. If they could keep some kind of balance, perhaps he could too, in order to use the power Bruce had allowed him. Would he then also be some kind of hybrid? What a disturbing irony, he thought. Eric was not so sure that he was totally ready to give up the life he had known, the friends, the family. The problems and trials of life were what told him that he was alive, he thought. The good times and the bad were real life, even through maddening horrors like these.

Chapter 30

Andrew and Taylor travelled along in their car through roads that were busy with night traffic.

'I appreciate what you've done, you know that? I am grateful,' Taylor told Andrew.

'She was a problem, and could be again, so you're just what I needed. He, though, isn't,' Andrew said to him while driving.

'He won't do too much. He can't, alone. And we didn't plan to. We didn't really know what we were doing at all. We were guessing, mostly. Shit, we didn't have a proper plan anyway. It was her, not him,' Taylor told him.

'You think so? We'll see. Miss him, do you?' Andrew asked surprisingly.

'What? God, no. Couldn't care less, but I mean we've only got a few hours now, haven't we?' Taylor asked.

'Right, less than that. So we're setting up the right back up. My tribe in the North can't be found or caught tonight. That includes you. He'll be caught. It's not personal, remember? Just bad luck,' Andrew explained. 'Alright with it all?'

'Fine, hell yes. No problem,' Taylor replied enthusiastically, but looking out of his window. He looked at the other cars driving past them. He thought about the people in the cars; who they were, how they lived, if they were happy and content with their lives. Some might be driving home, to families, lovers, friends, while he was a passenger on a road so close to Hell, or perhaps purgatory.

Minutes later, they arrived somewhere close to Byker, by a schoolyard and a row of office buildings. They left the car and walked toward the second building of offices. Andrew knocked intently at the front door and pressed the buzzer on the intercom. A door opened, and a rugged man peered through the gap, before slowly opening it.

'Andrew. Good evening. How are things right now?' the man asked. He looked unwashed and dirty, with slick, greasy hair and tired eyes, and seemed jittery and paranoid.

'Could be a lot better. How's the night?' Andrew asked, stepping inside.

'Things are backfiring all over the area. No stop to it. Some sicko out there we have to find, A.S.A.P. Grizzly things,' the greasy man told him.

'Not good to hear. Actually, that's why I came. I've picked up some news from around my area in the last couple of hours,' Andrew said to him. They walked on into the shadowy corridors.

'There's a guy who's been killing us and those with Bruce,' he said.

'What, a human, you mean?' the greasy guy asked in disbelief.

'Yes. Same one doing all of it. Some have seen him at a few different places. Got a description, too,' Andrew explained. Taylor saw that Andrew was holding back a good few things, twisting the truth.

'Do tell, then,' Greasy said.

'About 5'8, brown hair, white male, handsome shit. Might even be called...Dean, or Derek...Eric?' Andrew said.

'Wasn't there a couple of them?' Greasy asked, with a look of unsure curiosity.

'Maybe, but this guy is in charge. Think he's been using others just to get the results he wanted,' Andrew suggested.

'We'll look out, then. Has he been seen recently?' Greasy asked.

'Yes. Thing is...he's met with Bruce and that lot. He didn't die,' Andrew informed him.

'What does that mean?' Greasy asked

'Could mean not much. Could mean they have something going on, somehow, in some way,' Andrew said.

'What? This one human guy?' Greasy said, spitting as he spoke.

'That's right. Kill him if he's found, okay?' Andrew said.

Greasy nodded. Taylor almost spoke out, but held back anxiously. Kill Eric, he thought. He should do something to stop it, but what could he do, after lying, leaving, taking Grace from him...he felt sick and guilty as hell.

'You've heard something too, haven't you?' Andrew said, and turned to face Taylor.

'What?' Taylor said in shock.

'About our satanic loner, the clever human stopping our kind?' Andrew said, prompting him.

'Yes, I have. He's possibly...wants revenge. Some deep thing, from the past. Personal thing. Someone said they'd heard him say so,' Taylor offered. Greasy looked at him then at Andrew.

'Okay, interesting. Thank you, Andrew. I'll go use this information,' Greasy said, bowing to them.

'Tonight is very important, Arthur, no mistakes. Okay?' Andrew said. Greasy nodded silently then walked across the room they had entered. He stepped up to a door on the far side, and opened it. Two uniformed police officers came through, casually nodding to them in greeting. Taylor was bemused and waited to understand this.

'What's this?' Taylor whispered to Andrew nervously.

'Let's go, we've business elsewhere now,' Andrew said, smiling, and turned Taylor away from the men, back toward the way they came. They quickly walked back out to the car again.

Chapter 31

'Mr. Philip Pollock?' the policewoman asked.

'Yes, what's up?' the man asked.

'Mr Pollock, I don't want to upset you, but we have some serious news,' the policewoman told him.

'Come inside, then,' Pollock said.

Inside his warm house, by a glowing fire, the police woman and her male colleague carefully told him the news.

'Your daughter's boyfriend, he's been seen alive,' she said to him.

'Really? Where?' Pollock asked, visibly interested.

'Yes, out near the motorway a couple of times recently. Again yesterday. He's been around a lot. Someone else with him, too. Possibly a close friend. A girl reported it yesterday. She crashed in her car. Eric saved her from it,' the police woman told him.

'Really? You don't know where he is right now, though, do you?' Pollock asked anxiously.

'We're trying to locate him. It's difficult tonight. There's been some trouble around the area, Tynemouth and then Byker. Just wanted you to know. We'll keep you informed when we get more news. That's all for now. You're okay, are you?' she asked

'Mmm. Quite as well as I could be. Coping in my way,' Pollock told her.

He walked the police officers to the door, saying goodbye. As they left, he thought about Eric. He needed to know where he was. He had been having all kinds of disturbing thoughts pass through his mind ever since the funeral. Had he seen things, deadly things? He was not mad, he knew this, not as far as seeing some things might go. And he thought that the young man, Eric, who had possibly caused his daughter's death, might also have seen similar terrifying things himself. In fact, it just might be likely, he thought. So much rested on the actions of his deceased daughter's damned boyfriend, he was beginning to realise, as rain began to come down like endless tears from the black clouds of the dark night sky above.

The taxi pulled up sharply by the roadside of the street where Eric and Taylor had been renting the cheap hotel room. Emma did not know if she would find either of them or Peter, but she had to try. She could change Eric's mind; she had to, she told herself. She was not entirely sure what he might have gone off and done since they had separated, but she did believe that he was ready to do almost anything without giving a damn about himself and what could happen to him. She knew that he seemed pessimistic, overcome by losing Grace. She saw that he was just about giving himself up to any other thing that might take his mind away from pain. They needed each other on this night, now that they knew that serious supernatural horror could threaten their lives wherever they went. She did not want to lose him, as he had been a close, dear friend, if never anything else.

If only she could just find Peter, she knew things would be easier. Hopefully he was already with Eric, she thought, persuading him to come back home and be with friends.

Emma walked up the narrow path to the front entrance and stepped inside. The reception desk was unmanned, but then she noticed someone to her left. A thin, bookish man looked at her while he arranged some furniture.

'Looking to stay the night?' he asked her.

'No, sorry. I'm not. I'm here to find a friend of mine; well, a couple of friends. Do you know if two young men called Eric and Taylor have stayed here in the last few days?' Emma asked in the nicest manner.

'I'm sorry. I just can't give out details of any customers who stay,' the man explained. She saw that he seemed genuinely sorry and apologetic.

'So that's yes, then, is it? Please, it really is incredibly important that I find them tonight. They could be in so much danger. They are very dear friends of mine. You have no idea at all where they might have gone?' she asked him. She almost even batted her eyes and trailed a hand around her chest to loosen him up.

The man looked at her thoughtfully. He was obviously considering just what harm could come from telling this very attractive young woman a little information. She waited until he finally decided to speak.

191

'They were here. Not anymore; they left this morning, one before the other. Think they might have fallen out, had an argument or something,' he explained helpfully.

'Really? Okay, thank you. But any idea where they are at all? Please, anything?' Emma asked. She pouted her lips, licking them just a little.

'Not really, sorry. Kind of kept to themselves. You could see the police if they're in trouble. You don't want to get into trouble looking for them,' he warned in a friendly way.

'Right. Thanks for your concern. That's it, then? Well, thank you anyway. Goodbye mister, take care,' she said. She winked at him as she walked away.

He reached out and touched her arm as she was going.

'There is something else. Another person was looking for them. A church guy, a youth person or something, he said,' the man added.

'Oh God, Peter,' Emma said, pleased.

'Yes, he said you might be here at some point. Said to ring him on a number. You're Emma, right?' the man asked

'Maybe I am,' she replied, as he took out a piece of paper from his pocket and handed it to her.

'Thank you very much. Bless you. Be careful tonight,' she told him

'You too, young lady,' he replied, smiling at her. He watched her leave, and sighed to himself.

Chapter 32

Two men stood outside a busy pub enjoying a cigarette each and discussing work, women and football. They were dressed smartly and were reasonably wealthy in appearance, with expensive suits, gym-honed physiques and strong tans.

'So that girl at second floor, you been in her pants yet?' the black haired man asked the blonde one.

'Oh yeah, great little minx, that one. And her sister. Trying for her mother, too. Just as tasty looking believe me!' Blonde man said.

'So how's the wife?' Blonde creep asked.

'Don't ask. Probably try that redhead behind the bar later. Unless you want her?' Black hair said.

'Really, how about we both enjoy that one? Been a while, hasn't it?' Blonde creep said.

'Could do, and pick up a couple more then over to my pal's hotel again?' Black hair suggested. They both smiled wicked grins at each other, along with dirty laughter.

A car pulled up suddenly beside the two men at the curb. Eric stepped out quickly and grabbed Blonde creep.

'Who? Hey, you little ba...' Blonde began, as he struggled with Eric. Immediately the friend tried to throw a punch at Eric, but he recoiled, hunching down in visible pain when Eric looked at him. The man tried to shout out, but only blood dribbled forth from his mouth as he fell to his knees. Even though Eric was smaller in stature and thinner than Blonde creep, he was somehow able to pull him toward the car with little effort at all. Eric covered the man's mouth and clawed his face. The opposite door of the car opened. Bruce stepped out, and quickly grabbed the second man. Bruce and Eric pulled the two sharp dressed men into the back of their car. Bruce sat at the wheel and drove them away before anyone saw the deed.

Icy cold night air blew past his face as Peter sat thoughtfully alone on the roof of the Newcastle University main building. He had been there a half dozen times by himself. He was not the sort to find strange places to ponder or watch folk normally, but since graduating he had returned to this secret place, finding it to be calming and peaceful. He even thought that he sometimes felt closer to God up there, alone with the vast, magnificent clouds over him. Out along the edge of the roof he could see the entire skyline of Newcastle at night, the darkness pin-pricked with hundreds and thousands of amber lights illuminating the blackness around. They signified life, energy, living, being. Hope in darkness, hope in dark times. People were alive in the darkness of night out there, he thought. They were people who could shine in the darkness that was always around.

He sat back then once again, closed his eyes and spoke to his God. He asked for answers to the night's problems; for strength, hope, courage, protection and guidance, for help to go to Eric, Taylor and Emma. And then for understanding of what was really attacking the place he knew as home. He opened up, acknowledged his fear, his ignorance, arrogance and guilt. He asked for forgiveness and help.

He knew that God might not provide an answer right then. It was not to his wishes, but to God's wishes, in God's good time. He knew that, even as frustrating as that could be. He did not hear God right then. He believed that he had, up there before: he was sure of it.

But tonight it was deadly quiet. He knew why. He sighed, shook his head. His right hand made a fist and he punched the concrete wall before him at the edge of the rooftop in sheer anger. He just wanted it stopped. He wanted intervention, salvation from above, but realised that it would come when it was the time and not before.

He saw blood trickle from the torn skin on his knuckles as his mobile phone suddenly rang in his pocket. It rang a classic rock ringtone loudly. Startled back into the real world, he felt inside his pocket.

'Hello? Who is it?' he said, having opened up the phone.

'Peter, it's Eric's friend, Emma,' she said coyly, overjoyed to hear him.

'Hi Emma,' he said in a slight daze. He wiped the blood from his knuckles.

'Sorry, is it okay to talk?' she said, unsure.

'Yes, fine, of course. Good, even. Where are you? Are you safe?' he asked.

'I'm near Wallsend, or Walker now,' Emma explained.

'Okay. You're okay though, are you?' Peter said again.

'Yes for now. I've been trying to reach you and Eric and Taylor,' she told him.

'Emma, what do you know about them, I mean what's Eric done?' Peter asked.

'He's not guilty of anything, really. Well, he's saved people, him and Taylor, but now there's something just so dangerous happening. I don't completely get it. Well, I wish I didn't get it,' Emma said all at once, being honest and open.

'I know. Right, you've confirmed my thoughts. I'm not out to get them, I want to help. I really believe you and what you say about them,' Peter said

'Could we meet up, as we're both looking for them?' Emma asked.

'Yes, we have to,' Peter agreed. He smiled to himself and thanked God for her call as he began to descend the staircase.

'Where are we taking these guys?' Eric said to Bruce as they drove along at a break-neck speed.

'To a suitable place. You're angry, aren't you?' Bruce said.

'What? Why do you think that?' Eric asked, though he admittedly was.

'Angry at a whole lot of shit in your life, aren't you?' Bruce asked calmly.

'I've lost people I've loved. That has pissed me off considerably. Other than that…everything's peachy. Well, I mean I can be the loud, happy guy, but I do currently have some things that fuel my fire,' Eric admitted.

'Of course. All strong men do. All the champions, kings, leaders, revolutionaries are powered by tragedy or clueless faith. We'll satisfy the anger. Men anger men in this world, fight, kill, use each other, and fool each other for…not much at all. The dictators, leaders, crazy men were all insecure and scared. But you, you're angry. Now you're more than the man you were. Tell me your worst, most savage thoughts of hate and anger,' Bruce said.

'I don't know…I kind of tend to suppress those thoughts mostly. Kick a ball around, get drunk or write music on my guitar. It's what I know to do,' Eric told him.

'I want to see it, the you that wants to scream, kill, destroy, control and make his mark. Let go,' Brue explained

He steered the car along and stopped it by the front of a vast, empty car park somewhere unrecognisable to Eric. Bruce stepped out of the car and opened the back, pulling out one of the businessmen violently with no pity. Eric stepped out, opening the passenger door at his side of the car and pulling out the other man. Eric and Bruce stood over their gagged, bound men among the desolate, empty industrial landscape.

'So what do these blokes know?' Eric asked Bruce.

'First, I want you to enjoy yourself. That man is a canvas for your anger. Paint the canvas,' Bruce told him.

Eric looked at him unsure, not particularly liking the idea of what Bruce was suggesting. Eric was hugely angry at the world, at God, at life, at the police, at nearly everything he knew. Was he angry at these two men? Why the hell not, he considered. They did seem to be a pair of very arrogant, macho, sexist bastards. But still...to just kill or torture them? That was not me, Eric thought. No matter how angry I get, I'm not Manson or the Ripper, he thought. He knew people often argued over whether those serial killer types are born that way or if they were bred that way by society. It's not in my genes, my family tree, and I was not abused by society, he thought. He knew Bruce and his kind slaughtered people like others buy groceries. That was them. It was him now too. And who the hell could stop them, or him?

Bruce suddenly grabbed the man below him, who squirmed as he tried to loosen the ropes that bound him. Bruce pulled him up to look into his face and blew air into his eyes then like some strange hypnotist. When he blew, flesh flew straight off the man's skull, like leaves blown down an autumn street. Blood flecked across and over Eric a little. The man cried and gave out a painful howl, as Bruce then prodded a clawed finger in around the loose, sinewy mess that covered the man's exposed skull.

'Now you,' Bruce said as he dropped the man to the ground like a ragdoll, 'but don't finish him. Do whatever, but make him speak.'

Eric looked at the horror that Bruce had inflicted on this man, visually unrecognisable from just a moment earlier. Eric felt his stomach turn, but he saw the opportunity before him. He needed Bruce that night. All emotions could be false. He should forget emotions and follow instinct, he thought.

Eric stepped toward the disfigured man shaking at his feet. He spoke quietly to him.

'You must cooperate with us, with me. This night unbelievable things are happening. I will spare you as much as I can, if you tell us

196

what you do know,' Eric said reasonably. The faceless man quivered and spat in Eric's face. Eric took hold of the man by the arms and flames sprang up, running along the man instantly from Eric. Bruce watched quietly, pleased, while Eric held the burning man, waiting for any words. The man screamed loud and horrifically, but Eric only stared right into his eyes, waiting.

'Speak to live,' Eric suggested impatiently. He looked at Bruce, who had begun to shake his head in dismay. Eric turned back to the burning man and held him up almost effortlessly.

'This will get much worse, if you don't talk. That might sound almost impossible but believe me, it could happen,' Eric told him.

'I... deserve this,' the man whispered in pain as chunks of his melting flesh dropped away.

'To hell with you,' Eric said, and shook the man around. The man seemed to shrivel, twist and melt in Eric's hands. Blood and sinew dripped and fell over the ground as Bruce approached Eric.

'I expected that. Let's try the other one,' he told Eric.

Eric looked at Bruce as he tried to understand just how he had burned and melted a living man with nothing but his own two hands.

'I think you'll be quicker than me, don't you?' Eric said, not entirely looking forward to burning a living man by hand again so soon.

'But this is about you tonight. Proving yourself, revealing yourself. The only time,' Bruce explained. Just as he finished speaking, they heard sirens wailing out from some streets close by.

'We'd better move the next one in the car. Get some place else before we try him,' Bruce warned. Eric nodded in agreement, and they quickly pulled the other man up back into car boot then drove away, just as two police cars arrived at the top of the street.

Chapter 33

After making arrangements, Emma agreed to drive to the place where Peter ended up. She drove along, with punk rock tunes keeping her spirits up as she moved between cars and lanes speedily. She knew the demon things were out possibly everywhere and anywhere right that minute, but she still knew very little about how to combat them most effectively. Knowing the danger was enough.

Five minutes earlier, Emma had phoned her parents. She needed to warn her mother, father and family, but without sounding crazy or making them too panicked.

'Hello Dad?' Emma said, hearing him answer.

'Emma, where are you?' he asked in a calm enough manner.

'I'm out with friends right now,' she told him. 'Dad, where's Mum?' she asked, trying to keep calm.

'She's on the computer to your Aunt in America. Do you want to speak to her?' he asked.

'Well, no, but...Dad, you're not going out anywhere tonight, are you? Any of you?' Emma asked nervously.

'We didn't have anything planned, no, why? What's the matter?' he asked.

'Nothing, just wondered. Could you stay in, actually? I think I want to see you all when I get back later. That okay?' Emma asked.

'Yes, I suppose. Emma, you're not in any kind of trouble now are you?' he asked. 'Be honest with me.'

'Oh no, not me, not at all. Of course not,' Emma quickly answered.

'Any man problems, then? You'd tell me? You know I'll help you any time, both of us,' her father explained reassuringly.

'Just please don't leave the house, okay Dad?' she said.

'Okay, if that's what you want, we won't. Be careful dear, please. You'll come home soon, will you?' he asked.

'When I can, yes. I might be a while, but...Dad, I love you and Mum, okay?' she said. She just could not help herself. She pictured them in her head, her family with their problems, opinions, advice. They were hers whatever. They knew and loved her, and she loved them back at a time like this. She held back tears.

'You're sure there's nothing bad going on, Emma? Tell me if there is,' he said.

'Dad, just please wait for me at home. Don't go out, any of you, please. I'll be there later,' Emma told him. She ended the call. She was starting to cry just a little, tears forming around her eyes. She cried for a moment before laughing to herself, then started the car engine and drove away.

Mr Donald Lewis sat watching the sports channels alone in his modest, old house, with a simple microwave meal on his lap in his small front room, a flickering dim lamp light at his side revealing the shrivelled food. A knock came to his front door, disturbing his focus on the football action. He cursed the person knocking, thought about answering, but then simply continued watching the football match.

The knocking continued. It really annoyed him, like an uncomfortable itch, or a yapping dog. After waiting another minute or so he finally stood and walked through to the door in a foul mood. He opened the door reluctantly.

'You again,' he said flatly, seeing Grace's father Philip staring back on his doorstep.

'Can we talk yet, Donald?' Philip asked.

Donald Lewis sighed and looked out behind Philip, then made eye contact.

'I'm sorry, you know I am. He's a jerk, my son. I'm just sorry, okay,' Donald said.

'I know you are. I also know that he genuinely loved my daughter too,' Philip added. Since the funeral, and really since Eric had started seeing her, Philip and Donald had not been good friends. There were obvious class tensions between them, but Donald was also simply a little jealous of both Philip's perfect business accomplishments and similarly perfect family life. Donald had suspected a condescending attitude from him, looking down on his more simple working class life as opposed to Philip's obvious level of wealth.

This would not normally have irritated Donald so much, but the real problem was what Philip thought of Eric. Donald himself fought with his son regularly, and they both had individual problems in their lives, but that was a private family thing between only Eric and Donald. This snob of a man had seemed to not believe Eric good enough for his precious daughter. Big headed, selfish fucking capitalist, was all Donald ever thought whenever he saw Philip.

'I know you're sorry. I really don't think that Eric was directly involved in the death of Grace, so please accept my sincere apologies, Donald. I do not wish any harm to come to him, really,' Philip told him.

'Well that's good to hear, I have to say,' Donald said, not totally convinced but wishing to seem understanding and civil.

'Can I come in?' Philip asked politely.

They sat in the front room and looked around uncomfortably, as if the appropriate words were somewhere in the atmosphere waiting to be found.

'Are things getting easier now?' Donald said.

'Not much, but just acceptable in a way. Sort of. Good to have family around,' Philip explained. He looked visibly irritated, extremely tired and slightly uncomfortable talking about Grace, but seemed to want to.

'She was very special. A good one, a really beautiful young lady. Very clever, intelligent, good sense of humour too. Eric liked that,' Donald told him.

'Yes, you're right totally. Donald, I came to talk about him, actually. Look, I see how it has hit him now. Poor young man. They were much closer than I knew, I now realise, or wanted to accept. I've seen her journal, you see,' Philip explained.

'Oh right,' Donald replied, feeling uncomfortable. He did not know where the conversation was going, and really did not want to speak much longer with Philip. They were not friends, and not the sort of people to be friends, as far as he could see. He was honestly sorry for the man's loss, but they would not be the kind of men to naturally spend much time together and so should not pretend otherwise, he thought.

'Grace really did love your son. They were making plans, to live together, travel more overseas, things like that. He seemed actually quite a stable lad; thoughtful, protective of her. Even, well, level-headed,' Philip told him.

'He's not much like me, it comes from his mother. God rest her soul. Eric rarely takes any advice from me, but that's probably for the best,' Donald said, and let out a slight laugh to himself. 'Glad you think he's a nice young man now.'

'I think he's very unique, a special guy. Have you heard from him? He's not here?' Philip asked.

Donald sighed then looked around the room.

'No, no I haven't, but that's not too unusual. The police have paid a visit earlier on, unsurprisingly. Probably will hear soon; he does call, but well...he's coping with this all in his own way...he's with friends, I believe,' Donald explained.

'Right. Well, that's a good thing. I hope he returns soon or phones to say...' Philip began, then he stopped speaking, distracted by the television news in the corner of the room.

'What's that?' he said, seeming shocked.

'What?' Donald asked, and looked over with him. They both looked at the television screen in stunned fascination.

The news reporters were explaining crimes around the city and around the motorway that night. This was the first either of them had heard of the terrible atrocities. There was a C.C.T.V. image of a man caught near a petrol station that seemed to look just like Eric.

'Hang on a minute...' Donald said, shocked.

'It looks like him,' Philip said amazed.

'I know...no, that's not right. Suppose you'll change your mind again now. Didn't think it would last. He's a bloody fool at times,' Donald said, not feeling too hopeful. They watched the news report together.

"In the last hour a number of truly shocking and uncommonly brutal attacks have taken place around various parts of Newcastle and the surrounding area. A number of people have been found dead and some are at present injured or still missing. Police are remaining quiet at present about the causes of these attacks, though a small number of people are suggesting strange, possibly occult activity, or a group of serial attackers with possibly political motives behind it all.

"People are seriously advised now to keep indoors and report any unusual activity to local police as soon as possible. There is danger out there, but police also wish to stress that they are out right now, addressing the situation. There is, however, speculation regarding the two young men seen near a couple of the areas where attacks have occurred. The police have not strictly confirmed the connection of the men, but are looking into the identities of both and urge people to contact them if they recognise the young men or have seen them elsewhere..."

'Jesus Christ...' Philip said, amazed and considering the likelihood of the image really being Eric.

'Bloody news media. Exaggerate anything. Just selling papers, and lies. He messes about but the news is all owned and made by rich old white men. A distraction from the real problems of our world. Capturing our idle imaginations, that's all. Making money on gossip, that's it,' Donald said in response, in some way defending his son.

'That's Eric, Donald. You can't deny it. Look, it's him,' Philip said, and pointed at the screen. He stood and began to walk out of the house. Donald quickly followed him, surprised.

'Wait, hey, what are you doing? Where are you going now?' Donald asked.

'I have to go and return to my family. Bad things are happening, Donald, like the news said,' Philip told him calmly.

'Oh don't believe all of that bollocks, mate. Look, that's not Eric, okay? I mean, I'm a fat old waste of space, but he's not! He's a good young man!' Donald shouted after Philip as he walked to his car and got inside.

Donald stood next to the car door as Philip started the engine.

'Don't do anything stupid, Philip. He loved Grace. You understand that, don't you?' Donald said. He gave up. He watched Philip drive away then returned to his house, punching the front door as he entered. His son was in trouble, he realised, his only damn son. The one who was the reason he had not drank himself to death years ago.

Chapter 34

The Williamson family left their house to drive out into the quiet dark night. Mr Joseph Williamson instructed his wife and two teenage sons to come with him across the estate over to the old church so that they could pray to a God they had almost forgotten for safety through this suddenly horrific night. In only the last few hours Joseph had learned that his close friend and his friend's wife had disappeared.

In the last half hour, the family had spoken quietly to next door neighbours, all of them extremely shocked and in severe panic about what was being broadcast on television and the radio and internet about the dangerous events in the area. It terrified them all, as only a short while before they had been relaxing watching repeat programs on TV, doing chores around the house as usual. Now the most unnerving tales, ones which only usually appeared across the newspaper front pages every few years nationwide, had come to their town.

They had all listened to the cautious warnings from the police and local authorities, and eventually the family prepared to leave the house, only because of Joseph's decision.

'Please, can't we wait longer?' his wife, Laura, asked quietly as she followed him.

'No, we've waited long enough already. This is all deadly serious, Laura. We need protection,' he told her.

'There are police out there. We've heard them. They're there protecting us now,' she told him.

'Can't we wait at home for you and mum?' the younger son, Chris, asked.

'No, you can't. You're coming with us. Staying with us. We're staying together,' Joseph told him.

'Dad, I don't believe in God. Neither does Chris,' the other son, Paul, said.

'Well, you don't have to do anything. Just come along,' Joseph said, they noticed curtains moving behind windows slightly, as some people were watching them, amazed at their courage or stupidity in leaving the safety of their home so soon.

'You don't believe, do you Dad? In God?' Chris asked.

'What?' Joseph shot back distractedly.

'I mean, it won't mean anything, will it, and all the scientists, atheists, all with their own clever theories...people worship TV, popstars, film stars, don't they?' Chris said philosophically.

'So I haven't been to a church in a while, but I've always believed. Just never much liked the organized religion aspect, but now...Spirituality, now that's different altogether,' Joseph told them.

'Mum?' Chris said, wondering about her point of view.

'Your father wants to keep us safe. We're going. Stay close now, both of you. Stop asking questions,' she said in a nervous voice.

They walked with a torch each, along grass and pavement toward a church that had almost been pulled down until recently. Joseph did hope that he was doing the right thing. He never did such random, brave things, but he felt it might just be worthwhile taking his family there. He did have a childhood upbringing of churchgoing, and, like most people, had drifted from the church, but never too far from belief or faith. The tales that they had heard in the last few hours made them sick, horrified and scared more than almost anything in their lives ever had before. They were all cynical at first, but as they saw that the reports were very really serious, they all became genuinely frightened.

Joseph knew there were police out there, but he did not believe that they might be enough to hold back or defeat this murderous, mysterious force. It was simply one of those rare times, he had thought. Only a very small number of times in his life so far had he known truly disturbing occurrences, and this seemed to be the worst yet. Worse than gangs, worse than riots, worse than life threatening diseases. This force was unknown, indescribable evil.

'Look. Dad, there's Mr. Norwick and his family down there,' Chris said, pointing out across the streets under the light of street lamps.

'Oh yeah. See? Not such a crazy idea,' Joseph said to them.

They then noticed another few people from around the neighbourhood walking along other streets opposite as they came nearer the town centre. The wind whistled by, a strange moan through the night air. With it came a similar but less familiar sound, and they looked around individually, a little more unsure and afraid. Chris then called out over to the son of Mr. Norwick.

'Hey! Dean! You okay?' he asked.

Dean and his father were walking, and suddenly Mr Norwick was jerked quickly into the shadows by a dark shape. He was violently pulled across a few feet behind bushes and trees. Dean and his mother watched in shock, and then Dean stepped in, thinking only of saving his father. In the shadows of oak trees, Mr Norwick screamed in agony, as he was twisted, torn and beaten out of view from others. The sounds bursting out intermittently were painful to know. When Dean came up, blood washed him, from his tattered father, as the mystery attacker quickly lashed out and grabbed him.

Chris and his own family could only see fleeting glimpses of horror between the trees and shadows, but the soundtrack of it all was enough to make them almost physically sick. Chris saw the blazing red eyes from within the deep black shadows, red blood splattering around, and heard the endless painful screams.

'Jesus above, what's happening over there?' Chris said.

'Run, come on. Run toward the church everyone now!' his father commanded.

Someone else screamed from another direction nearby, on the other side of the road. Chris and his brother looked around to locate the origin of the screams.

'Just ignore it. Come on, quickly,' their father urged.

Chris looked back. He saw the red eyes sparkling in deep shadows, looking right at him, or so it seemed. The moonlight picked out the blood spilled along the road and pavement across the road.

'My God...' Chris said. This was insane, just unbelievable, he thought. It could not be happening, to them, so close, right then, but it was. It was a horror film come to life, an ultra-violent video game that he could not escape.

Another scream erupted from some other streets very close to them.

'It's all over,' he said, thinking about the unknown danger surrounding all of them in the streets. These damn red eyes. Do the two guys in the news have red fucking eyes like this? No way, he decided.

'Come on Christopher, now!' his father said sternly. Chris just had to look deep into the shadows, wondering what was really killing and why.

'It's not them,' Chris said slowly to himself.

There was a growling noise as he joined his family in running. The old church was in view, reliable, humble and waiting. The closer they got, though, the more screams and cries burst out loudly from around them.

'Dad, these people...people are dying, Dad,' Chris said.

'Yes, well we could be next. Keep moving,' his brother told him.

'Shut up, I'm just...' Chris started, giving up. He knew his family had to look after themselves, but he wondered if they did not also have time or responsibility to try to save others from around their town. This was life, he thought. Like people in more extreme situations overseas he had heard about, in countries where people were threatened and terrified daily, oppressed by corrupt governments, abused, denied human rights. But his family, they had to save themselves before others, apparently. The strong survive, it seemed, no matter where, no matter what.

'Jesus, what now?' Chris said in shock.

'Wait...' his father said.

'We've no chance. Shit, this is it,' Chris's brother exclaimed.

'Bullshit, look, they've got those people over there. We...we can go now, can't we?' Chris asked. His father nodded and led Chris, his mother and brother quickly across the road past the horror on the streets behind.

'Keep quiet, run now. Don't stop at all,' he told them all.

'Claire!' A woman shouted in a loud whisper out from the street to the left. She waved and began to run out toward them.

'Who's that?' Chris's father asked in frustration.

'It's Sheila, from my poetry class,' his wife told him.

'Okay, well keep moving,' he said.

'Wait,' his wife said, pleased to see her friend.

'We have to go. Seriously, now please, Claire,' he said in a nervous, quiet voice.

'Shit, Mum!' Chris said. He took her arm, gently pulling her.

Sheila came out into the quiet road, and before she crossed to the other side, something with claws ran out instantly and grabbed her.

'Oh my God!' Claire said, frightened, and put a hand over her mouth.

'Come on now,' her husband advised.

'We have to help her...' she said.

'No, we can't risk it now. We just can't. We can't,' he told her.

'No Samaritans, now,' Chris said. They began to run on again.

Claire took a brief glance behind her and saw her friend and her friend's husband being taken apart, their blood on the road everywhere in seconds. She threw up uncontrollably, but her husband pulled her on with the two teen boys. They heard cries, screams in every direction just as they finally approached the sanctuary of the church, waiting for them like it always had been.

These killings were psychotically repulsive and vile. This was not a normal time, though, and they all acknowledged it. Even demons like these felt vulnerable and paranoid, with a heightened need to exhibit their brutal killings.

It was an example, not really for most humans, police or other institutions, but specifically for Eric and Taylor. They had angered both separate tribes of demons, who now were showing what they had gotten themselves into.

Chapter 35

Behind these savage random attacks on the streets of North Shields, Andrew walked up with a couple of fellow hybrid demon brothers, inspecting the carnage and waste, the spilled flesh and blood in the gutter of the streets.

'Unholy shit, this is wild. Glorious fun, this wasting human clay,' one hybrid by his left said to him.

These two hybrids at either side of Andrew seemed to continually be shape-shifting, deforming their appearances between a myriad of ugly, disturbing amalgamations of dog, wolf, goat, ape and some kind of man. The only constant was their piercing red eyes, like Andrew himself had.

'Can we do more of this? We never do enough. We are demons, aren't we?' the other murmured.

'I need to remind you, do I, of the past attacks and confrontations we have encountered?' Andrew said, looking at his companions with dismay. 'Listen, these past centuries have allowed us to gain our own place. We have challenged the stronghold of the dominant original demonic tribe. We have our own ways of existing around the humans of the North. As they have seen industries rise and fall, economy dip and jobs disappear on mass scale, desperation and poverty, we were there. In this country, they think these people are less, they are considered lower because of where they are, what they had been doing. We kept them alive, we saw their pride.'

'Bruce knows our way, he's been setting us up to fall for years now. This could be it right now, don't you think?' one suggested.

'You really think so? I think those demons are desperate. I think they fear the humans are more confident and assured than they've been for many decades now. Confident humans will not easily fall for simple traps and temptations. So Bruce and his kind will attack us, yes, due to simple bitterness and aggression. We can use this,' Andrew replied calmly.

Andrew knelt down by one of the gutted and blood-encrusted bodies on the road. He touched it, feeling the warmth of the skin, the wet blood dripping down the clothes. They never usually killed like this if they could help it. He tried to always make sure of that. He and the hybrid demon men and women at his command were proudly skilled and more used to manipulating people, hurting them and torturing them psychologically. Andrew had been taught from his early days as a hybrid the new, challenging ways of dominating and controlling mankind, which used their latent human nature and characteristics.

Bruce and the original demons only ever butchered like this haplessly, like simple predators in the wild. Andrew was more than a predator, he knew he had been a man and almost half of him still was. This, he believed, gave him and all the other hybrids unique ingenuity, cunning, objectiveness, and a thoughtfulness that the original demons were devoid of and always would be. Seeing these results of their unscheduled wild attack brought him down, made him remember his distance from his old human life. The evil in him had festered, grown, creeping over his humanity. As a hybrid, those emotions and traits were pushed back while lust and aggression took control.

'Is it enough? No, let's keep doing it. To Byker next?' the first hybrid suggested.

'Perhaps. We are good at this, aren't we? These souls are ours. No deals, no blackmails this time. No deals,' Andrew said aloud. He stood and kicked at the body on the ground in anger, entrails scattering on the road.

'Down we go,' he said as he continued to walk down the road with his distorted demon hybrids.

Byker had been ignored for decades, with its broken down houses, crumbling school buildings, its abandoned shops. Like a smaller but still proud sibling to the larger Newcastle beside it, the people of Byker always lifted their heads high in defiance of the bad economy and job losses. Now they were forgetting about dole ques and grey futures. In the streets there, like those all across the North that evening, people either hid in their homes or tried to reach them as fast as they could.

By now, police were responding to the reports of attacks and dead bodies found that early evening and afternoon. The people of Byker did have still a certain amount of confidence and hope amongst the horror as a number of police cars appeared from Newcastle and Gateshead. A number of respected, police detectives and officers arrived to protect the people, to save them and meet the dangers head on. Like almost everyone, they were assuming and believing the deaths and attacks to be the acts of these two supposedly deranged men, as the rumours and reports were telling them.

Eric and Taylor were wanted in connection to some of the earlier events, but somehow, now that these rumours had circulated, they were the only main suspects, and voices high up in police departments communicated this opinion.

A handful of people wandered along the Byker city main streets, with fear and dread pushing them on. Seeing the police cars parked at the end of the street, a couple of people walked up to meet them, hoping for answers. A thin, ginger haired man named Thom greeted two police officers, who stood by their car watching the streets around.

'Hello. What's the latest? I mean, what's really happening? How many have died now?' he asked.

The two officers stood silent and still, watching him until one of them eventually spoke.

'Too many already. Two young men, dangerous killers. Get home now, we advise it. How far do you have to go?' the officer asked him.

'Oh, a couple more streets. Are there many more police around across town?' Thom asked.

'Yes, enough. We're working on finding these evil bastards and protecting all of you as best we can. Be very careful. There should be another couple of our cars and more officers down the next few streets now,' the officer explained.

'Why are they doing it? These killers, I mean?' Thom asked.

The two officers looked slightly annoyed, even a little angry.

'We really can't take time to talk about that, sir,' the second officer told him in a stern voice.

Thom and a blonde woman walking along near him then heard some sort of loud wail a street or two away.

'What's that?' she said, turning to look around.

'You should both continue on home now. Don't worry about that, and don't stop for anything,' the second officer told them.

'Is that them? The noise? Could that be the killers?' Thom asked curiously.

'Just go home. If it's those two men, you'll regret standing around too long,' the police officer said.

'Okay, okay,' Thom said. He and the blonde woman began to walk off, watching the officers as they talked into their shoulder radio sets.

'It's frightening, isn't it?' the blonde woman said to Thom suddenly.

'Sorry? Yes, very. Many kinds of danger around tonight,' he agreed. 'Do you have far to go home?' he asked.

'Well, a few more streets, yes. I'll be okay, I suppose,' she said.

'Plenty of police all around. Do you think they're doing what they should be?' Thom asked her as they walked on quickly.

'What do you mean?' she asked.

'Well do you think that's those two guys somewhere over there who we heard?' he asked.

'I don't know. What are you saying exactly?' she asked, sounding confused.

'These murders happening are literally all over. How are two guys doing it all by themselves so quickly?' he said.

'You think there's more people involved?' she asked.

'Absolutely. But the police don't seem to let on.'

'But people are dying. We should keep going,' she reminded him politely.

They heard some kind of scream or howl to their right, and looked at each other.

'Come to my place. I'm okay, really. You'll be safer than continuing on much further alone,' Thom said. 'I'm a decent bloke. I promise.'

'I'm Sarah,' she told him while she looked around, visibly fearful.

'Come on,' he said with a polite smile.

'Are they around us, the two of them?' she asked.

Thom looked around. He could still see some police officers running down a street behind them, and could hear a siren wailing loudly.

'Police are around us. Maybe something else as well. I don't think the two guys are near. But we still need to move now,' he stressed to her.

They walked on under the thin light of street lamps. They then saw other people running out across an opening before them beyond the main road and a grassy area ahead.

'Oh shit, oh my God,' Sarah said quietly.

'Might not be anything,' Thom told her. 'Look, let's turn that way,' he said, pointing.

The sounds in the streets nearby were certainly bizarre, he thought, all kinds of unpleasant howls and depraved moans. This just is not two guys, no way, Thom thought. The police won't tell us, or they don't know themselves, he thought.

A police car drove right in front of them and Thom waved at the driver.

'Hey!' he shouted. The police officer at the wheel wound down the window as he stopped his car.

'Are you alright?' the officer asked them.

'They're all over, in every direction. We hear them, what does that mean?' Thom asked.

'Just get home to safety right now. Behind locked doors. You're okay?' the officer said.

'Yes, we're fine. Just wanted some answers,' Thom told him.

'Can't give any yet. Just get to safety, okay? We have to go. Do you want a lift?' The officer asked.

'Well...okay,' Thom said, looking at Sarah as she nodded silently.

They got into the police car and were driven toward Thom's flat, as he instructed the officer on directions.

'Do you know why these guys are doing this?' Thom asked after a couple of minutes.

'We can't say much, sorry,' the second officer in the car told him.

'Right, of course. It's very strange. It seems to be dangerous all over at nearly the same time,' Thom told them.

'They may have help,' one of the officers said.

'You are near enough along here now, aren't you?' the other officer said.

'What? Well, alright. Thank you,' Thom said with suspicion.

He and Sarah got out of the car and watched it drive away, leaving them alone on the street.

'I've got no idea what's happening right now,' Sarah said to Thom as they continued to Thom's front door.

'The police are lying to us. To everyone. People are dying, and they're not stopping it. They're doing something else,' he said. He turned the key and he and Sarah entered his flat.

Chapter 36

Philip walked back inside his home, saddened and frustrated from his unsuccessful meeting with Eric's father. He walked on through the hall, and met his wife and daughter, who sat in the kitchen together drinking coffee.

'Hello, are you alright?' his wife asked with affection.

'Oh, I'm alright. Just seen a friend. How are you two?' he asked.

'Philip, some horrible things have happened around the area,' his wife said.

'What do you mean? Like what?' he asked.

'People are dead, Dad,' his second daughter Lilly exclaimed.

'Why? Anyone we know?' he asked in shock.

'No, I don't believe so. Not yet,' his wife said quietly and looked out of the window.

'Dad, I'm scared. It's on the news. It's all over; Tynemouth, Byker, Newcastle, everywhere,' his daughter told him.

'Is this right?' he asked his wife. She nodded without looking at him.

Philip walked through to the lounge and switched on the television. He flicked the channels for a minute, and then found the local station news.

There it was. Many reporters all scrambling around in the dark streets, police keeping them back from the glimpses of blood and damage to walls, fences and cars around in the background. Philip sat forward, watching.

"...unbelievable events around the North East tonight. At least five people have been murdered in similarly brutal and outlandish ways in the last few hours across the region. The reasons for and perpetrators of these most horrifying occurrences are open to debate, and police are offering few details. No official police statements are being..."

Then, on another channel:

"...told to keep safe at home, with doors securely locked, alarms on, and answering to only people you actually know. Phone police if any..."

And another channel:

"...unbelievable, truly shocking. Police seem terribly unfocused, maybe that's why..."

Then on the first again:

"...the churches and temples are uniting, it seems. Local priests and vicars of various denominations and faiths are taking people into their places of worship. Families are praying and wanting spiritual protection, guidance, safety from what many believe is some unexplainable dark force at work..."

Philip's wife walked in and saw him staring with fascination at the reports.

'It's so shocking. I was worried for you while you were gone,' she told him, putting an arm around him.

'Listen, I have to go out again. I won't be long but I really have to...' he began.

'No, Philip. You can't. Are you mad? Why? You don't have to,' she said, a look of fear and concern on her face.

'I... a friend needs me. I have to be a good friend,' he told her.

'No, you heard the news reports. It's a killer or a gang just murdering people, anyone at all. It's too dangerous, Philip. People are dying on the streets outside. Don't go out. Not you too, not after Grace,' she said, pleading with him.

He pulled his arm from her grasp, and walked out. As she followed him to the front door, Lilly came to see them arguing.

'Lock the doors, all the locks. Curtains closed, and keep your phone on you. Don't answer the door unless it's me or someone we know well,' Philip told her as he opened the door to leave. Lilly watched, horrified, while his wife closed the door.

Philip took his car out back along the coast road, drove for a short time, and then slowed down by a row of quiet pubs and buildings, some closed and some disused. He pulled up along the end of the row.

Many more police cars and officers were driving around, some looking for Eric and Taylor. The genuine police officers spread and mixed with the many unknown hybrid demon officers. The law of men was no law to trust for certain now, though many still would with doubtful hesitation. They looked for people who could easily die, who might be useful dead.

After a short while, as deaths mounted, rumours began to spread. No two people could agree for long on exactly what was out there to be afraid of, they could only agree to be very afraid. From the city station, a commanding superintendent made a televised announcement, saying that it seemed likely now that the two suspects had at least another two or more helpers, which could explain the events so far. This new theory kept people insanely frightened and fearful for even longer.

Everyone except Eric and Taylor, when they heard the news, though they individually had other things to be just as scared of in the coming hours ahead of them. They were each in deep between the darkest powers around the land.

Sometime after ten o'clock, the streets of Newcastle, and the other Northern towns and boroughs were just about deadly quiet, with only a very small number of lost or foolish people still walking or running for their lives. Dozens of police cars drove along the silent roads, patrolling and sending back and forth news and information between groups of police. Just outside of Newcastle, along by Jesmond on the coast road, a number of police cars parked up by a service area and stopped inside. After collecting coffees and some sandwiches and snacks, they sat around out by their cars discussing the search for the killers and the night's events.

'This is a huge fucking mess, Arthur, it really is,' one tall, elderly officer exclaimed to another near him.

'Don't blame me. I didn't ask for all of this. We're all out here to end it. We will, too. It's a big night, we all know this. It's bloody confusing, and it's our jobs to end it, and we will,' the grey haired man in the brown jacket by him said.

'But where the fuck are they? They're a clever couple of shits. They're like ghosts, apparitions or something...from Byker, to Tynemouth, then Walker, then Gateshead...there's a few of them, right?' a blonde policewoman said.

'Yes, we've agreed this. I know we're not all completely agreed on it, but it really seems like they have a team of some size with them. And all the stupid occult theories aside, they are probably a gang, or it's between gangs. Poked a big fucking wasp's nest of crime or some shit somewhere, somehow, and now it's gone insane,' the brown jacketed man told them.

'And we keep telling people it's them? Nothing else?' she asked.

'No, just that. Fine as it is right now. Less panic on the streets,' he replied.

'Well, can we get extra help out from nearby? Sheffield? Or Manchester, maybe?' she asked.

'No, they wouldn't reach us in time. Just have to see how the night pans out. For now, it's our problem alone,' the older man told them. 'Look, Brian is getting news back from Tynemouth, he's told me. They're finding some things there. We're getting to some truth now,' he told her.

'Are we really?' she said doubtfully, and threw the rest of her doughnut in a waste bin. They all walked out toward their cars and then drove off in separate directions.

The man in the brown jacket got into a police car with two officers and looked back at them.

'This is a huge fucking mess tonight, right?' one of them said.

'I know, but Andrew has it planned out. It's moving smoothly. We've a very interesting night ahead,' the brown jacket inspector told them.

'But we could...everything we have, how we all live...' the police officer said in a nervous and angry voice.

'Don't think about it. Do your job as you always do. Leave it to us, and Andrew,' the brown jacketed man told him.

They drove off away, and all four of the police cars spread back out in opposite directions along the motorway.

Chapter 37

Bruce drove the car along the motorway with almost careless boredom, his attention straying across to the dark outline of buildings in the night sky and the ominous full moon over head as he and Eric travelled on.

'Are others onto the ways of the hybrid demons as well?' Eric asked him.

'Yes, but we have the best, most significant part to play,' Bruce told him.

'Really? Don't you let others do more of the work? I thought there was a kind of hierarchy?' Eric asked.

'That's...very human. This night things have come to a final point. I sense the work going on, I can get there if I need to. But you are with me now,' he explained. 'Turn here, then next left up...and over the lights...' he commanded.

They came to slow the car down at a long street with closed shops and quiet pubs. The whole street seemed abused, battered and bruised, as if it had been repeatedly targeted during the war and never recovered.

Bruce got out of the car and then walked around to pull out the wrapped up and bound man from the back. Eric looked around, worried about being seen by anyone, but complied, and retrieved the gagged second man with Bruce. They dropped him out on the pavement at the opening of a back alleyway, pulling him deep in.

'What now?' Eric asked.

'You tell me. We're going some other place now, so this guy can't waste our time at all. Get what we need so we can move on,' Bruce urged.

Eric took a look down at the genuine fear and confused panic on the face of the man on the ground, in the man's alarmed eyes. This was a big, well-toned, strong man. A man usually in control, controlling others, hitting women, bullying weaker men, Eric thought. He's embarrassed, afraid, and obviously scared. Good. Eric had never been a sport fan, a football nut, one of those loud, obnoxious blokes, so irritating, insecure and threatening to others, as he thought this guy must be. They always irritated the hell out of him, he thought. He did try to tolerate almost everyone, even those he would not naturally hang out with, but some folk were just too much. It was just a man, he thought.

'It's not personal; well, not much,' he said flatly to the man who just looked back at him. Eric then lifted up a hand over the man. As Eric moved his hand up, he saw around his fist an only just visible slight haze of smoke, so unnatural and bizarre. He took in a quick, deep breath. He could feel within himself some unusual, strange force, tugging, almost moving inside him in some way, like another, second heartbeat suddenly pounding alongside his own. It felt like new organs inside him, like he was breathing in some new way for the first time. His senses seemed quicker, too; more acute, more alert to changes in the light and to sounds around them. The man suddenly tried to kick out at Eric and succeeded in knocking him over a couple of paces.

'You damn shit, hey!' Eric said. He held out his hands over the bound man.

'Don't move at all, you big arrogant arse, okay?' a voice said from behind Eric. He froze, uncertain.

'Bruce?' he said.

No answer came from Bruce.

'Not now. What's your plan, butcher boy?' the voice behind him asked. 'Hands behind your back, slowly now, and step away from the man'

Eric had no idea who it was giving him the orders, but logic suggested it most probably was police. Where was Bruce? Had he been caught by police somehow? Was that really possible?

Eric put his arms in the air, slowly behind his head, and moved away from the bound man at his feet.

Thoughts and visions began to swell to the front of Eric's mind. He was internally presented with moments from his past. Some of it seemed very random, some possibly more meaningful. He was seeing in his mind parts of Byker, Wallsend, the coast, North and South Shields. There were buildings on fire, billowing smoke pyres, and sparking wild fires. There were visions of war-time bombings, but in between on the streets he could see demons running, creeping among shadows. Other distinct visions in his mind showed him possibly times around the turn of the century, the extreme poverty and destitution. Families were begging, crawling for food and medical help. After this, he saw visions of the 1950s, and then briefly after this. Political and social changes and attitudes, protests and strikes on the streets, royal celebrations with street parties and parades. The sixties psychedelia and hippy free-love movement opened up the views and beliefs of many, with a casual loss of interest in old values and move toward embracing and connecting with Eastern spiritual perspectives. The fear and respect for what many believes to be evil or spiritually dangerous before was changing, and it posed a challenge to Bruce and the originals. Andrew and the new demonic tribe stepped up and saw their direction ahead with the changing times and cultures. As the masses became more cynical of organized Christian religion, open-minded to Eastern ways and recreational and hallucinogenic drugs, the demons had to finds other ways to retain their power and control. The bad trip was the way in for a demon and darkness around the North.

'That's it, keep nice and calm now. Up against the car,' the voice told him

It was police, he thought. It already looked bad enough for him but getting caught like this...he had done nothing wrong himself, he thought. The opposite, in fact. He had saved nearly a dozen lives and probably many more, and they catch him?

I've saved them all from bloody demons from Hell or someplace, trying to kill us all and take our souls and they take me in, he thought, outraged. Goddamn police are just like they say, like everyone believes, he thought. Everything was coming straight down on him and no one else. If I'm put in a damn police cell, they'll see just what real living nightmares will be reality soon enough, he thought. No good had come to him. Even joining with some of them to get them against each other had not stopped someone ruining his plans. He slowly began to turn around.

The policeman closest of the group of four came up behind Eric with handcuffs. As he reached for Eric's wrists, smoke appeared suddenly. The fingers on Eric's hands began to spark, and then flames burst up and flickered, growing in size.

'Oh really...' the policeman said to himself, not apparently shocked but intrigued. He suddenly smacked Eric in the head with his elbow hard enough to watch him fall to the ground at his feet. In seconds Eric was gone, into a deep darkness of unconsciousness.

When his vision returned, with the moon above illuminating his view Eric could not be too sure if minutes or hours had elapsed. Before him, he saw a large, empty room with badly painted beige walls. In some low corners there were cryptic scrawls on the walls. There was no furniture other than the simple bed which he sat up on. He stood slowly, his mind still heavy and aching from the blow and stress. What the hell had happened? The policeman had damn well hit him, he remembered. What kind of policeman does a thing like that? Jesus, they can't do that shit, he thought.

He realised that he was possibly in a police cell, but it seemed there were no police around. It was deathly quiet as he walked up to the locked door, which had a small but thick window at eye level. He peered out, but just saw more white walls. There was no one to be seen or heard. Was anyone there with him? He sighed to himself and eventually returned to the low beaten old mattress at the far wall of the cell to think. It had all been going well, he considered. Did he simply underestimate Bruce, he wondered. Perhaps Bruce owned those police; he had said that they were deeply involved in the institutions around the North. No, wait, he thought. That policeman, he hit me. The police know, Eric thought then, with a sharp epiphany. They know about the demons, maybe know or work with Bruce or the other ones, the hybrids. The police will not save us, they don't want to, or they will not have the chance, he thought.

Another vision filled his waking thoughts. He was seeing the various secluded and hidden sanctuaries where the demonic tribes existed. Men had made deals with them, had known about their existence and ways of cruelty and torture. Not even holy men of churches or temples, but men of business and commerce. The deals were kept secret, as they required deaths and the ruin of lives and communities at times. The sorrows and fears maintained the strength and power of the original demon tribe.

Eric coughed and even cried briefly, feeling the genuine loss and tragedy experienced by so many families for decades. He saw then in a more distant and blurred way some vague vision of a lush and peaceful land, trees and fields, calm and sunshine. In seconds a change took place, and dark rain and serpents engulfed this vision. He shook his head, clenched his fists and opened his eyes.

The door to the cell clicked, and opened to reveal two smartly dressed men with two police officers beside them, all looking serious and angry yet with curious caution as they entered.

'You're a very interesting young man, aren't you?' the closest man told him.

'Been travelling around a lot, have you? Been up to all sorts of shit, haven't you?' the older, shorter man said.

'I've done nothing wrong at all. Can I make a phone call?' Eric said.

The tall, suited man leaned in close.

'No, clever shit. No, you can't phone home.'

'It's my right. Get me a phone please, Columbo,' Eric said sardonically.

The other suited man looked around the room vacantly. Suddenly his left hand came from nowhere and slapped Eric hard on the cheek. It hurt like a bitch, Eric thought, but he took it quietly.

'None of that, you. Tell us what you know now, or believe me you won't last much longer, okay?' the suited man told him, pointing a thin finger in his face.

'What the hell kind of police station is this? A bit fascist, isn't it?' Eric said

'Talk straight now, what were you doing out there? The bloke tied up, where's he from and why did you have him?' the older man asked loudly.

What should he tell them? What happens if he lied? What happens if he told them everything he knew? Should he join with the other ones, the hybrids, if that's who these blokes actually are, he wondered. But then surely Bruce would catch up with him soon enough, and what would that offer? He did have the power that Bruce had given him, he remembered. Could that get him out of this place in one piece? It might just be the only option, he thought to himself as he looked the guy in the eyes.

'There's a lot going on right now. That man, the one tied up, he knows about some unbelievable things going on. The truth is...I've been trying to find whoever is attacking people around here. I think this bloke might have known some of them, because of his job; talk to him, interrogate him, and let me go,' Eric told them.

'Is that what you know, is it? You're the Sherlock, it seems,' the first suited man said, nodding thoughtfully.

'More like Van Helsing,' Eric said under his breath.

'Sorry, what?' the shorter man said angrily.

'I've done nothing wrong, you know that. Let me go. Look, a load of bad shit has happened, but a whole lot worse might too. I'm sure you have worse people to catch and spend time with than just me, right?' Eric said.

The two detectives looked at him then at each other briefly, swapping secretive looks and thoughts. The older detective faced Eric then.

'We actually don't care too much about you at all. Who are you? Some weird, schizophrenic young man trying to get some attention, get in the press maybe?' the detective guessed 'We can, and will, do anything that we like to you. No bleeding hearts or sympathetic souls to help you here. If you ever believed, I advise you say your last prayer now. We'll return soon,' the detective told him. He watched Eric for his reaction, then turned and walked out with the other detective. Two police officers came along into the cell and kept watch on Eric.

After the detectives had left, one of the police officers leant in and pushed Eric back against the wall suddenly, and Eric banged his head with a loud crack.

'Hey, damn it!' Eric shouted, but then held back, knowing he would only receive more for any remark. The police officer sneered at him, his partner laughing quietly. They both then left the room and bolted the door securely.

Eric felt cheated, lost and alone. Had everyone ran and deserted him? Say a prayer, he thought. Give me a break God, you hear me, he thought. Silence tormented him. Outside the night was filling with all kinds of murder and bloodshed. He had been too damn sure of himself, leaving Taylor and Emma when he should have let them stay by his side. He had been such an arse, he thought. What a fantastic friend. Only a thin strip of light illuminated his cell for him to know where he was and that he had been caught and was unable to continue, abandoned or forgotten.

'Eric, how are you?'

Eric shook his head, at hearing a voice close to him somewhere. Did he hear that?

'Eric, are you there? Speak,' the voice said. It was the voice of Bruce.

Eric looked around the cell, confused. There was still only himself in there, and the dirty bed he sat on.

'Where are you?' he asked.

'I'm close by. Bad luck. It's not the end, though. You want out?' Bruce asked. Eric could not tell where Bruce was, but continued talking to him. The silence returned.

'Hello?' Eric said in the silence.

'You impressed me Eric. Stamina, determination. We like that,' Bruce told him.

'Great, I'm pleased. Can you get me out?' Eric asked. 'The police are coming back and they don't seem to be really keeping to any strict rules anymore. They're doing whatever they fucking want and it bloody hurts!' Eric explained

'Still angry,' Bruce said

'Damn right I am,' Eric replied. Silence again. Eric looked around. He could hear something out in the corridor.

'Bruce?' Eric said again, waiting.

No reply. Then a slight rumbling behind him. He turned around and saw the bricks of the wall behind moving, shaking, the mass and brick reshaping unbelievably before his eyes. It came out in lumps, growing in shape and size. The bricks seemed to be actually somehow morphing. Eric watched in awe as two muscular, dark blue arms came at him through the wall.

'Jesus!' Eric said, shocked. They were Bruce's arms, he realised. They grabbed him and pulled him toward the wall.

'Wait! Hold on!' Eric said, but he was pulled right up against the wall.

Another sound; locks in the door being turned, undone. The keys turned once, twice. Bruce then pulled.

Eric suddenly fell through the wall, out onto the grass outside the police station at the feet of Bruce, who looked down at him.

'Welcome back,' Bruce said, and pulled him to his feet. The expression on the face of Bruce was disappointed and serious. Eric could see, even in the dark of night, just how unnatural Bruce really was. The pallid amphibious skin, the strange tightening of bizarre musculature around the neck and face, and the almost hypnotic red eyes that looked at him. They immediately ran over to the car waiting on the roadside and drove off away from the police station just as the detectives came out of the front entrance.

Bruce drove the car with Eric in the seat at his side. Eric wanted answers but began to think he should play things down.

'Where did you go back there? When they caught me?' Eric asked, 'They were going to tear me to pieces if I had stuck around,' he explained

'Just unlucky, that's all. Bad timing,' Bruce told him

'So what did I miss, then?' Eric asked, though not at all satisfied.

'Not much. Act one is over. Intermission and onto the killing of men demons. We gather now, I give my orders, we move out. No more mistakes,' Bruce said, suddenly very serious once more.

Chapter 38

With death escalating in all directions around the North, it might have been surprising that somewhere a kind of love was beginning to bloom unexpectedly. Peter opened the door to his flat and found Emma smiling back coquettishly at him.

'Hello again. Are you alright?' Emma asked him.

'Hi there. I have a grasp on some things so far but...please come in,' he said, looking at her eyes. They really were very dazzling, bright eyes, he thought. Like diamonds, so bright. They lifted his mood, and he was very grateful.

As they drank cider together, Peter asked about what Emma knew about what was attacking people and about Eric and Taylor.

'How much danger are your friends really in right now?' he asked.

'Too much, honestly. But they're in deep, just them I think. Eric wouldn't tell me everything, for my own safety I assume, but he needn't have,' she explained

'You believe that it actually is supernatural, do you?' Peter asked.

'I surprise myself by saying so, but yes. I'm glad you will listen, you seem to kind of understand. Can you actually help us?' Emma asked.

'I certainly hope I can, but there's no clear way apart from my background. The way of God. I hope I can help you, Eric and Taylor,' he replied, smiling back. They looked at each other, seeing that they both seemed to be on the same page. Emma began to suddenly cry, which surprised Peter slightly.

'What's up? Hey don't worry,' he told her and stepped close to her, putting an arm around her. She whimpered a little then managed to speak.

'Yes, just...it's Eric's girlfriend, Grace. She was my close friend, too. She died over a week ago. I introduced them to each other. It's all happened, all this death since she died. I swear it is significant...and...it seems to be all connected too,' she told him.

'I'm sorry. You think it's connected? How did she die, if you don't mind me asking?' Peter asked.

'We...we're still not really sure,' Emma said quietly.

'Oh right. We'll find out what's going on. We will,' he told her, hugging her gently.

Emma looked up at him, feeling comfortable.

'You're such a good person, Peter,' Emma told him, as she stopped sobbing.

'Not much more than most people,' he replied modestly.

'No, you are. And plus being involved with the church and young people, that's great. Show me how to be good, to help people,' she said to him. She held his hands softly.

'I don't know if I can. I think you are a good person, a very good friend to others,' Peter told her.

'We're friends, aren't we?' she asked him.

'Well yes, but...' Peter began, but his words stopped as they kissed each other. Emma leaned to him and the lust brewing in both of them came out suddenly. They could hold back no longer and kissed with intense passion. Emma then peeled back his shirt and rubbed her hands over his chest and arms. Peter stroked her hair and kissed her neck as she then touched his belt bucket, and began to loosen it. With the high emotions and strong cider, they fell into making love together on the floor, euphoric joy hiding the nervous fear, for a while at least.

Peter and Emma fell asleep after their unexpected but satisfying sex for the next hour or so on Peter's bed. He woke first. Seeing Emma asleep by him, he feels embarrassed, guilty and regretful. Though he honestly was absolutely sincerely attracted to her, he was ashamed of himself. He did not mean to act on his feelings, or at least not that night.

He did like her, he knew that. Emma was not like most regular young women he met, he thought. She was different, funny, intelligent, but very caring and in ways mysterious too. She was captivating and engaging when she spoke to him. He was not meant to just sleep with any girl he liked. He really did mean to stick close to his idea of finding someone then marrying them before sleeping with them, which fitted with his religious life. He had not grown up that way, but had been trying to stay on that course until now.

Emma began to make a sound as she lay sleeping. Peter panicked, wondering what to do. How did this change things? Could they both still look for Eric and Taylor together like nothing had happened? Eric and Taylor could be fighting any number of unearthly creatures anywhere right then, Peter thought. He had to leave. He began to dress in haste and then Emma sat up naked under the duvet.

'What time is it?' she asked, slightly sleepy.

'About ten o'clock. We should leave,' Peter replied, looking elsewhere as he put on his shirt.

'Are you okay?' she asked him.

'What? Yes, fine. Don't worry. You should get dressed,' he told her.

'You're not fine. Was it wrong that we made love? Is it really bad for you?' Emma asked.

'What?' he said, sounding irritated. 'No, don't be...God no. Oh shit...' Peter said, and walked out of the room quickly. He looked around the lounge for his car keys. Emma got dressed fast and followed him into the lounge.

'It felt great Peter, lovely actually,' Emma said.

'Great. Seen my keys?' he said, ignoring the complement and avoiding eye contact as he looked under cushions.

'Peter, it was wonderful really. I really like you a lot, you know?' Emma told him with honesty.

'My damn keys...shit. This is not good. We're late, all hell's breaking loose around us...death and sin, and more sin, and where are my damn keys?' he said, mostly to himself.

'You're upset about it?' Emma asked, feeling guilty and ashamed of seducing a decent Godly man of faith.

'I just need my damn car keys,' Peter said aimlessly, looking vexed and anxious.

'I'm sorry I came here,' Emma said quietly.

'Oh no, look...it's me, really...' Peter began, but he was just so confused and angry at himself.

'Just forget about it,' Emma told him with sad eyes, and she pulled on her top and left.

'Oh my God, Jesus...help me, please,' Peter said, shutting his eyes briefly. He punched the lampshade beside him on the coffee table, smashing it and drawing blood from his knuckles. Blood dripped down onto the cover of his bible on the bedside table.

Alone and confused, Peter made a phone call.

'I'm going to help this young, troubled guy, father. He's being called a killer, a serial killing monster among men. It's wrong, there's more to it all. There are serious forces around him, I believe,' Peter said to Father Gaskill.

'You are...sadly correct, Peter. Be extremely careful. May the Lord follow you as you go,' Gaskill told him.

Peter heard a nervous falter to the tone of Gaskill's voice.

'Are you alright, Father?' Peter asked.

'Peter, I personally believe the two young men hold serious connections to prophetic words and visions this church has experienced in the past. This is a tremendously dangerous time of supernatural challenges Peter. I believe evil is out on our streets. Remember the prophecies,' Gaskill told him.

'I... you only told me a few. Nobody would acknowledge them, would they? We never spoke of them, really. I understand, though,' Peter said.

'Holy Island. Lindisfarne, the saints and the monks who defended the earliest translations of the gospels into old English from the Viking attacks. Many spoke of strange forces tempting them, attacking them on the island. Forces that tried to stop the translation and spread of the gospels all those many years ago. The people of the North have been vulnerable for a long time,' Gaskill explained. 'They travelled. They travelled North, as the monks defended scriptures and our country. The monks were attacked, some brutally murdered, but much more was prepared than most ever really knew about.

'The righteous journey and then the steps taken to protect this land hundreds of years ago by the saints are more than most ever knew. Some holy men themselves did not believe or give time to consider the extreme serious threat that continued to exist. I knew, I believed. I have spent so long learning all I can. I prepared for these times now, believe me. No others have,' Gaskill explained solemnly.

'Some of the most infamous and sickeningly brutal of the Vikings were demon possessed. Halflan, Ivar...some called them 'thingmen'...some did not and would not believe. All true, but all forgotten,' he said.

'Alright. I will pray to know these visions and words. I must go now, Father. Thank you for your support,' Peter said as he walked away.

Chapter 39

Bruce drove the car down through tight dark streets as Eric thought about what he had agreed to be a part of. Could he actually trust Bruce at all? This was a fucking demon.. People had feared things like Bruce for centuries now, trying to lead good lives so as to not meet them. Now, though, no one believed in them anymore. Bruce was not human, Eric thought, and he should not confuse him with mankind or the way men act. He probably felt few actual emotions, which regularly crippled the average man in times of trouble, Eric considered.

'Bruce, can I ask just how many innocent people could die tonight while we stop the hybrids?' Eric asked him.

'Enough. As many that get in the way or need to die in the infinite pain,' Bruce told him

'Do you know who? Or is it just going to be random? I mean, some people should be spared, I think...' Eric suggested.

'Too many questions. Soon you will ask less, do more,' Bruce told him. Bruce steered the car along past a street where there were some open spaces, more disused buildings, derelict car parks. They passed the car parks on their left, and then came the shock.

'Oh God!' Eric suddenly said. He looked out of his window and saw a scene of depraved, bloody torture on the street.

'What's going on there?' he asked Bruce.

'Some of my own, working hard,' Bruce told him.

'But they were...skinning people, bleeding them, tearing them in a line...' Eric said his voice faint and wavering.

'Has to be done. It's how we work. That's how,' Bruce said.

'Just killing people, they're butchering people, are they random kills?' Eric said.

'Plenty of governments do that. Liberating people, apparently. No, killing just the same,' Bruce explained. This was something to consider, but even so, Eric saw people dying out on the street there in the most shocking manner possible at the hands of these beasts.

'Get used to it,' Bruce told him.

Eric looked at Bruce with disgust.

'Death can be anywhere, anytime, like us,' Bruce added. 'Get used to these images; it's what you've chosen.'

'But this is Britain,' Eric said, as if it changed anything.

'Britain, America, Africa, Cambodia...all the same to us. We've been all over. Now we're here,' Bruce informed him.

Eric looked out of the car window, considering the unlimited pain he could see out on the streets only a few feet away.

'Stop! That woman, I think I know her!' Eric said quickly to Bruce.

'Forget her,' Bruce told him, the car continuing along.

'No, wait, she was suffering!' Eric said.

'You're wrong,' Bruce argued casually.

'Stop the car. Come on!' Eric demanded. He looked at Bruce, then at the two demons in the back of the car, who simply sat chatting between themselves.

'No time,' Bruce said simply.

The car moved on, Bruce letting Eric absorb the scenes of horror and realise that it would just be one of many such occurrences. This would be the future for Eric if he truly was to stay with the demons and keep his side of the deal. He would be indifferent to any suffering, agony, violence or deaths brought upon anyone familiar to him. His human life until then, his friends, family, anyone he might have felt or cared for, must now be forgotten. He was giving up emotion, feeling, and love of all kinds. But not for his dear love Grace. He would not forget her, or forsake her. No, no matter how much he changed, how much power he might be given in order to help the demons. Surely, then, it would not work, if he could not and would not forget Grace. The demons must be able to sense this, he thought, sooner or later. Was he being insanely selfish or pessimistic? What other way could he go, he thought. He kept his head down as the car continued towards Newcastle. He stopped looking out of the window for a while, avoiding what he knew was happening.

The stained glass was illuminated again in the church as Father Gaskill returned to the front altar. The reasons to be there at such an unusual time of night during the week were mounting by the second. He had switched his mobile off for a brief time, which he usually did before personal worship. He was there to pray intensely, like he never really had in many, many years. He closed his eyes as he knelt down by the candles at the front altar side.

There was a sudden knock that echoed loudly through the church and he turned toward the door. The knock came twice as he walked to the doors and answered it.

'Gaskill let me in, quick. We need to talk,' a middle-aged Asian man said in a nervous, serious tone of voice. His eyes held fear and worry.

'Deshi, why are you so troubled?' Father Gaskill asked, concerned for his good friend.

Gaskill quickly let the man inside the church, closing the doors behind him, and they walked through to the private back office of the church.

'Have you heard about the bad things happening? Really bad things, you get me?' Deshi asked him

'I... yes, I did hear some things. You are very concerned?' Gaskill asked.

'Oh my, yes. People have been killed in the last few hours. Police can't give any definite answers at all. Many families are upset and seriously scared for their lives. This is a concern for both of us right now, and many other local religious leaders in the area,' Deshi explained.

'What are you doing at your temple, then?' Gaskill enquired.

'Probably just what you will be doing very soon. We are praying, consoling and discussing actions to prevent more of these serious tragedies. Gaskill, this is very serious, really,' Deshi implored.

'What do you think is really happening?' Gaskill asked him.

'It could be very big, dangerous things, or maybe not. Have to see just what the police do, if anything. Are you expecting me to get all super religious?' Deshi asked.

'Don't we all in times like these?' Gaskill replied. 'Not to say that we shouldn't. Why come to me here?'

He sensed another angle from Deshi. They were old friends, which used to surprise some people. Despite Gaskill being an Anglican Church vicar and Deshi being second in command at the local Hindu temple, they both got along well, and both liked similar music, films and jokes. They respected each other's beliefs, and never pushed their own faiths upon each other, often helping each other whenever they could in the community. It helped to unite and show people around that people of different faiths could coexist peacefully.

'This is more than just random attacks or accidents. These are evil things happening, Gaskill,' Deshi said.

'Really? Define 'evil'?' Gaskill said.

'This is where we are conflicted, in times like these. Alright, these things, they are either the evils that my people fear or the evils you fear and know, do you understand what I mean?' Deshi asked

'Yes, I do know. I needed you to say it. Alright, I do agree,' Gaskill replied gravely.

This made him think of Peter then, out there with a chance those unknown evils might catch him soon enough.

'What more do you know?' he asked Deshi with renewed interest.

'I know of the deaths, the families of many races and areas, all horrified and seeking answers and help. Many are at my temple now. Many pray who never have before. They are truly scared and in need of God and spiritual protection,' Deshi explained.

'Right,' Gaskill said, holding back his own opinion. 'You haven't heard of specific people or groups being linked to any of it?' he asked.

'The police, they actually are looking for a couple of young men. Trying to convince us that these two are the cause of it all, which honesty seems unlikely to me. I don't think that's it at all. Just not logistically possible. There are more than two of them. Of course, those two could be involved, but I think there's a lot hidden from us. Some say strange things, they've seen strange things,' Deshi told him.

'Such as?' Gaskill asked.

'Don't laugh, but...shape-shifting people, people with burning red eyes and worse,' Deshi said. 'I must get back to the temple now. Be prepared, Jeffery. Be safe. I'll call you later,' Dehsi said.

He patted Gaskill on the shoulder as he went to leave.

'Okay then. Take care,' Gaskill said as he walked his friend to the doors and waved goodbye. He watched him leave and wondered about how different their religions and belief really were. When it came to worrying times like these, all prayers must be good prayers.

The phone rang again then and he walked over to answer it.

'Hello, Father Gaskill,' he said.

'Father, is Peter there?' Emma asked.

'No, not right now. Who is asking?' he said.

'Oh I 'm Emma...a friend. We...I am concerned for him. He could be in trouble. Do you know where he is?' she said.

'There is much happening now, isn't there?' Gaskill said.

'I'm sorry, I don't understand...' Emma replied.

'You know, in the church, quite often actually there can be words of prophecy, prophetic vision from church members, even now, not just centuries ago. It still happens. Some times in the future these words and visions can come to reveal things for us to be aware of, things to follow or even sometimes things to be careful of. In recent years, though, many others holy people who I know tended to discard prophecies as irrelevant, redundant, or embarrassing, even. I believe many religious people only go through the motions, pleasing people but failing to please God, failing to question God or evil and our own potential to change things or see things. This church and I have collected a number of words and visions. Some have rarely been spoken of in the years since being given,' he told her.

'Emma, I myself nearly three years ago received visions. Visions of a near future time. I saw evil things rising while men and women of Newcastle slept spiritually distracted, disheartened. I saw this. This year, this month, right now. Two young men in danger, spiritual warfare in some real way,' he said. Emma could hardly believe what he was telling her. It was so bizarre and strange. People only said things like this in old horror films or cheap paperback novels, she thought. It could make some kind of disturbing truth in a way, though, she thought as he continued. Was he really honestly telling her the truth? He seemed to really genuinely believe what he was telling her, it seemed. What would it really mean if what he was saying really was true?

He spoke quieter then.

'Not only this. Two times long before this, two other vicars at this church were told word of connection to the past in Newcastle and the area. Holy Island was spoken of as being significant in the past, and with significance for the future. It is where the earliest known translation of the gospels into English appeared, and monks there defended it with their lives many times. Two others had visions of Lindisfarne on Holy Island, the monastery there, the monks, Lindisfarne castle, and the Viking raids on the island. The saints there...some said the Vikings...well,' he said, looking drained and tired. 'Dark times, but the gospels continued in Old English, the word of God survived across to the North and the rest of England. The word of God will save us, I pray,' he said.

'That's a lot to take in. I hope you are right. I hope we will be saved,' Emma told him.

Chapter 40

The room still very much stunk of a wretched aroma. Taylor walked in small circles, talking to himself at first then looking at the body bag on the table beside him.

'So speak, then. Tell me something I don't know. I'm with them. I've got everything I could have ever dreamed of having; the most gorgeous sexy women, any amount of money, guitars, cars, anything. And I'm public enemy number one, but they don't know it at all. They think something altogether different,' Taylor said to the motionless body bag, which sat slumped in the position in which he had left it.

It was Grace's body inside. He had been careful and considerate, looking after the body most of the time; he knew that he had to, for the best results. He had just taken her out of the large freezer cabinet where she had been staying. Now was time to try to interrogate her once more. He did feel foolish, but he knew that Eric had been speaking to her, as hard as it had been to believe at first. Now that Taylor was with Andrew and the hybrid demons, he had stolen her body just after the funeral with their help. He had been left to speak to her, after convincing Andrew that he would have the best chance of communicating as he had known her when she had been alive. Not that they were exactly the best of friends.

He knew to think hard and focus on speaking to her, like Andrew had explained. There was a kind of chant that he was told to say, over and over if nothing happened at first. Failing that, he should call Andrew and they would just have to shake up her poor, weak soul to hear her.

None of that was necessary, as suddenly the essence of her drew up from within the body bag. It was like a flickering bad photocopy of her, and it sat up on the table and leaned towards Taylor.

'You...don't...want it. Andrew...has it...all. He paid the price,' she told him with a fragile whisper of a voice.

Taylor sneered, wanting to almost punch her or smack her. Not that it would even hurt her, he realised. She knew how he felt, and that annoyed the hell out of him. Was he so obvious? So transparent?

'So did I, I did. And I could do all that,' he replied

'Not...like him...not tonight,' Grace told him.

'Why? Why did you die, Grace?' he asked her. Would she tell him the real truth about her death so easily? He had the uneasy feeling that she knew or had a very good idea what he was thinking, why he wanted to know, what he had been doing and even what he wanted to do. She was in some other realm of existence, and he just knew that she could sense things in different ways. He had to ask anyway, he thought.

'Want...to hear? It might...ruin your good...times,' she said honestly. She had not told him everything yet, and he had not wanted to hear it all, until now.

'Go on, tell me. Not for them anymore. Just for me. Tell me how it happened,' he said quietly, patiently.

He looked at the beautiful corpse, opening the body bag. She still was in very good condition after nearly two weeks dead. He did respect her enough to try to maintain her youthful beauty. He had not exactly ever wanted her, but would admit that she really was very beautiful and that Eric had been a lucky guy, very much so. It was the relationship that Taylor was jealous of more than her.

She had revealed very little to him in the past couple of days, even while he had threatened her on occasion. He had to get the information from her, the reason for her death. Andrew needed it, for all their safety. They knew that she had done something, gotten close to picking apart their world, their hidden lives. Her truth would unlock it all, would reveal so much to him about the whole thing, the entire darkness within Newcastle.

He had realised that so far she had tried to play with him, tease him, and make him angry. She had said things that were misleading and cryptic, but now it seemed that she had listened to him, now it seemed she was cooperating finally. If she really could see into his troubled mind, surely she could see what he wanted to do now, how he intended to continue. He barely doubted anything, and believed that she could probably see his recent sins and debauched gratification, but also see how he was contemplating going against Andrew and his hybrid people. He might just be easily tempted again, but hell, he honestly wanted to leave it and help Eric if he could. It pleased him, as he did not really enjoy shouting at her continually, warning her and threatening her of the many things he and Andrew might do, the ones they might harm if she did not soon help them. He sickened himself in many ways, he realised.

What was he now? He was insatiable, a self-serving, devious creep, anxious like some addict or madman. He was lonely. He ultimately knew that Andrew was no real friend, only a business man, conman, and parasite. He was some unholy demon parasite, Taylor thought. The kind that he and Eric were on the verge of changing into if they could not save each other.

'Are you...sitting comfortably?' Grace asked softly.

'Go on then. Spit it out,' he said.

She moved around a little, as if her dead body was a tight fit, uncomfortable to her.

'What you are...doing right now...been doing...with Eric...is because of me,' she began.

'Yes, I realised that. What else? Why?' Taylor urged.

'Yes, of course. It is not what you might think it is. You were stopping the demons, the devils, Finding them. They...were finding...you. Not for any reason you expect,' she explained.

'Oh really? I knew enough of you. You're playing me, but I knew. Eric would always do just anything, poor bloody sap,' Taylor told her.

'Andrew showing you the good life now?' she asked him. He knew what she was implying.

'Yes, actually. Damn right. It's fucking marvellous, it is. He knows life. Knows a good damn time, that's sure right,' Taylor told her defensively.

'Going to stick with it, then?' she asked, moving around over the table, over her motionless corpse in the bag.

'It's better than regular life most of the time, around these useless towns. It's all lies, no jobs, no hope, no money being a good person, a regular damn fool. This is it,' he told her proudly. They both knew he was lying.

'Look, stop messing around now, tell me more. You know who'll die, who'll pay for it if you don't spit it all out now. Time's up,' he told her.

'The good things, good is always dangerous,' Grace told him. Had she heard his threats, or did she just not care?

'You might be right. So I'll go out now, and do what I spoke of with Andrew and the others? You won't like it at all. They'll meet you in your limbo,' he said bitterly.

236

'Andrew killed me. But why? You should know, I think,' Grace said.

Taylor stood looking at her in silence. He could only think about her words and focus on restraining his frustrated anger. He took a deep breath then stormed out of the room.

Outside on the street, Taylor walked to his car and took out his car keys. There were whispers or kind of faint sounds somewhere around him. He looked around, feeling uneasy. Was he crazy, so desperately nervous and guilty as to hear voices of reason from within his own head? He got into the car, quickly shaking his head in denial, and started the engine.

He drove off down the road, the darkness a gift to sink deep into. Heading back out, he realised that he knew more now. He was a man who knew many more kinds of useful, supernatural things, secrets of the universe. And now he knew more about Andrew. In the last few hours he had been taught tricks of the hybrid demon pleasures only known to Andrew and his extended gang. In his own way, he realised that he really might be useful very soon.

As he drove along, Taylor thought about Andrew in a different way. Now he knew that Andrew had actually murdered someone he himself knew. He and Grace had not always been the closest of friends, but she had been his good friend Eric's love. Taylor was seeing Andrew in a very different light. He could use this knowledge to his advantage, perhaps, he thought. But in what way? Grace had filled his angry mind with questions and unfocused rage.

He drove around Walker, past Wallsend and up toward the coast road towards where Andrew spent his time. After a few minutes, the traffic piled up close to Jesmond. There seemed to be something happening near the Jesmond Bridge and the lower park area. Eventually his car could move forward, and he looked ahead with great curiosity and annoyance. A number of men were stood around arguing outside of their cars, the cars parked haphazardly, causing traffic to slowly navigate around them, with drivers shouting out and cursing. For some reason, Taylor decided to pull over and join them.

As rain began to come down again, he got out of his car to meet the trio of arguing men.

'Excuse me, good evening gents. Nice night,' he said, smiling at them. They looked at him curiously but continued shouting at each other.

'Hey! Stop yapping for a minute, will you all? Jesus help me,' Taylor said loudly over them, drawing their bewildered attention.

They all stood there speechless and eager to individually ask him who the hell he was, butting in to their argument.

'What's this all about, this pathetic shouting here?' he asked with no fear of the large, brutish men, rain dripping down his face.

'Bloody murderers, mate. People dead is what it's about. You want to go hide your little bony arse, I reckon,' one of them told him.

'Someone or something is down there in that park. A couple have died. It's still down there and police wouldn't do a damn thing at all. Someone has to kill the fucker,' the man in the baseball cap and jeans jacket said.

'It's his fault; he bloody sent them in there!' the young Asian man argued.

'Okay now guys, let's calm down a little. Anything could be happening right now. Let's go down, all of us, how's that sound?' Taylor offered. He knew more to the story than they could imagine, and it gave him a feeling of power.

All three men nodded solemnly in agreement, not wishing to look cowardly to each other, and they all then began to walk tentatively down the sloping pathway into the entrance of the park below the bridge.

Taylor walked down the path with these men, whom he did not know or fear. They each held serious looks on their faces, only looking forward as they walked. Each of the men clung tight to their own weapon which they had brought along; a car jack, a spade, a crowbar.

'How long is it since they took away the bodies?' Taylor asked them.

'Well nearly an hour, I suppose. They had to leave because of other things happening. Apparently there just aren't enough police around these days. Bloody joke,' the baseball cap bloke said.

'Really? Could be anywhere. How about we split and continue in pairs? Gives us a better chance, I think?' Taylor suggested.

The men simply looked at each other as if they could barely make simple decisions by themselves. They nodded in agreement once more.

'You and me,' Taylor said, pointing to the Asian man, 'and you two take the path as it splits a few yards up. Here's my number,' he said, showing them his phone display. They individually copied it into their own phones quickly.

They moved on, and the four men split into two pairs down the winding, dark paths of the huge park. Minutes later, Taylor took his chance. He slowed down behind the baseball cap guy.

'Hey come on, what's up?' the guy asked.

'Did you hear that?' Taylor asked, straight faced.

'What? I don't think so,' Baseball replied quietly.

'I heard something. Definitely something, you know, strange,' Taylor said.

'Well where from?' Baseball asked, growing paranoid.

'This park, it gives you the chills, doesn't it?' Taylor said, and then pulled a joke frightened face.

'For God's sake, you're a weird one. Get it together, man,' the baseball guy told him, not amused.

'Right. Okay. But it is strange, isn't it? Must hold many secrets, many dangerous things, many dark tales from through the years,' Taylor suggested. 'From a corner, something hellish and evil might jump out and rip us apart,' he said.

'Christ, man, are you mental in the head?' the young Asian man asked, incredulous.

'Oh if I were it would be so easy...' Taylor said. He moved toward the man slowly. Baseball stepped back, wary of him.

'What's that?' Taylor said, turning around and pointing behind baseball guy. The man turned around with a nervous step to see that there was nothing behind him. He turned back to look at Taylor.

A putrid, man-sized beast confronted him, tore out his throat in one violent movement and sucked at the wound as it sprayed the man's blood across the long grass.

Along the other quiet pathway, the two other young men and the man in the parka jacket moved along pretending to be unafraid, with proud, masculine posture.

'Who is that bloke, anyway?' the one in the parka jacket asked, making conversation.

'Him? God, yeah, taking charge like that. We were just about sorting things, right?' parka guy said.

'Exactly. Just came from nowhere. Damn weird as well,' the Asian guy added, 'So you think we should keep going down ahead or try going down that side next?'

'Nowhere,' a voice told them from within the trees. Hands or claws suddenly came from within the shadows of the trees and snapped the

Asian man's neck. Parka jacket man stumbled, wailing in shock. Still mostly hidden by shadows of the trees, the thing came out toward him. Clawed hands grabbed out at him, as he suddenly caught the red eyes staring at him intently.

'Get away...if you...you'll pay,' the guy said in a wavering voice, losing his nerve right away.

'Are you a man?' it asked. Then it launched out quickly, claws slashing out, cutting the man as he tried to hit it with his spade. The beast followed him down a trail until the man stopped, nearly running into a tree in his nervous panic. He looked back at the unreal, monstrous thing coming toward him. He decided to stand firm and take a hard swing at the thing. They hit at each other, and within seconds parka jacket guy knew he really had no chance. The beast was immensely powerful, it seemed, and it effortlessly began to tear into him against his hits, ripping flesh in all directions. The man was torn to bloody pieces in a tattered pile on the ground. Splattered in his blood, the beast inspected the torn man, then lurched suddenly. It fell to its knees, producing a pained groan. It bent out of shape, clawing at the sky above. As seconds passed, it contorted and stretched in different directions, and finally collapsed in a heap of tired limbs. It held up its head eventually, and it was Taylor once again, with a satisfied grin upon his bloodstained face.

Taylor pulled out his mobile phone and dialled up a number as he walked along.

'Emma, how are you? Seen Eric anywhere?' he asked, sounding faint.

'I'm okay. Could be much better. Couldn't we all?' Emma replied.

'You sound like you need some of my uncomfortably funny apolitically correct jokes right now,' Taylor told her, as he wiped drying blood from his chin.

'Well, maybe. I met a guy. He's lovely, haven't met a bloke like this in a long time. He's caring, deep, intelligent, a gentleman, spiritual,' she explained.

'Spiritual? How?' Taylor asked, curious.

'He's a youth pastor at a church, training to be a minister or vicar, But I'm ruining things big time,' she told him.

'Well, that's really great. I'm pleased, but we need to find Eric immediately. You think you're ruining things? No chance. Let's meet up, okay, I'm not far from Deansgate. You got your car?' Taylor asked.

Chapter 41

Police car sirens moaned across the night while people drove home in fear to their families. Taylor walked back up the side path of the park and returned to his car on the roadside behind some tall bushes. He found the carrier bag on the back seats and took out an old shirt, and then wiped the drying blood from his face, checking that he was clean in the driver's mirror. Then he drove away again with renewed confidence and aggression.

As Emma walked up to the police station she was surprised and intimidated by the amount of people crowded around the entrance shouting, ranting, screaming for attention. They filled the doorway entrance as she entered. People were shouting, bickering, crying. It was bizarre and distressing. Normally, most people tried to stay away from getting involved with police at any time, but this night it seemed not enough people could get inside the police station.

Emma could see the reception desk and managed to squeeze past a group of rowing people and a couple of visibly stressed police officers.

'Hello, I need to speak to someone, it's really important,' she told one of them.

'Everyone has something important to say right now, if you could please just wait in line,' replied the taller officer.

'I actually have information that could be very useful to you now,' she told them.

'Alright. You and all the rest. Take a seat, madam,' the female officer told her.

Emma looked at her, sighed in frustration, then made her way past a few people to a chair by some other women, who sat looking either angry or hysterically sad. Emma sat down and listened to the many scared, arguing people around her being consoled or interviewed by several police officers and detectives.

'Dead, just like that. Unbelievable,' one man said, crying.

'It didn't look right. Just weird, I mean really bizarre and horribly weird. I don't know how to describe it, I saw something strange, will you listen...?' another was saying.

'That killer is coming and no one knows how to catch him. He's doing it, isn't he? There's a gang of them, right? Just stop them! Use guns, rifles, grenades, any damn thing!' another man said dramatically.

So many screaming, intense people were surrounding Emma. She was so glad that she herself had not yet lost any family or friends. She tried not to think too much about that, knowing that anything could happen, good or bad. These people were so angry, lost, manic, and sad. People who they loved were so suddenly and horrifically murdered or had died mysteriously, and for some their loved ones were still just missing. She could be waiting there for a long time, she began to realise, looking at all of them, each wanting to talk with the officers. Was it worth waiting?

Emma looked over to her right and saw a middle-aged woman crying so hard, with a man, probably her husband by the look of it. He too looked so frustrated, helpless and angered, but loyal, there for his wife at such a terrible time. He could do nothing but be there beside her, whatever they were experiencing.

Emma stood and walked back through the crowded foyer, past the arguing people, the crying families and officers.

'Aren't you going to wait?' the receptionist called out to her. Emma turned to look at her.

'I'd never forgive myself if I do,' Emma said, and then quickly left the building.

Chapter 42

Screams could be heard from somewhere near as Bruce drove Eric and himself up the long coast road, with no other cars around them. He turned off at signs for a service area.

'What are we doing?' Eric asked.

'I need coffee, a break. Make some calls, too,' Bruce explained.

They parked in the quiet car park, where only a couple of lorries sat silently, and walked across, entering the shops and cafes. Bruce took out his mobile phone inside and prompted Eric to go walk around or get coffee.

'Go relax for five minutes, while I talk to some friends,' he suggested.

'Okay, I'll just go to that coffee shop,' Eric told him.

Eric walked over casually, looking around at the shops and food chains. It was always strange to see these places very late at night, almost like a ghost town vibe, like that Dawn of the Dead film. He half expected the undead to jump out and bite into him. He went through the coffee shop toward the toilets. Inside, he entered a cubicle and, closing the door, pulled out his own mobile phone and dialled.

He waited, thinking about how long he could spend in there before Bruce noticed.

'Hello?' a voice said.

'It's me, Emma, Eric,' he said

'Oh God, where are you?' she asked, surprised. She sounded distracted for some unknown reason.

'I'm close to hell. Very close. Are you okay?' Eric asked her.

She simply made a faint stammering whimper.

'Emma?' he said, worried.

'Eric you're in so much danger. Don't trust any police,' she told him.

'I know, but I have to be with these...people just for tonight hopefully,' he explained

'With who? Tell me more please,' she asked.

'The ones doing all of this, all the killing, they're not human. What do you know now? Anything new?' he asked.

'What? Well I met the church guy, Peter. He wants to help. He thinks it is a supernatural thing; it is, isn't it?' Emma asked.

'What does he know?' Eric asked.

'Eric, this is too hard now. Too dangerous. Maybe Peter and the people he knows might be able to do something. I don't think that I can really be much help now. I don't think that I should...' she said, unsure of her feelings.

'This is for her Emma, all for Grace. And for everyone else around here. She has the answer, and us,' he told her. He could hear her crying a little.

'What's the matter?' he asked.

'I... shouldn't do this anymore,' Emma said between sobbing. She hung up on him.

'What the hell? Oh Goddamn it,' Eric said aloud to himself. He turned around, looking for something to punch. Bruce came into the toilets.

'You here, Eric?' he asked outside the cubicle.

'Hang on a minute,' Eric told him and flushed the toilet behind him. He came out to meet Bruce.

'I was going to puke but...no luck yet,' Eric told him

'Come on, toughen up. This is it now. We'll tear the others to pieces soon enough,' Bruce explained confidently. 'Let's be off,' he said.

They left the service area shops and returned to the car, continuing through the quiet, ominous night.

'So, how much death have you seen in the North, or how much have you caused?' Eric chanced.

Bruce took a slight casual glance toward him then back at the road as he spoke.

'I have witnessed all kinds of deaths. Many reasons were specific to the North-East here. In the decades in which I have been above, I have seen your businesses collapse. Men fighting men, very entertaining. You say you all want to be equal, but...no. We moved in, taking, using, abusing the opportunities. There were suicides, murders, killings, and a good number which we assisted. There are also deaths which we have no hand in, and we simply witness your own evils. You wish you could say that we did it, but you have your own fallen freedom,' Bruce explained.

'You watched people and families struggle when their jobs were cut? Factories closed and businesses taken elsewhere, leaving hundreds lost and desperate? And you moved in for the kill?' Eric asked.

'We are not human. We do not stumble on pity, empathy or sadness. We have other things to do,' Bruce said, his red eyes sparkling under shadows.

Eric looked at him in silent anger, frustrated and feeling a deep sorrow for the lives ruined. Bruce was very right when he spoke of the men of this country seeming directionless, afraid and then fighting each other, never seeming to agree on things. Was that how he should now be viewing the world? An environment to simply destroy, break, and use, then watch the chaos and sadness set in? They drove on, Bruce smiling with a look of sinister confidence.

Were the people of the North really weaker, more confused, than down South? Did the demons choose here because it really was much easier to conquer? Were we all much easier, less confident, less driven or organised and ready for something like this, like them? Fuck no, Eric thought.

Driving along together, Taylor knew Emma could help him through. She had to understand what he had been doing, if he could actually confide in her. How much was too much to reveal? He did want to help her and Eric again; to be good once more, a regular person if he could be, but too much truth could ruin every chance to stop the demons if Emma did not accept him.

'Everything going to be okay with you and Eric now?' Emma asked.

'I hope so. I honestly do. You will help me, won't you?' he said. 'I mean tonight. Even if tonight is all I'll have, as long as he might be okay with me. We did fight these beasts that no one really ever expected to exist,' he told her.

'What exactly were you two doing?' Emma finally allowed herself to ask.

'Can you suspend your disbelief?' Taylor said.

'Taylor, I've already personally seen a whole load of sick shit in the last few hours,' she said. 'Go ahead, tell me.'

He hesitated, then began.

'After Grace died, it all began. Eric was so upset, so torn up by it. She disturbed something I think, she shook up the evil of the North. Her mysterious death did not totally mess him up, but he did want the real answers of why and how she died. In the days afterwards, he then told me of things, places that he wanted to go check out. He disappeared one night. When he returned, he told me a shocking story. I thought that her death had finally pushed him, his sanity leaving him finally. I accompanied him, and my doubts were gone soon enough,' he told her.

'What happened? What did you see?' Emma asked, genuinely wanting to know everything. Both Taylor and Emma knew that she had a very good idea of what he and Eric encountered.

'All of this happened. We witnessed what man has denied for decades, disowned. Things changed instantly,' Taylor explained.

'So what has happened between you and Eric since then?' she asked, understanding and sympathetic so far.

'We both had problems, fears. We were suddenly chasing these actual demons. I should have helped him more, but I was distracted. I was a fool, really.'

That was all he told her right then. Emma nodded, glad to finally know more of what Eric and Taylor had been through and why. It had obviously had a huge psychological effect upon both young men, she realised. She drove on thinking about all of this, and then broke the silence.

'Taylor, I'm doing this now because I know Eric so well. You do too, and we knew Grace,' she told him.

'Oh God,' he said, quickly steering the car around a few feet to the left of the motorway road. Behind them on the road stood something shockingly vulgar and grim, an inevitable scene. The car brakes and gearstick jammed, as Taylor wiggled it manically in frustration.

'Oh Christ, what now?' Taylor said.

They were not hiding any longer. A group of figures stood ahead, vaguely human in form though other elements suggested more. There was blood glistening on them and they strolled on right across the road ahead of them. Further along, Emma could see a group of people running to stay alive, with the bizarre figures she knew were demons chasing behind.

Taylor moved the car again gradually toward the lurching demon group, who were focused on their prey.

'Don't stop. Go back or something,' Emma told him.

'No, don't worry. They must be like animals,' he said, confusing her.

'Yes, fucking wild rabid animals. Go, or ram them!' Emma suggested.

'You're right,' Taylor said flatly as he drove. Then he stopped near enough, and opened the car door.

'What are you doing?' Emma said in shocked disbelief.

Taylor did not answer but stepped out and walked quickly along in the direction of the people. As he walked closer, they heard his footsteps. One of the group looked over. The wild red eyes stared with merciless insanity at him.

Taylor waited. Was the demon hybrid or original, Taylor wondered. He knew that they could tell each other apart a mile off, but anyone else had trouble making a difference out to begin with. He wondered if they would recognise him. The demon nodded slowly at him, and then simply continued along with the others to chase the running victims down the road. Taylor returned to the car and sat back in his seat, relieved. His quickened heartbeat gradually began to slow back down. He started the engine, and he and Emma drove away once more, leaving the demons free to kill.

'What happened there?' Emma asked quietly when he drove them away.

'I don't know. I think they know me and Eric. We made our mark. We might just have what it takes to finish them. Can I meet this spiritual guy you know?' he asked Emma. Inside, he hated himself.

They decided to make a quick stop at the next service station. They were well aware that time was escaping them, but they also needed to catch their bearings, and refresh themselves briefly. When Emma went alone to the ladies' toilet at the service shop mall, Taylor walked around the car park outside under the heavy black clouds.

He felt out of place. He was a different person than he used to be. He realised that he had played with the devil, literally, and escaped. But he saw that he had learned things, useful things. He had seen things that others did not know of, and he now feared less, knowing the evil around. What he did fear, though, was possibly more significant than anything others feared. He looked around at the tall, thick trees around. A cold chill came by him.

'You're getting there...' a voice told him. He turned to see the hazy image of Grace shimmering a couple of feet away from him.

'Get away. I don't need you now,' he said in a low voice.

247

She watched him as he walked near the service area front entrance. He looked back and she was gone. Taylor was relieved, but only slightly so. Looking through the doors, he saw Emma returning up the corridor.

'You will sacrifice much,' he heard Grace gently say to him from somewhere.

'I am sorry for what I was doing. I wish I hadn't done it,' he told her quietly before Emma came outside.

'And you will...sacrifice much,' Grace repeated calmly.

'I have done,' he said with resentment. He scowled and cursed quietly while Emma came out into the cold, rainy night again to meet him.

'Let's go,' he said with an angry, bitter voice. Emma looked at him curiously.

'Well stay here if you really want to; do you?' he said.

'Let me drive, okay?' Emma said. He looked at her contemplatively then nodded. They returned to the road, trapped in the old car with each other.

Chapter 43

Peter sat on the bus into Newcastle, which had practically no passengers, other than some strange old lady at the back, a couple behind him and the driver. He looked out at the streets as the bus moved along, and thought about what might happen that night. It was an unbelievable, shocking time, he thought. His life felt like it had suddenly become in just as much danger as many of the people overseas. Every day of his own life until now had been very comfortable, peaceful, free and blessed, he knew, and he thanked God for that. He had been hearing stories which strangers on the streets outside had been telling each other. Sitting on the bus, he still could hear others mumbling, whispering, gossiping and arguing about things they had heard in the last couple of hours on TV, radio, from friends, relatives. Man, people can certainly elaborate things in order to tell a story, to get attention, he thought. He then heard someone mention Eric. He almost turned right around to put them right in their misunderstandings, but managed to hold back, resisting temptation.

He stood as the bus came to approach the top of Newcastle City Centre. He stepped off next to the university. Looking around, things seemed normal, quiet, though he knew to be prepared for anything nasty or unexpected. He remembered Emma's talk of some hidden special places in the city that she had been researching. What she had briefly spoken of did actually connect with some other bizarre things about Newcastle history that he had heard a while ago. It even seemed to fit in with some strange old tales and rumours connected to some city churches he had heard about. This night was about the unsaid, the taboo things and places, stories and prophecies that many denied, ignored, tried to forget over time. Things don't go away if you simply just try to forget about them, he thought. They stick around, fester until some else finds them or they grow and come back worse.

Talk of these things had split some local churches, he remembered, Gaskill having told him. His own church had been born from two previous churches that closed after disagreements and accusations. That always felt stupid to him, just the idea. He knew that everyone should be able to come together for God and for love. The fighting and arguing looked hypocritical to outsiders, and made him angry and sad. It was times like this that all believers needed to be united, he thought.

Father Gaskill was almost like his mentor, and they had become close friends in the three years that Peter had been at that church. In that time, Gaskill had revealed some of the elements of these sinister past events and stories that many chose to ignore. Gaskill was no great fundamentalist, but he did not think man should forget or fail to consider the more strange and unworldly happenings around them, knowing that not everything was fully explained. He knew to focus on uniting the community, but never forgot to acknowledge existence of powerful and often rarely acknowledged dark forces, as well as the force of good in the world. This he had instilled in Peter as they had worked together, and they studied and debated Bible scripture. Gaskill himself did believe in the myths and prophecies that had appeared over the decades in the North, which other vicars and church men had forgotten. Among the local holy men and women, he was largely viewed with scepticism as the overly dramatic 'fire and brimstone' preacher who was always wildly off track in his opinions on the spiritual needs and dilemmas of the community. The prophecy had been very dark, disturbing and tragic. Many had not wanted to explore the meaning or even think about such things ever occurring. Now, though, it might finally come to save them, Peter thought.

The streets of the city centre would now have to look different to him, Peter realised. He had to ignore the places he knew from everyday life; nightclubs he knew, restaurants, pubs, coffee shops, and concentrate upon where the places he was looking for were. Parts of the city had been marked out as holding future evils, sanctuaries for ones who would harm mankind. Just when you think you know a place, he thought to himself. Beyond or among these places that held demons of both kinds, was allegedly the place that was built to work against it all. It most likely would be very hard to find, but it was apparently some kind of church, built specifically for combating the local supernatural evils of times long past, but hopefully could still be of great use on this present dark night. Gaskill said that he had heard it was built only in a loose sense, no real church structure like any other, so as to keep it unknown, but it still successfully served its purpose. Unfortunately, the group who attended the unknown church were separated, killed, taken mysteriously. That, Gaskill had told him, was now around twenty-five years ago.

Peter walked on with bold concentration. People passed him; groups, couples, young teens, all continuing to go around between pubs, clubs, behaving as if it were just another ordinary night in the town. Peter received puzzled, curious looks, some laughter, even, as he noted street signs and names, turns in the road, buildings ahead of him with vexed focus. He wanted to shout out and tell every one of them to run to safety, to hide and pray for help. He knew that would likely reward him with even louder laughter and possibly police or medical intervention.

He came to a road that split off between the back of the large shopping mall and the older streets with many grubby pubs and offices. As he began to make a decision on the direction to take, he heard some people arguing near him. A woman seemed to be pleading with some men. Peter slowly turned the corner to look up the narrow, cold street. There were the group of men and two young women. They all seemed in their twenties and each one was highly panicked and arguing with another. One of the women ran suddenly and fell into Peter.

'Oh my God, I'm sorry,' she said, looking at him. She was taken by the strange seriousness of his face, like he was on a mission.

'It's alright. Everything okay here?' Peter asked.

'Don't tell him!' one of the mean-looking young men shouted down to her. She looked at Peter thoughtfully.

'There is evil danger, back up there,' she said, pointing behind. 'It attacked us,' she told him.

'Really? When you say evil...' he said.

'I don't know, not man or animal...something else. Like both at once, just fucking horrible,' she said. She turned to her friends, who looked at her disapprovingly.

'I'm off, I'm not hanging around. I'd go somewhere else if I were you, mate,' she said to Peter as she ran off alone. He looked up at the remaining young people then walked up to them.

'What's happened?' he asked them.

'You will not believe any of it,' one of the men said, shaking his head.

'Oh really, I just might. Tonight is a bad night. Was someone taken or attacked by something?' Peter asked.

'Yes. Our friend Alex is gone. Down that alley,' the remaining blonde girl told him.

'He can't do anything about it, Sarah!' one of the men said to her.

Peter looked up at the opening of the alley and saw the street sign. Wyndorf Street.

It was one of the streets Gaskill had mentioned, he realised. Peter took a breath, and then took a step towards the street. As he came near the black darkness of the alley, he heard some kind of moan or call from someone. He looked back at the young men, who watched him quietly.

'You're not going in after your friend?' he asked them.

They shook their heads with fearful exaggeration. He stepped into the dark of the alley alone with caution.

The alley was not completely dark; there were small pockets of light from behind various dirty windows along the alley. So this alley held some of the hidden evil, he thought. He had no idea how powerful it might be, though, he realised. He would have to be realistic in a way, be prepared to arm himself to fight, as well as pray for help. He examined the ground at his feet closely in the hazy shadows of the alley. There was dirt and mud, but no footprints were clear to see. Then a door suddenly swung open, spreading a thin layer of light through the alley, and it banged hard against the wall behind loudly. A couple of tall, thin men came out of the doorway, looking angry and ready to attack anyone that got in front of them.

They started down the alley and in an instant spotted Peter. They grimaced, then the man in front laughed at him.

'Shitty night, isn't it, bro? Going to get much worse, too,' he told Peter, then pushed past him, as did the other. They stormed on back out to the main street and disappeared around the corner. Peter let out a sigh of relief as he watched them go, but it confused him greatly. He turned his gaze to the door that they had come from. It seemed that it was the back entrance to possibly a pub or nightclub building, he thought. There was a strange, thick smell that suddenly sunk into his lungs.

Unbelievably, the door had been left open by the two men. He just could not believe his luck. He had nearly stuck his foot or a stick nearby into the gap as it closed, but it simply stayed lazily ajar. The two men did not seem to care or mind about him being there or walking right in. He thought carefully, but then that was what he did.

There was a dim light shining around inside from deep within a long, twisting corridor. There were voices nearby, arguing but jovial, and then a sudden scream. Part of Peter wanted to walk away, but another part of him felt he was where answers lay waiting for him.

He walked in deeper, closer to the voices he could hear. It seemed that the two men, possibly demon men, thought he was with them, maybe a demon also, so he now was not too weary of confronting more inside this unknown hiding place. The conversations were becoming much more audible gradually, and he stood discreetly by a dark corner and heard snatches of dialogue.

"...down Tynemouth, Jackie over at Byker, Athena down Walker way. Only an hour or so, really..." one voice could be heard saying.

'... part is easy. No problem. Always fun, too many regulars anyhow. Time for change, right?' another said.

'...move out over the city now. Shock, scare, kill a few. But make him the martyr now. Distract all of them. That's key,' a low guttural voice ordered.

'They have him still?' another asked.

'Seems like it. But it's his image that counts. The masses react to it. Leaving us to move in easily,' the low voice explained.

'Has he helped us?' another voice asked.

There was a silence, then someone spoke.

'Yes. This man has brought on what was needed. Build him as a demon now.'

It was Eric they spoke of, Peter knew. It was them; it was the place, or one of the places. He quickly tried to think of what he could possibly do to stop them or slow them down. He was one man, and they were many, like cockroaches that had long ago infested the North. Peter felt he had to leave, even if the young teenager was actually inside. It was a painful moral dilemma, a painful struggle with his conscience. Something told him to continue. Was it God? Was it fear? No, he thought, not fear, but hope. He felt terrible about leaving, but part of him thought he should move on with the information that he had just heard. He stuck a hand in his coat pocket, and found a small candle. He placed it on the floor of the corridor and lit it with his lighter, then quietly walked back out to the alley, then out onto the main street again.

Peter came out and saw the waiting teenagers under the street lamp.

'Call police now. Don't go down there but have faith. Your friend is safe. You should all get to a safe place too now,' he told them.

'What do you mean? Where is he?' one asked.

'I can't say, just get to safety please, there's no time to talk,' Peter said.

'Some men came out before you, we hid from them. Did they see you?' one of the girls asked.

'No they didn't see me. Now please, go!' Peter commanded.

'What? Why didn't you stop them? Why not?' she demanded.

'It's not right. Not that way,' he told her, with frustration in his eyes.

'Bullshit! What do you know? Why didn't you do anything?' she asked, grabbing his arms.

'I do feel your pain. Believe me. This danger is all across the North now. Everywhere. Go and find safety. Police are coming,' he told her and her friends.

They started to go off, and so Peter also walked away with heavy thoughts and guilt.

After walking up a few streets, Peter could hear the police sirens, and an ambulance came hurtling along the road ahead of him. His fear grew against his stamina as he watched it move along. There were less people out on the streets, but there were more cries, he noticed, the screaming and shouting rising louder in all directions. It was a continuing audible terror which he could not ignore. Off to his left, he could see people fighting, punching and beating each other brutally. It really was beginning to resemble almost some kind of apocalyptic vision. He could not reach everyone, could not help more than one at a time, he thought. Where the hell was his God right now? This was simply too much. Was God just blind or ignorant to this?

It was a test, or that was what Peter told himself. Like many of the stories in the Bible, these disturbing atrocities must be testing his faith, his hope, and his idea of God. Bad times come before the good times, he told himself.

He realised that he was then only a few streets from the city police station. Could any police really help out on a night like this? Could they fight unnatural, inhuman things like those on the streets at all and win? Throw a demon in a police cell, right, that'll stop it, he thought. No, he realised that it was mostly likely full of hysterical, angry souls, demanding answers, truth and salvation. They might be looking to the wrong people for help, he thought.

He turned his back to the police station, and walked on. He would not ignore the death and horror around, but he realised that he should invert the actions of the demons. Their lies and fear should be bent around, exposed, and Eric held up and acknowledged for his brave actions.

Police cars sped past continually and people ran along shouting. He heard some mention 'red eyes' as they screamed past. He kept noting the areas and street names that he passed. A group of three people ran out of a street to his right, and one man looked at Peter in disbelief.

'Get away from here, mate, there's some fucking mad things happening. There's a killer down there!' he said wildly.

'Really? Well, it's under control,' Peter told him.

'No chance, mate. How do you know?' the man asked, his friends pulling on his arm.

'I just know,' Peter told him.

'Who, police? They won't do shit all. It's gangs and that bunch of murderers,' the man told him. He shook his head, then ran off with his friends as fast as they could.

Peter found it a challenge, but nothing new. Coming from a church and believing in the trinity in a world of cynicism, denial, and consumerism, it was just accepted for him to come up against disbelief, fear and lack of hope.

He was walking between the streets allegedly owned by the some of the dark forces, he remembered. He might not have too much power there, but he was sure that he could arm himself, be practical, and improvise. He knew that prayer was not all he should rely on, and was ready to find himself a decent, strong weapon to defend him with.

More police cars raced along the main road beside him as he walked. He wondered where they were all heading, and it worried him deeply. He thought of some huge, bloody and violent scene erupting all over the streets further down the city somewhere. Was he already too late to help? He could not think like that, he knew. The cars seemed to be going toward a certain place. He wondered if they could lead him toward Eric and Taylor. It did seem that the few people around were quickly heading in the opposite direction. Perhaps they had only been called toward the individual deaths and attacks he thought. A woman came up near him without him noticing. She was crying when he looked at her.

'Are you alright?' he asked.

'I've lost him,' she sobbed helplessly

'Who? Who've you lost?' Peter said.

'My man...he disappeared. Gone. I heard some scream. I'm so scared now. It could be that killer off the news, the young man, you know?' she said.

'No, it's not him, he's okay. It's...there are other dangers, but don't worry. Police are around.'

'That man has killed dozens of people, they can't stop him, he's still on the loose,' she said. 'Help me, please.'

'I am helping...listen...' Peter said, frustrated in her misinformed views. Damn the news media and television, he thought. He looked around, flustered.

'I need the police to come,' she said, looking around them. They could both hear the sirens in the distance.

'No, shit, don't. You don't need them,' Peter told her. As he said this, a police car actually came up around the top of the street, and the woman gasped in relief. She began to wave and managed to draw the attention of the officers inside the car. The car came right up close to Peter and the woman, and a police woman stepped out.

'Hello, is there a problem?' the policewoman asked.

'Yes, there is. My husband is gone. The young killer has got him! Just streets away from here. That killer, the young man. Help me, please, find my husband!' the hysterical woman urged.

'Oh, for God's sake,' Peter said

'Who's this man?' the policewoman asked, looking at Peter as if he was contagious.

'He was just walking by, I asked for help. He thinks the killer is not the young man. Can you believe?' the woman told the policewoman.

'You are very wrong if that is your belief, sir,' the policewoman said.

'What?' he said. 'He's not the one killing. I mean, he's involved...I know that's not what is being reported, but it's all wrong,' he told her. He felt trapped. He knew that none of what he had said sounded good. Both women seemed convinced that Eric was the newest national icon of fear and dread, a horrific legend in the making. He wanted to say more, explain things better, but knew it was not doing any good, only wasting valuable time.

'Madam, you can come with us. Tell us what has happened properly. We'll find your husband,' the policewoman said, then she turned to Peter. 'You, sir, think about what you're saying to people. There is a dangerous man out tonight, and we are trying to keep people calm while we find him and stop him,' the police woman told him quietly so as not to frighten the woman as she got into the police car behind them.

'So tell me just how this evil young man is in so many different places at once?' Peter asked.

'Don't be smart with me, okay sir? Besides, there is at least one other person with this psychotic. Be careful on your way home. Don't want any trouble, do you?' she said with a dark smile, and watched him as she got into the car. Her attitude struck Peter as bizarre. The policewoman watched him as she drove the car back down the road.

Peter looked around and ran on. He had to find this mysterious church ground, as Eric was most likely there. He slowed down again a couple more streets up the block, the streets dead and lifeless. He hoped it was for the best, people tucked away in their homes behind locked doors. Many of the street names were ones that he knew Father Gaskill had mentioned; Tabor Street, Basquiat Street, Bickers Avenue. He was right in deep amongst it all now, he thought. If people like him had even believed sincerely in evil existing as it was written, this was a breeding ground, a nest for it.

He was either in way too deep or in just the right place, he thought. Two men came around from his left suddenly, looking pleased and confident. They walked along near him and made eye contact.

'Are you okay there, pal?' one of the men asked him in a friendly manner.

'Hmm? Yes, thank you. Just taking a walk. I'm fine,' Peter said, struck by their bizarre attitude.

'No, you should get to a pub or something, man,' the other told Peter.

'Right, yeah. Might do that. See you then,' Peter said.

'We're not afraid of anything out there,' the first man told him.

'Okay, fair enough,' Peter replied, knowing he should move on.

The two men continued along beside him as he went, so Peter finally turned to face them again.

'Where are you fellas going?' he asked

'Wherever we like,' one told him.

'Look, seriously, there are some really bad things happening around tonight. You know, right?' Peter asked.

'What kind of crap are you talking, mate?' one of the men enquired.

'Listen to me, you damn fools. People are dying tonight. Get to a safe place, okay?' Peter said, frustrated.

'Who is this freak?' the other man asked, looking at his friend sarcastically.

Peter could not believe these two arrogant men. They almost deserved to get caught by some stray demons. Peter did sense they were trying to wind him up, even mess him about. The last thing he needed right then was trouble from some men wishing to prove their masculinity.

'I think you'll get into trouble, not us, you freak,' the slimmer man told Peter. Peter snapped, grabbing the guy by his shirt collar and pulling him up close.

'Get out of here now, or you'll most likely die. I wish that I was mad, believe me; I damn well wish none of this was occurring. Not one part of it,' Peter said into the man's face with furious anger.

The smaller fat man pulled at him suddenly, grabbing his neck. The man Peter had hold of smiled as Peter released him, due to the other man gripping him.

'You wish you were mad? Just ignore it all. Everyone does. Turn a blind eye, friend,' he told him. The shorter man pushed Peter down to his knees as he looked up at them. He wondered how this was going to play out. The streets had finally given him some trouble.

'You two busy tonight, are you?' he asked them. He watched them and their body language. He could probably take the fat one and escape somehow, he thought.

'Only as busy as you,' the slim one replied, smiling. They began to walk apart and Peter stood slowly, ready to fight or run.

'I will do what I have to,' he replied.

'You will? Yes, you're that sort, aren't you?' the slim man said.

'Thank God,' Peter said quietly, and took a step away.

The eyes of the two men burned deep, changing from green and blue to crimson red suddenly, and then both men rushed at him.

Peter moved and then one caught him, slashing his arm. A knife? No. Peter took a look down, and saw strange, long holes. The two men were demons. Both looked at him with their glaring red eyes like wolves from hell. The other lurched over at him, but Peter punched him in the face. A crack sounded, and blood flowed out like wine. Blood for blood, Peter thought. Whatever it takes. The other man came back and grabbed Peter by the arm. Peter moaned and leaned over, caught.

As the other one came back again, Peter pushed a hand into his face, then knocked the first man back too. As he hit the ground, Peter turned and punched him again, full force. He looked down at the thing below him. Once man, now some wretched beast of sin and savage murder. The man was bleeding heavily, though looked right back at Peter.

'What are you doing?' he asked accusingly.

'I... don't...' Peter said, bewildered and shocked at his own actions. He had never really been a fighter, or made someone bleed like that before.

'How could you do that?' the other red-eyed man asked.

Peter looked to one side, ashamed of himself. It was not like him at all. Where was his trust, his faith, he thought. One of the demon men smiled ruefully, then suddenly jumped over to deeply cut into Peter's neck and face, ripping flesh. Peter reeled back in pain, putting a hand to the wounds. He strained to focus, then once more simply beat the life out of the demon men as they came at him. He floored them, one unconscious, the other on his knees, gasping but coming back up to take another swing at Peter.

'Fucking try it. I'm in no good mood,' Peter told them. This was how it worked now, he thought.

He watched them and they watched him. A second passed, then the standing demon reached quickly to claw Peter, and Peter swung out once more. The demon fell back over the other in a heap. Peter took a moment to catch his breath. He looked down and saw the blood covering his arms, hands and legs. He was a killer now. It was only the start of what was to come. He felt no better, but he had stopped them before they had taken him. It was how it had to be now, and he had to understand that. Dangerous times, like the prophecies, he thought. He walked on.

As Peter walked away from the defeated demon corpses, he was watched secretly by two more men nearly two streets away, standing under the cover of shadows.

'Hey, look at that bloke, is that blood on him?' one of the men asked the other.

'Shit, it...drive, drive, now,' the other man said. The car began to quickly move up the street toward Peter.

'Is it him?' one of them said.

'Could be, or his pal. Maybe he's another one,' the other man said, while driving the car slowly across from Peter.

Peter could feel the cold air drying the blood on his arms and face. In the quiet air, he heard a car somewhere behind. He turned to look, and saw a police car coming towards him up the street. He ran then, like a criminal. Like a blood soaked killer. God help me now, he thought. From then on, Peter saw that he too was wanted, along with Eric and Taylor. He was running and hiding like they were. It made him sick to think he was being cautious and the demons were going about freely, disguised in their deceitful ways.

Chapter 44

Sitting at the steering wheel, Emma at least felt reasonably in control with Taylor next to her. He had been giving directions, as she had not actually driven around some parts outside the city much, but they were finally approaching the outer roads.

'What are you thinking?' Emma said to Taylor. It was the first thing besides directions that either of them had spoken about for fifteen minutes.

'Hmm? Thinking? My mistakes. And about Eric, and... her. Let's see,' he said.

'Got a good idea of what we're going to do, then?' she asked.

'Where's this guy you know?' Taylor asked her.

'What?' she said, embarrassed.

'This church bloke you mentioned. Is he going to be exorcising anyone?' he said with a smirk.

'Fuck off, no. I don't know. Leave it. He's a good guy, just...' she said but did not finish.

'Sorry. Just wanted to know. Here we are,' Taylor said.

Up ahead, they could see the towering civic hall centre building. Emma drove on, with only fragile thoughts of hope as she crossed traffic lights.

'Are we going in a few streets or what?' Taylor asked.

'I think we'll be okay to walk. Maybe better, really,' he told her.

'Why's that?' she asked doubtfully.

'I've been here with the worst of them. We're probably fairly safe, for now at least,' he said.

They drove in for two more streets and parked just next to the taxi rank behind the shopping centre. Getting out, they looked at each other briefly.

'Lead on, then,' Emma said.

'I know where to avoid, and you know where to go, I believe,' Taylor said. Emma realised that he was probably correct, so she took the lead as they walked through the quiet city streets. It was void of life, unnerving and unnatural to her. She did not really like being alone with Taylor out on the streets, but then she knew she preferred to be with him than by herself on this night.

Chapter 45

The car pulled over suddenly, Eric waking from a heaviness that had come over him. He looked around outside the car.

'Where are we now?' he asked.

'We're stopping here. There's trouble,' Bruce told him abruptly. He got out of the car and began to walk, before looking back at Eric.

'Come on, get out, follow me,' Bruce called back. Eric followed without saying a word. He knew to be careful, to keep Bruce happy for a short while until things began to happen.

'I've had my kind moving around to hold back the hybrids, but there's been some problem. You damn humans,' Bruce explained while walking on.

'What problems?' Eric asked

'Over reacting, being curious. Sound familiar?' Bruce said.

'Bruce, how long have you been around, you and your kind?' Eric asked. He didn't know how much truth he would get in the answer. Bruce turned to look back at him.

'It was this place. This cold, wet, miserable part of the country. Perfect. Souls so low, depressed, angry, disappointed. Lost people, bitter. The South, London, I mean, were too strong, too much for now. All you people, easy. Easy to break in, enter, use you, use the life, the land. Take what we wanted. Thing was, after a while you are all angry at God, at yourselves. You were the best ones. But one man helped before. Very helpful, but he had ideas. Then us, you and... hybrids,' Bruce explained.

'What? The North was easier? We're strong bastards, we fight. We're just as determined as them down South. We're...different, just different. No better or worse. That's my belief. So how long?' Eric asked

'Decades now. At least,' Bruce told him. 'Only one part of it. Now complications.'

'Yes, complications. We're not so simple,' Eric said.

'I disagree. Very simple. Come on, help. You are the exception,' Bruce told him.

'Listen to this,' Bruce said. He held a palm flat on Eric's forehead. It surprised Eric, but then he began to see images in his mind vividly.

He saw parts of Newcastle: streets, corners, roads, pubs, fields. Then faces, people...blood. He saw groups stalking around, other groups fighting. Taylor, Emma, Andrew and many demons. People with wings flying also, and hunched people crawling, and more between. He fell back, dazed.

'What was that?' he said in stunned shock.

'Follow me now. That's all happening. Streets from here. They're all involved, them, us, and many others. We're losing grip now,' Bruce told him. 'I want you to take a few streets, and I'll go along with the other lot. We'll meet up in thirty minutes,' Bruce said.

'What? What do you want me to do?' Eric asked.

'Do what you have to do. Whatever you think is needed. I believe you are close enough to my kind to know,' Bruce told him. 'Until the agreed meeting, of course, at the Quayside streets.' His eyes held on Eric with wild purpose, burning red. Eric almost felt sick looking into them. Bruce pointed down an alley, and Eric nodded before beginning in that direction.

'They'll know you, my workers,' Bruce said as he walked out in the other direction, leaving Eric.

Chapter 46

Walking with caution in the safety of shadows, Peter did feel a mysterious kind of positivity. Finally, as a man working for God, he felt like many biblical apostles and Old Testament figures that had faced the corrupt Pharisees, unbelievers and oppressors. It gave him a kind of courage, and he tried to wonder how the fuck Moses might feel put in this situation. He almost forgot any troubling personal thoughts or doubts.

There were figures moving a few streets ahead of him. He could not slow to help them, he remembered. It was like the old superstition of walking on cracks in the pavements; any wrong street, and he was suddenly vulnerable. He heard the police sirens, and saw a police car roam along suddenly. He found that he had come to be what he believed was a good few streets in the wrong direction, away from the goal. He stopped, unsure of the right path, and looked around. Was he trapped?

He was on the wrong side of the city high streets, and police cars moved in all directions. He was alone. He thought of Gaskill, then Jesus, then knew that others were praying for him. The thought lifted him. He then took a run straight out into the main road ahead, under the street lamps. It exposed him, but he moved on quickly, with determination.

He was seen as he ran. From the streets around, a number of dark figures came out in pairs and began to follow behind him. Eventually, he heard a couple of the footsteps, the noise, but it was too late. He only looked ahead as he ran back in the right direction. The footsteps grew louder behind him, faster too, and he only thought of getting to Eric and the secret church area. He turned a few streets to confuse his pursuers, at risk of confusing himself. The darkness taunted his senses, suggestive yet vague. He quickly looked down an alleyway as he went. As he looked back ahead he stumbled, nearly falling over onto the ground.

'Are you okay?' a voice asked.

He stood nervous and hesitant, then focused on the shape before him.

'Emma?' he said, relieved.

'Oh God, Peter, it's you?' she asked. She reached and helped steady him. He looked around nervously.

'What's wrong?' she asked.

'They're coming,' he told her.

'Who are?' she asked.

'All of them; police, demons, the ones who...' he started, but did not finish.

'Is this your man friend?' another voice asked from within the shadows behind. Taylor came forward, and Emma and Peter looked at each other uncomfortably.

'We can't hang around here long. I'm being followed. Is he alright?' Peter asked Emma, and pointed to Taylor.

'He's just a bit unpredictable,' Emma told him.

'What? Jesus, can't you trust anyone?' Taylor said. 'Is she as two-faced with you, church man?'

Peter turned to Emma.

'We should move. I'm very sorry about...you know,' Peter said.

Emma seemed slightly embarrassed and blushed. While she was angry, she was still very pleased to see Peter was unharmed.

'Some shit went down between you two did it? A little lovesick, are we?' Taylor asked, joking. Emma turned to him.

'Close your mouth, okay? You've caused enough goddamn problems by yourself, so just shut it,' she told him, finger pointed sharply.

'So this is the one with Eric?' Peter asked.

'Yes, this is him. Perhaps you should leave now, Taylor,' Emma suggested. Taylor was being incredibly irritating, but then Emma was not sure Peter really wanted to be alone with her again.

'So am I left by myself now, is that it?' Taylor asked.

'Yes, it seems like it. We're at the right place now, anyway,' Emma told him.

No sooner had she finished than a group of loud wild figures came crashing right into them. Noise, shouting, laughing, howling and screams came to confuse and terrify them.

'It's him!' a voice shouted.

'Which?' another asked.

Dark shadows moved, blurred as Peter fell across onto Taylor, when two strange shaped men fell over them. Emma moved away, with an echoing whimper. Taylor punched out into the darkness, hitting no one at first. Peter was more cautious, backing up, but then something pulled at him violently. He pushed back, and then something scratched across his cheek. He lashed out and caught a hand. He tried to catch the person properly with his other hand, but then some other force pushed him hard. He fell and was touched, clambered over by half a dozen hands, then feet kicked him and more clawed hands scratched, grabbed at them.

A flash of light from a car driving past the street corner revealed some colour and shape to the motley gang of attackers among the darkness of night. They were a mixed bunch, though red burning eyes and china-white skin united them as a gang.

'Emma?' Peter called out. She did not reply, and it sent a colossal fear into him.

'Emma? Emma?' he called again, to no reply.

'No escape yet for you,' he heard amongst the noise.

One huge scream penetrated the cold air above them all for an extended moment. It was extremely tough to tell who it was. Was it Emma screaming, Peter thought, or Taylor, or even a demon? The more he heard, the more it could barely be defined as male or female, man or demon in origin. It simply sounded so pained and strange.

Peter stumbled in the chaos of the attacking hands

'Emma?' he called out again.

'Over here,' a voice said. Peter recognised it as Taylor.

'Where is she?' Peter asked him.

'I don't know. Fight these things! Stay close!' Taylor urged.

Peter hardly felt like trusting Taylor, and was already a little suspicious of him, but he had to in order to save Emma. They could hear the hissing and murmuring of the demons around them.

'Listen carefully,' Taylor said. Peter did, and heard steps very close to him. He waited, as did Taylor. Seconds passed slowly, then came a sudden aggressive noise. Both men swung fists out in front of them. Peter connected and hit something hard, hearing a crack and moan. Then he heard Taylor moan painfully. There was hissing, barking and loud menacing screams from around them. The sound of Taylor seemed to move away from Peter. He was caught, taken, Peter thought. He carefully stepped forward, hands ready to punch and knock any of the damn hellish things to the ground.

'Peter?' he heard.

'Emma? Oh God. Where are you?' Peter said, glad to hear her voice. He stood as cold and vulnerable as the simple flesh and blood human he was. Feet were roaming around in many directions, he could hear. Demons moving around but weary, staying back for some reason, he thought. He felt simple and naive among the mysterious, deadly predators.

A hand reached out and took him suddenly by the shoulder.

'Found you,' Emma said.

'I... think they've gone. Let's move, quick. You alright?' he said.

'Yes, thanks,' she told him. She clung close to his arm.

'Taylor?' she called out in a low voice.

'Just...leave him for now. We should go,' Peter said with regret.

The moon came over their heads, shining light upon small patches of ground around them. Emma held Peter by the hand and they quickly ran on together through the narrow back alleys of the city centre.

Chapter 47

The small group of writers and reporters from the Evening Northern paper travelled along the coast road. This was a very different night for them, having heard the news of wild sadistic attacks from some sort of man, or duo, the unsettling information from friends in the police. They all agreed that the things which they were hearing were at once unusually bizarre, hard to believe, and contradictory, but ultimately deserved their full attention. They were hearing of murder and sickening attacks, but also sightings around the same places of hard to describe figures, creatures even. They argued about just how much could really be true, and how much was simply unprintable rubbish, but they all wanted to know the reality behind it all.

'So we're heading along toward the coast, North Shields, right? Tynemouth first?' asked a blonde man to the man sitting at the driving wheel of the car, who focused on the vacant roads before them.

'That's right. That's where the last couple bits of info and sightings are from. You all still good with that?' the driver asked everyone behind in the car.

'Yes, sounds okay. Let's get a bloody great scoop, right?' one of the two women cheered.

'Suppose we should,' the other, brunette woman answered beside her.

'No, wait,' the first woman suddenly said, 'I hear from Alex in North Shields of a couple of people fighting, there's been a serious attack there.'

'What? You think it's these guys?' asked the driver.

'Okay, we'll check this place first, like we decided, then maybe go along there too, if we'll even need to,' the other told him.

'Hey, look, all of this isn't the usual kind of front page or even any page kind of news we get. How do we know how to cover it best?' one of the women asked.

'Look, we'll use what we can, how we can. Do the usual; be creative, be entertaining. What we do, for God's sake. So it's all a bit Halloween, well we just have to deal with that,' the driver answered calmly.

The women became quieter thereafter as they drove along, the sole vehicle on the long roads. Seeing the roads so empty around them did not give them much courage.

'Ladies, don't worry, I'm sure that what we have been hearing was embellished and elaborated a hell of a lot, usually is in some way, isn't it?' the driver told them, trying to keep them level-headed and ready for what they might find.

They parked up along the town hall of Tynemouth. The roads were deadly quiet, potent with latent danger.

'Here we are. We're apparently only a couple of streets from the place of shocks and scares,' the blonde man, Jeffery, announced in the van to the others.

'Don't joke please, Jeff. This is different. Let's just get what we need then fuck right off away,' one of the women, Diana, told him anxiously.

They left the van as a tight group and walked closely by the side of the tall building nearby.

'So we have this Clive, a taxi driver, and Beth...Alsop, is it, the florist who should be around near the pub,' Jeffery reminded them, but only really talking to ease the atmosphere.

'Yes, that's right. They should be waiting there hopefully,' Diana replied, a slight tremble in her voice.

They all knew the direction and stuck together, an uneasy group with a job to do in the face of the mysterious dangers. A street lamp suddenly flickered overhead.

'Okay...John on the city police tells me they have been along here a short while back. James Kerouac also came by with his gang. So, we should be pretty safe now, I'd say,' the other woman, Jen, said as she read the message from her phone. 'They do say that the guy seems to have passed through, attacked possibly. How far do we want to go?' she asked the others.

They looked back at her silently, then Jeffery spoke.

270

'Well, let's meet the two we have here first, then decide, right?' he said.

'Also, a business connection of Kerouac's, Derek someone, from the Vladeer House business saw a lot somewhere else,' Diana continued. 'You know that John and the police guys are minutes from here, do you?'

'Yes, he's giving us a chance to do our thing, you know. They all are. But they'll come in seconds if needed, promise,' Jeffery told her.

Diana looked at him, wondering how well she knew him as a trustworthy friend.

'We're not simply bait for this guy, are we?' she asked.

'What? Come off it. We're the best, right? Let's just do this. Time's getting the better of us,' he replied, with a confident grin.

These reporters would find an award-winning angle, the right shocking but fascinating parts of the tale to print. They would earn almost too much money for it all, and too many awards, for wandering these cold dark streets like no one else wanted to that night. That was what they told themselves. They just needed to be fearless.

They heard a quick, sudden patter of footsteps either from behind them or from the alley to their left. They all looked at each other, then at Jeffery for a response. He stepped forward ahead.

'We report what we see, then we get the hell out of here,' he said, a visible cold sweat on his brow. He began walking out and the others followed behind.

'Get John on the phone,' Diana urged him.

'Wait a minute,' he told her, distracted by faint and unusual moans.

'Stop, Jeff,' she said, her nerves almost taking her voice from her.

'Don't be afraid, we're just observers,' he told her, and stepped on around the street corner.

They came out at the wide open grass area, fenced off before the town library and shop entrances.

They saw him running alone. A brutal, wild scream sounded, then another. To their far right, two lurching figures slumped down on the ground. They saw Eric. He was just another young man at first, like any other. They watched silently from across the grassy lawn area under the trees. He ran out, determined, focused and chasing someone or something up ahead. He seemed to be charged with a fevered anger and aggression in his movement, looking around him, cursing.

'That...it's...is it?' Diana asked the others. They stood unsure, and then Jeffery nodded in response, still watching this crazed young man. The other woman, Jen, spoke.

'It is him. The one...but look at him...' she said, strangely fascinated by him.

When they moved out, following him slowly from a distance, they then saw the two figures he was trying to catch up with getting away from him. He was exhausted. but he would reach them, he knew he could. It was like sport now, hunting, catching these things. There was a unique thrill and rush of energy to the chase, he thought.

Bastard things, he thought. They would not stop him; they were just a couple more he needed to stop on his trail towards the truth, towards saving his Grace. There were so many, though. Like a hidden breed of insects, multiplying in their nests. Then they broke off, escaping his sight. He cursed them loudly as he stood in a rage.

Eric looked around him as the strange energy pulsed within him. He looked around and his eyes suddenly met the gaze of the journalists by the trees.

They all stared back, shocked, frozen in fear. As they watched him, and he watched them, they saw his eyes. The eyes suddenly burned a bright red before them. It was shocking and unnatural. His skin seemed to lose colour, turning deadly white, and a strange orange aura seemed to emanate from around him

The two women stood holding the recording equipment, frozen in fear. Jeffery and Karl were hesitated, but stood in front of the women, as that was all they could do. On seeing these curious observers, Eric quickly bounded across towards them, enraged and uncontrollable.

'What are you all staring at?' he asked, his eyes burning a hellish crimson. 'Take a damn good look, won't you!' He moved in close, creeping so near to them that all of his ghastly appearance could be witnessed clearly.

'Stay back, now. No trouble here,' Jeffery told him, clutching his camera tripod tightly. Eric looked him up and down, unimpressed.

'Oh, reporters are we? Want a darn good story? Top headline of tomorrow?' he asked.

'Jesus Lord, I've not...seen such...' Jeffery uttered.

'Oh Christ, God...' Diana stammered, watching.

He looked at each of them with their shocked faces. I must look a real horrific mess, he thought. But he had no time to think. He simply growled at them, like some rabid creature, and they all stepped back, terrified. Karl, though, clicked off half a dozen quick photos discreetly, his camera held down by his waist, and Diana had recorded audio on her small device. Knowing that he was letting his more important victims escape, Eric then ran off once more, alone up the dark street ahead. Goddamn news reporters. This monster is not the one for them to fear, he thought.

'We have to go,' Karl said in a quiet but defined tone. Jeffery stood watching Eric disappear down the darkness of the street, then he and the others ran back around to their van. As they climbed inside, Jeffery called up a number on his phone.

'Hey, we've...we've seen him, just now...yes, really. He butchered two on the street. He's...he's just dangerous, like nothing else. Dangerous. Some evil in him, really. Honestly,' he said quietly to the listener on the end of the line, while Karl began to drive them away, back to the newspaper offices. They had the news of tomorrow and days to come.

Chapter 48

The city of Newcastle held a good number of secret lairs, meeting places, dens, hideouts and clubs which had been found or built by both groups of demons over the decades. Any other local gang culture had nothing on the evil soaked deep within the back streets and seedy businesses around the towns. Gangs were either taken over by demons, or run down.

If Eric was walking along the right path, he deemed he would be safe, in some respect. He was due to work with the demons that corrupted the North, and it tore at his heart thinking about it as he walked on. Footsteps approached from nearby. Eric spun around, and there before him under a dim street lamp stood a tall, muscular man in a crumpled denim jacket. The eyes glowed lucid red at Eric.

He waited to see what the demon wanted from him. He felt confident in his power to fight it, thanks to Bruce.

'Follow me now. These streets are ours. Help me with your knowledge,' the demon said. 'I'm Sirius,' he told Eric.

'Evening. Lead the way,' Eric said as he began to follow the demon guardedly.

There were questions Eric wanted to ask this demon minion, but he was not certain if it would endanger his opportunities ahead. Eric wondered what this demon thought of Bruce and how things were run. How did the rest of them view their leader? What would they prefer if they were to find themselves a new one? He had crossed over in a way, between both groups of demons to be able to know them, their ways, and their deeds. Now venturing deep in among the places no men had seen, he was careful not to ruin his chances, having come so far.

'So what has happened?' he asked Sirius while they stepped along a back street.

'The other ones have been meeting us with surprising force. They are clever, part-human shits. Even since agreeing to the coming meeting on the Quayside, some have killed, some trying to trick others. Not all can wait for the battle. Some just kill when chance arises,' Sirius explained.

'But it is still going ahead? The meeting? Battle, you call it?' Eric asked.

They had to, he thought. It was how his plan was to work successfully.

'We believe so, yes, but there is rebellion. We expected some, but not like this. The lead hybrids, with Andrew, claimed miscommunication of news. Both groups have to maintain mystery, you see,' Sirius told him.

'So it should not be so hard to calm them, right? Until the Quayside?' Eric asked.

'You might think. They are from humans, the hybrids, so they are stupid, confused wretches. They are a mistake, fucking experiment gone wrong. Dual needs and desires, that is the threat to us,' Sirius said.

'Okay, I understand,' Eric told him, and was glad then to not be of either group, but then he came to thinking that he himself might be some kind of hybrid now. A few painful regrets clouded his mind. Either way, he came to see possibilities to confuse and manipulate all of them once more. That was a good thing, he thought to himself while walking with the demon.

Sirius sniffed the cold night air around them like an intuitive dog on a trail.

'The street up ahead, they are to the left, near the car park. They killed some of us. I killed some earlier. Now, you and your big man mind helps me-right so?' Sirius said.

'You want me to do something here?' Eric asked.

'Yes, you are with us, right?' Sirius asked.

'I am. Where are your...others?' Eric asked.

Sirius turned and made a strange gargling noise, with his head twisting around from side to side. Three figures emerged from the shadows, coming from opposite directions.

'Here; Oreb, Keelar, Robin,' Sirius said, introducing them to Eric. They all resembled Sirius quite closely, and it was difficult to decide if any were at least pretending to assume male or female gender in some way at all. No small horror was hidden, their bodies blistered, crooked, though muscular and strong.

'Follow my lead,' Eric said to them.

Less than five minutes later, Eric ran out into the street ahead and turned the corner. He then stood looking around, acting naïve, though hopefully convincing. He tried to look desperate, lost, confused and simply pissed off enough to draw interest. After a few seconds, he continued to curse to himself and pace around tightening his fists in anger. He had never acted in school or college, and worried that it might just not be convincing, that he might be giving away the truth. He had only planned for a couple of minutes and yet no one had emerged to greet him.

He thought of calling to Sirius or going back to the demons unsuccessful.

'Clever man, are you lost?' someone asked in a weird, guttural voice.

Eric slowly looked around, but could see no one yet.

'No, but I wonder what is happening,' he said aloud. He waited. He felt stupid, trapped even

'Where do you stand now?' the disembodied voice asked him.

'I am between tribes. A connection, a shared interest. I became aware, and have my reasons for being involved but mine alone,' he stated.

'These are our streets. Not theirs. Their time has gone. We are the next step, we are the future. Man released,' the voice told him.

'Maybe,' Eric said. 'Aren't you meeting them, every one of you? The big showdown by the Quayside?' he asked.

Before an answer came, Sirius came surging quickly up the street with the three other demons. They ran out at Eric, as if they wanted his blood. It made Eric nervous, but he was ready, as time was moving on. He walked out further, keeping distance from the coming pack. As Sirius and the others came up to meet him, the hybrid men demons stepped out suddenly at him. Eric waited in defiance, while Sirius and the demons joined him. He ran up out of the street, leaving both sets of demons to confront each other.

The two groups of powerful opposing demons saw each other as they both watched Eric escape alone. The groups then watched each other, each group desperate to rip, kill, tear the other, but they simultaneously stepped back into the deep shadows of the opposite sides of the street once more. They would wait.

Within the demonic community that had been built up secretly over the decades, there were dangerous friends and dangerous enemies of many kinds. The many hundreds of demons around the North had worked their way into and under mankind, behind regular perception. It had not taken long at all. It may have been due to the recession, the social collective depression, man's trust in technology, the evolving culture of people in the country, but they sunk in deep and took real control. Politicians, councils, even gangs and criminals of all kinds, still continued to believe they were most powerful, but in reality the demons were changing everything and everyone.

The original demons were in some ways just like the biblical stories. They could shape shift, occasionally fly, and sometimes influence human minds telepathically. They would sometimes reveal their real, unmasked appearances when attacking, chasing and fighting men or women. As in legends, they could appear to have elements of wolf, goat, dog and other strong wild beasts, and then more indefinable features, as if haphazardly moulded by some blind sculptor.

They could usually control these changes, though frequently they might change due to their mood. This often came to explain and create many of the ghastly camp-fire stories, local urban legends and Halloween tales over the decades. This rarely happened to Bruce, though, who had been one of the very earliest true demons to rise to Earth and begin the stronghold in the North of England. He was not the sole original demon, however. At the start there had been four of them, with specific orders, a mission, and a time limit. Although rarely discussed, and to humans little was ever known, the four demons arrived knowing to cripple the human species at the best time, unseen and with no intervention. The true fate of those other original demons was debated and not entirely certain. Those original four started the chain of events decades earlier. Mankind unknowingly helped welcomed them in, to claim buildings, lives, communities, and souls.

Chapter 49

Years before, in the late seventies, there had been a secret meeting of three intelligent, curious entrepreneurs wanting help in gaining even more wealth and power in any way possible. These were young and brave men, but all of them egotistical and having climbed to a respected level, desperate and addicted to power. They had gained money, business deals, friendship with others, who exchanged thousands or millions daily, and they needed to maintain their success. Other businesses lurked around them, other people who were just as talented, if not more so. None of them could find any other options that could be counted on, no more friends who they could trust any longer. Between them, they had found many bizarre, macabre interests, and with these they saw some potential hope. Dark arts and evil writings of sinister poets, prophets and madmen led them to try outlandish things.

Their power and success made them foolishly arrogant and paranoid, and the taboo of evil ways beckoned them. They had eventually managed to summon Bruce and his demon brothers. It was a sign, an invitation to Bruce and the others to take up residence in the North. The men believed themselves to be powerful and intelligent, but within hours they were shown how things would be. The demons revealed their own plans, their powers and the horror and death to come from then on. The curious men who had evoked the demons found they would not immediately be kings or presidents, but that they would instead be used, tricked, abused, and tormented along with all the others. The men were eventually killed in the sickest, most unbelievably painful ways. These men who stumbled into dabbling one night with black magic and the occult had individual problems leading them to do so.

One man was losing faith in his business dealings, and jealous of his partners taking control. The next man was older, and extremely bitter at young businessmen, as well as being bitter at God. He wished to live for many more decades, if not forever, and do many more things; he wanted to torment the youths and tempt more and more women and men into being with him from all over the land and beyond. The last man could be said to have joined the other two accidentally. Perhaps he was pressured into it by them. All three knew each other loosely through business deals over time. The other two valued his opinion, his skills in business, and friendship. He seemed to live a pleasing life over all, more so than the others. He had problems, but was aware that he was not starving, disabled, or oppressed in any war-torn country. He knew he could definitely have things worse, but he knew he could have them much better, too. He wanted the highest quality, finest living that could be found, pure luxury better than anything known. This provoked his curious and intelligent mind. He, more than the other two men, was a pragmatic, modern-minded man, and logic and reason drove him.

Between his logic and his common sense, curiosity managed to keep him in the same place as the other two men. It was a simple, ghoulish night with the three of them testing the boundaries of this world, our known dimensions and known spiritual beliefs. He personally was testing the legends he had been forced to believe as a child and his own interest in the unknown realities of the further cosmos around our planet and beyond. Another nail on the coffin of organised religion, faith, superstition, fear and any Heaven or Hell or God at all. That one night over two decades ago, this man had cursed his own family, his species, and had ruined the lives of many all around him and those to yet be born around the North-East of England in future.

Life continued after that night, but that life was a kind of secret Hell, gradually tormenting and taking lives, for all three of those men. One of them disappeared only a few days after that unholy night, another practically became certifiably insane, and the last man, the one with reason, logic and weary common sense, remained almost unaffected, or so he thought. Though able to absorb all of the increasing suffering, terror and mysterious deaths, he watched with interest and eventually became personally involved. That man was Philip, Grace's father.

Expecting much pain and horror to follow himself, his wife and family, once he had become involved with the demons, unbelievably thought they had been left unharmed. The horrors that he witnessed around the North entered his head, crafting some kind of continuous nightmarish guilt over the years but only after many deals, killings, and deeds had been committed. He could not, and did not, speak of what he and his two friends had beckoned forth years before on that chilly night to anyone while the evil still moved in the streets around the Tyne.

The danger was out there, all around him and everyone. It had escaped, and he certainly did not know how to capture it and send it back to where it had come from. But he did not want to, for many years. The demons that came joined with him once he had saved himself by bargaining with them; offering ways for them to do much more grand, elaborate evil by working with him. He helped them, and they elevated him in his business life to a much more feared and respected man, who others listened to and would do anything to work with. The other two men barely existed by then, but he had found a way to work with these creatures that benefitted them and him, with mutual respect.

Philip lied, and watched things happen all around him over the next decade. He could do nothing, it seemed, without knowing an equal evil event could be taking place somewhere. He found his punishment for the God who had hated him, if he could even believe that a God existed, which was to simply let Him watch the evil tear apart the hope and life of the towns around and know that it was almost certainly because of the political and business decisions of Philip.

As he had watched the deaths mount up around him, one day suddenly his wife was pregnant again. It pleased him at first, but then he realised that he did not want another child to enter the dangerous world which he had helped to create. He spent some time awkwardly trying to speak to his wife about what they wanted in their life, hoping to persuade her to keep their new family down to one child. After coming near discussion of abortion, his wife would not ultimately consider such an act, and so their second child came into the world nine months later.

As the years rolled on, his secret fear for his children weighed heavily upon his mind, tormenting his thoughts daily. Though he was working in secret with these inhuman creatures, he did not entirely know if he could always trust them forever. Among humans, he was respected or feared. With the demons, he was merely used and accepted. There was an affinity, an understanding between him and the beasts, but they were a different breed, not even born of this Earth, he remembered. So how could he trust them, he often wondered. So far, they had held their side of the deals, rewarding him in business and pleasure, and he continued to set out more paths for them in return. With years passing, he began to wonder just how alone he really was. He had to help himself, he eventually came to see. He wanted to free himself of the never ending fear of them ultimately doing him or his family harm, but he could just never find a way, or the courage. Behind the image of a powerful man stood a fearful and guilty creature.

He never came close enough to considering suicide, and believed that he would find a way to rule over them. He almost ruled over all the humans, he knew, so that would be the crowning glory. He had observed for years that while the demons were indescribably supernaturally powerful, they constantly lacked sharp focused intellect, or simply did not bother to plan much at all. This eventually gave him some hope that he could perhaps in future trick them, and switch the balance of power.

He became a more spiritual, God-fearing man, though admittedly only because he had to further his own plans. Local vicars and clergymen and women came to know him while Grace and her sister were growing in Jesmond. Philip became good friends with two or three of them, but others were hesitant due to his material wealth, political stature and moral attitude. At the same time, the many dozens and dozens of demons in the night time shadows of Newcastle watched his moves with suspicious interest and dismal disgust.

Grace entered her teen years, and Philip came to gain respect and advice in protecting and being there for his family from his holy friends of the churches around the North. This became useful to him as he continued to research all forms of black magic and dark worship, books about restraining evil and controlling it. He decided that he would use the demons more than they might ever use him, and then would banish them to their place of origin. He wanted to eventually perform a complicated region-wide exorcism with help of the vicars and clergy he knew after having gained the friendship and close confidence of some.

Troubles came to find him and his work eventually, though, slowing his progress; he was faced by men with questions, local vicars, even young Satanists and certain curious police officers. He held back for a period of time, unsure if the demons were still actually out around the towns after some distance had come between him and them. There had been a long period of quite peaceful calm, with much regional violence and crime falling in numbers. Philip began to wonder if it had ended a while back, if the demons had had enough souls to last them, to satisfy them finally.

Before her mysterious death, Grace had been a spritely, beautiful, bold young woman. She had only months earlier begun her university degree in English literature and language and moved into student halls in Central Newcastle. Her parents had brought her up to be a questioning, independent young woman in this new multicultural England, with opportunity and equality there to take hold of in her life. Because of the lives her parents had led, and their work, she had opportunities which they never had at her age, and she was of course grateful, though she did sometimes feel pressure and expectation.

She admired both her mother and her father, and had built up an interest in what they did. Her mother was keen to tell her about her career as a journalist and photographer, but her father was increasingly more restrained about explaining his work life to her. Her mother had encouraged her with tales of feminist demonstrations for rights and equality, travelling around Europe, and experiences with men. Philip had remained a strong but quiet man to her, revealing little of his work details, early career, or experiences to her, which frustrated and surprised her continually, though she eventually ceased asking.

Grace's mother told her this was his way, he was a private man, but she sensed more behind his silence, and wondered why he was so secretive, what there could be to hide and why he was such a mysterious man. When no answers came to convince or satisfy Grace, the danger returned. Though Philip loved her dearly, he underestimated how resourceful and skilled Grace could be when she wanted answers to the questions that had been building up for such a long time.

She broke into his room and found things that offered strange answers, but gave her even more questions, though she feared that any real answers might just be too unbelievably shocking to handle. She began to follow the clues of her father's secret journals, from his documents and computer discs and memory sticks, confused and fascinated. His admiring daughter had watched and followed him, and quietly found keys and passwords which led her into the secrets which he hid from the family and all others. Over a couple of weeks, she learned much more that was disturbing, strange and darkly bizarre. Seeing her father after learning of these hidden things, his secrets hidden from his whole family, she wondered what it all meant. These were dark, confusingly disturbing things. He was, it seemed, involved in black magic of some kind, possibly even sacrifice. It was absolutely shocking, almost unbelievable, if not for the words, documents and pictures she had found. Why, she wondered to herself over and over. She realised she just had no real idea of who her father had ever been at all and wondered if her mother did either. Why was he involved in such dangerous, bizarre things? What did it make him?

At that time, only days before her death, she had not told anyone of the things she knew about her father, not even Eric. He did in time come to detect her reoccurring restlessness and time away, with only vaguely believable excuses given. She was at the city library often, then going to unusual parts of Newcastle and the North alone, and she was simply much quieter when they were together. Eric felt ignored and neglected a little, but it had been his own way to be a loner on occasion so he was fairly okay with her wandering ways.

Then Grace had died.

Chapter 50

Between murdering, killing, and other macabre deeds, Andrew continued along with parts of his previous human life. He had been a bar manager for a few years before he changed, and still kept up much of the work at his bar and club, alongside his hardworking human co-owner Marcel. It was located down the lower back streets of central Newcastle. It was quiet a scruffy, fatigued building, but it had a unique character and charm in its indie, retro vibe; all black, silver and corrugated chrome along with mirrors and neon on the walls, along with framed old etchings and Celtic imagery of folk tales.

He checked back in, sullen and pensive. He had been sure that Taylor was willing to join with him. They had so much in common, Andrew had thought. There was a connection; that same anger and dissatisfaction with the rules, and mysterious morals of society. He knew Taylor was trying to leave now, and it offended him greatly. He understood, was even jealous, but pissed off too. Looking back he had nearly expected Taylor to leave, but the timing could have been better. He and Taylor had very similar outlooks and characters, they had found, but not similar enough.

Andrew knew Taylor would not discuss what they had shared, but he knew Taylor would do anything he had to soon enough. He sensed a change. He also knew that Taylor still had the body of Grace locked away, which could still be of great use. If Taylor might come in his way then Andrew would not spare him now. He would spare no one.

The bar was lively with small crowds, who must not have heard of the deaths around them, or simply did not believe it. Andrew walked through the crowds considering the people around him. Were these simple, jaded, desperate men and women actually content, or just drunk? It was a bar, and like all other bars people drowned their personal or collective sorrows and eased the troubles of life with a drink or three. He had often thought about what happiness actually was, knowing that in real honesty he rarely had ever been happy. There was always the guilt and shadow of evil things behind his actions. With old friends, yes, but even then they were collectively desperate and lost, just pushing the limits, the taboos and each other.

Even as a hybrid demon man, he drank, popped pills, got stoned, got high while frequently killing, slaughtering with other hybrids down back alleys or in fields and parks. Now, though, his ways made him again feel sick and regretful. He wanted out. He was a parasite, he knew this. He had hoped Taylor might have been the one he could trust to do this. Taylor had wanted the hybrid life, but Andrew no longer did. They were going to exchange roles.

Among all of the smiling, flirting faces around him a beautiful face was twisted up with anger.

'What's happening for God's sake Andy, tell me?' the woman said to him loudly.

'You're back,' he said, genuinely surprised to see her. She took his arm, and walked him over to the quiet corner of one side of the bar full of regular freaks, players and hangers on.

'Yes, I'm back, and I'm hugely pissed. Why the killing all over?' She asked, looking upset though not completely serious.

'What?' Andrew said, not understanding her. She normally giggled constantly around him, telling dirty jokes and flirting shamelessly.

'People are being wiped out, too many people. Tynemouth, Byker, Gateshead, Newcastle and in between. Why?' She asked.

'It's happening, Lucretia. He left me. He was with the one who managed to kill demons. They both did it together. It's all on tonight,' Andrew told her in a low voice.

'No, it can't happen. What will happen to all of us? That guy...don't they know too much?' Lucretia asked, worried. She really was stunningly beautiful, amongst her thick, colourful, gothic make up. She had a mild Asian complexion, with dyed red hair. She dressed alluringly, though stopped short of resembling a total fetish prostitute.

'What did you say to him?' she asked. 'Shit, Andy, are you still being all morose and maudlin?'

'He was just hanging around a while really,' Andrew told her, referring casually to Taylor.

'So can you get him back? Do you know anything about his friend, this trouble maker guy, the demon killer?' she asked.

'You could try. You and your ways,' Andrew told her with a knowing glance.

Lucretia smiled, her eyes widening.

'Alright, then. I will, I'll get the slippery shit and get him to tell us what we need to know, then I'll end the bastard like only I can. Where'd he go?' She pulled on his arm for them to leave the bar.

An old-looking car pulled up outside Jesmond police station, alongside dozens of others not usually parked there, all crammed in tight and close. After a couple of minutes, Eric's father Donald got out of his car and walked up and through the station entrance. He did not enjoy being there at all, but this was it; he was going to try to defend his strange, distant but hopefully innocent son.

He walked in and immediately was squeezing past through crowds of hysterical, arguing and melodramatic people being calmed and restrained by a handful of policemen and women, who were left there while many others went out to find the potential killers. He was going to make some enquiries about 'the evil young serial killer'. As he stood near the reception desk, however, he decided to first casually listen in to the conversation of the police officers near him in the large crowd.

'The bodies must be near the field next to the motorway at Wallsend. Yes, the golf course...' one voice said.

'...down the Oakley Road after eight o'clock. He looked insane, crazed. Going to get someone else...' another explained.

'I pray for my own. Those poor souls did not escape,' said another.

'...on the high street just around ten to nine...could be anywhere. What? It must have been him. Who else?' the first policeman said.

So many people believed that his son was pure evil, one of these sick killers that comes around from nowhere every decade or so in England. Could he ever make them think otherwise? Was the damage done for good? He knew that Eric had been dealing with Grace's death in a peculiarly solitary way. His father had let him go. They had been apart for nearly a year before this, after their personalities continually clashed. A crumbling relationship, once Eric's mother had died two years before in suspicious circumstances, which Eric almost accused his father for. Donald had felt bad enough for that and now Grace had been taken from Eric just as he was coping with life again.

He had wanted so desperately to be a good father, but life was testing both of them with the most terrible, tragic experiences.

Donald listened for another couple of minutes and then decided to move on. He had a few good clues by then about the direction that Eric was taking if he read between the lines. He returned to his old car outside the police station and started off along the road to the motorway. From inside the police station entrance, a single police officer watched him drive away.

Eric stood cold and sniffing in a small, narrow back doorway. He held out his phone before him, checking it for a call or text. He looked at the city streets at the end of the dark alleyway. This town was some kind of hunting ground now, he knew. It had been like this before, or had it, he wondered. It probably had, he realised. While he had hung out shopping, drinking with old friends there had been danger all along, hidden but very close to them always.

'Looking thoughtful there,' someone said suddenly. Eric looked up.

'Sirius. I suppose so,' Eric admitted.

'Good to know. Come, we must go. We think our act worked, but there are others around. The whole city and more is at risk. There are many angry confused minions and hybrids ready to end each other without orders,' Sirius explained.

They began to walk off once more, Sirius leading the way, though Eric had a good sense of where they should be heading. The other two demons joined them as well, following quietly alongside them.

'What do you suggest for the next few that we encounter?' Eric asked Sirius.

'Similar thing. You weren't meant to happen, you know?' Sirius suddenly told him.

'Well, you know, we men don't regularly expect things like you lot in our everyday world either. You know how human nature works, right?' Eric said. 'Just being a good Samaritan, really.'

They walked on in silence for a few minutes watching around them, cautiously moving forward. As their minds began to drift individually, Sirius stopped suddenly.

'Wait. Listen. Here we are,' he said in hushed tones, an arm stretched out before Eric in warning.

Eric and the two other demons strained to make out any sounds, but then sounds grew louder, clearer.

'Is it them?' Eric asked. Sirius nodded.

The three demons looked at Eric, and so he stepped out alone and moved toward the end of the street.

He could hear some people speaking, clamouring around, things being knocked over. He was not entirely sure if they really were in the right place. Had they gone too far, or taken a wrong turn in the dark, foggy night, and now ended up too far off course, he wondered. He waited. A quick glance back and he saw Sirius nodding to him, urging him to continue. Eric turned the corner.

He saw a sickening sight before him. Was it cannibalism? Was it some kind of sacrificing or dark offering? Whatever the reason behind the thing he saw it had to be stopped. It was unnatural, immoral and evil. He approached the group of blood-splattered men and women.

'Having fun?' he said. They all stopped their devious, sick work and turned to look at him. They began to move in his direction very slowly, creeping up. One of them spoke.

'What's it to you?' a crazed-looking, black-skinned man said, blood on his hands, while the four others watched, twitching, licking their lips, and smearing blood over their clawed hands as they held their captives.

'I'm interested in tonight's goings on. Some big thing down at the Quayside, isn't there?' Eric said, testing them.

'Do you want the pain for yourself, man?' one woman with red eyes asked as she held her clawed hand against a petrified young man's face.

'Wait, it's him. It is,' another told her with caution.

'That's right. Here I am, but that's not what's important. Aren't you lot disobeying rules here?' Eric asked with confidence.

'No, no! We're simple like you. Not at all,' one shouted back at him furiously, defiantly showing the blood on his hands and chin and body as a warning.

No, you are all even more animal than I am, Eric thought; worse than any animals.

'You haven't long, man,' the black demon man told him. 'Don't bother hiding. And don't stop us. Do your own thing. Kill like us, you might as well now. We're everywhere,' he said.

'You'll be punished, won't you?' Eric said. 'Your anger and violence is out of order, not for here, like this. Even by your kind's standards,' he told them.

The black demon man walked up close to Eric so that they were face to face.

'And what of you? Why do any of this now?' he asked. 'You're not perfect. No redemption, that's bullshit,' he told Eric, smiling with red eyes.

'No, you might be right. Want to see what might happen to me? See me butchered by Bruce and others in grand, bloody style?' Eric asked. 'Be at the Quayside, after midnight. Stop these worthless killings until then; witching hour, right?' Eric told him.

The black demon man struck out at Eric, but some invisible force stopped him. As Eric watched curiously, the black man fell, clutching his stomach tightly and groaning in pain. The other demons then quickly ran over, jumping out at Eric with fists and claws held high. Eric braced himself for the attack. As the first one came to meet him, he put out a hand in defence before him. These were evil creatures, he remembered. They might look like men and women, talk and act like any normal average people he might meet, but they could transform and inflict deadly pain unlike any man or woman, he thought. He would not be killing people, he told himself. He watched their inhuman, piercing eyes before him. They did deserve pain, punishment. He was angry and this was a justified occasion to put his anger to use. Practice before the big showdown, he told himself.

The first attacking demon man reached for Eric and came to a stumbling stop instantly before him. He stood looking confused and sheepish. Eric wondered if anything was happening, then a shock came. The demon man shook disturbingly before Eric as the other demons came right up behind but slowed, noticing more strange reactions. The man shivered and shook, then Eric saw the changes. The man's skin began to shrivel on his bones, stretching back over the hands, arms, face. Then the flesh burst into flames in different places in an instant. The eyes, lips, face lit up, bright red and orange flames dancing and burning through and black and grey smoke quickly clouding up from the man.

Eric looked down and noticed the same thing was beginning to happen to the first man he had stopped. The other demons also then fell to their knees, screaming, shouting, and cursing Eric. He was again impressed and fascinated by the things that he appeared to be doing. He could not believe his supernatural strength and abilities; they were Godlike, he thought. What could he do with power like this? He thought about when he would reach the Quayside. Could he burn them all up in smoke, just like these wretched things? The possibilities might be endless, he considered. He could almost be a kind of superhero. He stopped then, stopped his mind and selfish ego from daydreaming of dangerous fantasies. Such thinking had already taken him too far down the wrong path, he admitted to himself.

There was no time and no need, he reasoned to himself. The demons were crippled, lying around by his feet, and their victims were gradually escaping off into the night with confused but grateful thoughts. As Eric took a deep breath and turned to continue his night, he saw a shadow move behind him. He turned and met Bruce.

'So you've been busy by yourself once again?' Bruce asked knowingly.

'Busy enough,' Eric replied.

Chapter 51

Many of the roads were strangely quiet as Eric's father drove along the motorway. He had never seen so few cars before the early hours like this, he thought as he drove. After a couple of minutes, he caught sight of some unclear accident to one side of the road. It was the worst night he could remember, since, since…

This night was just so unnatural, the brutality and relentlessness of it all, he thought. Could it be stopped by the police that they had, who were always so criticised, ridiculed and distrusted? He heard police sirens somewhere behind. There was never a finer example of the police managing to do jack all in a bad situation than right then, he thought. Even if his wayward, wild son might actually be guilty of some sort of strange crimes, they just did not need to spread around so many lies, myths and rumours. He often never knew what to believe from the newspapers and TV news, knowing how they fabricated stories, distorted truth to scare the masses. This is my damn son, he thought in anger. I didn't ask for this, he thought. They might not have been close or getting along at all really but he did not wish his son to been chased and hated by people, with his life in danger. He didn't want this, but did Eric?

He took some turns in the road with his car, crossed roundabouts and continued on. An expensive-looking car suddenly raced past him, inches from knocking his car as it passed. He cursed it as he watched it get smaller and farther away and turn off up ahead. Two police cars appeared close behind in his wing mirror. Good God, he thought. Are they following me? No, they must be tailing that crazy arse in the sports car, he thought. They stayed close behind him, though, and seconds later signalled for him to pull over. He realised that he could not, and probably should not, try to outrun them, and so made his way over to the hard shoulder a few yards ahead.

As rain poured down his windscreen, the police cars parked up behind Eric's father and walked over to his car. He wound down his window as they approached. Cold wet rain spat through his open window as he waited for them. He had much to say to them, much anger to release. Any police officers coming near him now would get a torrent of negativity and his opinion about how they were treating his son and how he was being depicted by them and the news reporters. The two police officers approached his door together and one leaned down to his level to speak.

'Hello, sir. Can I see your licence?' he asked.

Eric's father held it up to the officer. The police man looked at it closely, then gave a look to the other officer and suddenly leaned in and opened the car door. Eric's father moved back, shocked, but the policeman went in and pulled him out as he struggled against them. The two policemen dragged him out of the car into the heavy rain on the motorway road, holding him tightly.

'What the hell is this? You damn loons! Tell me why?' Eric's father shouted. 'Are you mad?' he asked as he struggled.

Two other police officers had walked over by then from the second police car parked behind the first and joined the other police officers. None of them spoke to him, only nodding and looking at each other quietly.

'What do you think he's done? He's guilty of nothing at all. He's a good young man, my son. Better than most,' he managed to tell them. 'We don't need this Orwellian fascism. Get the wrong files on hard drive, wrong numbers, did you, like always?' he asked, laughing a little to himself. No answer. They looked at him, watching the anger on his face. The policeman nearest punched him hard in the stomach, while the others held him still. He felt the pain twist in him, sickening and awful. He almost threw up, but looked back at the police officers.

'Why? If you did your work right, you'd know...he's...innocent...damn you,' he said, suffering.

A different officer punched him again in his side, then twice in the face. They all studiously watched him bleed and groan, as if they were listening to their chief or writing up reports. Eric's father coughed blood out onto the road and down his shirt.

'What does he know?' the officer who initially punched him asked.

A heavy daze moved Eric's father, but he had heard the man.

'I know...barely anything. You...know...more than I...' he told them.

Another police officer stepped up to him, and after studying him, suddenly smacked him straight in the face, busting his nose easily. Blood streamed down around him as he continued coughing violently.

'Lies. You can't save him, or his love. What did she tell him?' the officer demanded.

Eric's father just had no idea what the man was talking about. Did he mean Grace? It suddenly made him think that he really did not really grasp the real nature of events. He was beginning to see that there might be even more the police chasing Eric

'I know nothing that can help you or him, God help me. I pray you all open your damn eyes before it's too fucking late,' he told the police officers.

The lead officer reached out and grabbed his head. He held onto Eric's father, and in the next few seconds the whole head burst into flames, and burned brightly, the flames and smoke rising high in the night sky. Eric's father screamed in pain as his face burned black, flesh peeling, crisping and disappearing behind smoke and flames.

The officer released him, and the burned up body dropped lifeless to the ground. The whole body continued to burn up in flames while the demon police officers watched with red eyes. They all watched for a couple of minutes, then returned to their police cars and drove off, leaving the charred remains on the roadside.

Chapter 52

The line of cars parked all around the street outside the small church surprised and shocked Father Gaskill as he walked around alone to collect his thoughts and say a silent, private prayer for help. The night was unpredictable, and had begun to challenge him in many profound ways. Many people had driven to the church that had never been in a long time, or even never at all. It pleased him, but then simply reinstated the seriousness of the night's events.

People sitting in his church then had come for sanctuary, safety, answers and help from God, if He dared show himself. Many had lost family members, loved ones, and friends, and were willing to try anything, even swallow logic, pride and fear and step into a building commonly ignored, rejected or mocked. They did believe that very unusual, sinister forces were out, things none of them fully understood, taking whoever they liked with no good or obvious reason. They were all beginning to see that whoever was killing, whether one person or many, they were obviously a vastly powerful, well organised, mysterious force and perhaps the police just would not be able to stop them.

Gaskill though that in over thirty years of being a respected local vicar at his church, he had never seen such a shocking string of events in such a short time in the community. Before he had fully become a vicar there had been issues around the North about spirituality, faith in modern times and even the interpretation of good and evil within the holy book that other elders and vicars had seriously debated, he knew. Then things had suddenly calmed, and just about remained that way. He had never had to console such a large amount of people in such a large-scale tragedy in the area, and barely knew where to begin. He lit a cigarette and began to smoke it as he paced the side garden path around the church yard. He took a deep draw, then another while looking out across the streets beyond and around the church.

He caught sight of something glowing, a couple of streets away then. Two small red marks in the darkness ahead. Was it cat's eyes he could make out? Not if they're red, he thought. The eyes moved along a little, a few feet high off the ground. The two red lights eventually rose to five foot in the darkness. No, the eyes were not bright like cat's eyes could be, he thought. They were eyes, though. Another set appeared then right next to the first pair, hovering in the blackness, then another. The three sets of eyes blinked at him from within the deep black shadows of the opposite street. The eyes unnerved him, but he watched them still, curious. He smoked his cigarette almost down to the very end absentmindedly. Feeling the heat prickle his fingertips, he put it out on the church wall behind him as he continued to look ahead.

The three pairs of eyes blinked at him still. Gaskill's heart sank, and he slowly took a deep breath as he walked back toward the church doors unsteadily, turning away. He took out his mobile phone as he entered the church.

'Hello Peter?' he said impatiently.

'Father, are you okay?' Peter replied almost immediately.

'Well...there are many people here at the church now. People have died all around the North in the last few hours. How are you doing? Any luck with what you wanted to do?' Gaskill asked.

'Things are...moving along, yes. Please pray for me and my friend Emma and her close friends. I pray for all of you there. Father, are you really sure you are okay?' Peter asked, suspecting from his voice that some problem was deeply troubling Gaskill.

'Of course, Peter. God be with you now. Good luck, my good friend, be careful out there,' Gaskill cautioned. He took a look outside again, before fully closing the church door behind him. Still the red eyes watched him from across the street, unflinching, unmoving.

The car was between Eric and Bruce as they stood and looked at each other with respectful hostility.

'Did you make me do that? Make me kill those ones there?' Eric asked.

'You wanted to, you had to, didn't you? You had the urge in you,' Bruce told him 'Hell, you even saved a few people in the fight then. Get in,' Bruce said.

'No, give me answers. What's my part here?' Eric asked, expecting some elaborate lie. Bruce smiled a wicked smile back at him.

'Am I using you? Are you using yourself? Eric, we're better than that. You know the truth. Am I wrong?' Bruce said.

'Our deal is set, Bruce. I have my limits. Do your own clean up after tonight,' Eric told him.

'Want to waste more time?' Bruce asked, looking uninterested. He opened the car door and motioned for Eric to get in. Eric gave him a stern glance then got back into the car.

As they drove closer towards the Quayside, Eric found he had a number of things to ask Bruce and could hold back no longer.

'Bruce, how much hold do you have? How much power?' Eric asked

'Enough, always just enough,' Bruce said

'And the hybrids, how much do they control?' Eric said. He had to wait for the answer, it was not immediate.

'Men want a little of what we can give. Your simple institutions have been useful to us over the years. Thank you,' Bruce told him cheerily.

'You've used institutions? What, like the police, the government, religions?' Eric asked, very concerned.

'Of course. Why wouldn't we? Our trick is to plant the fear, the guilt, the sin. Works a treat,' Bruce replied while watching the road.

'Are you in the media too? Printing lies and warping minds, I suppose?' Eric asked.

'Everywhere that can be used has been. Only problem was the hybrids, not man. Well, except you. Not now though, right?' Bruce said.

The words woke up a new perspective in Eric's mind suddenly.

No, he thought. He was man's problem; man against man, all understandable, obvious, and tragic. He was enjoying the killing, the freedom and power given to him. He actually had become what the police and news reporters had been hoping he was from the very start. They would be right; he was a merciless serial killer to be afraid of. It was so very easy for them all now, he thought. He would be written up on the front page headlines as a disturbed youth; product of modern society kills many as cry for help. Typical case, they would think; just another one, another martyr, another tragic freak side effect that the teachers and doctors had missed years before. The politicians could use him as a great case to prop their policies and reforms before elections happened, blaming the opposing party of years earlier for producing this kind of dangerous young man. But he could not be anything more than an actual man, which would not be possible or practical for anyone, Eric thought cynically.

It was not just himself, though, he thought. There was Emma, Taylor and Peter, and they were only the ones closely involved. Whatever they could do they were out there doing it. He hoped so, anyway.

Chapter 53

Taylor was alone and miserable. He had lost everyone he cared for all at once, and it stung. He cursed Peter and was jealous of Emma for all her work she had done for Eric. He had ruined every part of living for Eric, and then did nothing to help him through the pain and damage done. He thought of Andrew and realised that he would probably be looking for him, to hunt him or get some kind of outlandish revenge. There were no paths left to him, he thought. He felt alone, with guilt and fear tormenting him. Alone save for the body of Grace.

It felt like he might be wasting time, Taylor thought as he ran down along the street and entered the metro station. Every second moved much too slowly as he waited for a metro train to arrive. He heard the shuddering rumble and then saw the light illuminating the long dark tunnel at either side of the platform. He boarded the metro and began his return to the flat, where Grace's body waited for him.

Taylor sat aboard the metro train in a corner of one carriage. Behind him, a few rows down, a group of arrogant teenage boys smoked weed, which was thick in the air around, and they cursed loudly to the annoyance and dread of the handful of other passengers around them. All that Taylor could consider was whether the body in the freezer cabinet in his flat was still there, still intact, and safe for him to collect. That was all he could think of, until he was then distracted by a flicker of bright light. He looked around the metro train carriage and then ahead of him he saw Grace, shimmering like the lights of the train.

'Thank you,' she said quietly. 'I knew you...would be good.'

'It's not over yet. Anything can happen in the next hour,' he answered, looking away out of the train window down at the dark streets as the train moved over ground out of the tunnel.

'Be careful, now...you'll be followed,' she told him.

'That's nice,' he replied quietly. One of the passengers looked at him curiously.

'I warn you...you are...so important,' Grace told him. He turned to look at her.

'Really?' he whispered. 'I doubt it, to be honest. You're dead, aren't you? Eric might be now, too. Everything's gone sour,' he told her in anger.

He then suddenly became acutely self-conscious and felt someone behind him.

'Who you talking to, nut job?' one of the teenage boys asked, a can of strong lager in his hand.

'No one. Myself, actually. Long day at the office. Need to have a good drink, y'know? Cold, isn't it?' Taylor said to him. The youth looked back then laughed at him.

'Fuckin' mental, you is mate!' the teen told him. He laughed and his fellow malcontent friends laughed in unison with him.

Taylor felt slightly worried in case they became violent. He did not like many of the lazy, drug-taking youths on the streets, and might like to kick a few up the arse. But here he might not be able to handle a gang by himself, especially if they were carrying weapons. They simply smoked and drank on, laughing loudly at him. His stop came up, and he left the metro train, smiling goodbye as the train took the stoned teens away. Was he mad? Perhaps it was karma or a suitable kind of punishment, maybe from God. He walked quickly along the quiet streets toward his flat with tormenting thoughts rattling through his troubled mind.

Chapter 54

There had never been a stranger, more bloody night of death and murder for David Raimi in his career as a police chief constable. Unholy sights were presenting themselves to him every quarter of an hour or so, as he drove around with his colleagues through the dark, cold night looking for clues and victims. All of his police colleagues were obviously nervous, anxious, and frustrated. He himself tried to keep an objective view on the events. This was admittedly a hard task, knowing that he personally knew of the real forces involved in the night's bloody deaths and attacks. His small close team of officers were not by any means perfect. Though he did count Jeff, Alex and Fiona as good friends who had been with him in many tough situations over recent years, they were individually guilty of possible homophobia, racism, accepting bribes, and other questionable activities.

As this bitter night grew on, Raimi found himself hiding more and more of his own opinions and personal thoughts in order to make best use of his team. He also was keeping back his own opinions about the mounting deaths and assaults. It seemed to be coming to some terrible escalating climax, and he wondered if he was really acting in the right way. He knew some facts which suggested that police would not definitely be the best ones to end the attacks. He had to admit to himself that quite honestly it could be holy men who knew best how to end it all. He considered the facts which he knew so far; in recent weeks, two young men had been seen near or possibly connected to a string of very mysterious though macabre attacks.

One of the two young men was very likely to have been involved somehow due to his girlfriend having died in the past fortnight, Raimi remembered. Though whether the man was doing good or bad things was still ultimately undecided. There was no real evidence of him actually being the murderer to blame him or even his friend either. He knew thought that Eric was guilty in some way, was involved in some sense in allowing these sick tragedies to happen. He did not necessarily believe Eric to be the actual murderer. He was sure, however, that Eric was keeping the truth to himself, holding back information that could help save many other lives.

With these secret personal theories, Raimi was tracking Eric as best he could. He had followed him in his car carefully across the city earlier toward the park, and then caught him again later with a young woman who seemed to be a friend. As the many shocking things began happening elsewhere, Raimi had to leave Eric to his deeds, but had been trying to keep check since by radioing across other police colleagues who were moving around the areas.

He had expected this at some point. He knew his job could be on the line if he acted too strangely or chased an innocent man openly with obvious personal interest, but he saw things coming together now. A dreadful, fearful kind of logic played on his mind as he rode along with Alex and Fiona.

'No one's going to want to come here in future for any damn capitals of culture bullshit now are they?' Alex commented sarcastically as he drove. He laughed a little to himself to loosen the atmosphere.

'We're going to take the shit for all of this, you know. Stop joking around you creep and think,' Fiona told him.

'Christ, calm down Fi, it's just this mad night is heavy shit, okay? I need to joke or I'll crack up totally on you two,' he replied.

'Really you two, keep professional now, can you? We have to, for everyone's sake,' Raimi explained solemnly.

'Check Mr In-control here. He's got a plan,' Alex said.

'What are you thinking, Raimi? Been quiet. You okay?' Fiona asked warmly.

'I'm fine, really. Just thinking about the possibilities,' Raimi answered.

'Gangs, isn't it?' Alex said.

'Really? No, not like regular gangs we know, no way. Organised, yes, but very different,' Fiona said.

'Could be. What's your thoughts on it now, Raimi?' Alex asked.

'Hmm?' Raimi said, caught deep in thought. 'Well I think it is something that has not been seen here, or at least not in a long time. Things go in cycles, don't they?' he said.

'Oh right. Okay, like what then?' Alex asked, curious.

'Well, let's just keep open minds, right? It's the best way to find the true causes of these things, I find,' Raimi told him.

'You think something more bizarre, then, more like a stupid Hollywood film?' Alex said.

'No, you think like something unfamiliar to us, to police, like what?' Fiona asked.

'I don't know exactly. You know, best not to jump to conclusions too soon. It seems deeper. Not just this boy or his friend. It's dangerously big. That's not two teenagers. And the circumstances of these deaths...let's just see, but be prepared,' Raimi told them.

Alex pulled the car over down by the side of a row of shops and newly built expensive houses.

'There have been some calls from around here. Let's see what we find. Be wary. Alan and Glen are on back up if this place is too wild,' Alex said as he got out of the parked car at the same time as Raimi and Fiona. Alex walked out a few steps before turning to face them.

'I think the call came from that pub over the street. Why don't you two go in, I'll look around the street? See you in a couple of minutes. If not, come and get the pieces of me,' he said, and laughed just a little.

'Why? Don't be an arse, Alex. No hero crap,' Fiona said.

'Alright, we'll go in. You be careful, bigmouth, okay?' Raimi said to Alex, and nodded to Fiona, who sighed. She rolled her eyes but followed Raimi toward the pub across the street while Alex walked down to the bottom of the street alone.

'Who'll die next?' a short, blonde, middle-aged woman yelled in a fevered crowd of people in the small pub as Raimi and Fiona entered. They were instantly spotted and many dozens of people moved over toward them.

'Okay, we're here to sort things out however much we can. Is anyone hurt?' Raimi said in a loud, disciplined voice as he looked at the many desperate and angry faces.

'Too late, mate, they're dead and probably many more are now,' a man said, almost squaring up to Raimi.

'Well look, we'll see what happened and what we can do about things here. There are many dozens of police out there right now let that help you now. We want this stopped right now, tonight,' Raimi told the large crowd.

A small distressed teenage girl stepped up to him between others.

'I called you...my brother...' she said, and burst into tears unable to speak to him.

'Her brother was attacked. I saw it with her. He's been taken...and two others. There was blood splashed all over the street. Go and see it for yourself outside if you haven't,' the wider lady next to the girl told them. Raimi looked at Fiona.

'You want to handle them, and I'll go?' he asked.

'Alex is out there. Go on,' Fiona told him.

Stepping out back to the street, Raimi looked down the road. The air around was cold as he looked for Alex, but he could not see him, and so cautiously began to walk a few metres down in the direction the woman spoke of. He looked closely at the ground ahead as he walked, waiting to see gore, blood uncontrollably splattered around. He reached the end of the street and had found no marks of any attack or blood that he could see easily. Was he at the right place? While he was there, he decided to take the chance to check on his other lead. He took out his phone and dialled.

'Hello Russell? It's David. Spotted him or his pal any place yet?' he asked.

'Maybe, David, but it's hard to keep track. There's too much going on all over now. Is he really guilty?' Russell asked.

'Not necessarily, but he knows. He's a key player, the one thing to unlock this all,' Raimi explained.

'You might have to just try to follow now if you can. Good luck. Sergeant needs us moving on,' Russell told him, and hung up.

'Shit,' Raimi said. He turned around and was shocked by Alex looking right back at him.

'Hello. Come to look for me?' he asked, smiling.

'What? No, looking for the blood and mess. See any?' Raimi asked.

'Can't say I have. Is it supposed to be around here?' Alex asked.

'Yes, on this corner. God, this is damn frustrating as hell,' Raimi said.

'Isn't it? You have some other things on your mind, don't you?' Alex said in a strangely sympathetic tone.

'Let's focus on these events, okay Alex,' Raimi suggested.

'Right, we will. What was it you thought was causing all this? Your big idea?' Alex asked.

Raimi looked at him, and wondered if Alex had some different thing on his mind that he wished to discuss.

'Let's go back to the pub. Did you see anything strange? Where did you go?' Raimi asked him as they began to walk.

'I took a look down the alley there,' Alex said, pointing in the direction. 'Nothing of any interest, I'm afraid,' Alex told Raimi, who nodded to himself. Raimi always sensed a resentful attitude from Alex but right then there was something else he saw to be wary of in him. Raimi could really not be bothered with more selfishness, but if Alex had some personal problem with the way things were Raimi would certainly put him in his place.

In the pub, Fiona had expertly managed to calm the crowd and appease their hysteria in a few minutes. In this case, she shocked them all by demanding silence, then proceeded to ask questions and give people tasks to do, after sending a number of them home together. As a few of the people spoke among themselves, she was talking on her radio to another officer.

'It's over here, that's right. We'll go to the next area. Much more to do. My two are behaving bloody weirdly. Raimi's still acting a little distant, unsettling me. I don't like how he is. He's thinking too much...right...when? Can that happen?' she said, while discreetly watching the people around her in the pub. Alex and Raimi walked back inside and looked over at Fiona. They approached and she finished her call.

'No trace of anything happening out there at all,' Raimi said.

'Really? You're sure?' Fiona asked.

'Let's keep our guard up and move out. You've calmed them, sorted any problems, have you?' Alex asked.

'Well, no thanks to you, yes. I don't like this,' Fiona told them.

'Let's just go, we have to,' Raimi said but Alex seemed distressed in some way.

'Wait a minute. We need to be sure that these folk here are okay,' He told them.

'They're alright for now. An ambulance picked up the girl whose brother is missing. The rest are dandy,' Fiona told them.

'Let's be off then,' Raimi said, looking at them.

Alex walked over to the barmaid who stood at the bar.

'How is everyone now? We're sorry we haven't been able to do more. Very sorry,' Alex told her.

'Yes, madam, regrettably we have to be away to now. Keep safe,' Raimi told her, and patted Alex on the elbow, receiving a harsh glance in return.

The three of them walked back out to their police car on the street, and Alex stood jiggling around with the car key in the lock.

'What's up?' David asked.

'Nothing. Hey Fiona, you got one of your hair clips on you?' Alex asked. 'My key is messing me around again.'

She walked around to his side of the car and took out a clip from under her hat. Raimi stood watching. He could not believe that three highly trained and experienced police officers were discreetly breaking into their own car. He looked around them and grew anxious. A sound buzzed out from around him, maybe from over his left shoulder. He turned to look around. Was it a scream?

'What's wrong, Dave?' Alex said from by the car door.

'That sound...hear it?' Raimi asked. He saw Alex and Fiona trying the car key in the door. The sound rumbled and lilted curiously, and so Raimi decided to venture out toward the direction of the unnatural noise. He stepped out quickly, looking down the street. It was still unclear what it was exactly, and then he heard a scream. He ran down and turned the corner.

As he ran along, a thing clawed out at him instantly from deep within dark shadows. He stopped, stumbling back a step or two, hands out in defence. It looked vaguely like a man, but pointed claws and smoking red eyes marked it out as some unnatural thing a breed apart.

'Keep back,' Raimi said. He quickly caught the clawed arms and wrestled them down from near his face.

'He's going to stop you. He's out there now,' Raimi told the inhuman beast. It stood silent and watched him. It sniffed and retracted the claws. Raimi chanced a quick glance behind him.

'Alex? Fi?' he shouted. The demon leapt at him as he saw it coming and fell back a few steps onto the main street behind again. It stepped towards him slowly with a kind of hesitation. Raimi observed how it acted, and was fascinated, but had no idea how to defend himself against such a thing, or even capture it. He supposed that he would use regular police procedure primarily, with a little improvisation, of course.

The police car came up behind him then, and Fiona swung the door open for him.

'Jesus Christ! Get in, David!' she shouted, seeing the clawed thing near him. Raimi took a chance, and quickly punched it across the jaw, knocking a spray of blood out. He took a look into the demonic crimson eyes of the beast as he dived into the car.

They drove off and a new argument broke out between them as they went.

'What the fuck was that?' Fiona asked, still loud and unbelieving.

'You don't know, sugar?' Alex asked.

'What do you mean by that?' she asked, slightly offended.

'It's what's killing people. What got that girl's brother. There's many more around. That's...our enemy tonight,' Raimi said, quietly.

'I can't believe what I just saw,' Fiona said. She had a look of frozen confusion and terror on her face.

'Really?' Alex said in a cynical tone.

Raimi listened and found a strange mood to the words between Alex and Fiona. Was he missing something? A part of the conversation from earlier?

'So are they mentally ill or diseased people? Like they have a virus?' Fiona asked.

'No, keep guessing,' Raimi replied. Alex laughed to himself for a moment then pitched in.

'How much do you know about these people, sorry, things, Raimi?' he asked, and drove extremely recklessly, swerving past cars and lorries with little worry at all.

'More than I'd like to know, I think,' Raimi answered.

'Maybe we should turn back toward Tynemouth. Let chief know about this, see if we're needed there?' Fiona said.

Raimi was very anxious. The creature that attacked him was horrific, but being in the car with Alex and Fiona was almost as uncomfortable. He knew what the beast was and that there were many more, and he was expecting much more danger ahead.

'Be honest with me, Alex, what's up with you?' Raimi asked.

'Some very nasty things tonight, don't you agree?' Alex said calmly as he drove erratically.

'Well this is just the kind of challenge that comes along for the police force every few years, and we will deal with it. This is our challenge, for our generation,' Fiona told Raimi.

'Who, Fiona? What do you know? Really?' Raimi said.

'I know as much as you do,' she told him.

'Bullshit. Stop the car,' Raimi said to Alex, who watched him in the rear-view mirror.

'What's wrong with you, Dave?' Alex asked.

'Wrong with me? I'm leaving. Things to follow up elsewhere. Stop the car now,' Raimi told him.

'We should stay together, Raimi, it's the best way for us to work tonight,' Fiona explained.

'No, I disagree. Alex, I mean it. Stop now,' Raimi said, losing patience. Alex did not reply at first, simply ignoring him as he drove wildly.

'Alex,' Raimi said once more. With no reply, he gripped the door handle by his side.

'Fiona, be very careful, okay,' he said to her.

'Of course I will,' she answered. In that moment, Raimi reached near to Alex and flicked a switch, then opened his door and jumped out, rolling violently over the road into deep bushes along the roadside.

Minutes passed by as Raimi lay in the cold dirt at the edge of the field, his mind closed and wounded. Images drifted over his consciousness, until as the rain spat down onto him for what felt like hours in deep black limbo, then he finally opened his eyes to the night again.

Raimi was not sure of much at all. Was he having a breakdown? He cared too much about society to let anyone or anything, even some hellish creatures, threaten life around his home. Realistically, he had come to see that he had been ignoring many signs around him for weeks, months and perhaps even longer, if he was honest with himself. He felt slightly ashamed of having rationalised it and ignored it all that time. And now all hell was breaking loose.

His very modern, secular logic had forced him to see only what he expected to see, or what he was allowed to see. He and his colleagues trusted and relied upon finger prints, hair, skin samples, and all other biological evidence. Then there would usually have to be witnesses or footage on camera. Recently none of these things had appeared, but he still had a sense of who was involved and why. All there was were his memories of older cases, strange old pieces of evidence, unexplained things that now came back to fit together with newer clues revealing a greater threat. How much had he let happen? Should he have trusted his senses earlier, and maybe he could have saved some of the lives now lost? Police needed evidence, and it frustrated the hell out of him. Damn bureaucracy and paperwork, he thought. He was a policeman, someone who protected others from dangers of all kinds, and yet he had not stopped these vile, bloodthirsty beasts.

They were the police force, Alex and Fiona. They were also much more, David realised now. He had known them both for nearly two years, perhaps but...all that time, he thought. He felt like such a damn fool. He wondered which one would have killed him first. They were on separate sides, he realised from watching how they reacted to him and to each other; two separate species, but both connected to the evil. It was a true shock to him as he realised that these things, these evil possessed people, were in his workforce. They could be anywhere else as well, he thought, in all work places, anywhere they liked. The thought made his blood run cold. He had no idea what they might do now that he had escaped them successfully, but he was sure that they would not forget about him. He stood, and began to walk along through the dirty mud-clotted field and tried to orientate himself.

He tried to think about where they were heading when he left them. When he jumped from the car, he saw that they were driving somewhere near Durham, close to the Tyne. His legs and head ached from the painful fall and impact when he had landed. He knew that he was bleeding on his shoulders and knees, and felt the cold air sting his wounds. He moved off painfully and began to feel around his pockets to see if he still had his mobile phone on him. Thankfully, seconds later he withdrew it from his side trouser pocket. He dialled and waited.

Even as an experienced, physically fit police detective, he felt vulnerable, nervous and at risk from all around him.

'Hello?' a voice said to him.

'George? It's me, Raimi. Where's the young guy, Eric? Find him?' Raimi asked. It was agony to speak, let alone to walk.

'Well, we have a good idea, I suppose, but there's a lot of strange things happening,' George told him, sounding troubled.

'Tell me about it. So what do you mean? We had him tracked, didn't we?' Raimi said.

'Well he was moving in near the centre of Newcastle, almost. The murders though, David, the deaths...' George began.

'What? What's happened?' Raimi asked.

'They're following him now, I think. It's turned around. He might be doing it, David,' George said.

'No, it's not like that, not that simple, George, I told you,' Raimi said, annoyed.

'Yes, I know. It's just the new deaths are closing in near him. But the trail does suggest that he is really involved, witnesses have reported him attacking people, and news reporters are telling us he really is psychotic and dangerous. He's being followed by another killer, or others maybe. Does that sound right?' George asked.

'It's not right, but there might be some truth in a way. Thanks for the help, George,' Raimi told him.

'Are you okay? Where are Fiona and Alex?' George asked.

'They're working hard. Keep him under tabs. Give me street names if you can and the other details as they come, yeah?' Raimi said, with a twinge of pain in his shoulder.

'Yes, I've a few names,' George said. 'I'll text them to you now. Good luck, Dave,' George told him.

'Thanks, we'll see what is really happening, and who will pay for these things very soon,' Raimi said with determination. He ended the call and trudged on over the dark field. Through tall, naked trees he could see the looming black silhouettes of St. James' Park football ground and the civic centre.

Chapter 55

As cold winds blew in over the Tyne, the streets of Newcastle were nearly totally devoid of any sane-minded people. The time was nearing eleven o'clock and many had been shockingly slain, their blood washing the North; some randomly, some specifically hunted down. There were few who were not fearful of being on the streets, only brave or foolish police officers, demons from both hidden tribes, and, in among them, the handful of souls who could just possibly end it all that night.

Taylor sat by the large freezer cabinet with more cheap whisky to help him cope with his anxieties as he looked in at the body of Grace.

'What was so special? The bastard tricked me,' he said. 'All of these crazy things... No God is helping, but then...I doubt I deserve it.'

He heard a faint sound above him. Looking up, he was stunned to see the returning vision of Grace, transparent and calmly laughing down at him.

'What...what the hell's funny?' he asked.

'Mankind is,' she said quietly.

'Really? Why do you say that?' he asked. 'Why can't Andrew speak to you like this?' he asked her. Grace looked back at him with a silent, sweet smile.

'Help me out. Help me help you!' he shouted, and threw the whisky bottle at her, which simply passed through her and smashed against the wall behind her.

'What's it like?' Taylor asked her.

'Strange. Painful. Sad. I haven't...reached...the end...haven't passed...yet...' she said faintly, her words getting quieter.

'So where are you, limbo?' Taylor asked.

'You...tell...me,' she replied, with a sad, helpless face.

'Why, then? You see them, don't you? You know what is happening?' he asked.

She nodded in agreement. They looked at each other without saying anything for a moment.

'I think I should be dead, perhaps. I can't help Eric; I've only done the opposite lately,' he told her.

'There's...time,' Grace said.

'Really? Because police have been tracking us. They're out searching for us. We're serial killers or something. Like they've got something to do now, an important occasion,' Taylor said, thinking aloud.

Strangely, talking to what could be an actual ghost or hallucination was helping him to sort out his thoughts and alleviate his uncomfortable dread.

Chapter 56

At the top of Eldon Square shopping centre in Newcastle City Centre, Andrew and Lucretia strolled down briskly, discussing their present plans. Neither had any strong fear of other demons or other attacks, knowing from their fellow kind that the area was clear. Lucretia looked around the street, slightly paranoid anyway, and still angry, but excited about these new battles with the original demons.

'So where? He's just a regular young man, right?' she asked Andrew.

'Two men. He and his friend. At least. They can be smart bastards, you know; -Malcolm X, Gandhi, and bloody Jesus...they keep coming. Knock them down, they get back up. Martyrs are a pain in the arse,' he told her.

'They didn't meet us. Are we near the others now? Their streets? I mean has any of it changed? Would they cross our streets?' Lucretia asked. 'They just better not try, right?'

They knew they might have to cross the original demons' areas in order to capture Eric and Taylor. Andrew knew he would lose a good number of his hybrid demon companions, and may have already, but he had to continue. He wanted change like nothing else.

Until this time, everything had been kept from human eyes by both demon tribes for all of their existence. Now, life was already going to be different for them, but just how different had not ultimately been revealed yet. Did Andrew really care much anymore? He was feeling different, ever since the funeral and seeing Eric and Emma there. Such painful sadness for them in losing Grace.

'You've been quiet for the last few weeks. What's been up with you?' Lucretia asked Andrew suddenly.

'Me? Just watching the mortals. How life was and is for them. Always entertaining in their way,' he said philosophically as they walked along.

'Really? I couldn't do it again. I was wasted. This is life we have, this is it; living totally, living free,' Lucretia told him. She fully believed this still, and enjoyed every evil, decadent day of her existence as a hybrid demon woman. She flicked her fingers and six-inch claws sprang quickly up from her nails, shining under the moonlight.

'Right, of course. But I suppose these two men made me think about my old self,' Andrew explained guardedly.

'Really? Why? Because they're stupid guys who make mistakes on a daily basis?' she asked, and smiled at him.

'Wait...stop,' Andrew said suddenly, and held an arm out before her.

'What is it?' she asked.

He looked carefully down the street past the closed shops and silent restaurants.

'I heard...smell that?' he said, detecting some unusual aroma.

'Them?' Lucretia asked.

'Perhaps. Blood spilled close by...' he stated.

'Another route?' she asked.

'No...' Andrew answered, and stepped out. A head suddenly rolled out from behind a corner, bouncing unsteadily, blood dripping from it along the ground as it came to a stop at his feet.

'Well done,' Andrew said.

'It's not him or the other one?' Lucretia said.

A shadow came over Andrew and Lucretia, spreading out wide over the ground. A sudden whistle of wind came from above. Lucretia stepped quickly to her left and Andrew only just moved in time to avoid the tall demon creature that landed down between them. Another scurried out from around from the same corner as the human head. Lucretia flicked out her claws, and her eyes flashed red. Andrew simply watched, unimpressed.

The two large demons stepped around Andrew and Lucretia, eyes hooked on them.

'Predictably a waste of my time,' Andrew said.

This provoked one of the demons to quickly jump at him, catching his arms and hissing in his face. Lucretia put up her claws as the other tried to grab her then.

'No way, you old sap,' she said, and scratched his face with ferocious joy. He recoiled dramatically and she laughed, but then saw Andrew held tightly by the others.

'Andrew? Can't you kick his arse?' she asked. She looked at the demons, who then gave her a quick sneer as the lead one thought about how best to inflict torturous pain upon Andrew. Lucretia watched, wondering why Andrew simply stood helpless and reluctant to fight back. She knew how powerful he could be. All other hybrid demon men and women respected and feared his strength and knew he had been the first. It confused and frustrated her, and even made her quite scared.

'Andrew...fight?' she said, hoping he was about to throw them off in all directions and kill them fast. He looked back at her, then calmly at the grotesque large beast that held him. He seemed to shrug, Lucretia thought. The beast snarled and clamped a hand around Andrew's face, moving the other slowly down toward his stomach. Lucretia watched, anxious and waiting, wanting to step in when it was safe enough. She had her own ways of fighting, and knew that she might not be able to handle these demons alone. She could not risk more harm coming to Andrew than could be helped, she realised.

'Andrew...please. Come on,' she said, frustrated.

The beast flicked out a long crooked clawed finger and aimed it at the top of Andrew's stomach. It smiled as it looked at Andrew. It pierced his shirt, then his flesh. Andrew grabbed the beast by the neck and flames burst wildly up around it, engulfing both of them instantly. Fire and smoke flickered and sparked uncontrollably around them. The demon let go of Andrew as it screamed and recoiled, falling down before Andrew and Lucretia.

The other demon then grabbed Lucretia by the legs and pulled her down. She screamed as she hit the ground, but then quickly punched the demon repeatedly in the face, and then clawed at it with her own bloodthirsty aggression, cursing it as she drew blood. Andrew came up by them. He pulled the beast away from her and sent fire and flames rippling over it. In seconds, it smoked and began to burn to nothing, along with the first demon near them. Andrew helped Lucretia to her feet and she looked him in the eyes.

'What was that all about?' she asked after catching her breath furiously.

'Are we lucky?' he said, contemplatively.

'What are you talking about?' she asked. 'Damn lucky to have survived that. You're so damn strange tonight. Thinking like a man, aren't you?' she said.

'Old habits...' Andrew said, and sighed quietly to himself as he looked away.

Lucretia looked around, weary of more demons waiting to attack them.

'If anyone knew about that you'd be so embarrassed,' she warned Andrew.

'I should be more than embarrassed,' he replied. 'Where are your old friends, your family? Do you know or care?'

Lucretia looked away from him, ignoring the questions. He was talking about forbidden things, useless thoughts and feelings. They all chose to forget their previous human lives when they became hybrids, and usually assumed new identities. They did not really have to, but it made things easier to cope with in some ways. For some, like Andrew, it had been decades, for others only weeks.

Lucretia had run from guilt and sin, a Catholic upbringing and unexpected teenage pregnancy. It could have been labelled a mistake by a kind soul, but most would call her actions murder and evil terror since. She had been completely out of control. It was a frequent reason for many of the converts to the 'middle-ground' of being hybrid. She was so sorry for the deaths that she had brought about, but she had been so scared. So scared that she ran to Andrew, knowing of some kind of safety he had whispered to her about one time in his bar, having seen her sad and alone. Anyone welcomed, anyone saved from their sins, and the chance to be who they wanted to be.

Here they were, killing the species they used to belong to themselves, hiding where they once walked freely. They could walk with men and women as before, though never for long, as they eventually would feel physically sick, their bodies rejecting such close proximity to that old life.

'I would have felt pain like a man, like I used to feel it so long ago,' he told her, wanting her to understand.

'Like a fool. You're being dumb. Too much man talk. Let's go,' Lucretia told him. She walked ahead without waiting.

Andrew had brought her in, saved her from jail or worse, he remembered. To mankind she was dead, forgotten. He had helped many since he himself had become part demon decades earlier. He regretted so much of it. He could let himself think that, finally. He had seen in

315

Taylor shades of human life that he missed and wanted to know again. He observed guilt, sorrow, jealousy and excitement, and wanted them back as his own feelings.

He walked on, Lucretia leading boldly onwards through the quiet streets.

Chapter 57

Raimi heard the sound of sirens once again as he stumbled on between shadows under shop fronts and doorways. To him, the sound was not to be trusted or welcomed any longer. Just as it could bring help, it could equally be rushing pain and death to some anxious, waiting souls. He was no policeman tonight, but a man with a sole prayer to be answered. He must find this persecuted young man and redeem his own apathy, mistrust and bad decisions by helping him any way he could.

'Hello? Hello, David?' a crackled voiced called on his jacket radio set. He hesitated before finally answering the call.

'Yes, what's up?' he asked.

'Are you near Newcastle? There's a man we need being chased by a mob. They're out for his blood. He's the young guy's father,' the officer explained to him.

'What?' Raimi said, 'Where exactly?'

'Around near the top end of Market Street by the university way. Hurry. We've got a car or two going as well,' the man told him, with great drama in his voice.

'Shit,' David exclaimed to himself, and immediately ran with a renewed purpose.

He noticed that he was at Saint Thomas Street, only a few streets away from the events. It should take less than five minutes to reach the place, he thought as he ran. The pain pulled from deep inside his chest and body. The cold wind and night air stung his bleeding wounds on his arms, knees and face, but he continued toward Eric's father to do some real good.

He turned down a street, then turned again, hearing voices. There was loud shouting and arguing, perhaps only one or two streets away. He turned one last time and came to face Market Street. The street was bereft of people, as were all other streets around. He wondered if they had given him the right street, or if the man was long gone by now. Raimi walked down the street slowly, looking deep into shadowy alcoves and doorways to either side.

'Hello? Anyone down here?' he said loudly. No reply came.

'I want to help...no need to be afraid. I want to help...Eric. I know he's doing good. I know he's innocent,' he said aloud in the street, alone.

He stood and waited. Seconds passed, and then a figure emerged. Right at the very end of the street, a dark silhouette came out from the shadows and stood silently. Raimi could not make out a face or any features in the dark.

'Is that Eric's father?' he called out.

The figure moved a couple of tentative steps near him. Raimi did not want to take any foolish chances and stayed where he was, waiting. The figure moved another small stride toward him.

'I want to help Eric,' Raimi shouted down to the figure. It seemed to move again, but right at that moment the noises returned, yelling and cursing something or someone. A lively crowd suddenly came out toward the figure at the end of the street from an opening and took it deep within as it moved along. The shouting and screaming continued. Raimi knew what it was then and ran again toward the crowd.

'Stop it! Stop everything now!' he shouted as he ran. He could hear punches, moans, the screams of terror.

'Police! Stop what you're all doing right now!' he shouted with urgency.

Seconds later, under dim broken streetlights, he could see the appalling image before him. Men and women stood in an open circle in near silence as Raimi came up to them. Below, at their feet, lay the bruised, beaten and bloodied body of Eric's father. The man was torn, bruised and battered. He would never live like he had ever again. Raimi looked at the people around in disgust and anger.

'What did he do?' he said to them, almost involuntarily.

'Not him, his son, the murdering bastard,' one large, burly man spat out with venom.

'His son is not...' Raimi began, but gave up. He ignored the quiet, guilty crowd around him, and knelt down to look at the broken old man. He could not have long left at all, Raimi thought. He looked close and could see the last few breaths expelling from him.

'I'll find him,' Raimi whispered close to him then. 'Be proud, a proud father,' he said, and watched the man quietly pass away.

The crowd stood waiting. Some had fled, but many still watched. Raimi stood as a police car came to park up along by them.

'Quayside club,' Eric's father managed to say quietly with agonising pain. They were his last words, and Raimi listened carefully.

Two police officers stepped out of the car and came to inspect the scene.

'He's the father. Murdered. Can't really say which one person did it. All of them, really. Take his body to rest in peace, please,' he told them, then walked off before any questions could be asked. One of the policemen began toward him, but was quickly stopped by the other, and seeing the sorrow in his eyes watched him walk away alone.

The struggle had exhausted Taylor. He sat slumped and tired on the floor of his flat backroom. The body of Grace was next to him in the body bag which Andrew had provided, crumpled and folded in a sagging pile. He looked at it, thinking. She had been a very slim, slender and beautiful girl while alive, but she was still quite a lot to move for him by himself. He had the car parked right up by the back door ready. He had to get her in the back of the car as soon as he could manage it.

'No time to rest now,' a voice told him.

'Grace?' he asked. He felt embarrassed and disgraced as he sat next to her lifeless body.

'I... don't mind. Do what's...needed,' she said softly.

He sighed and began to pick the body up again. He struggled and fumbled away with her arms, directing her out toward the car with serious effort. He heard voices speaking from somewhere near, and panicked, almost dropping the body. After regaining his hold on her, he heaved her up with force and landed her successfully inside the back of the car.

The voices were loud from behind the next door fence at the left side of his garden. Did one of them say his name? He pushed her further inside the car boot and then ran around to the driver's seat. He started the car and quickly drove away, with a corpse in the boot of his car that would hopefully be his salvation.

Chapter 58

The car finally came to a rumbling stop as Bruce parked it up along a narrow alley by the top streets at the side of the city centre. He and Eric got out and he turned to look at Eric.

'Walking from here. Gear ourselves up. See what has been happening so far,' Bruce told him.

'Alright,' Eric replied, 'Not long now, is there?'

'You will be good for us,' Bruce told him, nodding. Eric could see the shining, pointed fangs in Bruce's mouth as he smiled at him. 'Sirius and the others should be around here. Hopefully they've done as I asked. You go check down that street,' Bruce said, pointing. 'If you don't meet Sirius or any others, come back.'

'Okay then,' Eric replied, and began to walk away around the dark street.

Eric did not know for sure how much control Bruce actually had over him or over the events taking place. Bruce seemed aware of more than was immediately around him at any time, but Eric felt there was still some level of secrecy from even his powers. While this demon creature with a man's name had been the cause of so much of this shocking horror, Eric was undeniably fascinated. He wanted to know so much about Bruce, about all of it. He knew thought that he had to stop those thoughts, control himself, and do what he intended.

There were so many of them, he thought. They seemed very much aware of their own strengths, as well as the towns, and how to control them and use them.

He looked around, along past the dark buildings. Silent shops and businesses closed up for the night were all around. He could faintly smell blood. The deep copper flavour was on his tongue, in his nose, in the air around. What have I agreed to, he thought with regret.

The night passed on, and time would not let up on the chase. Things would reach an end soon enough, in whatever way was fitting, before sunrise over the Tyne. It was honestly exciting and maddeningly terrifying for all who lived around the North. One group of reporters suddenly witnessed someone running out ahead, between the looming city buildings. The figure began to closely meet their known description of the serial attacker.

'Hey, Bill, do you think...?' one man quietly asked

'Well, I'm not sure, but...'

They watched on, waiting, all of them frozen in fear. They moved in a few feet closer as a solid group.

'Hey, Brian, wait,' the red-haired woman protested in a whisper.

'What? We're okay.'

'Shit, look, really. Look at...what the hell...'

Brian took another glance across the street ahead. They all saw something very wrong with the figure moving ahead.

'What is that? What's up with him?' one of the cameramen asked.

'I... I am just not...sure,' Brian replied, mouth open in awe.

They all watched in fear and repulsion.

'The eyes...it's him, but...the eyes?' the woman stammered.

'His eyes are...burning,' the cameraman whispered, voice dry.

The eyes of Eric did burn like red, blistering coals in his head, and his hands gave off some strange flames as he walked out ahead of them.

'We have to report that?' the woman asked 'What...is he?'

'We, we have to...we will...' Brian told her

'That's no man, good Lord,' she replied

They observed the unnatural vision of Eric as he walked on away from them, his crimson eyes and burning hands so frightening yet so visibly real. This was their new report; this was the evening news, and tomorrow's front page.

A man fell out from between an alleyway over some bins. Eric, returned to his normal self, and looked down, shocked by the clattering noise.

'Jesus!' Eric said in shock.

He looked at the man, who was bruised and bloodied, and who stared back at him with wild, grateful eyes.

'Thank God. Oh my God. It's you,' the man said, in a weak, heaving breath.

'Who are you? How badly are you hurt?' Eric asked with caution. He held up a hand ready for any attack.

'Your father is dead. Tried to save you,' the man told him. 'I'm David Raimi. Remember me, Eric?' Raimi asked. 'I've been watching...' he said, with diminishing breaths.

Eric took a long, careful look at him.

'Oh, Jesus above. You...' Eric began to say in shock. 'What's happened to you?'

'Some...crazy shit has happened...you know that. I know you are doing good now. All this happening...what are you doing?' Raimi asked. Eric looked around, nervous.

'I can't talk for long. They're all meeting soon down at the Quayside. It's set now. Police can't do a thing. Demons, two tribes of them. Pray I kick their fucking arse back down. So much evil...' Eric said. He sighed to himself as he looked at the detective police inspector.

'Are they around?' Raimi asked.

'Nearby, yes. So are friends of mine. We're the ones who have a chance, any chance at all,' Eric told him. 'Take our car, top of the street. Drive away. It'll slow us down'

'Of course. I'm sorry...about his death, and for all I did,' Raimi said to him.

'Don't be. You're a good man, I see that. Working class heroes,' Eric told him with a smile. They shook hands and then parted ways one last time.

As David drove off, Bruce came quickly along to Eric.

'Who the fuck was that?' he asked.

'Damn, I don't know. What a ball ache,' Eric said, holding back a smile.

Chapter 59

With the roads empty for the most part, Taylor took the opportunity to speed up, a true man on a mission. No police or anything else was going to stop him then, as he drove on like wildfire. He could after a couple of minutes hear police sirens close by somewhere. Should he stop? Any other night he would have considered potentially being a good citizen and pulling up to the hard shoulder. Tonight, though, being a good citizen involved getting this dead body to a secret church site before the worst kind of horrors became permanent nightmares.

He continued. His hands gripped tight hard onto the wheel, he suddenly saw the small flashing lights of police cars in his rear-view mirror. He began to sweat and shake profusely, telling himself to just drive on. He tried to keep his eyes tight on the horizon ahead, but they drifted back again and again to the police cars following behind. He remembered the infamous old rap tune from years back about the police, and he chanted it repeatedly to himself to keep focused. He did not really hate police, just any kind of arsehole, but he had met arsehole police officers.

The cars came close on him, sirens screeching deafeningly. He would not stop. It was his only chance to redeem himself, to eclipse his sick selfish deeds. Even if it did not work, he would damn well die trying.

The police cars came up roaring close behind on him as he approached a large roundabout. He took a quick turn and edged around it, swerving the car at angles to confuse them. He sped out at the end of the roundabout and ricocheted sharply against another car from out of view. His heart beating like a drill, he gasped as he held on and steered against the phenomenal force of impact. Taking near all of his strength and pulling tightly on the wheel, he just managed to cross the car safely over to the adjoining roads and continued.

The unpredictable crash stopped the police cars from following, but also possibly claimed someone's life. Taylor questioned whether he should stop and turn back to investigate. It took less than seconds for him to decide to just keep driving towards Newcastle. Was he continuing for the greater good? If he had hit someone, how important were they, he wondered. That was a sick thing to think, he realised, but he simply had to continue. He knew he should probably think of everyone as being equally important. Was it only Eric, Emma and a few others that he drove on for? Maybe even just for him, and his own crushing guilt and the growing fear of God. He was extremely sorry for anyone hurt by his actions, he thought, but this was one short night, such a short time to save as many as could be saved. Others would die, and already had, he thought. He prayed forgiveness, but tried to retain his focus on the road.

Not too far up the road, to one side near a forest, demons had witnessed the cars collide against each other. They saw Taylor come along, and the other car which drove away from them. It hit off the other car and spun violently, in a thundering cycle over and around, then tumbled down along the side of the forest before finally stopping. The driver was beaten around, tossed and broken again and again inside the metal coffin. Blood stained the upholstery of the interior of the car. The airbag blew up faithfully on cue, but did little to save the already heavily injured man at the wheel.

As the car sat crumpled and wrecked, he managed to unlock his door and fall half out of it. He painfully gasped and spat out blood as a cry of pain chocked in his throat. He looked to the dark sky above, at the stars and cosmos above him spread out over Earth. Raimi looked up peacefully as he died.

Wild shock kept Taylor alert, with fresh aches in his neck and shoulders. The impact on the other car had bruised him heavily, but he had escaped predominantly fine. He could hardly believe his luck, and knew to drive more carefully from then on. Newcastle City Centre came up on the road signs before him, with less than ten miles to go. He hoped that the encounter had not caused much damage to Grace in the car boot, as he had heard her fall and tumble around. Not that she would feel the discomfort, he thought.

He heard the sirens once more. Would they not leave him? Did they actually know it was him they were following? Did they see the collision? They must have done, he thought, and yet they still continued to follow him, ignoring the crash. What kind of police were they? Did they believe him to be Eric, was that their mistake? They probably thought that they were both just as suspicious and dangerous to society at large, whoever they were.

The police cars grew larger in his rear-view mirror. He considered the accident, and how they were acting. He slowed down, and in a few more seconds they knew that he was stopping for them. After a moment, two police officers walked up along toward Taylor in his car. He thought about driving off, but thought that a bad idea. One of the policemen leaned down by his window.

'Good evening, sir,' he said to Taylor.

'Hello! How are you?' Taylor replied, with an indifferent smile.

'Could you step out of the car, please?' the other police officer asked.

'You want me out?' Taylor asked.

'Yes, sir, that's right, if you could, please,' the first agreed.

'Okay then, no problem,' Taylor said.

He held the door handle and then opened the door. Both policemen watched him with what he observed as slightly threatening looks. Taylor stood and looked at them, trying to appear harmless and friendly. He watched the first one, who was looking toward the back of the car.

'Either of you two circumcised?' Taylor asked.

They looked at each other, not sure they had heard right, and Taylor quickly punched the first with all his might, then stepped back fast. He knew the second one would then try to hit him, rightly ducking a fist to one side, then curved around and kicked that one in the stomach as he came at him before pushing the first one back. Both police men fell back in pain and surprise.

'You're following the wrong guy tonight,' Taylor said to them.

The eyes of the two policemen changed to deep red as claws sprang out from their fingertips simultaneously. Taylor reached into the car and flicked out blood across them, then quickly scrambled back into the driver's seat. They both moved in, jumping at the door with furious aggression and scratching the windowpane. Closing the door quickly, he then began to start the car engine. He fumbled frantically to get the key in the ignition. One of them punched and successfully smashed the side window, glass scattering over Taylor as he turned away in time. One of them grabbed at the door frame, revealing many sharp, crooked fangs.

Taylor looked back nervously then punched it in the face. His fist hurt like hell, but it felt so good.

'You let yourselves down,' Taylor told them as he started the car, and it successfully took him away from them with a sputtering roar of the engine. He looked at them in his rear mirror, demonic law keepers hissing with wild, clawed hands, waving at him from the distance. He was off again with luck and Grace.

Chapter 60

For the first time that night, Bruce had a glimmer of worry over his artificially moulded human appearance. Eric observed this with interested and amused curiosity.

'Do we need the car?' Eric asked.

'No, but...' Bruce said, but then became quiet. Eric did not want this to change the circumstances too much or it might ruin everything too soon, he thought.

'Well then, let's continue,' he suggested.

Bruce looked up at him suddenly. His appearance was unfurled, wild hairs outgrown over his face, his red eyes dilated, veins over his neck pulsing dramatically. His true, inhuman origins were showing. This was a legendary powerful demon still, and all would know it.

'Your father has died,' he told Eric suddenly.

'Sorry, what?' Eric asked.

'He's dead. One of my followers saw it. Not too far from here. It was the other ones,' Bruce told him.

'Why? How? Why was he out here?' Eric asked, his face a mess of confused fear and sadness.

'You. Don't let it in. They play with us now,' Bruce explained.

Eric gave it serious thought. He and his father had not been the best of friends before Grace's death and had not seen each other in nearly two weeks. Before then they had only possibly met up less than a dozen times that year. Many wild, unbelievable things had been happening recently, many which Eric would never have believed possible if he had not been right at the centre of them. These things had possibly driven them even further apart than ever, but he could not be sure.

His father had come to help him, he knew this. While they were last arguing about Eric's lifestyle and lack of commitment in his life, he knew the kind of person his father really could be. For friends and family, his father in the end would do anything, even swallow his own stubborn pride to save them.

'You see what they do?' Bruce asked. 'These new men with demon lust. They have no boundaries, no limits or control. We must kill them all tonight. A mass slaughter,' he said.

'I... think I have to agree,' Eric said, with uncertain hesitation but immense anger.

Even without listening to the words of Bruce, he felt cheated, used. There was so much he wished to know. He so wished he had spoken to his father before he had died.

'Bruce, how do you use us? I mean, your kind; how do you exist alongside us all?' Eric asked.

'We live secretly. We need less than your people want, but we need your people. You know how the species live? Kill or be killed,' Bruce asked.

'What, survival of the fittest, and all that? Or like the food chain of life?' Eric asked.

'Yes, almost like that. Your people know little of us, wish to know little about us now, but we are alongside you,' Bruce told him.

'So do you need to kill all of us or just some? You want control over us all, is that it?' Eric asked.

'This must be finished. This is how now. Many years passed, but now it ends. Men did step in years ago...they need to be finished. It was a mistake, the man who crossed us as one,' Bruce said.

'What man was that?' Eric asked. This was a strange new thing, he thought.

'A fool of a man. You will do this with me. For your father?' Bruce asked.

'You? What have you achieved?' Eric suddenly enquired.

'Meaning what?' Bruce said.

'All this time, the decades, all these angry words, deaths and vitriol...and what have you got? What have you done?' Eric said.

Bruce took a step around him, looked at him with an evil glare. Eric might have just said too much, asked one question too many finally. Were they going to fight now, finally, Eric wondered.

'You know this. You are part of it all. Be thankful...' Bruce told him quietly.

'No, listen to me, what? Just what?' Eric said, unshaken.

'You have ideas. The fury, ambition and hate,' Bruce said.

328

Eric was a human who he had hunted down after many weeks. An intimidating, unstoppable, man of flesh and bone who managed to stop them more than once. Few men ever had done that, Bruce thought. Eric had respect and admiration from Bruce but would be hurt if needed.

'Let's see how we can continue,' Bruce said, and began to walk out down the street.

'No, no, there's more I can do,' Eric said defiantly.

'Not tonight, though,' Bruce answered.

'I might do many things. I might make a mark, leave my scar, become myth and urban legend like you all. I might alter the lives of the people of the North in my way,' Eric revealed.

Bruce turned back and stared straight at him.

'No, you won't. Not until we finish tonight. I like your energy, your spirit, but focus now,' Bruce warned him.

Eric began to wonder if Bruce had been challenged ever, in his reign and dominance as the leading demon of the North. It did not seem like it had really happened, but maybe he had not always been leader. Eric wondered if Bruce could be easily displaced. If other demons had not, perhaps he could do it, as a human with demon energy in him, with a different view of things; with a human heart.

'I have to do some things. I'll meet you at the Quayside on time. Do you trust me?' Eric asked him. They watched each other in the deathly cold silence of the dark alleyway.

'Meet you there,' Bruce agreed with quiet indifference.

They began to walk off then in separate directions, each with their own deadly serious plans for how the night was to end.

Chapter 61

Emma was so grateful that she was with Peter once again as they drove up toward Newcastle deep within the fog and rain of the black night. Peter was a unique kind of young man, Emma thought. She had rarely met a guy with such strong, focused beliefs and opinions, yet who was so gentle, kind and compassionate. She did not entirely have complete faith in the true power of his faith. She did have faith in him, and he had faith, so maybe that was good, she thought. There were so many crazy, illogical things happening around them that she had to re-evaluate reality and what was possible in the world, she knew. But then, he had given her hope, and she was beginning to think differently about many things. Philosophers and scientists thought about things, but nothing was ever fully explained, was it, she thought. Peter had a faith, and however critical she might have previously been she was beginning to think that faith might be a very good thing for her.

Despite her opinion, Peter was now incredibly confident and inspired, or determined, at least. His faith in God outweighed his fear and doubt.

'I believe this is a night that has been spoken of for a long time, a really long time. These things just don't get acknowledged or put right out there in the press. If the majority of a nation are agnostics, that does not change what is going on behind the plastic sunshine, the manufactured reality,' Peter stated.

'Peter, I'm glad I'm with you now. Can you listen to what I know?' Emma asked.

For the last twenty minutes he had been mostly continuing a strong theological debate with himself as Emma looked out of the car window, approving but frustrated.

'Yes, we need to think about that,' he said, still deeply caught in his own thoughts.

'No, really, listen to me; you are very gifted, but what I've found is very significant to us now. For Eric and Taylor, you and me and all of Tyneside and further around,' she told him.

'Right, okay, I'm sorry. You spoke of the history of Newcastle,' Peter said, remembering.

'Grace picked away at some very dangerous things. Your church and all the others ignored it completely,' Emma said.

'Not everyone ignored it and not any more,' Peter replied. 'Look, the car needs petrol, we'll pull in at this next service station up there,' he said.

They arrived at the car park outside the petrol station. They each left the car, Peter filling it up at the self-service pump and Emma walked around the car a short way.

'So you knew Grace very well, did you?' Peter asked her.

'What? Yes. Best friends. We went to high school together. We drifted apart a little but then came back together over a year or so ago. We would tell each other very private things, share problems. Be there...' she said. She stopped her words, Peter thought, because she was either embarrassed or finding it difficult to discuss her friend.

'I... she died, Peter,' she said. He could see that she was right on the verge of crying unstoppably.

'Yes, well not for nothing, right?' he asked. He did notice that Emma was then seriously emotionally overwhelmed. He walked over and hugged her tightly, holding on for a long moment.

'It's okay, really. We're going to find what she was caught up in and sort it out. Finish it. She has helped people, I believe. Come on. The car's ready to go. What do you know that can help us?' he asked.

'Hear that?' Emma asked. 'Sirens. Police are out, and ambulances. How bad do you think things are getting now?' she asked.

'I wouldn't like to dwell upon it right now. Tell me then, if you want to,' Peter urged.

They stood in the car park free of any other drivers, or even any staff in the service shops. Emma looked around them at the motorway that stretched out far in either direction and the tall trees and fields between.

'I found information which Grace actually obtained. I don't know where she got it, but I suppose she got it from her father's things. It actually involves her family. Her father is involved with these dark things, these monsters that are killing us all,' Emma told Peter.

'How exactly?' he asked.

331

'It was not really specifically clear, but it seemed like, well, he's a much-respected businessman around the North, you see. It looks like some of the business deals and things...somehow he has got where he is with help from these evil forces. I know it sounds...' she said, but did not know how to describe it to him.

'No, I understand, I do. So you think she got involved or caught looking into it all?' he asked.

'In some kind of way, yes. I don't think she knew until she found all of this, though, and then it was just too late. Her father did business with a few people who she found. There are strange mistakes, dates, numbers, bank records, names. It doesn't make sense. She found that because it didn't make sense, well, it kind of make a different kind of sense. Just as she saw the reality of it...' Emma said.

'Okay, I think I understand,' Peter told her.

As Peter listened he saw movement somewhere behind Emma in the darkness.

'Wait,' he said, and peered over her. She turned around, worried, and they both then saw the two police officers coming towards them fast. Peter stood firm and held Emma by the shoulder.

'Good evening,' he said aloud to the officers as they came right up to them.

'Hello. We saw you here by yourselves. Just wanted to check that you are okay,' the female officer said to them.

'Yes, we're okay, thanks. Just filled up our car. We're moving on now,' Peter told them.

'Wait. You do know of the dangers around the region right now, don't you?' the officer asked.

'Yes, we're aware. It's very shocking. Unbelievable,' Emma told them. She looked at Peter, who seemed nervous.

'Better go, then,' he announced.

'Where is it you are going to exactly?' the female officer enquired.

'Home. Aren't we, dear?' Peter said quickly. Emma nodded and they got back into his car, with the police officers watching.

'Have I seen you around before?' the male officer asked Peter.

'Maybe, it's a small world. Goodbye, then,' Peter said, smiling back.

The officer screwed up his eyes in consideration, then spoke again.

'You're religious,' he said.

'Yes, I am. I'm a training minister in youth work,' Peter told him.

'What do you think about this all, if you don't mind me asking your opinion?' the officer said.

'It's...tragic. There's always hope, though. Please pray, it helps I find,' Peter told him.

'Good idea, of course. Very good. We've all been pretty confused and shocked, all of us. What is your church doing?' he asked. The other officer simply looked bored and sceptical.

'My church?' Peter said. 'Well, my vicar is consoling many dozens of people right now, I believe. Supporting families and people who have been affected by these events,' Peter explained.

'Let's go, Frank,' the female officer prompted quietly.

'Okay, I'm just talking to...' he said, and stopped looking at Peter.

'I'm Peter,' he said, helping.

'Talking to Peter. He's one that might be able to do more than some of us. These things, Jess, they're unearthly. I'm serious,' he stressed. 'The churches and temples around Jesmond and Newcastle are having trouble, I hear. More bad things, tragic things. Good luck, friends,' he told them seriously.

'I'm sorry about him,' the female officer told them, and pulled at his arm. They began to move toward their police car.

'There's one good police soul,' Emma said to Peter.

'Not the only one, but one among many bad ones,' Peter said.

'Don't feel pressured at all, though,' Emma told him.

The police officers got into their car and drove away while Peter and Emma sat in theirs about to do the same.

'We might take a detour,' Peter told Emma. She looked at him with surprise.

'Along Jesmond? Do we have time? I don't want anyone to die or get hurt, Peter, but we only have so much time to find Eric,' Emma reminded him.

'I have a feeling we should,' he said.

'I don't know, Peter. Are you sure? There's feelings, then there's guilt, or instincts or God telling us to do things to. Which is it?' Emma said. 'Because of what he just said? Really?' she asked.

'I know we're short on time, but I believe we can do it. I think I have to see what is happening. You can tell me more of what you know on the way, okay?' Peter said, and started the car engine. They drove away, turning back in the direction of Jesmond.

'Interesting couple,' the police officer Jessica stated to the older male officer as they drove.

'Yes, nice couple,' the male officer agreed.

'Good work, Frank. Very good job,' she told him, and stroked his hair.

'Let me go now, please,' he said. Beads of nervous sweat rolled down his face. He looked in absolute dread at her as she smiled back happily at him.

'Work's not done. You know we can't clock off early on a night like this, can we?' Jessica asked, and twisted his earlobe tightly in her fingers. He winced.

'I want to see my family,' he told her. He was scared and praying for release from this disturbing and wicked woman. 'I've done what you asked of me,' Frank told her meekly.

'You have and more. All this time. You stupid saps. Thank you, though. It's been so useful, really so damn useful,' she told him. She kissed him as her eyes flashed red.

Chapter 62

One of the many groups of fearful rushing people who moved along in the dark streets toward their homes slowed down a pace as one of them stopped. A man to the right of the group looked out across the streets, past the crossing in the main road and some cars parked by houses.

'Look over there,' the blonde man said quietly to another to his side.

'What's up? Keep moving, come on,' the other urged.

'But look, it's him,' the blonde man said.

'Who?'

'The guy off the news. One of the goddamn killers. I mean, who they said is a killer,' the blonde man said.

'Really?' the other asked. They both then looked over the streets and saw a lone man marching alone.

'Do you think so?' Blonde said

'Well, it does resemble him, I suppose,' the other agreed, 'So we should move, right?'

The man looked at him uneasily.

'Come on, everybody's moving on ahead now,' the other said.

'Right, okay then,' the blonde man replied, eventually taking his eyes away from the shadowy figures walking off some streets across from them.

'You're the guy, aren't you?' the weary person asked.

'I'm a guy,' Eric replied to him.

'Have you killed people?' the guy asked him bravely.

'I've done what I thought was right. Tough night ahead. Wouldn't stay on the streets much longer. There's some crazy bastard around killing, isn't there?' Eric said.

'Yes, that's what it seems like. People dying,' the man agreed nervously. He watched Eric. He really was not sure if his friend had been right. Was this just another guy and not the real killer?

335

'Wonder why? Do you? I hope there is some reason for it all,' Eric told him.

'What kind of reason could there be?' the man asked.

'Could be revenge, or justice, or some bigger thing that we just won't understand,' Eric said, and then quickly ran off away from the man, continuing on alone with his plan. The two men watched in quiet confusion and moved on quickly, with a fearful dread in their eyes.

Chapter 63

Getting out of his car, Philip noticed how dead the streets around were. He cautiously stepped up to a doorway deep in the shadows of the tall buildings nearby. He knocked and pressed a bell on the doorframe. He knew the place, though it had been many years since he had stood there on that step.

The door creaked, and bolts and chains could be heard from behind. A few seconds later, it slowly opened. Behind it stood a very dirty, greasy man. He was thin and deathly grey like a corpse, and had the most paranoid, crazed eyes, which stared hard at Philip.

'I know Bruce,' Philip told him.

'Really? Name?' the man asked.

'Philip Spruance. We go back a long time. You know my name, don't you?' Philip asked.

The man stared still, hesitating before speaking.

'I...do know that name,' the thin man said, and then gasped, with a strange, dirty smile forming on his face. 'Perfect timing,' the man said.

'I need to see him now,' Philip told the man, his patience running low.

'Wait there, please,' the man ordered. The door closed on Philip, leaving him alone in the cold of the deadly night.

He knew about the things killing people on the streets around the North. He had expected it sooner or late. It made sense to him. He really did not want to consider the real reason for her premature death. He knew it could very well have been now caused by a select few beings; Bruce was one of them, alongside others. He had been waiting, really. He just knew that sometime, even so many years later, they would interfere with him and his life, but he never wanted anything as truly horrible as losing his daughter. He would make Bruce pay so painfully if he was the cause of losing Grace. The door opened to him again.

337

'Come in now, if you will,' the returning thin man said, with a painful-looking smile.

He led Philip down a repulsive-smelling corridor, past nearly half a dozen doors with chipped paint and loose locks hanging on them, mould growing along cracks in the old walls. At the end of the corridor the man opened a larger door, with a series of keys to locks on the front. On entering, Philip saw a number of strange looking, intimidating people of many kinds, shapes, sizes. Most were playing poker at small tables or reading tattered pornography or poetry books, while drinking whisky and rum from the bottles. A couple looked in the direction of the doorway and looked curiously at Philip.

'So Bruce is busy tonight?' he asked the thin man.

'Oh, very much so. We're actually all waiting for the call. Much butchering and snuffing to be had soon enough,' he told Philip.

'I believe you know a good few others around, and many would like to speak to you. If you want to talk with them, have a drink as you wait for him,' the man offered.

'Right. Okay,' Philip said, looking over the many strangely mutated hell-spawn around in the long, open room. Philip had often tried to forget faces such as these demonic, distorted expressions around him. He walked through the crowded table area to the side of the room and waved to the couple of beings who had seen him.

'Long time, Phil. How's it hanging?' one said, and laughed dirtily to himself.

'Come back for more help, have you?' the other asked, interested.

'I need no help, but I do need answers. What's going on out there?' Philip asked, sitting down by them at their table.

'Drink?' one asked, offering some suspicious liquid in a tall bottle.

'Go on, then, yes,' Philip said. 'So tell me, because I'm not sure about why some nasty shit is taking place now all of a sudden,' Philip said.

'Out in your world?' the one with the tattooed face said 'Not us. Not our fault. This bigshot idiot messed with our routines, you see. Every next one, he's there. Bruce and the others are really pissed at it all. Caught him. Made a deal. Remember when you came calling?' the demon creature asked with a wry smile. 'He's human, see, this bigshot, did you know that?' he asked.

'No, I didn't,' Philip said, curious.

'So Bruce made a deal some way or other, for some reason we can't see. Then other bad shit starts going off around. Not this human, it's the hybrids now,' the ugly demon man explained.

'They don't like that Bruce has a deal with this man?' Philip asked.

'Yeah. All big and brave now. Think they own places, getting too clever. Their fault all this shit,' the tattooed man said.

'So you're attacking them, are you?' Philip asked.

'The human is with us. He's supposedly valuable somehow. There's a showdown tonight. After midnight, down at the Quayside,' the tattooed man explained.

'But innocents are being killed. How is it being explained or covered up?' Philip asked

'Hasn't been much thought about all that,' the second one told him and smiled. The demons began laughing rowdily among themselves.

'But you don't kill people in the open so obviously like this. It's not your way. And this human, who is it?' Philip asked.

'Hey, you don't know everything about us. Don't forget that. A few years being all sinful with us for your interests, you saw nothing. Tip of the iceberg, buddy. Drink,' the thin pierced one said to him.

Philip necked the hot, strong shot glass of mystery liquid quickly, and then looked at them both with anger.

'I need to see Bruce right now. He's let me down. He owes me a huge favour,' he told them.

'Really? Get in line, then. Or get involved again tonight, now,' the tattooed man offered.

'You're all fighting the hybrids, are you?' Philip asked.

'Bruce is leading the slaughter. Ending their short time on top, ending their control over the North before it really takes hold,' the tattooed man said.

'Without a thought for the people killed carelessly along the way?' Philip asked.

'Yes. Don't forget what we are, Philip. After all the civilised discussions and times with Bruce and others back then, we killed and murdered still. That was how your work was done. Your success, new vision and reputation were thanks to organised bloodshed,' the pierced one explained, smiling. He emptied his own bottle of whiskey while looking through a book about delusions of some kind.

'He's up near Newcastle?' Philip asked as he finally stood, done talking with them.

'Yes, where are you going?' the pierced man asked him in surprise.

'I'm going to find my old business partner,' Philip told them. 'To get some answers, if he's not too busy.'

'He's training up the human,' the tattooed man told him quickly.

'Really?' Philip asked.

'Yes, this Eric the Serial Killer' Tattoo told him.

Philip stood, not shocked but impressed.

'Good luck,' Pierced told him.

'Bruce needs luck,' Philip told them, then walked off and out of the smoky, stale-smelling room.

Philip walked down the roadway back toward his car in thoughtful silence. As he gripped the car handle he heard something: footsteps. He turned around quickly on the spot.

'Want some company, pal?'

Tattoo smiled back, with Pierced by his side.

'Okay, but I'm not in a whimsical mood. I mean business,' Philip warned them.

'Fine, we'll just direct you to the action,' Pierced told him.

Philip started his car with the two demon men in the back seats, and drove away.

Chapter 64

Peter drove the car to a stop near the upper end of the main streets opposite the Jesmond Dene Park.

'We can't hang around too long, Peter. I know you might want to...' Emma began to tell him again as they got out of the car.

He looked around the streets in the deep dark of night, at the quiet shops and ominous long bridge ahead.

'Okay, can't blame me for being a compassionate soul. You're stuck with a good Samaritan,' he told her.

They began to walk out through the Jesmond high street and Peter wondered what they might investigate.

'So tell me what you know,' he said aloud to Emma.

'Right. Well, when Grace died I found out then about it all. I had to know what killed her but even though I began to do some snooping I didn't actually know the real absurd truth until tonight. It's the churches too, isn't it?' she explained to him.

'Really? How so?' he asked

'These dark connections I have uncovered to do with Grace's father and his businesses, the deals. There was something from a news article years back which I connected to her father, I'm pretty sure. He denied being connected, blaming bad press and other things. But local vicars, one or two in particular, made a thing of it, suggesting that he and some others were doing bad things. These vicars, the couple of churches connected to them, they did something...' she told him, trying to remember the exact details from the library articles she had seen.

'They created a defence against any danger. They built a special kind of church, a tabernacle like no other to protect against new dangers,' Peter said, finishing her speech.

She looked back at him with silent surprise.

'I know about some things that I think explain much more. Emma, I think I know what we're doing next,' he told her with a brave smile.

'That right? Oh my God, yes. You know more?' She asked.

'I think I do. Much more,' Peter said. 'So Grace was your good friend as well as Eric's girlfriend?' he asked.

'Yes, a very close friend of mine,' she said, 'but she had a persistent, curious character. Maybe that helped it happen.'

'So do you know how she became involved in all of this? Is it to do with Eric?' he asked.

'No, Eric did not know either until both of us tried to find out how she really died and why,' Emma told him.

'So why is Eric out there somewhere accused of murder and attacks?' Peter asked.

'He had gone about finding out the answers. And he did find answers to why she died, with a price,' Emma said.

'What price?' he asked.

Emma looked at him, and then looked around at the bridge.

'These people, well, creatures, have a hold on Newcastle and the North altogether. They are based in a number of key locations, streets and areas in Newcastle, Tynemouth, Byker and elsewhere. There were a few small investigations over the years. Interestingly, the most valuable information I found was in a number of paranormal and strange local magazines, and journals,' Emma said seriously.

'But nothing was ever done about it?' Peter said.

'I don't think so. Or they found out and ended the investigations before serious attention was paid. These things practically control the North. It's evil, unbelievable stuff. I mean, really dark horror film shit, you know?' she told him.

'Look, I know about this. I've heard about this; the special church built years ago, the secret one. It was a controversial thing among church people, vicars around the area,' he said. 'Anything else you know of?'

'I think so, yes. There are weak points to their work. They seem to have existed in specific places and stayed there. Any change came when local churches closed or were ruined somehow; fires, attacks, sicknesses. That was when they had some belief. Now, most vicars, preachers, pastors don't believe their own words so the others rule,' Emma said.

'Some of us really believe in the Lord, in salvation. Some of us have real faith,' Peter told her with true confidence.

342

'I know, and I'm very glad you do. So Grace found out about it all. She disrupted their work and... someone had to. She's gone. They stopped her,' Emma said. She was quiet for a moment.

'So these areas where they are, can they leave the places at any time, at free will, or only certain times, like after dark?' Peter asked.

'Maybe, or only with permission. I'm not absolutely sure; sounds very clichéd, right? Like some old horror film?' Emma said.

'Well, yes, but it's tragically real. Got to have an open mind about it,' he said. 'Let's go along here. I think the church is near now.'

A couple of minutes later, Peter led Emma out to another street. At the end they could indeed see the tall steeple and roof of a small church at the other end of the street. Thick fog lingered through the street between them as they walked down toward the building. As the approached, Peter thought he heard movement behind or near them. A hand clasped down upon his shoulder before he turned. He gasped, turning around.

'Please help me, for God's sake. Such sick things I've seen...horrible shit, I tell you. Help me,' the short, middle-aged man urged. He was hysterical, yet deeply sad, and appeared to be exhausted.

'Come with us, don't worry. Safety is ahead,' Peter told him. He patted the man on the shoulder. The three of them walked on together, and in a few moments reached the small church gates.

Peter let Emma and the hysterical man walk ahead and into the church. He looked behind them, sure that he had seen someone or something moving. Perhaps he was simply more paranoid now, as they were now both very certain of how real and powerful these ancient evil forces were. They entered the church together, closing the door behind them.

Inside, there were many dozens upon dozens of people again, like in the other churches in the region. They prayed, argued, cried in whispers and spoke with the vicar and chaplains, who consoled them.

'What can we do?' Emma asked.

'Learn of what's happening, where, when,' Peter said.

He approached a couple near the vicar.

'Hello, I'm a youth pastor in Tynemouth. We've been travelling by. My vicar has the same turnout of people like this. What kind of things have happened?' he enquired.

'One family massacred...two lovers separated, possibly dead...an old lady pulled to pieces,' the vicar told them with regret. 'These atrocities occurred across a number of streets. I wondered if there is any significance in the area or not...' he offered.

'I believe that is very possible. Absolutely. The...force, the evil moving around the area comes from specific places. We know this,' Peter testified.

'The areas were Brooke Grove, Achilles Street, and Markson Avenue,' the vicar told him.

'Emma? What do you think?' Peter asked.

Emma stood pensive and tapping her lip thoughtfully.

'Markson Avenue...Brooke Grove...I'm not sure...this area, and Jesmond had some relevance to what I read, but, no, I'm not exactly sure,' she admitted.

'Alright. Doesn't matter,' Peter said, and walked away towards some of the unhappy people sitting with grief and sorrow in their eyes.

'Good evening, I'm Peter. I work for another local church,' he told them. They looked up, one of them scowling back.

'You haven't been working very hard then, or He's got other things to do right now,' the bitter man told him.

'I understand how you must feel, I do. But we are not perfect people, we are fallen, confused, lost. We're vulnerable. We're lost from God, and all kinds of dangers are hunting us down,' Peter told them.

'We do need faith and hope,' the smaller lady in the crowd said. 'But they're too strong, there's too many of them.'

'You want help, ask Him, but it's his timing, his decision,' Peter replied solemnly.

'Really? Maybe it's just messed up, psycho-crazies on the loose and that's it,' the bitter man put in.

'I disagree, for good reason, with respect. Try a prayer. You see, what can it hurt?' Peter suggested sincerely.

Peter put a hand on the shoulder of the hopeful woman before him then turned to Emma. The man who had entered with them had begun talking with others, and seemed a little calmer, so they left him. They looked at the grieving groups once more, and walked out of the church. Peter and Emma strode on back along the street, in the dark fog.

'It is safe in the churches, I know,' Peter said positively.

'I don't doubt that,' Emma replied. 'So back to Newcastle?'

'Yes, I... wait,' Peter said, and stood still, listening. He turned around, squinting hard through the darkness and fog.

'Hear that?' he asked Emma.

'Hear what?' she said nervously.

He took a step further, and then looked hard out ahead of them.

'Anything there?' Emma whispered to him.

There was a silent, prolonged moment, and then bright, red eyes flashed out in the darkness. Emma gasped. Peter stepped back close with her. The eyes came toward them in the dark fog, suspended in air but coming closer. Peter and Emma stood unmoving. Would they now always see these crimson eyes when they closed their eyes, Emma wondered. In the unnerving moment, the eyes found a body as the fog thinned out. They rested on a face, gaunt and weathered on heavy shoulders.

'Evening, all,' the man said to them.

'Stay back, I warn you,' Peter said.

The man let out a quiet laugh, and Emma noticed two other pairs of eyes arriving, also with bodies below in the fog.

'Do anything you can. We're together now,' Peter told Emma. They jumped apart when the three figures moved in suddenly. Between the men they stood preparing to defend themselves in any way they could.

The three strange men each grimaced and howled as their bodies heaved, twisted and contorted into shockingly repulsive shapes and sizes before them. Seconds later, three abhorrent, mutated beasts stood in their place, red eyes glaring insanely at them.

'God have mercy,' Emma said quietly.

'The streets weren't familiar...' Peter said.

'No, no they weren't,' Emma agreed, understanding him.

He grabbed her by the wrist and they ran up the street, moving quickly with the rabid demons behind them, scratching to tear them apart, clawing and howling loudly. One only just missed grabbing Emma by the hair. Another swiped out at Peter, cutting his side. Peter moaned, but continued running with Emma, seeing their car waiting a few yards ahead. Emma looked around at the hideous things that chased them. She knew Eric and Taylor were also running from these things, fighting them elsewhere. She held Peter's hand, her faith and trust in him, but reached into her pocket at the same time.

They arrived by the car, stumbling around it with the demons close behind. Emma swung out her arm over them. Water splashed out on them in a long arc, and they recoiled fearfully.

'Now,' Emma said to Peter, who nodded and unlocked the car doors. They clamoured in quickly. Peter gave a look of total astonishment as he started the car engine.

'What did you throw?' Peter asked, while driving the car away.

345

'It was water, from the font. You might call it holy water. It's done something, anyway. I don't know,' Emma replied.

'I did nothing?' Peter asked

'You scared the damn things,' she told him. He put the car up a gear and swerved from one side of the road to the other, as he drove to confuse the demons running up the road behind.

'They are men...were men,' he said, thinking aloud. The demon hybrids continued to run behind the car at an impressive rate, as Peter steered it onto the motorway.

'They're restricted, these demon men and women, to their usual hidden homes, streets they occupy. Specific areas. They couldn't follow us; they're not allowed,' Peter said.

'They were men and women?' Emma asked.

'Afraid so, yes. They were tempted by the real demons, to greed, fear and weaknesses. Lost their souls, to dark lies at some point,' he explained.

They drove on thinking about this new revelation, and it caused them to re-evaluate the way ahead.

'So you know the areas of the original demons of the North, but there are the men demons in places that we do not know of for sure,' Peter told her.

'I don't, but you might. You're in the church and the families of those affected are in local churches right now. Can you contact some of them around the North?' Emma asked.

Peter turned quickly to look at her.

'I can phone Father Gaskill. He does know a lot about this whole thing. In fact, he probably knows more than we could even guess. He can then probably give us numbers that we need. Maybe he has heard things that can help us by now,' Peter said.

'Great. We're getting there. I'm scared of many things, but I'm glad we're together now,' she told him finally. They looked at each other with a comfortable affection.

They drove on, along cold streets, some with dried blood over the pavements, some with demons creeping through the deep shadows. They felt safe with each other driving through the dangers of night.

The other churches and temples all welcomed in victims, and their vicars and elders, pastors and wise men all tried to console and understand the events to help others. Gaskill knew things from Peter and

346

Eric which helped him in understanding; others, though, reacted in more dramatic, aggressive and foolish ways. Gaskill had been viewed as the fool, the heretic, the rambling fundamentalist prophet. Some had even whispered that he might have been some dangerous cultist. He became quiet on his controversial thoughts, even when all the time he believed the words and prophecies to be highly important to the community around. Now he had been proven right.

All knew of him, and he knew that some might soon seek him out, including demons.

Chapter 65

A large, contemporary church near Byker found nearly two hundred distressed people entering through its doors in a couple of hours. Father Furnier was hugely sceptical, but shocked on hearing tales of horror and death. He listened with interest, but a level of strong personal disbelief, having in recent times found his own faith fading increasingly. With a couple of his supporting elders, Jim and Evan, he shortly stepped out, while the remaining elders stayed with the mourning families. Though he knew he should really leave the police to look around the area, Father Furnier has painful doubt of faith, almost to point of insanity.

He expected to possibly meet criminals, psychopaths and schizophrenics, but was aching for a confrontation of supernatural quality. He led his pack down the streets that he had been warned of, prepared with a crowbar, a cricket bat, and flasks of blessed holy water. Evan and Jim did seem obviously concerned about the unexplainable sightings, and so Furnier prompted them to be strong in their faith, as he knew they would be, at least.

'The police must be around here very soon, Father,' Evan quipped.

'Precisely. So let's keep moving,' Furnier replied, with the cricket bat gripped tightly.

'Father, maybe the ones in the church are simply very traumatised. We can tell them anything, really...' Jim offered.

'So let's tell them the truth. And we'll find something positive, too,' Furnier answered. He nudged Jim with his elbow and they continued.

They entered the area where one family believed their son had been butchered then taken off into the dark alley where they themselves stood.

'So, the boy could be down here?' Furnier said. They looked around the area. There were no immediate clues of an attack; no blood to be seen, no torn clothes.

'Father, if it was some gang we should really not mess around ourselves...' Evan suggested.

'We'll just look. You're right, could be a gang, an almighty serious gang. Or some other thing. Maybe something must connect all of the bad things we heard. A big, bad reason,' Furnier said. 'A gang just isn't it. Should be, but isn't,' he said. He looked deep into the dark of the alley then for what he could not explain.

'Want to take a look?' he asked the other two.

'Come on Father, why?' Jim said. 'I know those people back there are hurting and need answers, but to really risk our lives?'

'Why indeed...' Furnier replied, and sighed. He gripped the cricket bat, smiled to himself and walked into the alley alone.

There was light emitting from a couple of windows high above, but mostly the alley was almost pitch black. Furnier stumbled a little as he walked in, but remained defiantly brave and curious. He prodded with the cricket bat at large rubbish bins that echoed as he hit them.

He did not really know how he might deal with any criminal, killer or other force, if he eventually reached one. He was respectably well-toned and physically fit for his fifty-two years, so might put up a good fight, he thought.

Minutes passed, and Furnier looked satisfied as he came back out of the alley. He looked out and around, but could not seem to see Jim or Evan anywhere close by on the street.

'You two, come out, I'm back now,' Furnier called out. He looked up and down the bitterly cold street as fog drifted along.

'Jim, Evan, where are you?' he called. He felt a bit nervous waiting for them. After a lonely, long moment, he walked down his left, towards town.

'Hey,' he called out, in isolated anger. 'Let's get back,' he said, but no reply came. He looked far off, and waited. Eventually he decided to return to the church, thinking that Evan and Jim probably had done the same. He turned around and a clawed arm lashed out near his face.

'Jesus Christ above!' he shouted.

He brought the cricket bat up quickly and stopped the claws tearing him. Behind the bat he saw some hideous, dark skinned creature glaring back at him. Damnation before me, he thought. It suddenly squealed and clawed back again.

'What are you?' Furnier asked while keeping it back behind the cricket bat. It tried to scratch him again, with a twisted face and demonic grin. It spoke.

'The real you,' it said.

Furnier thought about the words then took a hard swing at the beast. It slid off to his left, dodging the bat, and then crouched down to claw again at him.

'Where's the boy?' Furnier asked.

The beast looked at him, snarling with fangs revealed. Red eyes blinked at him.

'As the others,' it told him. Furnier looked at it with careful curiosity, then understood. He turned around with the cricket bat held out tightly and smacked the beast successfully. He tried to do it again, but the beast managed to knock the cricket bat to one side. Two more demon men approached from somewhere suddenly, two more pairs of red glaring eyes on him.

'Lord, do what you can now, if I will ever be convinced,' Furnier said quietly. The beast sneered as they prepared to fight or kill with no exceptions for holy men.

Furnier swung at the three demon men recklessly, hitting them with surprising success. He caught two as they moved closer to him, beating out cuts and splits of their strange blue tinged flesh, drawing black blood. One fell, and the other howled at the wound in its side. Furnier revolved and immediately hit the first beast, but it also caught his wrist tightly. Furnier kicked it in the ribs twice, and it growled before rolling back to the ground.

'You're physical beasts in my world,' Furnier announced, and moved on, striking out at all three of them. They crawled up at him, claws still out for his blood. He managed to hit two of them again.

'I'll break your damn bones, your fallen limbs and bastard grins,' he told them, swinging the cricket bat.

They hissed at him. The first one came up at him again, then punched him in the face. Furnier fell back a couple of steps, but shook his head and growled back at them. He swung out once more, following the demon men around. One of them he missed, but the second he grounded with a hard strike of the bat.

'You do not belong here,' he told them, and hit the floored beast with violent glee. He connected, and heard cracks as he hit, sounding like dead meat. The strange, dark blood poured forth from the demon's mouth as it convulsed dramatically. The first came back at Furnier then, but he knocked it back, struggling against it, then kicked it down further.

A car came slowly around the top end of the street, headlights turning and illuminating the bloody fight. Furnier and the demon creatures all looked at the car, all distracted. In that moment, the first demon reached out and pointed a hand toward Furnier. 'You've the anger,' it told him as it convulsed. 'You're one needing more. Accept us.'

Furnier slowly shook his head in his paralysed state, some force holding him still.

The car continued driving towards Furnier and the three demons. Inside, Peter drove as Emma watched in shocked amazement.

'Jesus, Peter; sorry, but look at this,' she exclaimed.

'Who is that?' he asked, seeing Furnier and the demons.

'Someone...fighting demons...look, he's got a dog collar on,' Emma said.

'A holy man,' Peter said as he drove close to the scene. 'Three of them against him.'

'Yes, but look at him. He's not letting up. Wait, something's happened to him,' Emma said, seeing Furnier struck motionless suddenly, the demons moving in on him.

'They've done something to him,' she said, 'should we help? Can we?'

'We could do something,' Peter told her. He looked out at the demons around Furnier. The lead demon was holding out a clawed hand, some strange, crackling green light that emanated from it merging into Furnier. Peter swerved the car and stopped, flashing the headlights a couple of times.

The demons took their attention away from Furnier and looked at the car. Two of the demons began to walk over toward the car, while the first continued to keep Furnier paralysed in extreme pain, continuing to inflict some mysterious deed upon him.

'Shit, they're coming at us now,' Emma said to Peter.

'Okay, let's see what they can handle, shall we?' he said.

'What?' Emma asked.

Peter kept the car going slow and steady. The demons prowled right up next to it, one of them scratching the paintwork. Peter flashed the car lights again once more to annoy the demons. This it did, as they shook their heads in anger, blinded and howling, and leapt onto the car bonnet, as well as hitting the sides and roof. Peter drove backwards and then forwards a few feet, shaking the demons off. The car reversed a few feet, and then Peter drove forward again, lightning fast. It smacked into one of the demons, who bounced loudly off the front bumper. The other ducked to the right, but was still hit in its side, ribs breaking as it fell down.

As Peter had guessed, the demon took its hold from Furnier and turned to look through the car window right at him.

'I'll keep it running, and we'll run them down,' Peter told Emma.

He checked on the two other demons, which had fallen down on either side of the car. The remaining demon stood tall and defiant before the car, stretching out its muscular arms and clawed hands. It nodded to the other two demons and they all then launched at the car wildly. The two at the sides jumped back up, catching tight hold of the car door frames. They easily punched the windows through easily, but Emma and Peter moved together and shielded themselves from the cascading glass.

The first demon bounded right up toward the front of the car, leaving Furnier to fall down in a daze. Peter stepped on the pedal, and the car sped right up at the demon. It stopped on impact as the demon caught hold of the car by the front bumper. Peter and Emma were stunned and shocked, but Peter continued to steer and change gears. Emma waited, speechless and nervously watching Peter at the wheel. As he revved the engine in anticipation, Furnier stood on his feet again slowly behind the demon. He quietly found his cricket bat on the ground, drew himself up, and took a strong, hateful swing at the demon.

The demon smacked down hard against the car bonnet, letting go of the car. The car then instantly buckled over the demon while Furnier stumbled to his right, out of the path of the car. It lurched noisily over the demon, and then suddenly burst over and down the street to the end. Peter stopped the car and looked in the rear view mirror. He could see Furnier standing and swinging the cricket bat again at the crushed and bloodied demon, who lay battered on the road. Furnier seemed out of control, hitting and hitting over and over with no remorse. The other two demons were beginning to stumble up and towards him then, but he did not notice. They had their eyes set tight on him, to avenge their demon brother. They knew the man of the church, a man who used to be strong in his faith, but they observed his doubt and fragile thoughts. He was weak and confused, they knew.

Peter could see them moving again in his mirror, and decided to take aim. He suddenly began to reverse the car as fast as it would go.

'What are you doing?' Emma asked, holding on tight.

'One down, two to go,' he said.

The car raced back in reverse, Emma and Peter peering around through the back window as Peter drove. They had been seen by the demons, which moved away a little, though they still made their way toward Furnier and the other dying demon.

Emma watched nervously as the car came right up towards them. She was surprised at how violent Peter was being, considering how he had seemed a very peaceful, contemplative man of faith. God needs strong men too, she thought. As they came to be only a couple of feet from the demons, one of them jumped high up into the air, and disappeared in the dark of night. The second leapt further away to one side.

Peter continued toward Furnier. The car came up near him and the battered demon at his feet, slowing. Peter wound down the car window.

'What are you doing? There's no need. It's dead, isn't it?' he asked.

Furnier looked at him and Emma inside the car, with little sane emotion showing upon his jaded face. Furnier knew what he was doing, knew that he should simply stop, but he also knew what had been prophesised over two years before to him. It was his end, this night, this fight with these demon forces on the streets of Newcastle. Only right then did it all make sense to him.

As Peter and Emma watched Furnier with the cricket bat, the two other demons landed with loud resounding thuds around him. Furnier hit the demon before him another half dozen times quickly, knocking all kinds of sinew and colours from it as the other two stepped up behind him. Furnier made eye contact with Peter then, as the demons came around him. He turned and hit out at it with the chipped and broken cricket bat. He hit them each once again, splashing blood through the air, but seconds later they caught him and began to end him, pulling, tearing, biting at him, until he fell for good.

Peter and Emma turned away, repelled by the shocking sight.

'We must go,' Peter said. Emma looked at him with pleading eyes, but understood. He drove them away, knowing as a consolation that Furnier had opened up the roads around for them and stopped those particular creatures.

Chapter 66

Philip sat in the back seat of an old but stylish Jaguar with two demon men. It was certainly not the first time he had been in the company of these hellish devil creatures, and would not be the last. They knew him from times before. Many demons and hybrids knew the fabled modern parable of the clever business man who joined with Bruce decades before, together controlling the Northern towns until they had parted for unknown reasons. Philip was a legend, an exception to the rules of interacting with the simple men and women around them. He had played with demons and become deeply entangled into a game which had almost killed him and his entire family. Now, years later, Grace had been taken from him. He would find out why. He would get any kind of revenge he could.

'Many things have changed since you've left us, Philip, you elusive old dog,' the demon Pierce explained from behind the wheel of the car as he drove. His eyes were bloodshot, burning deep red, his skin flaking and scabbed over his face as he grinned.

'You going to step in again?' the demon Tattoo asked, sitting beside Philip.

'Why don't you simply take me to the others. I will see what I think then,' Philip told them in a calm but serious voice.

Both demons in the car smiled to themselves knowingly, as Philip wondered just what had changed. He had just about taken back his own humble human life after years of trying to be more than human. He had seen mistakes, tragedies, horrors. Friends, business partners, family, innocent men and women had died because of the hungry and insatiable devils that he had bargained with. None of that had pushed him enough into reconnecting with them, until now.

'We made you, didn't we?' Tattoo asked. Philip was silent, but agreed to an extent.

'Our work, our lies; we created who you are now,' Pierce continued.

'Who I... was,' Philip said, correcting him.

'Perhaps. Whatever. Damage done, right?' Pierce said, swerving the car across the road ahead with little concern.

'Men have messed with us since you left... men have killed us, and the hybrids. What do you think will happen?' Pierce said to Philip.

'What men did this?' Philip asked.

'Two men, you've heard I'm sure, haven't you?' Pierce said. 'You, if you are returning to us, will continue your special kind of work that you used to be so good at. Your place in things once again,' he told Philip.

'You had that kind of death so sweet...' Tattoo said cryptically.

'I helped him, Bruce...then Andrew. You know him well?' Philip asked.

Pierce swerved the car aggressively along the roadside, tearing dangerously close up next to buildings and fences.

'That's a yes, is it?' Philip asked.

'Problems, so many problems for us...' Tattoo said.

'You'll kill with us,' Pierce told Philip in a low tone of voice. Philip looked at them like they were next on his list.

'That is not on the agenda. I've left that behind,' Philip told them.

'Bullshit. No way. You've been waiting,' Pierce told him.

'You will,' Tattoo said, smiling at him.

'How are the businesses?' Philip asked.

'It was good. Was...until the two young men,' Pierce said.

'I left Bruce to it. Not my problem,' Philip said.

Tattoo leaned in close to Philip.

'You were the one who connected it all. Now, men have stopped us. This never happens! Never! Not ever!' he yelled hysterically.

'You're a damn beast. You're all monsters of the truest kind. Can men really stop you?' Philip asked.

Pierce and Tattoo were silent then.

'What? Tell me what I'm missing?' he asked, looking at each of them.

'You are in this now once more. Bruce has you back in. Welcome back,' Tattoo said.

'I'm not back at all. Listen to me. I'm just sorting things out,' Philip said.

'You can do it. You did it before, you stopped men, helped us keep control. Stop these men now,' Pierce said.

Philip looked at him. Thoughts came back that he had left alone for years deep in his mind. Memories of guilty deeds, regrettable jobs, lies that killed, which he had tried to forget.

'You liked it really, you did. Loved it, you did,' Tattoo said, teasing Philip.

Philip listened against reason.

'Just take us to the place where it is happening, where Bruce is,' Philip said.

'Or do you want to see Andrew?' Tattoo suggested.

'Shut your mouth! You fleshy beast bastard!' Pierce told him, annoyed.

This gave Philip something to think about immediately.

'What has Andrew done?' he asked.

'Enough. The wars continue daily, the humans only messed up what was between Bruce and Andrew. But Bruce is back now, has plans to regain everything like we had it. You'll help, indeed. Your bloody hands will work again,' Pierce said solemnly.

'Do you want to see how things are going these days, since you left us?' Pierce asked.

Philip thought about his answer and thought about his past. He had achieved many things over nearly two decades. He supported his lifestyle, his marriage and his family with deeds and deals conversing with creatures which people had forgotten to believe or chosen to deny completely. His many experiences and successful life had tortured his mind in private ever since; the danger, the deaths witnessed, the occasional tragic ruin of lives caused in part by himself and his actions and choices. He was a different man back then, living a darker, more intense life. Consequences ultimately catch a man, he thought. No man escapes his demons.

'If I am going to meet Bruce tonight, then yes; show me the changes you all know of,' Philip said.

These two mischievous demon men were irritating to him, but he knew them and their behaviour. He believed that Pierce and Tattoo were both probably as predictable and simple as they were when he last set eyes upon them nearly fifteen years ago. Even as Philip still inhabited the same region and town as the plotting demons he had known, once he had announced his leaving them, they had become very much invisible within hours from his decision. He no longer saw any of them, nor they him, for the intervening years until this night, and until Grace had died.

Pierce drove them along quiet roads, through streets where there had been rumoured drug gangs and sex trafficking. Philip was not afraid of the reputation of these parts of town; he had seen such things, and believed the demons were very likely involved with most of these activities.

'I remember these streets. Was it Christoph? The groups of demons who caused death in the schools and factories?' he asked.

'That's right. They haunted the coal mines too. Christoph is around, but very confused these days. He's one of them, though. The ones against Bruce and the past,' Tattoo explained.

They drove on past closed factories and overgrown park fields. Pierce suddenly drew the car to a halt, parking and stepping out. He leaned down by Philip's window.

'Come, I'll show you the changes you've missed. Our confusion and misguided adventures,' Pierce said cynically.

Philip and Tattoo got out of the car and followed Pierce along a narrow path beside boarded-up buildings.

'When you left us, we continued as normal, continued the bloody chaos. But we forgot how to keep control, how to do it...your way,' Pierce explained to Philip as they walked in the cold night air. Misty air blew out from Philip's mouth as he breathed, though none came from the mouths of Pierce or Tattoo.

Pierce stopped then, standing before some tall, blocky buildings with locked doors and boarded widow fronts.

'You were going to partner up with the councillors and crime lords of the North. Connections were made, this was going to be the base. Large scale control, manipulation. Wicked deaths. Testing the people of the north. Your plan, remember?' Pierce asked Philip.

'It was up to you. All of you, if you wanted it badly enough. I accepted that you were all still out here, doing what you all do. Not myself, not with you any longer. I gave you the ideas, plans, the start. There must be other reasons why it did not happen as you wanted,' Philip suggested.

'They came. Many of them, lots. All from Andrew,' Tattoo told him.

'That was it. But you owe us still,' Pierce said.

'I did forget about it. It explains much I suppose; the deaths that came after were plainly horrific, with little reason or meaning,' Philip said, remembering.

'That's right. We still did what we know best, but not like you had made us do it,' Pierce told him.

They stepped up to the entrance of the building. Pierce lay his clawed hands on the locked large doors and, with a pulse of sudden electric light sparking, the doors opened wide. All three of them walked deep inside the large echoing hall.

'The building does get used, but for no grand reasons nowadays. Only the expected disgusting deeds. Shame, right?' Pierce said, walking towards the beginning of the staircase to the left of the dusty hallway.

'So the others - Asher, Sarah, Dirmund - they are around still, are they?' Philip enquired.

'They fight like children with bloody fists,' Tattoo told him excitedly.

'They are here still, yes. Sarah and Dirmund are lovers, I think, if you would call it that,' Pierce said.

'They know Andrew still, do they?' Philip asked.

Both Pierce and Tattoo looked at him as if he had offended them deeply. Tattoo looked at Pierce with anxious anticipation in his face.

'They know him. Everyone knows of him,' Pierce finally said.

As Philip stood watching the two demons, he suddenly felt something on him. Finger tips touched him. Claws clasped down on his ribs and shoulder from behind.

'Welcome back,' a voice said into his ear. He knew that voice from years before.

He turned to see over his right shoulder an old acquaintance. Dirmund looked back with crimson eyes. He stepped away from Philip, and they looked at each other, a couple of feet apart, seeing how time had aged their faces.

'Pleasant surprise, this,' Dirmund stated with a deep sneer of resentment.

'Flying visit. Can't stop long. Come to see Bruce, things to be discussed,' Philip told him.

'Really? That all?' Dirmund asked.

'It's all I have to do. Nothing more now,' Philip told him.

Dirmund sighed then stepped up to him quickly.

'No! No, that's not all, damn you to hell. Thank you. Oh thank you so much, grand Mr Businessman. You damn legend. You have a royal big fucking mess of shit and blood, lies and deception to clean up. Your fucking mess that we've all lived with!' Dirmund told him, fuming.

Philip looked at him, and then at Pierce and Tattoo, who silently listened and watched, entertained.

'You know I left you all because I had to. I am a man, always was. I left you and Bruce and Andrew were in control. I was gone. You think me, a simple human, is to blame for any screwed up plans concerning your dark deeds?' Philip said.

'Please, you and I, and all of us know what you achieved. Well done. As for Andrew, curse you. And him, as we have many, many times,' Dirmund said.

Philip looked at Pierce and Tattoo for their reactions.

'I believe I am missing out on some important unexplained events,' he told Pierce.

'You don't understand it?' Pierce asked 'What just happened in your life? Your daughter,' Pierce said. Silence between them. Now the conversation was serious. Now Philip might just act without thinking.

'Andrew,' Pierce said. 'Grace met Andrew.'

Chapter 67

In less than forty minutes, Pierce and Philip drove across through places that used to mean something different to both of them. Though Philip never actually decided to become a hybrid like Pierce, Tattoo and others, he did stay close beside Bruce exclusively as the only human who helped the demons to infect the society around them.

Philip knew the psyche of mankind, the modern culture and sway of religious faith and atheism, from his own work in marketing and advertising before going further into local politics with business. As he had helped Bruce get deep into the lives and businesses of men and women, he had not realised what a deep hold Bruce had achieved over his own life. It had been another life, a sort of addiction for Philip, each new plan a dangerous gamble, though usually resulting in fresh success. Though never personally guilty of killing or murdering, Philip spent years advising the many groups demons and Bruce on their plans, getting them deals, access, meetings, and opportunities around the North. The memories had all stayed and festered in the dark halls of his mind over the years. Time with his wife and daughters had always been mired with thoughts of the sickening dangers and deaths happening elsewhere.

Philip sat up next to Pierce in the car once again as they travelled on. He sensed that Pierce was acting cool, but thought there were emotions being held back, along with certain truths. They were always such cunning devils, Philip remembered. That was their nature, after all. He did not know just how honest Pierce was being, which then made him wonder if Pierce might try to harm him soon. It did seem very possible, he realised. He could see that so many of the demons resented his leaving, and how he had brought Andrew into being those years before. What Bruce would give to the demon that killed him, Philip wondered. But hopefully he was worth much more alive for Bruce. He was almost certain of it. They had history, and a wicked legacy which he sensed Bruce would remember fondly.

'You think I am interested in returning, do you?' Philip asked.

'Is that my business? I would be lying if I said I was not interested to see what happens. I am sorry for your loss. That's what they say, isn't it?' Pierce asked.

'Yes, they do. Thank you,' Philip told him.

Philip saw a change in the expression on Pierce's face then. He looked up the road ahead, following Pierce's eyes. He saw cars suddenly coming up out of the intersections ahead. Two, three, then four cars sped quickly by.

'The road's busy now. Why do you think?' Philip asked Pierce.

'Don't like to guess...' Pierce answered quietly.

'That's up toward East Walker, near Byker. We were going close by, before Newcastle, right?' Philip asked.

Pierce did not immediately reply, but moved the car up in gear and focused on the road. Rain poured down through the black clouds over them.

'What's happening now?' Philip asked. 'Tell me.'

'A hell of a lot of things are coming together tonight. Been building up since this couple of two young guys. Unexpected things that should have waited. Now all this shit to deal with, in our way,' Pierce told him. 'You'll help me, right?'

'What? To do what exactly?' Philip asked.

'Whatever needs to be done,' Pierce answered.

They approached the entrance to the town of Byker beside Walker. Once again, all kinds of nightmare visions could be seen. Grim scenes moved before them; police chasing men, women, demons, and people with weapons of many kinds, vicars, priests, and children screaming between them all.

'It's not as simple as it looks,' Pierce told Philip.

Pierce then parked the car up along the high street and got out, with Philip following.

'What's all this?' Pierce said to one of the policemen near them, who was walking after a group of people with a colleague.

'Everyone is fighting everyone. People blaming others, attacking each other. We're...hey, Pierce,' the policeman said, and smiled.

'But what's really happening?' Pierce asked.

'We're herding folk in the places we want them. Their reaction is a bit surprising and a pain, but they're just stupid, right?' the policeman said with sarcasm. 'What are you doing?'

'I'm looking for Bruce. You don't know Philip here, do you?' Pierce asked.

The policeman took a brief glance over at Philip, nodding with a quick 'Hi,' then shrugged.

'Don't believe I do, sorry. Should I?' he asked.

'Philip here is responsible for a good deal of death and destruction, though he's loath to admit it himself. A part of history. Modest fellow. Good luck anyway with all this. Can we take a quick look around at it? Don't know if Lucretia is around here?' Pierce asked, looking behind at the hysterical masses running and shouting.

'She's out somewhere. She was around down by the Manors area, but you could try the bar you know?' the policeman suggested.

'Right. Thanks, good luck again, red eyes,' Pierce said, and walked away with Philip.

'Lucretia?' Philip asked curiously.

'She is the one who has kept the human side of Andrew strong. Both used to be, and they seem to inspire each other. She's wicked and unpredictable with it. A lovely, sweet girl,' Pierce explained.

'He still acts human, does he?' Philip asked. He could only imagine how Andrew was now, years since they had last seen each other. Andrew had in a strange way been a sort of son that he had not had. He did feel responsible for what had happened, but Andrew had made his own choices.

'Yes, they both could possibly regret their choice, but they keep each other wild and wicked. Strange couple, really,' Pierce said. He walked along through the crowd of barbarous people fighting and shouting at each other.

'Look at all of this madness. Glorious. It is full of potential, it could lead to many outcomes, am I right?' Pierce suggested. 'You could control this, this wild evil mess. You were waiting for a time like this all those years ago. I'm right, aren't I?' Pierce said pleased with his opinion.

'You know me, but not that well, Pierce,' Philip told him.

'Look around. You're missing out now. This won't last. I know about the competition between Bruce and you. Andrew's there now, and these shitty two men. That's no fault of yours, but leaves less freedom, doesn't it?' Pierce said.

'There's a thing with Andrew and Bruce?' Philip asked.

'He's stepped in where you didn't dare. But you stayed human, unlike Andrew. Thus, hybrids against the original demons,' Pierce explained.

'Don't think you can push me easily into action, I'll see it around me. I can guess much of it too,' Philip warned 'You've been working for Andrew since I left?'

'Yes. Always hope in a new way. Bruce was so basic, predictable, old,' Pierce said.

'What's Andrew done?' Philip asked.

'He's bridged the gap, merged lines. Distracted men, women much better. Modern ways, modern fears, and desires; he knows it all,' Pierce said.

'He and Bruce both after these two young men, are they?' Philip asked.

'Yes. One big witch hunt tonight,' Pierce answered.

'I know some people,' Philip said, and casually stepped out toward the arguing crowds. He looked around, noticing men in suits, police, and regular people of all kinds. Some faces were very familiar to him. He pushed on through, with Pierce behind him. He waved then to a couple of men near the number of police officers.

'Hey Donald! Anthony!' he shouted, and the two men looked toward him. He and Pierce approached them through the crowd.

'How did you end up around here, Philip?' Donald asked.

'I was driving by here. Heard about these things happening tonight. Just awful,' Philip said.

'Absolutely. We've been trying to organise things here with much of the local police authorities. It's just chaos right now. People are angry and want the ones responsible caught now,' Donald told them.

'Maybe I could help out in some way. Do you know some of the police personally?' Philip asked.

'Yes. You know Andrew Sutcliff and Inspector Barry Fellows, don't you?' Donald asked. 'They were at the charity conference last month?'

'Yes, I remember them. I'll go see how I might help,' Philip said, and left with Pierce.

They squeezed on past more people being held back by police, arguing and crying. Finally, Philip reached the chief inspectors.

'Hello Barry. It's me, Philip, remember?' Philip asked. They recognised each other immediately. Philip knew Barry was a hybrid demon, as did Pierce.

'Good to see you. Very shocking, all of this,' Barry told them.

'Yes, could be any kind of reason behind it all, right?' Philip said.

'We suspect some young men, actually,' Barry said.

Philip looked around them then spoke in a lower tone.

'Can we talk more privately?' Philip asked. Barry looked at Philip and Pierce, and around them.

Of course. Tell me what you think,' Barry replied.

They moved away and discussed the events around them, the murders, attacks, the past, and the groups of demons around the North. Philip offered some suggestions to Barry, who listened and agreed with him. Things could happen very quickly, changes could be made in the blink of an eye, Philip thought, if only the right people wanted change. Philip had since his time with the demons achieved an extremely respectable level of business and personal life. He had been grateful until very recent times. Nonetheless, Philip still had trust on his side from people who kept the North alive and prosperous, people who supported it economically and socially. Like many rich wealthy and successful people, he could influence others whether he was morally right or not. Money talked, and the money came from Bruce and the demons. Not only was he wealthy and connected now, but he had so many demons from his past that would listen and help him just as willingly as before.

In the next twenty minutes, Philip spoke to and was introduced to several other politicians and police officials who had come to the area of Byker. They listened and wanted to make plans with him, with help from a number of them being hybrid demons themselves. As the police calmed the crowds in the high street, Philip stood with two councillors and a number of local politicians and the chief police inspector.

'From what you say, Philip, we should be successful with the police along by Newcastle going towards the East, with the descriptions you know of. We can send these people home and focus on the suspects with confidence now, I think,' Inspector Willis told him.

'You're welcome. Like I said, the young men were near our area, they sounded confused. They'll make a big mistake, I'm pretty sure of it,' Philip said.

As easily as that, he was back in. They welcomed Philip like a veteran sporting hero, and he did have much to offer and suggest that could help the situation. He would use them all again, like in the past, only now he had no selfish and evil plan beneath his actions. He just wanted truth and justice, no matter how hard that might be to find.

Officially, he had helped the police and authorities with their present search for an extremely dangerous pair of young killers. Philip secretly knew, however, that he had spread his message all around, from Wallsend to Gateshead, Byker to Tynemouth. The hybrid demons would know he was back, and they would all move towards catching Eric and Taylor for the respect and reward that Philip and Bruce, and even Andrew, might present to them.

After finishing his plans with the many respected figures and police officers, Philip returned to meet Pierce, who had been talking with the distressed families.

'What have you been up to while I've been gone?' Philip asked.

'I've been listening to the poor folk affected by the deaths and attacks. Tragic tales of people taken before their time, people horrified beyond belief. Oh well, all's fair in life and death. How about you?' Pierce asked.

'Things are moving along. We have eyes on the street. We should know where everyone is in a very short time. You enjoy this tonight, right?' Philip said.

'Perhaps 'enjoy' is the wrong word, but it is familiar, that's for sure,' Pierce answered.

'What are you doing, Pierce?' Philip asked.

Pierce gave Philip a strange look.

'I'm getting into the car. We're heading to Newcastle, aren't we?' Pierce said.

'How's it been for you, since you changed? Being less human?' Philip asked him.

Pierce looked at him, and his expression changed to one of angry fury. He stepped right up to Philip's face.

'Listen, I've lost nothing...I'm me, I'm more than I was, even. It's a better way. Try it, I dare you. Ask Andrew, okay, your damn Andrew,' Pierce said.

Philip stood and simply listened, not entirely convinced of Pierce's opinion.

'Was it worth it? How many have you...seen die?' he asked.

Pierce looked at him, then walked away quickly through the crowds in the high street. Philip heard his mobile phone ring in his pocket.

'Hello? Yes, me...Philip, yes...you have? Yes, just for tonight. All of them, yes...yes, I'll see you soon,' he said to the caller. He looked around, hesitated, then opened the car door and got inside. He tried to look through the crowds for Pierce.

'Come on,' he said in frustration. A moment later, Pierce came pushing back through the people with someone by his side.

'I'm back. Are we going? This is Lee, he knows a few of the streets where we're heading. He can help us,' Pierce explained.

'Okay then,' Philip replied.

The three of them got in the car and began to drive away up the motorway roads again. Pierce sat with a sheepish smile on his face.

'You've seen some bad things tonight, haven't you Lee?' Philip asked as he drove.

'Yes, I have. I know people who've lost their husbands, wives, children...it's just fucking appalling. It frightens me, it does. It just should not be happening, any of this kind of thing at all. It's always someone else, isn't it? Until now. Why, though?' Lee said.

'That's the question. I heard it might be some young gang, just gone mental, lack of good parenting, bad peers, all that. Mind you, some other people believe in some really spooky ideas about it all,' Pierce said.

'What? What do you mean?' Lee asked.

'Well, things not being so clear or explainable,' Pierce said.

'What? Supernatural kind of stuff? Like black magic and all that shit?' Lee asked, with a look of scepticism.

'I'm thinking more demons, devils, all that jazz,' Pierce told him.

In that moment, his eyes flicked to bright crimson pupils, his fangs extended, and he suddenly clawed into Lee with visceral violence. Blood exploded over the inside of the car, as Pierce tore and wrestled with the dying Lee until he finally stopped resisting.

'Oh, Jesus Christ, Pierce, you shit! What are you doing?' Philip asked, shocked and distracted from driving. Pierce looked at him and smiled, with blood over his lips and chin.

'See this? He's finished. I'm still here. Don't worry; I know he's actually a criminal, and a woman beater. One less, right?' he said, laughing a little.

'That's not the way,' Philip said, taking a deep breath, his eyes on the road again.

'You know it is. It's power, freedom, it's my life and your past. You dress it up, but this is it at the core. Below the deals, the handshakes, whispers, and lies. Blood gets spilt, souls get taken,' Pierce explained.

'So we've a dead body in the car now. Now what happens?' Philip asked, looking at the body of Lee in the rear view mirror.

'Watch and see,' Pierce told him.

In the following seconds, the body began to crackle, smoke and then disintegrate before their eyes. The blood on Pierce and the car vanished just as quickly.

'No trace. I did that Philip, for myself. I'd do it for you. If you returned, I and many others would do that as much as you need us to. Guarantee it,' Pierce told him.

'I don't need that, not in future...' Philip said with an ambiguous tone.

'But tonight you do?' Pierce said.

'Tonight I do,' Philip agreed.

Philip took notice of the streets around Byker as they moved on towards Newcastle. He had not been through those parts much at all in a few years, the very troubled working-class areas, with constant unemployment and alcoholism draining any hope and courage.

'Who moves around these parts now?' he asked Pierce.

'Andrew is rooted in some of the streets and a couple of pubs, but then Bruce was in Byker early on. But he has lost his touch, for a number of reasons. Perhaps years ago. His minions here are weak and confused. We should have no trouble passing now,' Pierce explained.

Philip was cautious to believe everything that came from Pierce. He believed that either Pierce was telling the white lies for his good or tricking him in some as yet unknown way. He did, though, realise that Pierce and Tattoo respected and admired him, and perhaps feared him as well. They knew what Philip had achieved in the past. So they should fear me, Philip thought. They knew what he did, and what he was still capable of if he chose to do it. Philip would work with these unholy creatures once more for this lone night, with the simple purpose of finding his daughter's murderers. But like anyone returning to the places of their past, he could not stop his mind from contemplating the many changes that had taken place in the years he had been away from it all. He then wondered about the changes to Andrew, his previously unsure but brave young friend who in the last time they were together had only just changed to a hybrid demon.

Andrew had been a very intelligent, cunning young man, though severely depressed and tempted by the things that Philip told him about, including power, liberation, freedom, adventure, limitless women and experiences, and much more. Philip did not lie at all, but he also did not tell the whole truth.

They became friends, Philip almost like a father figure for Andrew as Philip orchestrated plans which used and abused the North inside and out. Then, one day, Philip suddenly announced his departure from business with the hidden demons, including Bruce, and left Andrew to wonder why, with many more questions mounting and left unanswered for years to come.

Philip had almost been the sole creator of the hybrid demon men and women, but he cared more about the safety of his wife and daughters once he had accumulated enough money and a fine reputation. He knew Bruce and Andrew were still out there all the time, and they knew of him, though none contacted the other, as Philip had requested. Bruce, being a true, pure demon from below, could not continue to keep interest in intricate and sophisticated plans involving businesses and tricks of the mind. He purely lusted after honest blood, death, souls, and destruction, as his evil nature demanded.

The hybrid demons, being part human, still held to the ambition of Philip, and Andrew had continued to use them toward plans and goals along those lines. They separated from Bruce and his primitive destruction, and sought to keep tight hold on religions, in the streets, in gangs, government, and businesses over time, and eventually made a stand against Bruce and the originals. When hybrids fought original demons, the number of human men and women found dead around the North dramatically increased, with no obvious answers for police and public. A great many of those deaths were tightly covered up or ignored for years to come.

The next decade saw the hybrids manipulate and use mankind in many selfish, inventive ways, while Bruce and the other demons kept a hold on the streets and buildings, and over a number of gangs and countless weak-willed people. They would eventually fight to regain complete control again, when the timing was right or unexpected. That time seemed to have finally arrived after the interference from Eric and Taylor. It was now or never.

Peter drove the car for the next stretch, but fought against his body's tiredness, heavy sleep encroaching down on him. It had been the longest day for all of them. Emma watched him and the roads as they continued, ready for just about anything now. Anything could fly out at them, jump out or attack them and they would fight with all it would take, knowing what depended on them.

Chapter 68

'I bet he's not the only one to do that,' Peter suddenly said.

'Who? That vicar?' Emma asked.

'Yes. I think lots of them must literally be fighting their demons for all to see tonight. Maybe that's a very important thing. The way society views church people, the hypocrisy... but now...' he began, then stopped and yawned then.

'It's like things always catch up with us. It is like karma, isn't it?' Emma asked.

'In a sense, yes. When we get close enough, you know what streets to follow, right? You read where they are, the demons from the old notes and maps you saw?' Peter asked.

'I do have a fairly good idea of where, yes. Trust me,' Emma said. 'Do you think it is just kind of a coincidence that this has all happened right now?'

'All this?' Peter said, not sure of exactly what she meant.

'These devils or demons out killing people on the streets of Newcastle. I mean, Grace uncovered things that have been going on for a really long time, but now they're out in the open. Now we know, and they know we know,' Emma stated in frustration.

'She was caught. I'm not saying that she caused this, but maybe they're fighting like this because they've been found out; they're scared, vulnerable I think. We're in with a chance, maybe,' Peter told her.

Two other cars came speeding alongside them on the road. Peter was shocked and startled, but remained focused.

'Where'd they come from?' Emma said, surprised. Peter kept his eyes on the cars in his mirror as they carelessly sped past them, erratically swerving across the road. One of the cars suddenly smashed hard up against theirs, knocking them to the right a few feet as Peter struggled to steer the car.

'What the hell? Goddamn psychos!' Emma shouted, and sat up, looking behind them through the rear window of the car.

'You okay? Hey, don't look out,' Peter said.

'No, I'm fucking pissed off. Who the hell are they to do that?' she asked.

'Look inside,' Peter said. She leaned forward into the speeding car, and she saw the red eyes staring out at her.

'More of them,' Emma said quieter as she moved back into her seat. 'They won't stop us, okay? Keep driving,' she told him.

'I intend to,' he said, looking ahead at road signs but nervous of what she was thinking. He had not expected that she could be so angry. It did turn him on, though, he thought.

They were not too far away from Newcastle, perhaps ten minutes or less, he judged. Anything could happen in ten minutes, Peter thought, but he immediately tried to block the negativity from his mind.

'Don't think about them,' Emma told him. 'Think about what we're going to do when we get to the hidden church grounds. We locate the area, and you can pray and I'll read over the notes I have on me. Maybe we can get Eric there soon enough, too,' she told him. She was still scared, with good reason. Two more cars came rushing beside them on the motorway. They had insane grins on their faces and broken claws on the driving wheel as they drove past them loudly.

'They're all heading in the same direction as us, aren't they?' Emma said, observing them pessimistically.

'I... don't know. Maybe not. I think...they might be heading to the city, yes. They want Eric and Taylor, I don't think they necessarily know of the old church grounds and its significance,' Peter suggested.

'Well I hope not,' Emma replied.

The cars shot past them on both sides, and Emma saw the red-eyed demons inside, screaming and howling their frenzied laughter as they drove on.

In no time at all, news travelled in all directions, into homes and sanctuaries, clubs and pubs, the dirtiest corners, holes and dens. Even as most of the demons moved toward the Quayside for the long-anticipated showdown, they gossiped, whispered and muttered the news that pleased many and angered others: Philip had returned. The man who had worked with demons before, who helped them to conquer, was back. To the hybrids, it was mostly welcome news for all but a handful of them. For the original demons, it was one more unnecessary problem on top of the night's dilemmas. Though the news was spreading secretly amongst the hybrids because of the nature of them, all other demons knew well before midnight.

Sirius moved in shadows down crooked, old city streets with his fellow demon brothers when they were stealthily surrounded.

'Sirius,' a voice said from some unknown corner of the dark street around him.

'Come out, hybrids, fight real demons, if you will,' Sirius answered.

He and his brothers stood ready, with their clawed hands out before them. A man came out from the darkness of a doorway nearby, and as he walked he effortlessly mutated half his torso into the unnatural demon form it knew. His red eyes caught Sirius.

'You should all give up now, because it is over again for a long time,' the hybrid told him.

'Don't speak foolishly, half breed,' Sirius told him.

'We will rule you all without question,' the hybrid explained with a smug grin.

'Is that all you can think of?' Sirius asked.

'Truth hurts. It will indeed,' the hybrid said.

Sirius watched him, deciding if he had heard any truth in the words spoken. They were all due to fight soon whatever the situation, he thought. So maybe they had decided to play games and try to trick us before the final battle.

'Talk all you want, we'll see you all finished by dawn at the Quayside. See the man with you then,' Sirius said.

The two small groups of ugly, snarling demon tribes watched each other closely with anxious caution, stepping away from each other but remaining ready to tear into each other on the slightest false move. Each group backed away, and again Sirius and his demon brothers were alone.

'What do you think?' one of them asked him boldly.

'I think we get to the Quayside. Tear the human smiles from their human heads to dead bloody pieces,' he told the demon, and walked on before them with a sour expression on his old, leathery face.

Chapter 69

After nearly fifteen minutes of lonely, nervous driving, Taylor reached Newcastle, with Grace's body in the car boot. He was close to streets he had heard spoken of by Emma and Peter and he considered the truth to it all. How could information grow and change so much, yet remain true over many decades, let alone centuries? The legend and folk myths connected to Holy Island and Lindisfarne could be true, but seemed stupid, like they were simply exaggerated stories stretched from distant truth. Everything was either stupid or deadly serious now, he realised. The monks protecting the island while translating the gospels many centuries ago had held off Vikings and evil forces. Legends and myths seemed to be more reliable against modern reality as time passed, so he decided to keep an open mind if he could. As he himself was struggling to escape the demonic strength given from Andrew, any help, any possible spiritual guidance or protection would be appreciated, he thought in his guilty desperation.

The car drove up towards a set of traffic lights, but on this evening Taylor would take no notice of them, and it felt good. His mission was not going to be slowed down by man's technology if he could help it. He changed gear, and steered across the motorway free of any other vehicles. The car coughed up a sudden, horrendous noise, a painful, stuttering rumble, and the wheel and gears stuck suddenly.

'Oh shit, no, come on. Not now, just no way. Howay, man! Come on!' Taylor said aloud. He banged his fists on the wheel, staring at it in frustrated rage. This just could not be happening right now, he thought. Any other night, and other time but now. It was some dark celestial joke from above - or below, he thought - and he shook his fists and cursed repeatedly.

With a couple of difficult attempts the car continued eventually, careening along with a loud squeal.

He drove the car with difficulty along to the roadside as he came toward the outskirts of Newcastle. He was near the old cinema and restaurant near Manors metro station, and he got out of the car and opened up the hood. He took out his mobile phone and shone a light down over the engine and various pipes and cogs inside.

'Keep calm, Taylor...focus,' he heard from somewhere inside his own head.

It was the voice of Grace with him again.

'This is pathetic. Come on, it's just a fucking joke. After everything else, this?' he said, pointing to the car as if she would see the problem. He sighed to himself.

'Having problems, are you?' another voice asked suddenly from behind. Surprised, Taylor looked up. Lucretia stood leaning against the car door. She smiled at him and his heart beat fast.

My God, who is this, he thought. This woman was absolutely gorgeous. Where had she come from? There had been no one anywhere near only seconds before. She was breath-taking, stunning, with her blonde hair slightly curled around her delicate shoulders, porcelain skin, high cheekbones, ruby lips, and wild, wicked eyes. He wanted to kiss those lips so much, and wondered if she would let him get closer. Her eyes watched him; big, brown, and full of secrets. She seemed just a little familiar to him, but not enough for him to really place her.

'My car is acting up out of the blue, a real pain in the arse. Excuse my language,' he said, and blushed a little.

'Oh, shame. Where are you heading? I could maybe give you a ride if you like,' she offered, playfully winking at him.

'I really need to get my car back to...where my friend is. But thank you all the same. You shouldn't be out right now, you know, it's actually very dangerous on the streets tonight,' he told her.

'Really? How so?' she asked, moving closer to him.

'Well, I hear there have been quite a few accidents. Are you with friends?' he asked. He could not take his eyes off her. She was just too temptingly beautiful. After dozens of lovely ladies had given him such gratifying attention recently it was becoming repetitively mundane, but this new lady he was very interested in knowing. He wanted to spend time with this gorgeous mystery woman, did not want to pass up the opportunity. He was not sure if he was in her league at all, but she did seem to be making a play for him, so he was confident enough to try his luck.

'No, I'm by myself right now. Like you are. It's very cold too tonight, isn't it?' she said, rubbing her arms.

'Hell, yes. I mean it is, you're right. You know it might take me a while to sort my car out. I'm hungry too. Are you? Would you fancy getting something to eat with me?' he asked, trying to sound casual.

'I fancy getting to know you,' Lucretia told him. She moved a hand up toward his face and touched his cheek softly. He put an arm around her, then his other, and squeezed her behind.

'Do you want to come with me?' she asked, and kissed him.

'She's a distraction,' Grace told him. He almost bit Lucretia's tongue as they kissed, and wished Grace would leave his head for five minutes of peace.

'You can do this,' Grace said in his mind.

He stood back from Lucretia, distracted and agitated. He looked at her as she stood, anxious to continue their lustful embrace.

'I've seen you,' he said, but then hesitated, looking around. He felt suddenly fearful, wondering what was happening. He had seen her. He remembered seeing her a number of times in Andrew's bar, stood in the background. She had looked different then, though, he thought; different hair, different eyes, different complexion. He looked uncomfortable and backed away.

'What's wrong, darling?' Lucretia asked him in a soft voice.

'I... don't have time, have to go,' he said, and turned back to look at his car engine.

'Oh, you do have time. All the time you need. I know what you want, so do you,' she told him, and bit his earlobe gently.

'Get away...sorry, I can't, I have to go. I'm sorry,' he said. He poked a couple of parts of the engine in the darkness as he looked away, nervous and scared.

'Don't be such a wimp, for hell's sake, Taylor. Show me a good time. I've heard you could,' she told him.

He looked at her, then turned and got inside the car again. He closed the door and desperately put the key in the ignition and turned it, praying for some luck. As he did so, Lucretia leapt up at the car door and screamed at him, clawing at the window insanely. She changed into something shocking as he watched, horrified. Her eyes sparked crimson, her skin turned pallid grey, and veins rose up on her face as she growled at him, clawing at the window.

'Drive away and we'll tear you up, all of you. You and your friend. Everyone,' she warned. 'You're nothing at all. A shitty insect, a roach. It's a fucking war!' she yelled.

'Fuck off, you crazy bitch! Go to hell!' Taylor said as he pushed the gear stick around impatiently. The car rumbled, clanged loudly, and miraculously began to move away. Lucretia spat and sneered as he drove back onto the long road behind.

Chapter 70

Philip was disgusted as he drove. He had witnessed many deaths at the hands of demons, but it had been years since it had happened right next to him. It had all just been the usual desensitising news reports on television, edited hysteria, confused facts and sanitised tales. The real blood and horror was before him. It almost turned his weak stomach thinking about it.

'Are you alright there?' Pierce asked.

'Yes, just a bit dizzy. It's been a while,' Philip told him.

'Don't worry; you never did it yourself anyway, did you?' Pierce asked.

His mobile phone rang, making his eyes flash red for a split second.

'Hello? Yes...I have, right with me...oh, okay. There's time? Great. Okay...right. Five minutes, then. Bye.' He ended the call then leaned towards Philip.

'We're meeting Andrew,' Pierce told him.

'That's very good. Great. Where is he?' Philip asked.

'He's in the city, in Newcastle. Very busy. Some things have gone a bit wrong, humans messing things up; not you, but you know how they can be, right?' Pierce said.

'He's doing well, then?' Philip asked.

'Has done, I suppose. He has been a good leader. A good example of our way,' Pierce replied, and chuckled to himself a little. 'Drive on up ahead, take a turn, go over two roundabouts then...left. You know behind the Domingo Restaurant and Pet Sounds record shop, yeah?' Pierce asked.

'Think so, yes. How's he doing?' Philip asked, wondering who was close to these humans who had messed up their routines.

'He's close to the area, planning an attack. The damn police and humans are the unpredictable factor in things. Even bloody religious folk are doing things now. Doesn't always have an effect, but even so...it's all fun now, fuck yes,' Pierce exclaimed.

Philip drove down the back roads towards the centre of Newcastle. They were close and he would have to really reprise his old role of the man who could sweet talk demons and persuade them to do almost anything. Before Philip could make the final turn that Pierce spoke of, he had to slow the car due to some commotion ahead. There were police and others stood around in the road, and police cars moving around.

'What's this bullshit?' Pierce asked aloud. He banged a fist hard against the inside car door in frustration.

'We might have to change our route,' Philip said. Pierce looked out of his window uneasily. He tried to get a good look at the police and other men moving around. As Philip slowed the car near the pavement, policemen came to the car. He wound down the window to talk to them.

'What the hell are you doing?' Pierce asked him in a quiet voice.

'Let's see what's happening. We can get around this, can't we?' Philip said.

'Can we? Who do you know?' Pierce asked.

'Let's see, shall we?' Philip told him, and looked out as the policemen came to stand by his window.

'Good evening, sir, can I ask where you are heading tonight?' The dark-haired lead officer said.

'Yes, good evening. We're going to see some friends in town. What's going on, officers?' Philip said politely.

'We can't really tell you much but it might be dangerous for you to be out in the city tonight. We are telling everyone to stay away, go home. There have been some very bad events, some murders, and attacks, so we seriously advise that you return home right now, sir, alright?' the police officer explained.

Philip looked out behind the officers toward the many other policemen and suited officials who talked and argued further up the road. Did he know any of them personally, he wondered. It was quite difficult to distinguish their individual features in the dark of night. There were a couple who could be familiar, but it was hard to tell. He watched them as the first two officers stood looking at him through the car window.

'Sir, excuse me?' the dark-haired officer said.

'Yes?' Philip said.

'Sir, are you returning home?' the officer asked.

'I think...actually, I know someone...can I just go and talk with someone?' Philip said. Pierce watched as Philip calmly got out of the car. The officers were quietly surprised as Philip began walking down the street. Pierce got out and followed him.

'Sir, excuse me, hey! Sir!' the officer shouted after Philip.

'What's going on?' Pierce asked, catching up with Philip.

'I know a man,' Philip told him.

'A policeman?' Pierce asked. He looked ahead at the number of policemen and suited men all talking together. 'Philip, hybrids are often in the police force and government now. And so are other demons,' Pierce warned.

Philip understood, nodding as he approached a police officer, who then saw him.

'Philip? Hello. What are you doing around here now?' the man asked, surprised but pleased to see him.

'I'm...visiting friends, hopefully. Old friends. Have you seen much of the things going on?' Philip asked him.

The man sighed with regret and a sorrowful face, shaking his head.

'There are some terrible things happening. I'm telling you, you should probably turn around...and...'

Before the man finished speaking, something jumped out from the shadows of the alley behind and clamped onto him. The man tried to scream, but his mouth was covered, and he began wrestling the thing as it clawed at him, blood spraying out in circles around them all. The many officers and men around looked on, shocked and terrified.

Philip watched, concerned for his friend and knowing what it was that held him. The demon which held the man looked up at Philip suddenly, with a wild, menacing stare.

'Who are you with?' Philip asked quietly. The policeman it held fell down in his bloody pool as it let him go. The many police officers around quickly armed themselves, and spoke on their radio phones, asking for back up. Philip looked at Pierce, who also watched the demon man. Pierce stepped up toward it with silent interest. His claws came out on his hands and he flashed red eyes at the demon.

Suddenly, another demon leapt out, then another, then another from within the many dark trees and shadows all around. A whole large group of them came bounding out surrounding the policemen and suited men, who looked back in terror. The demons came around with their red eyes, clawed hands and hunger for the blood and souls of all and anyone. Only a couple of the police had guns pointed, as the others held out

378

batons and Taser guns in defence. The demons did not care, knowing they were beyond the impact of most weapons that men fashioned.

They individually moved in on the police and clawed in straight away. Some men simply ran for their lives, while most of the police swore and fired at the demons and lashed out helplessly. The demons jumped on them, bullets and beatings barely affecting them.

'Are they with us?' Philip asked Pierce, who seemed distraught.

'Let's move,' Pierce told him.

They were seen by a couple of the demons who had already slaughtered their prey.

'The car, Phil, the car,' Pierce said.

'They're killing them all,' Philip said, watching the bloody chaos.

'I know. Nothing new. We should leave,' Pierce told him.

Philip nodded, and together they ran towards the car, with demons very close behind. They ran, and Philip almost fell twice. Pierce looked back at them, with his red eyes defiantly glaring at them. They saw this, but kept on after them right up to the car. Pierce stood before them with claws out in defence as Philip got inside the car first.

'Start it up, Phil!' Pierce said, looking at the demons in front of him. Behind them, there was a couple of policemen and suited men still standing while the demons tore at them.

The car started and Pierce scrambled around to his door, but the two demons clawed out at him. Pierce struggled to finally get inside the car, and on shutting the door he began shouting at Philip.

'Go, mow them down, whatever you need to do!' he said.

'Straight through them?' Philip asked.

'Knock them down, they won't stop, right?' Pierce said.

'You think I should? Philip asked.

'Just fucking drive, please!' Pierce shouted.

Philip put his foot down as the two demons clawed at the car doors and then fell away as it moved fast. In front, many of the other demons walked towards the car, then ran at them.

'I can't just...' Philip began to say, nervous.

'Go! Hit them!' Pierce ordered. The car was moving forward at only around fifteen miles an hour, and Philip hesitated. Philip and Pierce watched through the windshield, trapped inside and left to wait as death came at them on many feet.

'We're screwed,' Pierce said flatly.

'No, we're not. Not yet,' Philip said. He pointed through the windscreen, beyond the approaching demons. There was another man coming up behind them. He seemed to be alone at first, then suddenly four more figures came out from another street, joining him. They all ran straight up toward the demons near the car.

'Here's the cavalry,' Pierce said. He and Philip watched and saw another unreal fight begin.

Andrew was in front, and he and the four hybrid demons came upon the demons near the car. They instantly began clawing and punching at the other demons with focused, relentless aggression. Blood hit the car windows in cascading splashes, and then demons landed hard against them, cracking the glass loudly. Andrew and his hybrid demons pulled at the others, scratching them, punching them, doing anything to get them away from the car. Andrew could be seen placing hands on them, with blue smoking pulses of burning energy flaming out as the demons growled with hostile pain.

The original demons fought back loudly against them. Philip could barely believe what he was seeing. It was like they simply no longer cared about being seen in public. Even years ago, things like this had never been so blatant and out in the open. After another couple of minutes, Andrew and his hybrids fought off and killed the original demons. They stood tired and defiant before the car, and finally Andrew looked inside.

In that moment, Andrew and Philip saw each other for the first time in many years. Philip sat silent as Andrew came over to the car and opened the door.

'Hello friend. A bad night to return,' Andrew said. They looked at each other, Andrew caked up and down with splattered dark blood over his expensive suit.

'I'm here to help,' Philip said. Andrew got into the car after ordering the other hybrids to continue into the city without him.

The next half hour and more was a unique, strange time for Philip and Andrew. Although Philip was oblivious to what the hybrids and original demons had been doing in the last few years, Andrew did know some of what Philip had done in his life. He had watched him occasionally over the last decade, curious and slightly jealous. In fact, there were many frustratingly strong human emotions causing problems for Andrew, and meeting Philip brought them all right into view.

'You've made your mark?' Philip asked Andrew as they travelled in the car.

'I would say so. In a big, enjoyable way. Demon in the nightclubs, that was my way,' Andrew told him with a proud grin.

'You've had fun, then, over the years as you are now?' Philip asked.

'I have, and there have been good times, bad times and all the strange days in between. Being a man, then, being...what I am now,' Andrew said, gradually ending his words. 'So you've been busy yourself?' Andrew then asked him.

'I have, but nothing as grand or exciting as this secret way of being,' Philip told him.

'How is your family?' Andrew then enquired.

Philip looked out of the car window, silent for a brief moment.

'We've known better times,' he said.

'I'm having a hard time with mine, too. Both of them. My old one, and this bunch of freaks I'm with currently,' Andrew explained.

'My daughter died, Andrew,' Philip suddenly announced.

'I'm sorry. How?' Andrew asked, genuinely concerned.

'Very good question. The only question, in fact,' Philip said quietly.

'You don't know at all?' Andrew asked, obviously curious. 'When did she die, if you don't mind my asking?'

'Just over two weeks ago. It is pure hell to cope with. It is,' Philip told him.

Less than three weeks, thought Andrew. This was his old human friend, the man who helped him to be the great, respected fighting hybrid demon man he was now. He could see the unmanageable pain in Philip's face. Well, this is only one small part of the way things are, Andrew thought. A curious thing, though, he thought. In less than three weeks, things had become unpredictably volatile for all demons across the North because of the two young men who had ruined the balance of things.

'Philip, what made you return to us tonight?' Andrew asked.

'Her death. And the death of someone else,' Philip told him slowly.

'Who else?' Andrew asked. Philip gave him a strange look.

'You didn't have to leave us,' Andrew said with sincere affection. He did have good memories of his early days as a hybrid demon with Philip leading him toward being the confident, powerful thing he now was.

'I did. I had a family that needed me. I'm their father and husband. You've enjoyed your time, then?' Philip asked.

'Of course. More than a rock star, more than a millionaire with all the women, parties, drugs, everything. Too much of everything. Funny, right?' Andrew said, revealing perhaps more than he expected to. 'Philip, your daughter...three weeks ago, these things began with us.

These troubles for all demons. We were followed and attacked. My demons, and those of Bruce,' Andrew explained.

Philip really did not like what Andrew was beginning to suggest.

'Don't even...I'm going to do things that I have to tonight. Whatever that is, and then I'm gone again. I'm sorry, that's it. How it will be,' Philip stated.

'Again. That's right. Thank you, Philip,' Andrew said.

They looked at each other and then out of the car windows by their sides. Andrew was quietly enraged. Philip was the man who justified his becoming a hybrid years ago, leaving a fractured family to find personal financial highs, respect, power and success in a world of supernatural danger. Then Philip had left him and the others. There were many other hybrids around Andrew, but Philip had encouraged him, legitimatised him, praised him, and used him in the initial new wave of evil plans with Bruce and the demons. The sex, debauchery, the drugs, gangs, exploiting, torture and murder were so unsatisfying and repetitive after a couple of years, but he was of course trapped in many ways. His human mind never stopped, never forgave him for abandoning his original God-given life so easily.

'You think my daughter knew?' Philip said eventually.

'Do you?' Andrew asked.

'I would hope not...Andrew, you know about all this, what's been going on? Who interfered with you all?' Philip asked.

'It's two young men. Maybe in their late twenties, brave, bold and irritating,' Andrew told him.

Philip knew. He knew then that Eric was involved; it made sense and fitted together in amongst the disparate pieces, fears and thoughts from his own life. It filled the gaps, it rang true. The real truth was there for him to confront; Eric was some kind of brave hero, fighting these demons like he himself had never yet dared to. However much he wanted to think of Eric as the young bastard that took his daughter, however easy and suitable that would be, there was much to him that he could not ignore.

'Your brothers were stopped by him, as well as Bruce?' Philip asked.

'Yes, this young bloke and his stupid friend were on a mission of some kind. So you came to stop them as well, if they killed your daughter?' Andrew asked.

'To find my daughter's murderers, that's right,' Philip agreed.

382

'Okay. I will help you. Of course, I owe it to you, don't I?' Andrew said. 'So do Pierce and the others. We will help you get revenge,' Andrew told him. They shook hands, and Pierce drove the car closer to Newcastle. After years apart, they had to trust each other like they used to once again.

Chapter 71

Eric could not believe his luck so far. It seemed to be working somehow, in some strange way. He was walking the line. He could do it. No matter what reporters printed, what pictures were seen of him in the news, none of that mattered at all. If it helped, so be it, he thought. He wondered what was to come of it all, or what should come of it. Taylor was gone, and Eric had almost begun to fear the worst, but manage to stop his morbid thinking. He had heard the rumours, but was hesitant to believe. But then, he was not sure he cared what still happened to Taylor; he had seemed childish, jealous, and manipulative for the longest time when it had been too damn difficult. Eric could do without that. He could do with the friend that Taylor used to be, if he ever could be that friend again. But would Taylor even want to know the new Eric, he wondered.

Would it help at all? Eric was working with Bruce now, at least in some form, but had his trust and had gained impressive supernatural powers. It helped with the pain, the problems, and the questions in his head. He was burning people, demons, and buildings in all directions, and was feeling great, at least for a while. He was in control; he was powerful and did not have to listen to anyone, not Taylor, not his father, the police, not his teachers, not anyone. He would just keep burning, blowing up things, killing people who crossed him to keep the pain away. Would he make national news, he wondered. This was to be a legendary time in the North, for good or bad. He thought then that he might continue to burn Bruce, Sirius and all the others later at the Quayside. Why not, he thought. It might be all he had left of all this dark, supernatural energy. Life without Grace, if it had to be, might not be the hell he had feared, he thought.

He heard footsteps nearby and ducked quickly into shadow. He watched as a number of red-eyed figures walked down the dark street. There were four of them this time, prowling carefully along in silence.

'He must have come down here; this is the way the man told us,' one of them said quietly to the others. They sniffed around like dogs, with their clawed hands catching the light as they moved. They could mean Andrew, Eric thought. Or they could also mean Taylor, or even him. It would make sense if they were searching for me, he thought. He must have angered so many, which only pleased him. Eric stepped out before them.

'Good evening, clueless beasts. Having a look around?' he said.

They instantly all jumped out at him and he stood firm in defence with arms out strong. One demon caught one of his arms, and another grabbed his neck tightly. The other two stood ready to cut him up in seconds.

Eric waited, watching them, and then focused his thoughts. He glowed a hazy red and then flames rippled and burst into being over his arms and torso. He set fire to the demons one by one as they fell away trying to escape him. Eric grabbed them back and pulled at them, their flesh melting in his flaming hands. They burned rapidly as he screamed at them in violent rage. He then engaged with the other two demons, who ran and began cutting him with their clawed hands. He took the pain and then grabbed them together, knocking them against each other hard, blood pouring around from them.

'See what I am? I'm the North you don't expect,' he told them. He had madness in his voice and a change to the colour of his own eyes was taking place.

'Is he around? This man who sends you?' Eric asked them. 'Is it Andrew or another one? Well?' he demanded.

They did not answer, but only tried to keep cutting his flesh as he held them out at arm's length.

Philip stepped out of the shadows, and Eric dropped the wounded demons to the ground.

'Jesus, what are you doing here?' he asked.

'Eric, what have you done?' Philip said.

'Me? I'm getting justice, finding your daughter's killer, that's what I'm doing,' Eric told him.

Philip could not believe what he was seeing. Eric still had folds of burning blue flames around his hands and an uncontrolled wildness in his eyes. It could, of course, create a good opportunity, Philip thought.

He and Eric had not exactly grown fond of each other at all while Eric and Grace were together. The old Philip might have very easily been too tempted to trap Eric in among the unknown demons of the North, to separate him and Grace. That was not Philip now, though, was it, he thought. Except for tonight perhaps, in order to get things done.

'Stop it, Eric, stop what you're doing,' Philip said.

'I don't think I should, don't think I will,' Eric replied. He saw the demons crouched before him, lurching in pain but still manically trying to attack him.

'You're not scared of them?' Eric said aloud, as he watched how Philip was reacting to the demons.

From behind Philip in the shadows of the alley someone else spoke.

'Keep back, I'll sort him,' the voice announced.

Eric heard the voice and stepped past the dying demons at his feet, punching the two before him, wrestling them away, then moved toward Philip.

'I loved Grace, I still love her, we were soulmates. Truly, no bullshit, we were perfect for each other,' Eric told him.

He grabbed Philip by the throat. Suddenly, Andrew stepped out of the shadows.

'I'm not guilty for anything to do with her death. I'm not, am I? Well?' Eric asked Philip, shaking him violently.

'No...no, you're not,' Philip said, shaking his head. Eric loosened his grasp on him a little.

'And there is a whole unknown story behind it all, isn't there? What's your part in this, Philip?' Eric said.

'Put him down, man boy,' Andrew warned Eric.

'You know each other, do you?' Eric asked. He looked at Andrew, equally repulsed and fascinated. 'Your secrets killed her, didn't they?' he said, looking at Philip then at Andrew.

'Put him down or you'll regret so much,' Andrew told him.

'I already do, but I won't give up yet. We're all sinners, right? Difference being I see my sin. I'm a bloody mess and so are you,' Eric said. 'I'll see you down at the Quayside very soon.'

Andrew looked at Eric, seeing the cold rage in his eyes, but then finally turned away and walked back off into the shadows. He looked at Philip, then was gone.

'Andrew, wait! Andrew...' Philip shouted, as Eric kept him in his grip. 'Eric...I loved her...' Philip told him.

'No, no, you did this,' Eric told him, pointing at the dissolving demons near them and the flames burning painlessly over Eric's arms

'Kill me. Please,' Philip whispered.

'What? Think it is as easy as that?' Eric asked. He looked straight into the eyes of Philip. This man was some strange puzzle, a guilty, evil piece of shit, he thought. But none of it was at all simple, was it, Eric thought.

'I understand,' Eric said. 'You want to be forgiven? You did so much, such evil things for your own success. She died. Do you know where you'll go after all of this? Reincarnation doesn't seem likely now, does it? Ever pray?' Eric asked.

'Not...for a... long time,' Philip said quietly.

'But you take chances, don't you? Now is as good a time as any. Can't hurt, right?' Eric told him. His shoulders, arms and hands burned brightly once more. He looked at the father of his deceased love, thought deeply about how this man might have acted years ago, and how he had acted ever since. Eric did not want to be some kind of savage demon beast, just enacting revenge. This man had his mistakes, his own lasting horrors and sins to take to the grave with him. He then engulfed Philip, with fatal black smoke and dancing wild flames burning into him, taking his life at last. A moment later, Philip was gone like the demons, and Eric walked away. A tear rolled down his cheek as he walked down the narrow streets toward the Tyne and the Quayside.

Chapter 72

There were minutes left to know how the night was to end. Between both groups of demons out to massacre each other and all who would confront them and the desperate souls chasing hope, Eric had thoughts troubling him. The death was on him like immovable tough stain. He accepted it as himself, his path, his future. He stepped along the pathway toward his car. Taylor emerged from the shadows.

'Eventful night isn't it? Full of surprises, recent times, aren't they?' Taylor said.

'Was it worth it, then?' Eric asked.

'I'm just a man. My choice, my bad decision. Lessons learned. So what do you think can happen?' Taylor asked nervously.

'I'm not going to fight you or harm you. It's back to the start again, isn't it?' Eric said. 'I've no fucking idea what is going to happen. If we're ripped to bloody pieces, well we're mates again, right? I've been a wretched shit, I'm sorry. I just want her with me.'

'I know. There's a way, I believe,' Taylor told him.

'No easy thing, now. And not one real person bloody knows still. Infuriating,' Eric said.

'I'm sorry for all I've done. She's still with us,' Taylor told him.

'Step away, Taylor. You should go. What will happen will just happen,' Eric warned him.

'I'll try my damnedest to bring my side down,' Taylor said 'We can do something, there are others out there. More help, not just us,' he explained to Eric.

'We need any help we can get in this damned game tonight, dear friend,' Eric said. He walked off to continue the final steps of the supernatural war.

That was the hope Taylor clung to, even as Eric rejected it. Whether he would speak again to this close friend at all he could not be certain.

He knew that he should not follow him right then. There was a way for it to go, a path to follow. A dark path, though with hope somewhere. It was a thought to hold onto at the back of his mind as he too stepped away to do whatever he could. It was for the North, for Newcastle, Gateshead and the towns around.

They were all on him, on his trail, the sinister merchants of torture, sin and death. They would string him up and make him experience endless agony, with only his own fear for comfort. Both he and Eric were on this path until dawn with no certain hope. He thought of her, he thought of Peter and prayed for his desperate soul as he ran through the night to overcome all demons.

Chapter 73
Quayside Nightlife...

Taylor walked down one short alley at the upper right side of the Quayside streets. He had been here on countless nights out, drunk, happy and on top of the world with old friends. He could see the familiar pubs and restaurants and clubs but there was no laughter, no screaming or giggling. The smells and the sounds of regular nightlife were absent to him, as if the human element had fled, knowing the horror to come.

Any thoughtless turn down the wrong alleyway could end him in seconds, he realised. There were bound to be many of them around, possibly hundreds, to go by the whispered talk around. He prayed that Peter had his own plan meticulously mapped out for his sake, and thought that Peter might have more luck somehow with his spiritual lifestyle. Though Taylor was still theologically cynical and sceptical of any benevolent higher power, he hoped that it helped Peter to believe while demons converged around them.

Taylor knew what Andrew was planning up until an hour ago. Just how much Andrew would possibly change now that he had finally betrayed him, Taylor was nervously uncertain. He was not sure of how much of a threat Andrew believed him to be, but he knew that he must be most inconvenient for Andrew. It would be his pleasure. He would offer himself with the knowledge that she had promised to be there to help as much as she could from beyond. It was all he had to count on.

He walked down the main road. He could hear the cars moving around, then chatter and conversation nearby. He saw them; dozens of men and women, but all unashamedly demons, with the smoking mist around them and the red eyes. Andrew stepped forward from the crowd and looked at Taylor.

'Welcome back, my indecisive leech, my fearful traitor,' he said, flexing his fingers and turning his head a little.

'I...will help you now,' Taylor announced.

'Will you? The corpse not so useful, is it? Are you out of offers? Because I recall you to be a shifty little leech who takes what he can get like a homeless dirty dog. Isn't that you?' Andrew asked.

'That would be a damn close description, yes. But the difference is that I actually will save your arses tonight,' Taylor began to explain.

Andrew stood near him, as many of the other important demons came up alongside him, curious and hostile toward Taylor.

'Okay then, explain how this is likely now after who you've been?' Andrew asked.

Taylor stepped close up to Andrew and whispered in his ear-

'Because I am what you want to be again. A crafty, sneaky, disloyal bastard human, who uses everyone and every chance before him. Only without the disease. Eric has forgotten this. He is always weak and sappy. I know his movements now,' Taylor said with impressive confidence.

Andrew looked at him, and his expression twisted a couple of times before he replied.

'You believe I'll spare you after this?' he asked.

'No. But I've nothing to lose anyway. This is it. The thrill, the experience, all I want now,' Taylor said with empty sadness.

'Tell me what you know,' Andrew said as he folded his arms and waited expectantly.

Life was never as precious as then, Peter thought. He drove around the outskirts of Newcastle towards the location described by Taylor. Doubt and belief were in equal measure in his mind as he turned down another road and prayed for guidance. He had to think beyond his own weaknesses, his mistakes, and any traces of doubt to think of something stronger. This was real evil, new yet ancient and unpredictably powerful. He had a good idea of the direction that might lead to Eric, as Emma had told him, and was contemplating turning around. What was his best option, he thought. He was only a simple man, with temptation and confusion close by him at that moment, as it was at any moment. He hardly knew much of Taylor and sensed that he was guilty of terrible things recently. All men and women were at times, and that was what dark forces depended upon, he remembered.

As rain steadily poured down, Peter reached for the gear stick in the car to change and take a different road. Blinding light cracked through the night sky, shocking his eyes shut. He missed the gear stick and panicked, looking up as the car skidded violently over the road lanes. Some ethereal images burned bright in the white lightning flash as he looked into the night sky before him. A woman, beautiful, slender, blonde and young, surrounded by birds and angelic silhouettes, motioned to him to look closer.

The dark night sky returned in a blink of Peter's eyes and he quickly regained control of the car. He saw that he was driving further down the direction that apparently held Taylor. He accepted the change, and drove on with a strange sense of assurance. As he drove, he knew to keep to smaller, quieter roads around the town if possible, as the corrupt local police seemed to be everywhere. He was sure that they were trying to stop the killings and crime as well, but they were only interrupting the real matter of war against evil powers, Peter thought.

He looked out of the car window to the left and could see in the distance the Gateshead bridges and Sage building, and there were a number of flashing lights moving along the horizon close to them. They were everywhere after a few seconds, and he suspected them to be police cars or ambulances, or both. He would get there, he thought. Despite the police, my doubts, my fear, the demons, I will reach Eric, he told himself, steering the car down into darkness.

One small backstreet pub on the Quayside still held a group of people, of sorts. Eric stepped in through the doors and looked up at Bruce and Lucretia, who were surrounded by a dozen or so other demons in surreal shapes and forms.

'Can we begin now, then?' Bruce asked Eric with sneering impatience.

'Yes, now it happens. You can continue to do what you do best. They will be easy slaughter,' Eric said, trying to hide regret.

'You work under me now, no questions?' Bruce asked.

'I'm just another human, right?' Eric replied.

They all quietly stepped out of the crooked old Quayside pub, one human and a line of demons. Each of them prepared to do whatever it would take to keep their hold of the North. Bruce, Eric and the many demons crept along the Quayside streets, only lit by intermittent, dim light from street lamps. They knew the place where it would all break loose. It was only a few dozen yards away. Yards beyond that, though not much further, came the new breed, Andrew among them, along with Taylor, who looked woeful.

'Has this ever happened before? Like this?' Taylor asked Andrew.

'Not exactly. This is it, though, the changeover. Stick near me if you want to live,' Andrew warned. Taylor thought about it, but silently nodded and looked ahead in nervous anticipation. Under the pale moon, wicked blood would flow profusely before the light of dawn.

A noise came across from the far side of the quay, Eric noticed. The area was closed off by the corrupt police, he knew, so any curious or heroic people were not expected. He and Bruce and the others all looked out toward the Tyne. The Tyne Bridge loomed over the many tightly-packed streets and small buildings around the Quayside. Tall and historic, well-crafted and symbolic to all, they saw the North and Eric saw his identity in it. They admired it as they armed themselves, claws out and ready, muscles stretching wider and strong in numbers.

'What is that?' Eric asked. They watched, waiting for something more. Then more came, words…a man speaking, but loudly, through a loudspeaker, perhaps. It was a prayer, or biblical scripture.

'Oh, mercy, that is sweet. Well, keeps it all interesting,' Bruce said with a chuckle to himself. Eric knew it was Peter. He hoped that it could actually have some kind of positive effect, even with his own niggling doubt. They listened. It seemed to come over the water from near the front of Gateshead, near the Sage or closer.

'I will fear no evil for I know what I know,' the voice said confidently and clearly over the water.

'Someone with a death wish. Do you know who it is?' Bruce asked Eric. Eric hesitated briefly. 'I can't really be too sure, to be honest,' he said to Bruce.

'We split now. Eric with me. Sirius take four, then Charles take six down out front carefully. Converge in six minutes…move forward. No prisoners, no personal fun or games,' Bruce warned. Sirius and his group dispersed, becoming smoke and floating away over the dark sky in the direction of the spoken scripture. Eric wondered if Peter's words would change things. He was about to find out if they would even protect Peter.

On the front of the small bridge, Peter knew that he had to move as soon as he finished saying his prayer with the loudspeaker. Not because of personal fear, but because he had to continue to follow the beasts and stop them in their tracks. He picked up his bag and moved on. He would take on whatever came at him, but he could not clear Emma from his mind. Their relationship, whatever it was, distracted him. He looked on towards Newcastle. He knew the death and evil was there, manifested in dozens of hellish ways. He could see many lights of the North in the dark sky; people at home, asleep, watching television, unaware of the dangers outside that held their freedom and their souls. Even by morning, suitable lies would cover the supernatural horrors of it all.

He walked on over the bridge. As he walked, the mist thickened across the bridge. He reached almost the middle of the bridge and the mist clouded all around him, before thinning out moments later. It cleared as he watched and left Lucretia standing before him with her fellow demon men around her. She walked toward him. Her hips swung seductively as she came, her curves hypnotically trying to tempt his masculine mind.

'Hello there, Peter...' she began as she approached. The accompanying demons, still mostly in human forms, merely watched her at work. Peter stood unflinching while she stepped close enough to bite him. She smiled a seductive smile.

'What are you up to tonight?' she asked.

'Busy night for me. Out of office work. And you?' he asked, reasonably sure of what she was.

'A night of fun and danger, care to join us?' she asked, still smiling.

'Afraid not, sorry to decline. I must pass now,' Peter told her, and took a step to her side. She moved near him then.

'Can you and I have some fun together? You'd like that, wouldn't you? So repressed, so frustrated, aren't you Peter?' she said softly into his ear. He shook his head and took another step past her defiantly. She gave the nod, and the demons moved in on him.

Chapter 74

The Tyne carried a chilling wind over by the closed restaurants, pubs and hotels of the riverside roads. Any other night of any other week the long Quayside road would have many dozens of loud, leery men and women out drinking all night long, fooling around, flirting, shouting, joking in all corners by the doorways, benches, stairways, and under the archways of the tall bridges that stretched across the River Tyne.

All the restaurants, pubs and bars were closed, locked from the coming terror and devastation to come. No sounds of laughter, or even arguments came from anywhere around the long stretch of road by the river. Deep within the streets which sloped dramatically down toward the riverside, demons of both kinds began to creep and lurch down silently from the opposite ends; some in pairs, some in threes, and some alone, but just as murderous. The battle was beginning, blood minutes away from spilling over the old cobbled roads, into the drains, into the moonlit river.

The roads higher up near Newcastle City Centre were closed off like never before, though most people had no intention at all of heading anywhere near the area, even though both tribes of demons wanted to keep all knowledge of their dark activities a secret. The hybrid demons had been successful in spreading potent lies and infectious fear through the local news media, and almost every human around was desperate to get to safety and away from the two young men believed to be on a mysterious but brutal killing spree. These plans of the hybrid demons and Andrew had been very successful, but in the last few hours and even the last few minutes, many things had come to undermine these lies, unforeseen elements interfering with the plans of both demon tribes. Now, as the Quayside was blocked for the demonic battle, Peter, Emma, Eric and Taylor could still potentially throw much of it into chaotic ruin, and both tribes knew this. The personal desire and guilt of Eric and

Taylor and the investigations of Peter and Emma had changed everything for both demon tribes, confusing and angering them further, enough for revenge of any kind as long as it could stop them.

Many dozens of true demons filtered down from the direction of the streets which they held power over, as did the hybrids from their own controlled streets at the other end of the city. As they all arrived, it was almost civilised, in some macabre way. All demons moved stealthily and precisely within the darkness, creeping behind doorways, arches, bushes. They all gathered in place, waiting, preparing for their signals expected from Andrew or Bruce. A handful of deathly tense minutes crept along, and demons gathered around one far end of the Quayside, hybrids hidden deep among the streets and dark corners to the other end waiting to claim Newcastle. Bruce and Eric walked along in the direction of the River Tyne with knowing caution. Only a few yards further along, Andrew, Lucretia and the hybrids moved down simultaneously, their own wicked ideas ready to be revealed in defiant bloodshed.

Movements were careful, prepared and ghostly, right until someone ran out into the Quayside road. Under the vast arch at the bottom of one of the roads leading to the Quayside, two demons began tearing into each other suddenly without any order from either demon tribe. It was too soon; neither tribe was ready yet. All others only watched at first, unsure if this was the beginning. It was extremely difficult to keep track of which demon was of which side, and who was being beaten and clawed with most success.

Two streets down, under the tallest archway below the train line, a number of hybrids watched the small fight, confused and angry.

'It's begun, hasn't it?' one of them whispered to the others.

'No, no real sign. No, this is a mistake. Their fault. It's not the start,' another said.

'Keep quiet. No word from Andrew still,' the other replied.

'We need to move out. We're too near the wrong streets. The talk of other strong energies is increasing. It's the streets around. Some are talking of the Holy Island,' one said.

'It's bullshit. Just nervous talk. We don't do that, okay? No one knows about that crap. It's all myth,' the second replied.

'No, Andrew agreed, there are links very close here. He agreed. The old Lindisfarne connection, the gospels from the island,' the first argued.

'Well, no, forget it. We move in,' the second said.

They looked at each other. The second then turned to look at a hybrid stood further back up the street, who looked back blankly.

'Two more minutes,' the other said.

Along by the opposite end of the Quayside, several more original demons crept out within the safety of dark shadows, waiting for their own signal from Bruce or Eric to move down in for the attack. Two more demons came down by the other five, who were waiting by some scaffolding on half-finished buildings.

'Where are Bruce and the man?' one of the first few asked quietly.

'On their way. Things are changing. Problems somewhere, not just the other ones. Unexpected things. We might have to just do what's right without any orders,' the new demons explained.

'No, not yet. What unexpected things?' the others asked.

'Not sure. They have been slowed down. It's the man. No good from him,' the first said.

'They are fighting, two down on the quayside too soon,' the other pointed out with a clawed hand.

'Shit to Heaven above. Damn the hybrid shits,' the second said.

'Let us launch on them now, like we should,' another said, eager to see bloodshed.

'Bruce decides,' the first replied with an aggressive stare.

'Bullshit! He's finished, confused. Had his time. We should take control,' the other argued.

They all looked at each other in a silent kind of agreement. They finally nodded together. As they stood, two hybrids jumped out to the main road below on the quayside, joining in the initial small fighting there, which was gaining size as others joined in, blood and claws met with hellish howls and screams.

'Shit, they're taking us down. We'll fucking lose it all,' the lead demon continued. The others looked at him, their eyes burning red in the darkness.

'We fucking move now. Fuck Bruce. For the damnation we know,' the lead demon told the others, and they all howled then, snarling as they began to run down the streets, separating down alleyways into more shadows and stairways further down.

Down on the main road area, the initial handful of demons fighting wildly were joined by more hybrids, punching, beating and tearing rapidly. Blood and green fluid spilled out chaotically over the roads and streets as they fell about, shoving and hitting as they fought each other.

'It's too soon,' one of the hybrids told another between punching and fighting back demons.

'I know but...something was coming toward me,' the other hybrid replied almost sheepishly before a fist smacked him in the face, busting his nose, blood pouring as he fell down. More hybrids came out then, down onto the Quayside road by the river.

They ripped and tore apart the handful of demons in their path gradually, and stood for a brief moment.

'We move on?' one asked.

'Where is Andrew? Or Lucretia?' another asked.

'We keep going now. No stopping. They're behind us,' one said.

'No, not them. Originals? Real demons? Or something else?' another said wearily.

'Some kinds of different energies around here, some movement, forces...' the other agreed.

'Whatever. Come on. Split up. Main street, weave, back and in. Lure, move, attack, kill,' the confident hybrid told the others. Most nodded and moved on, spreading out onward. As they went, killing and attacking, they did all acknowledge some strange level of unknown energy moving around them. This did nothing to stop the bloody death the hybrids were enjoying.

As the hybrids split up, the original demons also were approaching fast, ready to rip and kill for their streets and their North. They also moved down, using their own strategy, shifting across the alleys and quiet passages. Both tribes moved in without their leaders, and both were unsure of the surrounding forces manipulating them towards the centre of the Quayside roads.

The original demons successfully began to trap the hybrids like easy prey as they entered the dark streets and alleys, catching them and violently clawing each other, biting, punching and attacking with potent supernatural flames. Flesh and blood was splattered over the roads, dripping into the Tyne. They killed with ferocious anger, though all were highly curious to know where Eric, Bruce, Andrew and Taylor were. It could not simply be a wild, directionless battle for no good reason. As angry as they all were, there had to be significance to it all. Their leaders were missing, leaving them to simply slaughter until they knew more. The demons would kill and take their inferior kin down as best they could. With predator-like skill, and instinctive brutality they roamed out, catching, fighting, with death their only objective.

The many hybrids fell on the cobbled road, convulsing as their remains returned to human forms, a grey mist emanating from the corpses.

'Only beasts,' a hybrid yelled as he jumped out suddenly down onto two demons. He clawed at them, dodging their attack, sweeping their legs and knocking them down.

'Beasts with no fear,' the first demon told him, and rolled quickly, catching him and biting into his side furiously. Another hybrid appeared then, looking disturbed.

'Get off him, there's more around us,' he tried to tell them.

The demons jumped out and latched onto him, ripping his face into pieces, flesh dropping to the ground bloodily as his body followed.

Back up the higher streets, more hybrids moved down behind the others. As they crept down, a few began to feel movement around them. Two hybrids walked down one street, cursing to themselves and concerned with the abnormal atmosphere around the area.

'The streets are closed off now, right?' one asked.

'Yes, our police have done so at our end of the city. Only possibly a handful of senseless humans wandering to their death, if that,' the other replied.

The night wind breezed along by them, a chill prickling their skin. They looked around, paranoid and unsure.

'We can't be ambushed up here, can we? The originals have not reached this far up yet, have they?' one asked.

'No, no way,' the other said unconvincingly.

'What, then?' the first asked.

'Nothing. Come on. We're the better ones. Our kind, our new breed. Perfect. Better than man, better than them,' the other said.

They smiled and walked faster. At the corner of the street they stopped, waiting. Tall, thin shadows loomed out across the street from behind them; shadows of men, or something of a similar shape. The two hybrids turned quickly but found no one nearby, the shadows having instantly vanished. Suddenly, bells chimed somewhere a few streets away.

'Where is that coming from?' one of them asked.

'I don't know. Church bells, but I don't know how or why,' the other said.

They looked around the street and then slowly continued.

Higher up in the city, Eric heard the bells as he walked down. He heard church bells ringing somewhere not too far away, which made things even more unreal and ominous. He was feeling changes inside himself, his own biological and chemical makeup shifting, rearranging. He might have control over his human mind, spirit and senses, but his biological make-up could be transforming him into a manifestation of permanent evil against his will without hope, he thought. He moved on as his atoms and genetic structure moved in mysterious ways.

Both tribes of demons continued to slaughter each other, and dozens of them filled the road by the river. There was a layer of blood and other fluid covering the ground beneath them as they fought, some of them falling over into the river. A few demons remained higher up, quietly waiting for Eric, Bruce or Andrew to lead them.

'Why isn't Andrew around yet?' one of the hybrids kept asking the others as they stood looking at the streets around.

'Who knows? Let's keep looking for these two men. If we find them, we'll get a damn good reward, you know it,' another reasoned.

'I know, but...should we be down on the Quayside now? It's all happening. The original demons have better physical strength, don't they?' the other asked.

'Let's look around a little. Andrew must be nearly here,' the other told him.

They then moved along the street past closed shops and dark alleyways. Black cats wandered out bravely in front of them, defiantly and mockingly.

'Maybe down across this street,' one of them suggested. They crossed the road. As they stepped closer, shadows enveloped them, darkening the whole street. The church bells chimed still somewhere beyond. From the other end of the street, some kind of light sparked, illuminating two thin silhouettes of hooded men approaching them.

'Let's move back, we should go down to the quay,' one hybrid said. The church bells chimed still as they fled.

Between the narrow, cobbled streets atop the Quayside, Sirius and Tattoo stood, looking down.

'We must control this. Nothing will go right with this confused bullshit. Like genocide between human cultures, we're better than that...' Sirius explained to Tattoo.

They then began to move down the winding alleys streets to confront the developing chaos of demon versus hybrid demon, clawed hands releasing so much evil blood.

'Here, between this alley,' Sirius suggested.

They stood a few foot up from a pack of three hybrid demons, who immediately noticed them.

'Oh, we've a challenge here,' one of the hybrids announced, smiling back at Sirius. The hybrids all walked apart slightly, visibly keen to fight these two powerful demons.

They launched quickly into each other, grappling, catching clawed fists. Sirius took a loud punch to the face, blood shooting from his nose. Tattoo bit the ear from a hybrid, and spat it across the alley, bloodied teeth in his savage grin.

'Too early for this! We want this...but too...soon!' Sirius cried out between punching and clawing at the demons, then attempting to hold them back. He hit one across the jaw then pushed the next violently through a nearby window pane, the glass shattering.

He and Tattoo eventually managed to stand back, and the third hybrid watched in silence, observing the brutal fate of his fellow hybrids as they attempted to crawl up again. As Sirius and Tattoo watched, almost satisfied that they had made their point, they all felt the strangest cold wind come along through their bones down the alley behind. Looking at each other, both hybrids and originals stepped away. They parted down through the Quayside, all with a nervous dread, not knowing what was moving all around them.

The high roads at the streets above suddenly cracked and split, gaping chasms drawn open between streets. The hooded, shimmering figures roamed on around the higher streets, as all of the many demons of both tribes moved finally down to the Quayside to join in the bloody battle. It was in a strange sense like the mysterious apparitions were herding the demons down into the Quayside, without any of them really realizing it.

Eric could not believe what he was seeing; there were dozens, possibly hundreds, of demons attacking each other, a great collected number of both kinds. All pissed off, all desperate, he saw. Some were in various kinds of official uniforms, dressed as police, security, the fire brigade and more as they scratched flesh and spilled blood. He took a deep breath and then began to walk on down toward them.

The Quayside was a place for unspeakable blood-soaked supernatural street wars that night, as Andrew moved along carefully. He observed some of the wild and unplanned panic down below on the dark Quayside streets. He witnessed brutal bloodshed, torture, massacring of flesh, limbs, energy. Evil attacking evil, almost primitive and savage in style. A general lack of sophistication, class, ingenuity, emotion, feeling. A lack of humanity, pity, empathy. He felt torn between his feelings, confused with himself. The times were obviously changing, and maybe so should he, he thought.

'Maybe I should go out ahead,' Taylor suggested to him.

'Really? This is a night of unearthly retribution. Humans are only insects in these problems, understand?' Andrew asked.

'Yes, but I actually signify something here. I can confuse them, now. You know that, don't you?' Taylor said with confidence.

'Go, then. Impress me once again,' Andrew said. They looked at each other for a second, Andrew subtly surprised by Taylor's courage. Andrew let him go with sad envy. Taylor turned and walked on nervously. He could be a sacrifice, for Eric, for her and for all men and women of the North-East. He might be unknown, a petty criminal and a lying sinner, but this could be the chance for redemption he so wanted. He walked out toward the middle of the long street beside the water, moonlight sparkling gently over the surface.

He heard a hiss. He kept walking, but heard a rumbling also, then whispers somewhere. He stopped and looked deep into an alleyway to his right.

'Hello?' he said cautiously.

There was no reply at first, then eyes pierced through the darkness.

'I am Taylor. I know their plan,' he said. His heart palpitated erratically as he waited for a response. It came down onto him from above, then another from the left, and another behind him. They grabbed him, and bit his flesh, and pulled him to and fro.

'You want them…wait!' he told them bravely.

'Tell us for your soul and your people,' one of the demons said, with a lizard-like rasp.

'They say they know your movements and…they speak with the grand darkness,' Taylor told them. He waited as they looked among each other, weighing up his words.

'Impossible. A lie. He left us to show our worth among mankind. To show chaos, fear, destruction, sadness, ruin. He takes some, but never…' the man demon trailed off, confused and angry with his own thoughts.

'Well, that's what they say. And I have to say looking at what has happened, they might be telling the truth,' Taylor said. He watched them, ready for a backlash of violence.

'And your heroic young friend, where is he?' the demon man asked.

'Isn't he with you now?' Taylor asked.

'No, gone from us. No trace. They have not killed him yet have they?' the demon man said smugly. He grabbed Taylor and shook him. Taylor clawed at the demon man's eyes, then the nearest other demon stepped in and caught Taylor by the arms. Taylor struggled aggressively, but was held tight.

'Our precious thing, now,' the lead demon man told him, grinning. He laughed and his face stretched out and bent in several places into a more repulsive form. He cast this honest demon grimace back at Taylor. He looked around, then spoke loudly.

'Move in on them now! Claim these cold streets as our own!' he yelled out.

As the last word left his lips, Andrew and a group of demon men sprang quickly from within dank corners onto the demons holding Taylor. Andrew grabbed the lead demon man and snapped his arm loudly, then clawed at the face, swearing bloody murder. The demon punched him in reaction, while all around them the secret war finally began. Dark blood spilled over cobbled stone, and howls and screams carried through the night air as many demons tore wildly into each other.

With chaos spiralling around, the bridge beckoned Eric alone. After hearing what sounded like biblical Psalms echoing towards him, he decided to run over in their direction. He guessed that it must be Peter. If anything, it seemed to at least distract the demons. Eric was not sure how much belief he personally had in the faith of Peter or his strange modern take on parts of old spirituality, but right then Peter was possibly the only other person willing and able to stand against these dark creatures.

On the bridge, the scene was horrific, yet strikingly bold. Eric came to reach the front of the bridge, where a thick cloud of greying smoke unravelled between an image he did not want to see but which held his attention. Peter was making his way towards him from near the middle of the bridge, but as he walked he passed the gang of mocking demons. Though somehow subdued, they still scratched at Peter from crawling on their knees alongside him. They cut his face and scraped his arms and legs with their claws in defiance as he walked to the other side of the bridge. It almost resembled a macabre and surreal wedding procession, for Lucretia appeared at Peter's side, whispering into his ear all manner of sexual promises, kissing his cheek and touching him temptingly with her evil, angelic beauty. He saw Eric.

'Leave him!' Eric shouted out as he ran towards them. Lucretia looked at him then and almost laughed.

'Another man for me? We will have some fun tonight, won't we?' she said, keeping up with Peter. She looked at him as he continued with a pained face from the many lashes and scrapes of the demons at his feet.

'Peter? Peter, darling?' she said. She began to grow frustrated in losing his attention.

'He's a strong man. Strong in his faith,' Eric called out to her.

'It's over now, anyway,' she said, looking at Peter. 'Over, and we can go and relax some place.' She touched his cheek with her claws.

'No, not yet. Hear me,' Peter drawled, closing his eyes to pain. The demons pulled at his legs still, while Lucretia watched him bravely walk away from them.

'Damned human in your mortal ways,' she commented quietly. Peter fell toward Eric then, weak and helpless. Eric caught him in his arms and looked him in the eyes.

'Forgiven...' Peter whispered, and clasped his right hand into Eric's tightly. Eric looked at Peter, concerned and seeing what was inevitable. Eric looked up at Lucretia.

'Pity, but that's the way it goes for ones like him,' she told him. Eric held Peter, and felt a strange sensation through his chest momentarily. It was probably sadness, a jerk of his heart weeping angrily for the loss of Peter. It passed soon enough, but it left him with a different sense of being. He felt not exactly fearless, but calmer in some unexplainable way. He looked at Lucretia and her demon group, who all watched him from a distance. They remained still, not approaching Eric as he held Peter in his arms. He looked at Peter and decided to say a prayer. Regretfully, he could barely remember any kind of prayer at all, but he thought carefully, and eventually fragments of various scripture and prayers came to him. He quickly spoke them to Peter, himself, and, well, God, if He could hear him.

He looked up at Lucretia, and she seemed to be sneering back at him, and then she turned away from him with the demons following. He looked back at Peter. He could not simply leave him there, but he could not physically carry the body either. He looked around frantically, wondering what he could do, then turned back. The body was gone. He looked in all directions around him, but saw no one, and heard no movement. His chest painfully tickled him once more. Something made him walk away and think about the demons elsewhere.

Chapter 75

Death On The Riverside

All the demonic evil of the North-East had now arrived down at the Quayside, and Eric returned with his own evil inner strength. What he saw when he walked down shocked him. It made him realise that he would need to make new plans, and very quickly.

It had finally all started, but it seemed one huge, bloody fight, chaos all around. The demons were out along the Quayside, dozens and dozens of them. He then suddenly noticed Bruce a couple of streets across and down on the right, and he could even see Andrew up on the other streets opposite, watching it all. Both saw Eric, and he immediately thought about how he could fight or destroy them successfully. He wondered if he really could use this overwhelming inner energy to finish them. This power was consuming him; his thoughts, actions, identity. He was one of them, well, just about, and he had to know when to stop, and just how far he could go. He had no idea, he thought. He would continue until Grace was saved, he thought, and he walked down.

'Change of plan,' Bruce said to him as he approached. Bruce was still discernible, though he had taken on most of his unholy form, wings and distorted shape, all crooked and inhuman.

'Predictable enough,' Eric replied. He looked around, seeing the mix of original and converted demons in all directions around him. So many demons, so hideous and in so many shapes and sizes, yet no Taylor. This made Eric wonder just what had happened to his shy, deceitful old pal.

'No weapons now, no tricks or help, you crafty, mortal shit,' Andrew said with contempt toward Eric from up on the other street. All the demons moved in towards him stealthily. This could get painful, he thought. He had messed with both groups over the last fortnight, and both would deeply enjoy finally taking him piece by piece torturously and slowly if they could.

It would come down to timing now, he thought to himself. After all the lies, deception and bluffing he had to time it right. Had he been too sure of himself in planning this end to the stronghold of the demons on the North? The years since around his birth and just prior to it had brought this on, and he would finish it like it was his entire problem alone; for his family, for her family and for people all around. The North was not a simple wound for these things to feed from so easily.

'Come and claim me if you can, but understand that I will be the change you can't stop. Andrew, your arrogance is going to be fatal. You are just a man who will be punished,' Eric told him. He turned slightly, but kept an eye on all of the demons around him to be sure that they did indeed follow him. Then he ran. Not from them - he had no fear of them, or for himself any longer - but to a place he wanted them to go to with him. He had to trust in Taylor, Grace, and the work and prayers of Peter until he had died.

Eric quickly headed down the long waterfront road, with dozens, perhaps hundreds of demons chasing behind him. They could probably materialise ahead of him or around him at any time, probably on Bruce's command, if they wished, but they initially seemed to enjoy the chase while it happened and were confident that he would not escape them. If history was what he had discovered recently, there had been many sad deaths in this area decades before, Eric thought, especially when Andrew surfaced and the tension began to build. Holy men, fearful of God and strong willed, had stood between Andrew and his plans to take the North down with terror, violent death, horror temptation and sin, but he had stopped them all until these last few days. They knew now of the hundreds of years in the same part of the country when valiant, holy men had fought these evils for God, had come up against these beasts and devils before. Perhaps it was meant to happen again, perhaps it had been inevitable, destiny even. Whatever the reasons, it was happening. Eric was no monk, no holy man for sure, but he had learned so much. He believed so much more now.

Could he feel anything different yet, he wondered to himself. He looked around at the quiet streets, closed doors, shuttered and locked for the night as ordered by police, some of whom were actual demons. It was not up to him anymore. He only could lead them toward the area and distract them, in hope that something more might happen somehow. He would have felt helpless, he knew, but he retained an incomprehensible braveness. He had an urge to approach each and every single demon behind him and take them on one by one, despite his weak, mortal form.

Eric found the lines described to him in the ground before him. The written tales and mad scribblings were all true. It was the area where the original mission and waterfront church had been decades before.

'Looking confused? Accept it. We might spare many, you know my opinion,' Bruce said in a deep tone. He placed a clawed hand down on Eric's shoulder. Eric spun around, and held a hand out before Bruce, nothing more. It made the difference. Bruce stared at Eric silently, fangs in his mouth shining, veins on his forehead and neck rippling.

Eric had no idea at all what he was doing or what was happening to Bruce, but he could tell that the moment was significant. Andrew looked on, shocked, and then stepped up to intervene. He quickly slashed out his claws at Eric, cutting the flesh from Eric's arm, and blood flowed like honey.

'Who do you think you are?' Andrew asked in anger. 'You'll only makes things so much worse, fucking human'. Bruce simply stood looking numb and pained.

'Bruce, this young man is not meant for demon life. Served his purpose now, surely, right? There's something happening, it's him. What we have, even with our differences, we don't need this...'

Bruce watched with solemn silence. This hybrid demon, with his sly enterprises and crooked business style, was asking him to see their similarities against what threat Eric could well be for all of them. There was a way of being, there were humans, then demons, after that the problem of hybrid demon kind, but now this...angry young man. Bruce had given him some tricks of the trade, in hope or in fear. But what should he really fear?

Andrew watched him for his response.

'No one special, but someone here, now, who will try to banish you vile shits from here. Now,' Eric answered. He held out his other hand toward Andrew, who watched then laughed.

'So you're some kind of holy man? What, an exorcist?' Andrew asked. 'There's a difference to my kind, you know,' he told Eric. 'We took her, but we knew...we knew what she was doing. God bless her.'

Eric quickly swung a fist and knocked Andrew swaying to one side. Andrew stumbled for a few steps, then caught his balance. He looked around at the many dozens of demons watching and waiting for the signal to tear into him.

'Feel...good?' Bruce asked through his numbed face. 'You want...to...end...him,' he said to Eric.

Eric felt the eyes of the many large, frenzied demons on him. He thought about the deed, finishing Andrew off for good. How much would that solve? Time was passing far too slowly for him. He grabbed Andrew by the collar, shook him to consciousness and looked him in the eyes. The demons all around watched and waited. He wondered if they might leave him if he killed Andrew, who was such a problem for them. No, he knew they would not, and that he had been the biggest threat to them in years. They wanted him. He held Andrew near to his face.

'I know you've had doubts about being what you are now,' he said to Andrew. 'I know you're going to use the churches.'

'Lies, bullshit. He's...playing you,' Andrew shouted out to Bruce and all the quiet demons, though he had a trace of uncomfortable anxiety across his thin face.

'I'll do what I can,' Eric said, and gripped Andrew by the face as he held Bruce with the other hand.

Chapter 76

The car swerved across the lonely road in the dark night as Emma strove to keep focus. Safety was gone for her. Peter was gone; safe, she hoped, but she had no confirmation of it or any messages on her phone. She knew she had to reach Eric and Taylor, she just had to. She knew Peter was going to them also, and that they were all going up against the hellish things she had witnessed that night. Times would be good when this was all over. There were good things to look forward to for them all. She wondered just how much she really could do to help them if she did find them in time. She was so mad at Eric and Taylor for getting Peter involved, though she understood that he must feel it to be a calling or spiritual destiny or something.

She did know the facts. She knew history, and she knew things that people had forgotten or chosen not to think about for a very long time. And look what had happened, she thought. While we all go to work, shop, have repetitive relationships, watch TV, hugely important secret things are at work beneath everything else. Always was, probably always will be. Some things had been rewritten, broken up, misplaced, hidden or discredited, and she had begun to piece together many of these old facts and details as she drove across towns. There were patterns to forgotten events around these areas, connections with old and new facts and myths which she understood now.

The shame remained in her mind, however. She almost wanted to turn around and go straight home out of guilt over her feelings for Eric and Peter. She told herself that she probably had not ruined it alone, but the thought lingered. She realised that she must seem like some kind of slut or heartless bitch to both of them. It was not personal, she reminded herself. That was the past, behind her, and others understood that, she was almost certain. Her own stupid feelings would wait, she told herself. She thought of the killings, of what she knew. They were demons, she admitted to herself. Personal demons, and real fucking evil demons all around. She drove on, to find her friends among demons. Apologies had to wait, she thought.

The sirens came. She was expecting police, even though she thought it was strange that she had not seen them nearer to the city so far. She quickly took a turn down an off road to a darker narrow road. Down the next narrow street she saw more; bodies, limbs all over, blood on the street, death again. They were near. They were police, too, she remembered, and she carefully drove nearer to the centre of the city with great caution.

There were plenty of oblivious people lining the streets of Newcastle as Emma drove around the university buildings then continued on. She saw shadowed figures stumbling along, shuffling around near the shops and clubs and pubs. They seemed lost, confused or different in some way. Probably the shock of the blood and death, she thought. She so wanted to be like the ones who still did not know, who were cheerful, unafraid of monsters, myths or legends. She drove along to the end of the city and could see the police barriers blocking off certain access roads and streets which led down to the Quayside. They had blocked up the streets, she realised. This was all planned out, she saw. She came along the street opposite the old boarded-up cinema and parked discreetly, then got out to run the rest of the way. She looked around, and seeing no one, ducked under the police tape and ran down the alley.

This is one big trap, a sadistic game for creatures who thrilled in the death of humans of the North, she thought. She was entering a place she knew, but the streets were now obviously ready to catch, kill or slaughter any who dared step inside. Emma had to make her way around the top streets near the Quayside area without being caught. She tried not to use her torch and stumbled along, skidding over the mud and cobblestones. She looked around as she went, highly nervous but in a way excited by the thrill and the unpredictable nature of the night. She walked along and racked her mind to remember things that Peter had spoken of, the street names and history of the Quayside streets. She remembered that she had felt very foolish until recently to believe in any of these things at all. The demons, hell or heaven, any of it was ludicrous normally, from fairy stories for gullible, insecure types. She had no idea how much was really true, and it blew her mind. She had been in deep conversation with a Jewish friend and a Muslim friend about their faiths and the similarities and differences and opinions of life, death and whatever next. This came next.

She had not though that they were wrong or naïve, exactly, but she did believe that perhaps many religions knew small pieces of a larger picture. She felt like she was now in that picture or even seeing more than any religion had so far really understood.

She noticed a group of strange people at the corner of the street that she was intent on going down. Moonlight revealed their ringed fingers, leather jackets and smiles. They were talking among themselves, but looked at her and smiled, sniggering and laughing rudely, she thought. They dressed almost like goths, but with hints of Eastern clothing and European elements in the jackets and hairstyles. One man, tall and muscular in his leather jacket, stepped towards her as she slowed down.

'Going someplace, are you?' he asked Emma.

'Looking for friends, actually,' she replied, stepping away from him as he came closer. His creepy friends moved after him. Emma looked around quickly, panicked and thinking.

'Streets are blocked tonight,' he said with a strange frown. 'Police are busy down there, some emergency. We're helping them,' he explained.

'Really?' Emma said, worried as they approached her.

'Maybe you can help them also,' he suggested, and then quickly reached for her arm. She moved away and immediately took off down a narrow alleyway to her left.

She ran, anxious and looking around in case there were others like them to stop her in her tracks. She knew the city streets, but some parts, especially those alleys filled with tall shadows, easily confused her perception. Darley Street, she thought suddenly. It came to her from nowhere, the place Peter had mentioned, the secret church address. She ran on, and could hear the strange group running close behind her somewhere. If she was right in thinking, she was then near the street where the Lebanese restaurant was, or at least it should be very close by, she thought. She came to the end of an alley into the light of street lamps, and took a second to orientate herself, before setting off again.

She heard shouts from behind her seconds later, but ran on, knowing that she had to get to Eric and Taylor.

In a ditch thick with blood, dirt and tears, Taylor held his hands clasped together and shook back and forth alone. Before him, the vision of Eric's dead girlfriend shimmered again.

'Can I do this? Will it make any difference at all?' he asked in a quivering tone.

'Do this and...I...can do something also,' she told him faintly.

'After what I've done to you?' Taylor said 'I'm wretched. I'm no man. I should be with them. Andrew needs me. That's me. It is,' he said with tears on his face and tight fists shaking. He shook his head in confusion and guilt. His fingertips clenched his forehead, ripping skin away, and blood began to drip down his temples as he rocked forward and back.

'You are free, always will be,' she said gently with forgiveness. He looked away. He heard the police sirens and voices further down by the Quayside on the other side, and turned to look with alarmed interest.

Breathlessly, Emma fell around the next corner and came to see Taylor on his knees in the dirt among stones and cracked walls at the rear of some nightclubs. It was the street, she saw, the place Peter spoke of, and she almost wanted to cry in relief. She cautiously approached Taylor.

'Taylor?' she said, as he heard her footsteps and turned to face her.

'Oh God, help me. I can't decide at all. I need exorcised, locked up or arrested, at least. Help me? Can you help me?' Taylor said to her. He reached out to her. Emma stood still for a moment, then took his hand.

'What's the matter?' she asked him. She could hardly believe this was the same person she had met earlier in the evening.

'She believes in me, but...me...I don't...' he stammered.

'Who? Who do you mean?' Emma asked, not following him. Something caught her eye. There was shimmer of light a few feet above them in the night sky. Emma looked above Taylor and she saw the astonishing fragmented image of Grace looking down at them.

'Oh my sweet God, my God...how?' Emma said, amazed, her mouth open. She fell back in shock. Tears came rolling down her pale cheeks as she saw before her the close friend who had been taken from her.

'She believes I can do good, me, now after all my evils...after that...' Taylor said cryptically, looking around at the dirt and blood from his hands.

'Help him,' the spirit of Grace whispered down to Emma.

'My God, it's you, isn't it?' Emma said in disbelief. 'Eric is going to stop them all. He's fighting real evil, things from Hell, if it's real,' Emma said.

'Yes, I know. Help him, both of you, please,' the spirit told them. By the light of the spirit, Emma could see markings on the ground below her and Taylor. They were on the place where the secret church should have been. Emma stepped out further and began to really take a careful look down at the ground around them.

'We're here, here it is. This is it, now,' she told Taylor.

At first it seemed to be just mud and cobblestones, but eventually she saw the unusual number of large, broken stones. She walked over and touched a couple, thinking to herself.

'What do you see here?' she said to Taylor.

She observed the stones and the spaces between them. There was a notable shape or pattern, she thought.

'We need to move along over...over there,' she said, pointing ahead. 'But this really is it, Taylor. It's the sanctuary. The place they made for this time.'

'I know. You're right,' he agreed quietly.

Demons moved in around Eric, finally deciding to support their paralysed leader and even Andrew. They would each take a torn fleshly piece of Eric, fighting over his irritating, mortal body. With one hand stopping Bruce, Eric prayed that the demons came then, clasping clawed hands on him. He strained to feel the same level of the powers that Bruce had given him from earlier.

'Rip him up, tear his mortal body,' Andrew demanded from a few feet away. Eric did not know what to do while he held Bruce. He seemed able somehow to keep Bruce under control with a minimal pulsing, flaming surge of energy from his hands, and felt that he should just keep holding him tightly. As some of the demons scratched at Eric and hissed at him, others stood nervously, hesitant still.

'What's he doing?' asked one to another. 'He's got power still,' the other murmured.

'Tear him now, just kill the damn man!' Andrew shouted, waving his arms at them but looking nervous himself. Eric could hear a voice. It echoed in his head and was familiar to him; comforting, even. It was Grace, and she spoke to him with urgency.

'Hold on, Eric...hold on...'

Did she know what he was doing, he wondered. He could not see her anywhere, only the demons and his own blood finally trickling, flowing as he gripped Bruce by the throat. He held evil before him, and looked it in the eyes.

'Hold on, Eric...hold on...'

413

Andrew finally relinquished and let the dozens of original demons tear him into dozens of bloody pieces before Bruce and Eric. He was a sacrifice, a humble martyr. His chance at life was gone, but some kind of peace was released from within, freed from his pitiful life of violent mistakes.

Chapter 77

'You've what?' Emma said, not understanding what Taylor meant.

'Her body. And I should bury it properly. Her body...' he said, feeling tremendous guilt and sadness.

'It's around here, near us?' Emma asked him.

'It's the place where she...it happened. Well, she found this. Then it all went to hell. Literally. She thinks this place can...I don't know,' Taylor said, losing faith in his thoughts and how to explain things coherently.

'It's true. It is. This is it. She can do something now, here?' Emma asked.

Taylor walked away to his parked car up the muddy bank nearby and returned as Emma watched curiously. He revealed a large spade.

'We...we bury her. Then she can...help me,' he said.

'It's not about you, you selfish shit! Bury her...here?' Emma said, angered.

'I know, it sounds weird, but it's right. The saints prepared this place, and she reached it before she went, didn't she? This completes it. It will release her.'

'It will?' Emma asked. 'And how do you know this?'

'You don't want to know. Just...trust me. A lot to ask, but please do.'

'Where is she?' Emma asked. He looked up at the car on the muddy bank. Emma took the spade from him.

A demon grabbed hold of Eric and pulled at his arm with mad aggression. Another pulled in the opposite direction. Eric held Bruce, but thought of defending himself. He felt confident somehow and took the chance. Letting go of Bruce altogether, he wrestled himself free from the gathered demons around him and caught one in the face. He hit the other near him as well, and noticed a strange effect happening. Where his fists made impact with the demons, their reptilian skin had burned quickly. He touched the next nearest one to him, and that too burned and hissed when he touched it. He stepped out and began to reach out and touch them all as he went, burning their faces, their arms, necks and hands. He was bewildered, shocked and thankful that he seemed to have maintained some of the power that Bruce had given him. He watched the look on Bruce's face as they remained still, numb and weakened by his touch. Lucretia appeared from behind all of the howling demons.

'What is happening?' she asked, visibly frightened.

'Still want to get close and friendly, do you?' Eric asked her.

'Perhaps I do,' she replied. He looked at her, judging her expression.

'See what I can do? Look at your kind here. I have...' he began, but dizziness took him.

'You have what, a decision to make?' she asked, approaching him. She slinked over like the deadly, demonic femme fatale that she was. Eric shook his head, the heavy migraine paining him. He held a palm out toward her.

'You'll burn, too,' he told her.

'Fire and brimstone. Quite the holy man now, aren't you? They never really got it right, you know, the holy men all those years back. All the rituals, the prayers and humble fear,' she said in a sultry purr. She came down by him, and took his arm, gently moving it aside as she kissed his cheek. Eric simply fell to his knees in weakness, just like the fallen demons that surrounded him.

Emma stood and leaned against the mud-flecked spade, exhausted. She looked at Taylor.

'Will you do any of this?' she asked. 'You might be quicker than me. Come on, Taylor. That gang are going to find us in a few minutes,' she warned. 'You feel something...around us?' she then asked.

'Like what? Here, pass the shovel,' Taylor replied, and took it from her. The body was in the large, deep hole which they had quickly dug, and they only needed to finish covering it for the spirit to be free.

'Right, whatever you say,' Taylor replied, digging away below her.

'I feel a bit...unusual again, like when I was at the cathedral. There's something coming,' she told him as she looked around. She closed her eyes briefly. In the darkness, she gradually saw an image of two groups coming, two dark groups, but with light shining not too far behind them. But the two groups were savage, deadly forces. When she opened her eyes, she saw that her hands were out, open and pointing before her. She followed the direction of her pointed hands, and saw ahead to her left a large, broken, weathered stone. She checked the arranged stones, which they had placed in a particular order to resemble what they hoped would have been the outline of the secret church grounds. She arranged them in as much of a tight curving line around them as she could, while Taylor finished digging.

Taylor was throwing the soil down, and shortly began to feel better. He felt like he was finally making amends. He kept heaving the soil into the hole, but knew that he needed to pick up speed.

'I can hear people,' Emma whispered. 'Keep going, faster if you can.'

He heard her and continued sweating and straining as he worked. Emma heard footsteps nearby, getting louder and closer. She moved to the hole and quickly started to push dirt down over it, and threw it with her hands while Taylor continued shovelling. The footsteps grew in volume, and voices came drifting nearer by the second.

'Maybe I could attack them with this?' Taylor suggested, tapping the end of the shovel.

'No, just keep covering the grave. There's not much to go. Go!' she told him.

The gang stood in the opening behind them before the muddy bank to the car.

'What do we have here, then?' the tallest, ugliest leader asked.

'Keep going, Taylor,' Emma commanded as she looked up and faced the gang.

'This looks very suspicious indeed,' the leader said to her. One of the gang walked straight over to Taylor as he nervously continued covering the grave. The leader grabbed Taylor, and pulled the shovel from his hands. Taylor looked at him, furious. This was his apology, his redemption. He looked at the gang leader and then kicked more dirt on to the grave in defiance and patted it down with his foot. They all looked at the mound of earth then back at Taylor. He nodded his head, satisfied.

'Dig it up,' the leader of the gang demanded suddenly to his gang. Two of them took hold of Emma and Taylor as the other two approached the fresh grave, laughing. There was a rumble beneath

417

somewhere, a shaking underground beneath them all. It grew, visibly unbalancing them on their feet, a small earthquake of sorts. They all looked at each other and at the ground at their feet, scared and bemused.

A glowing light surfaced from the grave and floated high above them, like a flickering, burning star. It grew and spread only a few feet above all of them as they watched. Emma knew, and Taylor saw a face in the centre of the spectral light, the trace of a person, swimming, flying in the light as it moved over them. The gang recoiled in shocked awe and confusion, and stumbled back over themselves to escape the ethereal, pulsing light in the night sky. They ran off into the shadows again while Taylor and Emma watched the starlight. It rose higher over Emma and Taylor, turning away. It moved off and then went at a steady speed past trees and along the alleys. Emma and Taylor followed it as it went down towards the Quayside.

A cold wind blew across the Tyne by the Quayside. Lucretia stepped away from Eric.

'It's all becoming much clearer now,' Lucretia said.

The hybrid demons covering the Quayside eventually succeeded in ending many dozens of original demons, who were distracted by the sight of a trapped, tortured Bruce before them. Lucretia climbed up over a wall to get their attention.

'This is us now! The way it was intended. Our evolution, we, the chosen ones, the luckiest bastards in the North! Andrew set us forward. The originals are finished here, finished!' she shouted proudly and defiantly, smiling and waving a severed arm over her head.

'We are a mix, we're the next step. We're strong, but know both sides. We can get through this, you and I, and rule. Rule, past Bruce and...past him,' she said, and looked at Eric hunched over on the ground with the many crippled demons and Bruce.

'Rise again, we have the command, we rule these towns,' she told them. The two savage tribes of demons watched her and each other as she spoke.

Bruce, meanwhile, leaned down over to Eric and pulled him closer by tight grip on his hair.

'What did you think you could do? You had your use this time. Just a man, that's all any of you are,' he explained to Eric, and spat in his face.

Then it happened, all too quickly. Lucretia could not have stopped it even if she knew how.

The demons around began to stand, regaining momentum and will. Eric closed his eyes to it all to make them all go away. He was sick of it all, sick of the pressure, sick of the brutal death.

The light flew in, soaring along through the sky over the Quayside from the nearby streets. It looked like a sulphurous spotlight filled with painted silhouettes, and it flew down onto the scene of damnation below. The demons looked up, shrieking as light-filled spirits tore into them, weakening them and burning them up. The ghosts of light began to defeat the things of darkness. Bruce came up with a loud roar and his eyes caught sight of Grace's ghost. She stared back, unflinching, and flew down onto him and through him. He raged, his arms beginning to claw his own body apart, dark blood spilling out, flesh splitting and smoke rising forth from inside of him. As all of the light spirits flew through the many demons, draining them of power, the demons fell, screaming and burned. A thick, pungent smoke bloomed out over the Quayside from the defeated demons.

Eric opened his eyes and saw Grace. She floated across from where Bruce had been to meet Eric.

'Are you free?' he asked her.

'All of us are free,' she told him. She held out a ghostly, thin arm, and they held hands once more. As tears ran down his face, she smiled, before slowly disappearing from sight before him. They all were gone, leaving Eric standing in the smoke as it cleared. He looked around, lost, and then saw Emma and Taylor standing a few feet away.

Taylor came down to meet him with a humble look on his face.

'I'm so sorry, mate,' he said quickly.

'It's okay, bud. You're forgiven,' Eric told him. They hugged and then smiled at each other.

'Is it all over?' Emma asked.

'For now, yes. Back to normal life again,' Eric said. He faintly smiled.

'Have you seen Peter?' Emma asked him nervously.

'He gave his life. He had no fear at all. A real saint,' Eric told her, and put an arm around her as well as Taylor. The three of them walked up from the area as a new dawn rose behind them.

Morning light shone promisingly through the Tyne Bridge as they drove away out of the city centre. They travelled along to the church that Peter worked at, and found the vicar waiting out in the church yard to greet them. They quietly walked up the path and into the church. Emma walked up to the altar and took from her pocket Peter's scruffy old hat that he had given her, placing it on the step. The vicar stood by and watched.

'He was strong in his faith,' the vicar said, smiling.

'Yes, he helped a miracle happen,' Eric said.

'I believe so,' the vicar nodded.

'You expected us?' Emma asked the vicar.

'Yes, I knew that after the horror we would be saved. The most unlikely saviours, always,' he said to her.

'They watch us. He's with them now, Saint Peter,' Eric said.

The three of them walked out of the church back to the bright sunlight of the new dawn.

END